IN sickness & IN health

BOOK FIVE IN THE PASTOR MAGGIE SERIES

ISBN: 978-1-68313-235-6
Library of Congress Control Number: 2021941652

First Edition
Printed and bound in the USA

Pen-L Publishing
Fayetteville, Arkansas
www.Pen-L.com

Cover and interior design by Kelsey Rice

IN sickness & IN health

BOOK FIVE IN THE PASTOR MAGGIE SERIES

BARBARA EDEMA

Books by Barbara Edema:

~The Pastor Maggie Series~

To Love and To Cherish

To Have and To Hold

For Richer, For Poorer

For Better, For Worse

In Sickness and In Health

This book is dedicated to Dr. Charlene Kushler. Thank you for teaching me how to see when "it's only the cow." You are an amazing healer of minds and souls.

List of Characters

New Residents of Cherish, Michigan and Surrounding Areas

Dr. Alan Cocanour – New doctor in Jack and Charlene's family practice office and at Heal Thyself Community Hospital in Cherish; from Ann Arbor.

Dr. Betsy Sneller – Social work therapist from Manchester

Dr. Aimee Van Dyke – Dentist from Manchester

Sofia Rodriguez – Dental hygienist from Manchester

Ednah Lemmen – Office worker from Ann Arbor

Dr. Calvin Siegers – OBGYN in Ann Arbor

Dr. Marna Wilson – Emergency Room doctor in Ann Arbor

Our Old Favorites

Pastor Maggie Elliot – Pastor of Loving the Lord Community Church (LTLCC)

Dr. Jack Elliot – Family practice doctor; on the staff of Heal Thyself Community Hospital; husband of Maggie

Hank Arthur – Administrative Assistant at LTLCC; married to Pamela Arthur

Pamela Arthur – Hospital volunteer

Doris Walters – Custodian at LTLCC; married to Chester Walters

Irena Dalca – Organist at LTLCC; fan of mini-skirts and vodka; engaged to Detective Keith Crunch

Marla Wiggins – Sunday school superintendent; director of Cherish Childcare Center; married to Tom and mother of Jason and Addie

Howard and Verna Baker – Recent newlyweds; devoted members of LTLCC

Officer Charlotte Tuggle – Cherish Chief of Police

Officer Bernie Bumble – Charlotte's inexperienced deputy

Martha Babcock – Nosy police dispatcher and a woman who has given in to her bad angels

Cate Carlson – Maggie's worshiper and a student at the University of Michigan; studying in Ghana for a semester

Cole Porter – Owner and proprietor of The Porter Funeral Home; husband of the lovely Lynn; father of Penny, Molly, and Samuel

Harold Brinkmeyer – Successful young lawyer; married to Ellen Bright

Ellen Bright – Nurse at Heal Thyself; good friend of Pastor Maggie; Jack Elliot's cousin; married to Harold Brinkmeyer

Mrs. Polly Popkin – Owner and proprietress of The Sugarplum Bakery

Carrie and Carl Moffet – Orphaned children adopted by William and Mary Ellington

Julia Benson – Reporter for the Cherish Life and Times; mother of Hannah

Lacey Campbell – Owner of We Work Miracles Beauty Salon; engaged to Lydia Marsh

Lydia Marsh – Co-owner at We Work Miracles Salon; engaged to Lacey Campbell

Dr. Charlene Kessler – Family practice doctor; partner of Jack's

Skylar Breese – Owner of the Pretty, Pretty, Petals Flower Shop; engaged to Sylvester Fejokwu

Mr. Sylvester Fejokwu – CEO of Heal Thyself Community Hospital; engaged to Skylar Breese

Jim, Cecelia, Bobby, and Naomi Chance – New family at Loving the Lord

Juan, Maria, Gabby, and Marcos Gutierrez – New family at Loving the Lord

Jennifer and Beth Becker – Sisters and owners of The Page Turner Book Shop

Jasper and Myrna Barnes – Parents of Myla, Mika, Misha, Manny, Milford, and Maggie; along with Myrna's mother, Myra

Sabeen, Mahdi, Amira, Iman, Jamal, Karam, and Samir Nasab – Syrian refugees who live in the parsonage

Charlie and Kali Teater – New church members; parents of Ryleigh and Zoey

Keith Crunch – Detective in Ann Arbor; engaged to Irena Dalca

Bryan Elzinga – Maggie's younger brother; works in Ghana at United Hearts Children's Center

Marvin Green – Dear one who lives at Friendly Elder Care

Nora and Dan Wellman – Pastors at Glory to God Church in Lansing; Maggie's best friends from seminary

Linda, Jerry, Sharon, Brian, Katie, Dave, Jackie and Ron – Volunteers at the food pantry of Glory to God Church in Lansing

…And a few others!

Prologue

God whispers through a baby's first cry.

God whispers through children's unfettered laughter.

God whispers through broken dreams and new chances.

God whispers in the middle of the night, when sleep is desired but remains elusive.

God whispers in an unwanted diagnosis.

God whispers in cures and hopes for cures.

God whispers in the drug addict's head as he hurdles toward his last breath.

God whispers as wedding vows are spoken.

God whispers as divorce papers are signed.

God whispers in anesthetized dreams.

God whispers in memories from the past, when they have become the only memories left.

God whispers to the preacher in the pulpit, and her sermon changes direction mid-sentence.

God whispers in the childcare center, the classroom, the eldercare center, the hospital, and the funeral home.

God never stops whispering.

But who listens? Who can sift through the onslaught of earthly noises to hear a holy, hopeful word from the living God?

Those with ears to hear. Those who sit in stillness and know God.

MARCH 2018

Maggie opened the door to the hospital room. A large sign was taped to the door, "No Visitors," but she had been personally summoned.

Machines flanked the sides of the bed. They beeped and blinked in a gruesome cadence. Tubes were inserted and taped to each arm. Oxygen was flowing, measured by a small clip on an index finger. A hole had been made in the neck and a tube inserted to aid with the breathing. Sleeves encased both legs and inflated and deflated as Maggie watched. She noticed a tube coming from under the sheet. Blood drained into a bag that hung from the side of the bed.

Maggie reached out and gently touched the sheet-covered feet. Eyelids began to flutter and finally opened. Maggie watched as tears slowly slid down the two pale cheeks.

"Good morning," Maggie said quietly, moving to the side of the bed and taking the limp hand. "It's good to see you."

1

Maggie peeked out the secret door into the sanctuary. The church was filled. She saw her in-laws, Ken and Bonnie Elliot, sitting with other family members in the front pews. It had been almost six months since they had all gathered, but that time for a much sadder occasion. Today they gathered to celebrate the marriage of Jack's cousin Ellen Bright to local Cherish attorney Harold Brinkmeyer.

There was an air of excitement in the sanctuary of Loving the Lord Church. Guests were whispering and smiling as Irena Dalca—perched on her organ bench with frosty blue hair, wearing a lime-green pantsuit, a hot-pink blouse, and a tangerine-colored push-up bra, which seemed to be overdoing its job—played surprisingly appropriate pre-wedding music as bridesmaids and groomsmen coupled themselves at the back of the sanctuary.

Maggie turned and looked at Harold with a smile. "Are you ready?"

"I've been ready for months," Harold whispered.

Maggie opened the secret door all the way and led Harold to the front of the sanctuary.

The couples, dressed in their finery, slowly walked down the aisle and placed themselves in a perfect V formation, thanks to small pieces of tape Maggie had placed on the carpet during the rehearsal. Jack, Maggie's husband, walked down the aisle with his younger sister, Leigh. He was the best man, while Leigh was the maid of honor. Irena stopped playing to change the music. As she began the processional, Ellen's mother stood up, and the rest of the congregation followed her lead. Ellen and her father glided slowly down the aisle.

Harold made a sound between a snort and a gasp. He was biting his lower lip, and tears brimmed in his eyes. Maggie gave his hand a little supportive squeeze. Even so, the torrent was unleashed. Harold let out a sob as Ellen came closer. Jack put a hand on Harold's shoulder, but it was no use. Harold was openly crying. He took Ellen's hand after her father gave her a kiss and a hug.

Ellen leaned into him, grinned, and said, "Have you changed your mind?"

Maggie welcomed and seated the guests, while Harold sniffed and tried to strangle his sobs. She handed him tissues from the pocket of her notebook as she said the opening prayer.

The ceremony continued with Harold barely able to control his unrecognizable feelings. Leigh, who had her own tissues hidden in her bouquet-holding hand, gave them all to Harold as his waterfall of emotion continued. Maggie soldiered on with the ceremony, abbreviated her wedding sermon, and carefully guided the couple through their vows. Jack handed a linen handkerchief to Harold, while taking the sodden tissues and stuffing them in his pocket. At the end of the ceremony, Ellen received a wet, somewhat-gooey kiss from her brand-new husband. Everyone else remained dry-eyed, unable to focus on anything but Harold's reaction to becoming a married gent. Ellen held his hand and looked at him encouragingly.

As Harold and Ellen walked down the aisle as husband and wife to cheers and applause, Maggie marveled at how emotions bubbled up in the most unlikely of people at the most unsuspecting of times. Harold Brinkmeyer was a no-nonsense attorney. He witnessed the most intricate and intimate human legal undertakings and always handled himself professionally. He was able to detach from the strong feelings his clients might be experiencing.

He'd had a mad crush on Maggie when she first showed up in Cherish as the new pastor, but she dented his heart (he wasn't in love enough to have it actually broken), and he eventually moved on to another young woman. Maggie had been surprised and relieved when Harold and Ellen began dating. Ellen was one of her best friends, as well as being her cousin-in-law.

The wedding party followed the bride and groom down the aisle. Maggie followed Jack and Leigh, but as they passed Jack's parents, Maggie could see Bonnie wiping away tears. Maggie suspected they were not tears of joy. Jack's brother Andrew and his fiancée Brynn were killed in a tragic car accident that past December, one week before their own planned wedding. They were cheated out of their wedding day. The combination of family being reunited and the celebration of a wedding was too much for the grieving mother. Having made it easily through the ceremony, Maggie's eyes now filled with tears as she saw Bonnie lean into her husband's shoulder.

Back in her office, Maggie removed her clergy robe and hung it in her closet. She put away her wedding notebook. Then, taking a moment for herself, she sat and rested her hand on her growing abdomen. At almost six months pregnant, she felt like she had swallowed a basketball.

"Sorry for the scrunched quarters, baby," she whispered. She closed her eyes and began to hum. She didn't know Jack had walked into the office until she felt his kiss on top of her head.

"I was just taking a second," she explained. "Baby Elliot and I thought we'd sit for a minute before the rest of the festivities."

"Good," Jack said, sitting on the edge of her desk. "That was quite an emotional wedding. We all need a break."

"I never would have expected Harold to be so overcome. It proves he's not a cold, calculating attorney after all." She smiled, thinking of Harold's reddened face and his leaky eyes and nose.

"You got them through the ceremony. Nice job. But they are doing family pictures in the sanctuary right now, and that means us. All three of us." He gave Maggie's bump a pat, then took her hand. "The first wedding since Andrew and Brynn," he said distractedly.

"Is your mom okay?" Maggie asked as they walked out.

"Nope. Will she ever be?"

The sanctuary was in matrimonial chaos. The photographer's assistant was trying to bring order to the family and friends of the bride and groom, and at the same time being happily ignored by said family and friends. Finally, she clapped her hands loudly and shouted, "Bride, groom, and bride's family on the altar, please. Yes, in between the candelabras . . . No, Mom over here, Dad right there . . . sisters . . . and, yes. Everyone, quiet please!"

The photographer took dozens of pictures while her assistant organized, clapped, and shouted her way through the various groupings. Maggie put her clergy robe back on for pictures, recreating the ceremony, now without Harold's unending tears. He was finally relieved of his intense emotional reaction to his nuptials, though his nose was still quite red.

Sanctuary pictures completed, the wedding party finally wended their way around the corner of the church and down Main Street to the Cherish Café. Harold and Ellen had rented the entire restaurant for their reception, where their happy guests were waiting with drinks and appetizers. The new Mr. and Mrs. Brinkmeyer, along with their families, entered to cheers and more applause. Music began, toasts were given, and dinner was served.

Maggie was seated between Jack and Bonnie. Ken, her father-in-law, was on the other side of his wife. The rest of the table was filled with Jack's siblings—his older sister, Anne, and her husband Peter, his younger sister, Leigh, and the baby of the family, Nathan. The family had carefully woven itself back together since the horror of "the deaths." Anne and Peter, with their two children, Gretchen and Garrett, had moved from the Detroit area back to Blissfield. Anne had taught emotionally impaired high school students in Detroit but earned her EdD and was now employed at Adrian College, teaching soon-to-be teachers. Peter, an engineer, commuted to Detroit for his work. Gretchen and Garrett had transferred schools with little fuss. They both loved Blissfield and being near their grandparents' farm. They did not realize they were the balm for their grandma and grandpa, who were going through the terrible "year of firsts" after the losses of Andrew and Brynn—first holidays, first birthdays, first Mother's and Father's Days. Then, days and days and days. Days always frayed at the edges. Always with someone missing.

Maggie slipped her arm through Bonnie's and whispered, "How are you doing?"

Bonnie looked into Maggie's eyes. "It depends on the second." She smiled. "Today is a beautiful day of celebration. It is a reminder of what we didn't get to celebrate last December. But it's also wonderful to see Ellen so happy and Harold so emotional. It's just that we're missing Andrew and Brynn at our table today, and we always will."

"We will. I'm sorry for the sadness that creeps in while others are laughing and making jokes and the music plays. It's almost an affront to grief." Maggie wanted to tell the DJ to turn down the music to protect Bonnie and Ken, but she knew nothing could protect them.

With a quick smile, Bonnie said, "September will be here soon enough, and a brand-new someone will join our family."

Maggie felt the baby do a half twist with a kick. "I think we should all get ready for action, the way this one seems to be training for the Olympics." Then her mind gently floated away on the dream to come.

For Maggie, four weddings and a baby would fill the second half of 2017. The first half had quietly tiptoed from winter to spring to summer. It was as if the entire congregation mourned with Jack and Maggie as the first weeks and months commenced following "the deaths." Now there was the forced merriment of weddings and the anticipation of a little someone to arrive at the Cherish Elliot's farmhouse. This thought filled Maggie's mind during her waking hours. She and Jack knew who was on the way but were keeping the delicious secret of the baby's gender to themselves. So much of their lives was for public consumption, but the baby was their private joy. She felt a hand on her shoulder.

"Will you dance with me?" Jack dragged Maggie back from dreamland.

She looked at Bonnie and said, "Your son beckons. I just want you to know how much I love you."

Bonnie blinked. "Love you too, Maggie. You'll never know."

Maggie stood up. "Yes, I'd love to dance if you think your arms can hold me. I'm quite round."

"You'll be much rounder by September."

"Thank you for that." She smirked, then took his hand as they danced slowly in a corner of the temporary dance floor.

Harold and Ellen had decided the reception would be a family event. Children chased each other around the tables after eating gourmet macaroni and cheese, hot dogs, and fresh fruit skewers. Maggie enjoyed watching the little ones play.

When she first came to Loving the Lord Community Church, Maggie had taught a small high school Sunday school class. They had all graduated, except for Liz Tuggle (a senior), Jason Wiggins (a junior), and two new high school students: Naomi Chance (also a junior) and her brother Bobby (a sophomore). Now there were so many children, taught by Marla Wiggins. The Nasab family from Syria had four, the Barnes family had six, the Gutierrez family had two, as did the Teater family. These children were in addition to Kay and Shawn Kessler; Penny, Molly, and Samuel Porter; Carrie and Carl Moffet; and Hannah Benson. The two newest members were infants Katharine Baxter and Maggie Barnes. Soon her own baby would be added to the nursery on Sunday mornings.

The younger children filled the church with laughter. A few months earlier, Maggie had designated one section of pews to be just for kids. Each Sunday, they ran to their pews after Sunday school—much to the chagrin of Verna Baker (*No running in church!*)—then settled in for the worship service. If they got a little squirmy, Maggie would stop the service and ask them to shush. With stuffed animals, coloring books, and crayons, they usually made it through "all of Pastor Maggie's words."

Dancing with Jack, Maggie watched as the children were ushered into another room to decorate and eat wedding cupcakes. The restaurant was packed with guests. White and blue twinkle lights sparkled around the large room. Many of her parishioners were there, most of whom were longtime friends of both the bride and groom. Ellen-the-bride was a favorite nurse of all patients at Heal Thyself Community Hospital, and Harold-the-groom knew just about every legal secret belonging to his church friends and the rest of the Cherish residents. Harold and Ellen were an easy couple to celebrate. The newlyweds circulated from table to table, welcoming their guests and receiving hugs and well-wishes. Everyone talked and laughed as they ate salmon wrapped in delicate puffed pastry and fresh asparagus. They clinked champagne glasses as they made impromptu toasts to the bride and groom. Maggie let the warmth and happiness of the room envelop her as she and Jack swayed back and forth. She closed her eyes for a moment and rested her head against his chest.

When she opened her eyes, Maggie caught a glimpse of Irena and Detective Keith Crunch dancing nearby.

"Oh dear," she whispered. "Jack, look to your right."

Jack glanced over, then stifled a laugh. Irena looked indecent as she wrapped herself around Keith and kissed him lustily.

"You better get those two married, pronto. When is their wedding?"

"August twelfth. Not quite soon enough."

Jack and Maggie watched in horrified fascination as Irena ran her hands up and down Keith's back. One leg was completely wrapped around his thigh. Keith tottered, tripped, then stumbled on the edge of the dance floor while Irena shimmied her way up his frame. Keith tried to regain his balance, but his knee went out from under him and he crashed down near the DJ, hitting his head on the sound system, then landing on a large speaker that fell over with a crash. Irena, in her high heels, teetered precariously while clinging to him like a Koala bear. This, of course, intensified the force of his fall.

The music stopped and everyone froze. Irena was splayed on top of Keith, who was awkwardly balanced on the toppled speaker. He put his arms around her and rolled them both to the floor.

"Are you all right?" he asked Irena gently.

"Yes. Yes. I'm fine. I tink." Her blue hair was hanging in her face. "Dat vas quite de bump." She looked up at Keith, as meek as a kitten. "Arre you hurrt?"

Maggie watched this interaction with curiosity and embarrassment. Irena and Keith were so . . . so . . . intimate. It was like they were the only two people in the room. Keith gently held Irena and put his hand on her stomach.

Good grief! Are they going to have sex right here?

Maggie began to turn her head away when something dawned on her—an unthinkable thought.

"Irena . . ." Maggie knelt awkwardly and whispered, "are you . . . pregnant?"

2

Irena's head jerked up as her eyes zeroed in on Maggie. "Vy you ask dat?" she barked.

"I don't know. I'm sorry." Maggie felt stupid. Of course Irena wasn't pregnant.

"What if I vas pregnant? Huh? Huh?" Irena crawled back up, dragging Keith with her, and glared at Maggie.

The other people on the dance floor stared when they heard Irena. Now others at tables near the floor also halted conversations.

"Tell me!" Irena screeched.

"You're so . . . so . . . Well, you know . . . You're forty-three . . . You're so . . ." Maggie faltered.

"I'm so *old*? You tink I'm so old and to nut hev a baby?" Irena spit out the sentence, mixing up her words in her small fury.

"Not too old. Well, maybe. Are you pregnant or not?" Maggie regained control of her embarrassment.

"Yes! I'm going to hev a leetle baby vit my Captain Crrunch! He's de daddy." Irena looked defiantly around the room.

"Congratulations! Hoky tooters!" Mrs. Popkin bustled over to the fracas on the dance floor. A large-souled woman, she was always one to celebrate life. She loved nothing more than to provide her bakery goods for any occasion where people gathered, whether in joy or grief. The Sugarplum Bakery was a fixed mark in Cherish, and Mrs. Popkin was the honorary loving grandma of the city. "Whoever would have guessed you, Irena, would procreate? This is great news." Mrs. Popkin enveloped Irena in a gigantic bear hug, lifting her off the ground.

Irena squirmed and squealed, her twig-like arms and legs flailing against the roundness of Mrs. Popkin.

"Let me go!" Irena's muffled voice could barely be heard.

Mrs. Popkin set Irena down as if she were a child. Maggie thought she might even pat Irena on the head, but hoped she wouldn't. Irena looked like a cat ready for a fight, her claw-like fingernails splayed. Mrs. Popkin's large, soft arms left Irena's hair standing straight up as she set her down. She had splotches of Irena's colorful makeup all over the front of her blouse.

"Dun't do dat again!" Irena screeched.

"Now, Irena, calm your little self down. Hoky tooters, this is happy news. You'll be a wonderful mother."

These words raised eyebrows around the room. No one ever imagined in their wildest dreams that Irena would or could be a "wonderful mother." Good grief, no one could imagine her with a pet. Or even a plant.

But the words hit Irena differently. Her makeup-smeared face quickly crumpled, and she brought her hands up to cover her eyes. Then she let out a sob that filled the silent room. Before Mrs. Popkin could swoop in again, Keith limped closer and slid his arm around Irena's shaking shoulders. He bent down and kissed her hands, which still covered her eyes. Then he whispered something in her ear. She took several deep breaths and finally lowered her hands. This final assault to her makeup left her face completely grotesque, but her eyes shone up at Keith.

Jack stepped over and shook Keith's hand. "Congratulations," he said quietly to the detective. "Who would have thought this could happen?"

Keith smiled broadly. "Not me. But I think it's going to be a trip. I'll be watching you and Maggie to see how it's done."

Keith ran his hand over his hair. He never allowed one of them to be out of place, and his fingers put them carefully back in order. His other arm was still holding Irena.

"Do you think I might take a look at your ankle?" Jack asked. "It seems like you might have given it a twist."

Jack grabbed a chair for Keith to sit on. Irena immediately sat on Keith's good leg while Jack removed Keith's shoe and sock and began a brief examination.

The room stayed silent as the excitement of the wedding was now completely hijacked. Maggie spotted Ellen and Harold standing near a two-tiered cake decorated in elaborate white icing and fresh flowers. Behind the cake was a large display of various gourmet cupcakes for the guests. The photographer had been ready to take pictures of the cake cutting when the dance floor had erupted in the Irena insanity.

I hope Irena hasn't just ruined the evening for Ellen and Harold. For such a small person, she tends to take up all the space of every room.

But the bride and groom were smiling at the news of Irena and "Captain Crunch" becoming parents.

"It's not broken," Jack said, "just a sprain. It would be a good idea for you to go home, put your foot up, and put a nice frozen bag of peas on your ankle."

"Frozen peas?" Keith looked up at Jack.

"Yes. I learned it in medical school."

"You did not," Bonnie said stridently. "Doctors would never know anything that practical. Only mothers. I taught him about frozen peas, Detective. He gave me many opportunities, and I've always kept bags of peas in my freezer."

Bonnie was smiling, and it almost broke Maggie's heart. *I haven't seen her really smile in so long.*

Irena grabbed an ice bucket from one of the tables and plopped Keith's foot into the icy water. "Ve nut leaving yet!"

The celebratory evening continued until children needed to go home to bed and Maggie felt herself dragging.

"It's time for me to sleep," she whispered to Jack. "Tomorrow morning will come early enough."

They said their goodbyes and made their way out of the restaurant. Their last vision was of Irena taking the microphone from the DJ as she prepared to propose a toast, probably to herself.

Once back in their farmhouse and comfortably pajamaed, they made room on the couch for Marmalade, Cheerio, and Fruit Loop. The three felines defied all cat facts by being incredibly codependent on their humans. They gleefully writhed, purred, curled, then fell immediately asleep. Marmalade loved to be touching both Jack and Maggie. His little orange head was smashed against Maggie's hip while all four white paws pushed against Jack's thigh. Cheerio and Fruit Loop had each taken an available lap, although Cheerio mainly got knees.

"There doesn't seem to be as much lap room for Cheerio anymore. I wonder if she notices?" Maggie gave Cheerio a pet.

"I doubt it. You give them way too much credit. They aren't that smart."

"Are you picking a fight with your pregnant wife? I don't recommend it. It won't be good for your health, doctor."

"I'm just flirting with you. But if you want to call it a fight, then I'm willing to kiss and make up."

"I would prefer some ice cream."

"You can have both."

Jack kissed her, moved Fruit Loop from his lap to the floor, laughed as Marmalade squeaked his discontent, and went into the kitchen. Fruit Loop immediately jumped up to Jack's empty spot and curled into a perfect puddle of fur.

"But hey," Maggie quickly switched gears, "can you believe Irena is pregnant?"

Jack laughed. "That was unfortunately the most interesting part of the evening. Irena definitely commandeered Harold and Ellen's reception."

"I don't think they cared. They looked so happy and both can't wait to be on their honeymoon. But tell me the truth, is Irena too old to have a baby? She's forty-three."

Jack walked back in with a pint of Ben & Jerry's Americone Dream and two spoons.

"She's not too old because, obviously, she's pregnant. She'll be carefully watched by her doctor. I wonder who she's seeing. She hasn't been in our office. Maybe she's going to Ann Arbor."

"That would make sense. I bet she'll move in with Keith. He has a house in Ann Arbor, and she just has her little apartment here. I'll do some reconnaissance. I'll give her a donut on Monday morning, and she'll spill everything."

"Are you ready for church tomorrow?" Jack asked, taking a large bite of ice cream.

"I think so. It's a service crammed with creativity, and one of the most exciting of the year. At least I know the kids are ready. We've been working on it for weeks. Ellen and Harold's wedding decorations will add a flare, but I must get there early to add all the red ribbons and streamers. Oh, and get the fans out of the basement."

"May I help?" Jack said as he crunched on bits of waffle cone.

"You have to. I'm pregnant *and* short. Normally, I would stand on a small ladder and hang all the red bits and bobs, but now you must do it. Sorry."

"No, you're not, but I commend your womanly wiles. Use this pregnancy for all it's worth and take it easy for a change. You're like a hummingbird. Your buzzing wings never rest."

"Ah, what a romantic thing to say. I think I'll buzz upstairs and curl up in my nest. You don't mind giving the kitties their treats, do you? I'm pregnant."

"I don't mind. I'll be up in a minute."

Maggie set Cheerio gently on the floor and headed up to bed. Marmalade and Fruit Loop sleepily jumped down and sat by Cheerio, who was fixing her fur. Then six eyeballs stared unblinkingly at Jack's face until he put the lid on his ice cream and walked into the kitchen.

"C'mon, beasts."

Of course, the piles of treats Jack put down were vastly inadequate in comparison to Maggie's lavish offerings, but the felines hovered over their individual piles and ate with relish. It was good to be a cat in the Elliot household.

Irena slipped into a soft, pink negligee. She slowly moved her hand over her abdomen and felt the small protrusion. Then she whispered, "Hello, you. Eet's me, yourr mama. Vat's eet like een dere? Arre you heppy? I em going to tek goot carre of you. I vill eat de vegetables, drrink goot melk, and no vodka foorr you. Vould you like me to sing to you?"

Keith Crunch finished brushing his teeth. He began to clip his fingernails, but he heard something unfamiliar. Was it singing? He opened the bathroom door just slightly and listened. Irena's voice was low and soft.

Hai Luluțu, dormi un picu', Dragul mamii, puiuț micu'
Oare când oi fii voinicu', Să n-am grijă, de nimicu'
Haida nani nani, Puişorul mamii
Domi in leganuț, Puişor draguț
Luna şi cu stealilii, Să-ți păzească viselii
Să-ți mângâie geanilii, Geanilii sprânceanilii
Haida şi iar dormi, Până-n zori de zi
Să creşti voinicel, Puiuț muțuțel
Haida Liulu Dormi in pace, Mămuca ție ți-a face
Aşternutu' pe pământu', Să dormi ferit die vântu'
Liuliu şi-ai dormi, Până-n zori de zi
Nu-i pe lume nu-I, Ca al mamii pui

Irena felt two strong arms wrap around her shoulders. Keith nuzzled her hair, then kissed her gently.

"Your song is beautiful. What is it?"

"It's a lullaby frrom Romania. My mama singed it to me alvays."

"What do the words mean?" he asked.

"Someting like dis:

Come Lulutu, sleep a little, Mama's dearr, leetle chick.
Ven vill I be strong, to not vorry about anyting.
Come nani nani, Mama's leetle chick.
Sleep een de cradle, cute leetle chick.
De moon vit de stars, to guarrd yourr dreams,
To carress your eyelashes, your eyelashes and eyebrrows.
Come and sleep again until sunrise,
To grrow strong, Mama's leetle chick.
Come Liuliu, sleep een peace, Mama vill mek for you
De earrth your bedding to sleep shelterred frum de vind.
Liuliu and you'll sleep until sunrise.
None ees een dis vorld as my leetle chick.

"De vords 'Liuliu' and 'Luluțu' are terrms ov love and endearrment parents use for deir childrren. 'Nani' ees de sound a modder makes trying to put her child baby to sleep. 'Leetle chick' ees an endearrment used in Romania. All prrecious vords for de baby."

"Irena, I can't wait to watch you be a mother."

Irena's eyes glistened. "I neverr tought I'd be a mama. You arre de daddy. And now ve vill hev ourr leetle chick. I'm so heppy."

She helped him limp over to the bed, and they cuddled in together. As he held her and felt her breath become deep and even, he was surprised when his own eyes stung. He never thought he'd be a family man. He'd enjoyed all the pleasures of being a ladies' man. His work took all his mental and emotional strength. Lighthearted relationships with lovely ladies took his mind off the darkness of work. He saw the worst of humanity, the ugliness and cruelty of what families could do to one another.

He had never been more surprised than when Irena Dalca clawed her way into his heart. He was besotted by her strength, her directness, her passion, and by an underlying pain he sensed she carried within. He wanted to know everything that made her the complicated woman she was. She was honest and feisty and didn't try to make herself into something she thought he wanted. She would never betray herself in such a way. She was nothing like the women he'd dated and bedded and ultimately left. She was exciting, dramatic, rude, frustrating, and wore her inner scars on her brightly colored sleeves for the world to see. It also dawned on him that Irena was the first woman who ferociously protected him. But tonight, after hearing her sing a lullaby to their baby, he knew more than ever he would do whatever it took to love and protect Irena and their "leetle chick."

3

The next morning, the sanctuary had a celebratory air, with the ribbon and flower decorations from the wedding still in place. Maggie and Jack arrived early to hang red everywhere and put eight electric fans in place around the sanctuary. Several thin red ribbons dangled down from the top of each fan. They hung red streamers in the doorway of the large double oak doors leading into the church. More streamers hung on the doorway to the offices, the nursery, and the secret door into the sanctuary. Jack set various-sized red candles on the altar table. Then Maggie put several sheets of paper on the lectern. Pentecost was ready.

As Irena began the prelude, Maggie put on her white clergy robe and red stole. She said a prayer, picked up her sermon, and walked through the secret door. At first, the streamers got caught on her robe, then her hair. She parted them with her hand so she could get through, then looked around the sanctuary and smiled as her parishioners watched her emerge like a round, white butterfly from her red-streamered chrysalis.

Irena was playing the organ in her usual gangbuster style, dressed from head to toe in firehouse red. Everything from her feathered hat, satin dress, push-up bra, fishnet stockings, and insane shoes were the brightest of reds. Her fingernails were shellacked in red polish, and her makeup did not disappoint. Gold glitter covered her eyelids, and a perfect circle of red blush was on each cheek, which made her look like she had some sort of virus. Her bright-red lips surrounded her small white teeth, and she smiled maniacally at parishioners as they entered the sanctuary.

Since her baby news was now common knowledge, she played the prelude to celebrate herself, her Captain Crunch, and her baby. Her fingers danced up and down the keys, while her feet meticulously played the pedals. The pedal-pushing always fascinated Maggie because Irena refused to wear organ shoes. She played in her stilettos. Finally, Irena finished her prelude by playing "Rock-a-bye Baby." The congregation broke into applause while Irena grinned and waved.

Maggie wanted to roll her eyes but refrained. Irena was supposed to play "Holy Spirit, Ever Dwelling" to set the tone for this special Sunday. *Good grief!*

The service could not be contained after Irena's organ extravaganza. Maggie looked out at the congregation and smiled. Almost everyone in the sanctuary was wearing red, as they had been invited to do. There were two new families, who had no idea what they had walked into and stuck out like proverbial sore thumbs in their ordinary, non-red Sunday clothes.

"This is the day the Lord has made," Maggie said. She began every service this way, and the congregation was now in the habit of saying the last part of the verse with her: "Let us rejoice and be glad in it!"

"Hear these words from Acts, chapter two."

Maggie paused as the younger members quickly came up from their section in the sanctuary. Each one knew what to do. Some stood behind the fans. Some stood near the candles and held lighters. Several went to the lectern, found their designated sheet of paper, and stood to the side of the altar table in an arc. Once they were all in place, Maggie began to read.

"When the day of Pentecost had come, they were all together in one place. And suddenly from heaven there came a sound like the rush of a violent wind, and it filled the entire house where they were sitting." Maggie paused.

The young people behind the fans flipped the "on" switches at the exact same time. The thin red ribbons began blowing cheerfully as the wind from the fans moved around the sanctuary.

Maggie continued. "Divided tongues, as of fire, appeared among them, and a tongue rested on each of them." She paused again.

The older children standing at the altar table flicked their lighters on and slowly lit all the red candles. The congregation was silent. The only noise came from the humming fans with dancing red ribbons.

Maggie read verse four. "All of them were filled with the Holy Spirit and began to speak in other languages, as the Spirit gave them ability." Maggie stopped.

The arc of children, each holding their paper, read one at a time. Maggie had printed out the seventeenth verse from the second chapter of Acts in different languages, including Spanish, Turkish, Romanian, Greek, and Ghanaian. Maggie had worked with five young people— Jason Wiggins, Naomi Chance, Iman Nasab, Ryleigh Teater, and Carl Moffet—for weeks ahead of time. She had help from Irena (Romanian), Amira Nasab (Turkish), Maria Gutierrez (Spanish), Pastor Elisha via Skype (Ghanaian), and Maggie had taught Ryleigh how to pronounce the Greek words. As the young people raised their fresh voices in different languages, the congregation took in the significance of the first Pentecost Holy Spirit sermon.

After each person read, all the young participants around the sanctuary shouted out in unison:

"In the last days it will be, God declares, that I will pour out my Spirit upon all flesh, and your sons and your daughters shall prophesy, and your young men shall see visions, and your old men shall dream dreams."

The congregation sat in absolute silence. It was moving to feel the fans blowing, see the red candles burning, and hear the voices of children reading about children prophesying.

Maggie saw tissues being passed between parishioners from the boxes in each pew, and she felt the Holy Spirit filling the sanctuary. Then the baby kicked, and Maggie couldn't help herself. She laughed out loud. As she laughed, she felt a tear slowly slide down her cheek. She wiped it away and looked at her flock. They seemed confused. Some were still wiping their noses and eyes, and some joined in with her laughter.

"I know the Holy Spirit is here. When our emotions get scrambled, the Spirit is afoot," she said.

The service continued with the fans and ribbons blowing and the candles flickering brightly.

The children were finally set free at the end of the service to grab punch and cookies and play outside on the lawn between the church and the parsonage where the Nasab family lived. The Nasab's were a refugee family who were resettled in Cherish by the kind-hearted people of Loving the Lord. Maggie regularly took the family to the mosque in Ann Arbor, and they regularly were in church on Sunday mornings. The two faiths coexisted effortlessly and respectfully.

After a lively coffee time—where Maggie's white clergy robe suffered a cup of orange punch splashed all over it by one of the "M" children of the Barnes family—Maggie and Jack walked home by way of the dry cleaners to drop off the soiled garment. They picked up lunch to-go at the local deli, walked through the cemetery, and then down their tree-lined drive. It felt good to sit at their kitchen table.

"Do you think the first Pentecost was in any way more exciting than our service was today?" Maggie asked, unwrapping her sandwich.

"No. They didn't have Irena. The first Pentecost was a snoozer."

"I think so too." She took a bite of her turkey and cucumber sandwich, chewed, and swallowed. "I think people were surprised by all the red we had hanging and blowing and burning in the sanctuary. This was one of my more creative ideas."

"It was almost like the Holy Spirit was *hanging* around." Jack grinned.

"Almost. We must make this a tradition. I can hardly wait for next Pentecost."

Maggie's phone rang, and she saw the familiar overseas number. "Bryan!"

Maggie's younger brother was working in Ghana, Africa. He and his girlfriend, Cate Carlson, were spending the summer working at what was now a bustling children's center. It was once called an "orphanage," but subtly the word was changed due to its negative connotation. The government didn't want "orphanages," so Children's Centers were where the orphans lived.

"Maggie." Bryan didn't sound normal.

"What's the matter?"

"It's Cate." He paused. "She has malaria again, but something is different."

"What?" Maggie kept her voice under control and pressed the speaker button on her phone. "Jack's here too."

"Hi, Bryan."

"Jack, Cate is sick with malaria again, but she is not right . . . She's not okay." Bryan took a deep breath, then Jack and Maggie heard a tiny sob.

"What do you mean? What are her symptoms, Bryan?" Jack was standing now and began to pace around the kitchen table.

"She . . . uh . . . She doesn't know who I am. She doesn't know where we are or what we are doing here. And I'm not sure, but she falls into such a deep sleep, I can't wake her to give her the medicine. I can't get her fever down. No one here can help her. Marta was with us all night. Pastor Elisha held an all-night church service to pray for her . . . I don't know what to do."

Now there was a full-throated sob. Maggie could picture her brother crying. He would drag his fingers through his hair and wipe his nose with the back of his hand, just like when he was a little boy.

"And I don't know," he continued, "but she began shaking and jerking. I don't know what was going on. Then it stopped."

"Bryan!" Jack leaned toward the phone anxiously. "Get her to Accra, to the hospital. You've got to hurry. Find the fastest car or taxi and move her *now*. You don't have time to waste. Have Elisha get you transportation. He's got connections."

"What do you think is wrong?" Bryan cried.

"Bryan, get Cate in a car and to the hospital. Tell them you think she has cerebral malaria. Just get her there." Jack lowered his voice to slow his own panic as well as Bryan's.

Bryan clicked off the line.

Maggie gasped, her eyes full of tears. "How did you know that? Do you really think she's that sick?"

"I only know because I studied possible diseases before we went on our mission trip. She is very sick. The longer it takes to get her to the hospital, the more danger she's in. They must get her to Accra. Now."

Bryan called Pastor Elisha. No answer. Bryan tried again. It went to voice mail. Cate was dripping with sweat, her face red with fever. She moaned in pain as she gripped her sheets with shaky hands. Bryan stood up, frantically ran his fingers through his hair, then turned and raced out the door and onto the red road toward the Children's Center. He ran as fast as he could over the rocks and ruts in the road. Only his heart was racing faster.

Maggie didn't know what to do. Should she call her parents? What about Cate's parents? They were her parishioners. But what would she tell them? She only knew enough information to scare them. She decided to wait until she heard something more from Bryan. She looked up and could tell by Jack's face that he was putting together the pieces of Cate's fate with the minimal information he had.

He continued to pace. Then he went to his study and pulled a book off the shelf. He began to read everything he could about cerebral malaria, now certain Cate was suffering from the disease. She had to get to a hospital so they could administer intravenous artesunate to stop the virus and the swelling in her brain.

Maggie stepped in and stared at her husband with huge, aching eyes.

"I'm going for a walk. I'll take my phone with me, but I can't sit here waiting anymore. What are you doing?"

"Reading. And praying that Cate is getting closer to the hospital." He looked up and saw her face, her eyes, and he quickly added, "I trust Elisha and Bryan."

"I do too. I'll call you if I get a call while I'm out. I love you." She walked over and kissed him.

She laced up her shoes, although it was harder with her baby sitting in the way, and left out the side door, walking down the long driveway toward the cemetery. She used to run to the cemetery from the parsonage next door to the church, but now she came from just across the street. Recently, her runs had turned to walks. Being outdoors usually brought peace, creativity, or clarity of mind, but now she only heard the panic in her brother's voice and pictured Cate suffering without medical help.

When she got to the cemetery, she veered to the left, then to the right, avoiding the familiar gravestones. She walked down Freer Road toward Cherish High School, passed Cassandra Moffet's old home—where Julia and Hannah Benson now lived—kept walking up the hill, then turned left on Meadowview, her favorite dirt road. As she walked, she breathed in Cate's name, then exhaled, "God be with you." Her mantra went on for a mile down the dirt road. When she turned back to go home, she prayed for Bryan, Pastor Elisha, whoever was driving the car Cate was hopefully riding in, and the healthcare workers waiting at the hospital in Accra.

Maggie knew prayers couldn't be used to manipulate God. Prayers brought comfort to the person being prayed for, if they were aware they were being prayed for at all. But prayers more often comforted the one who prayed. Maggie kept walking. She wound her way past the middle school, turned right onto Madison, then left on Middle Street.

23

Instead of going home, her feet brought her to Loving the Lord. She entered the sanctuary through the beautiful oak doors, stopping for a moment to take a deep breath of the familiar smells of holiness—Old-English-oiled pews, hymnals, well-worn carpet, the musty velvet drapes at the back of the altar, and the lingering smell of coffee. Maggie took off her shoes in the gathering area and quietly walked to the altar and up the steps, then awkwardly sat on her knees. She breathed in deeply with one word, then out with another, repeating her four-word sentence: "Thy. Will. Be. Done."

She slowly walked home, then spent almost three hours trying to distract herself, when the call finally came—four hours after the first one. She was in the pantry, reaching for a bag of flour, when the phone startled her back to reality.

"Bryan, what's happening?"

4

Jack sprinted down from his office when he heard Maggie's phone ring. She put it on speaker, and they both listened.

"We're here," Bryan gasped. "They've got her on a gurney, and they've taken her back to the emergency department."

"Did you tell them about the cerebral malaria?"

"Y-yes." Bryan moaned.

Maggie waited. Jack looked at her. He was just about to speak when they heard Bryan again.

"She's unconscious . . . She's been unconscious for two hours. I . . . I tried to wake her up in the taxi, but . . . there was nothing . . . She couldn't wake up. She couldn't wake up." Bryan was crying now.

"Bryan," Jack said, "you've done the right thing, and she is with people who understand this disease. You did exactly what you needed to do."

Bryan blew his nose and regained his breath. "It took so long to get here. It took too long to get the taxi, and then we hit every traffic jam on the way. We stood still more than we moved. She just kept slipping further and further away."

"Is Pastor Elisha with you?" Maggie asked hopefully.

"Yes. He's talking to a nurse right now."

"Good. He will be a great help. Bryan, do you want me to call Mom and Dad and the Carlsons?"

Long pause. "No. I can call them. I should be the one to call them," Bryan said with ragged breaths. "I'm going to wait until I have talked with the doctors. It still might be a while. I want to be able to tell them something . . . definitive. But you ought to be ready to hear from them later."

"I'm ready. Make sure you take care of yourself, Bry. The doctors will take care of Cate. Call when you can, and remember we love you both."

The call was over.

Maggie took a deep breath. Then she went back to the pantry and got down the flour, sugar, and other baking supplies.

"What are you doing?" Jack asked.

"Baking. We need something warm and comforting to take to the Carlson's later tonight. They'll be out of their minds with worry."

Maggie got to work. She sifted, mixed, kneaded, and finally set the dough to rise.

Jack sat on one of the kitchen stools and watched his wife. The methodical push and pull of the dough soothed him. He watched, but did not see. His thoughts were three thousand miles away.

As the dough rose, Maggie pulled out cleaning supplies and pink rubber gloves. She went upstairs and cleaned the bathrooms. She got out her Swiffer and cleaned the floors in the bathrooms and bedrooms. She dusted the furniture. Then she went down to the guest bathroom and Pine-Soled away.

Finally, Jack, who had ascended to his study when the cleaning commenced, descended to the kitchen and saw his wife wipe her forehead with one drippy pink rubber glove.

"Maybe you should sit for a minute. You are going to wear yourself out."

"Well, you did all the vacuuming yesterday."

"And you cleaned the bedrooms and bathrooms on Friday. The house is clean."

"I just need my phone to ring."

"I know."

Maggie put her cleaning supplies away and washed her hands. She checked her dough, then formed it into cinnamon rolls and let them rise for another hour. When they were ready, she slid the rolls into the oven and got more ingredients from the refrigerator: milk, cream, eggs, and butter. She whisked together a simple custard, which she put back in the fridge. When the cinnamon rolls were golden brown, she took them out of the oven and set them on a cooling rack.

She needed to stay busy.

She needed her phone to ring.

Maggie's phone lit up with Bryan's international number.

Maggie hit the button. "Bryan!"

Jack, pacing around the house, came into the kitchen and stared at the phone. "Hi, Bryan. We're both here. What's happening with Cate?"

"Hi. She's in the ICU." Bryan sounded under control. There was only the slightest shake in his voice. "She's still unconscious, but they did a blood test which confirmed it's malaria. It took a while to get the results. She's hooked up to an IV with an antiviral medicine. Something called artesunate-amodiaquine." He stumbled over the unfamiliar words. "All they said was now it's a waiting game. She must wake up. The doctor said she has a fifty percent chance of coming out of this with no side effects, a twenty-five percent chance of having some sort of residual effect in her brain, and a twenty-five percent chance of . . ."

Silence.

". . . of dying." The shake in his voice turned into a sharp intake of breath.

"She's getting exactly what she needs," Jack said. "Bryan, you must believe me. She is young and in good health. She's getting the treatment required, and the doctors there know this disease better than any American doctor."

"Thanks, Jack. I'm so scared. She's got to be all right."

"What are you going to do now?" Maggie asked. "Can you and Elisha get something to eat? Is there a place you can get some rest?"

"Elisha brought me some food. He knows a lot of people we could stay with in Accra, but I don't want to leave the hospital."

Both Jack and Maggie understood. To leave the hospital meant to leave Cate all alone. He needed to be there until she woke up. When and if she woke up.

"Try to find somewhere to lie down. You will do better tomorrow if you get some rest tonight. Cate needs you to be rested, Bry."

"You sound like Mom."

"Good. You'll do as I say."

"I should actually call Mom and Dad and the Carlsons," he said, tiredness hanging heavily in his voice.

"We'll call if you want us to. Otherwise, we will take good care of them once they are aware of Cate's condition."

"I'll call them now. But thanks, Maggie. And thank you, Jack. You're a handy brother-in-law, being a doctor and all."

"I'm glad to help, Bryan. Now make your calls and get some rest."

They hung up.

Maggie turned back to her baking task. "This will take a little bit longer," she said as she tore the cinnamon rolls in pieces and placed them on a baking sheet. She dried out the rolls in the oven for a few minutes, then dropped them into a greased Dutch oven. She poured the creamy custard over the sweet rolls and added more cinnamon on top. Into the oven it went.

"What do you think, Jack?" she asked as she worked. "Do you think Cate will pull through?"

"I *hope* Cate will pull through. I especially hope she will pull through without any permanent damage. But it's in her brain." He stopped and shook his head. Jack knew how very real this outcome could be.

Maggie sat down on a kitchen chair. Exhaustion enveloped her. It was suffocating. The oven made the kitchen too hot. She wanted to walk out to the field behind their house, but her feet ached. Her back ached. Then she remembered dinner. She was so involved with her baking, she forgot they hadn't eaten since their lunchtime sandwiches, which sat half-eaten and dried out on the kitchen table. During her cleaning frenzy, she hadn't noticed the mess on the table.

"Jack, you must be starving. Dinner never crossed my mind. What would you like?"

She threw the sandwiches in the trash, then stood up straight and stretched, pushing her hands on her lower back.

"Does your back hurt?"

"Yes. Everything hurts. From my head to my heart to my toes."

"What if I make a couple of omelets and toast?" he asked.

"I would eat an omelet and toast. Will you put cheddar cheese in my omelet and jam on my toast?"

"I will. Go sit in the living room and put your feet up. You're in my way." He kissed her on top of her head.

Maggie took her phone and went to the couch. Before long, three sleepy, stretchy felines found her and arranged themselves around her baby bump. She laid her head back on one of the pillows and took a deep breath. She could hear Jack cracking eggs, then getting the toaster out of the cupboard. Her eyes closed as she drifted somewhere far away.

"Do you want strawberry or raspberry jam?" Jack called from the kitchen.

No answer. He looked in the living room and saw Maggie fast asleep—head back, mouth open. She and the cats were in dreamland.

After letting her sleep for a bit, he went back to the kitchen counter and continued his omelet preparations. He diced tomatoes, onions, and peppers, then shredded white cheddar cheese. Next, he heated the pan, added oil, and poured in his egg mixture. After adding his fillings, he began moving the egg mixture slowly around the edges until most of the egg was cooked. Then came his magnificent flip. Whereas Maggie always ended up breaking omelets into two jagged egg splats, Jack's careful precision created omelet masterpieces. Toast popped up, and Jack made the serious decision between raspberry and strawberry. Raspberry. He plated his lovely creations and added some fruit.

Maggie jumped as her phone rang. The startled and disgruntled cats launched off her lap with their back claws.

"Ouch!" She rubbed her legs, then looked at her phone.

The timer for the oven went off seconds after the phone rang. Jack removed Maggie's cinnamon roll pudding.

"Jack, it's the Carlsons." She felt her throat catch. She cleared it and touched her phone. "Hello, this is Pastor Maggie."

"Pastor Maggie, it's Ann Carlson."

"Hi, Ann. How are you and Mark doing?"

"I'm here too," Mark Carlson said, his voice heavy.

"We just talked with Bryan, and he told us we could call you. We're just absorbing the news." Ann sounded surprisingly calm.

"Yes, it's a lot to absorb." Maggie paused and waited for Ann or Mark to talk again. She wasn't going to dump a platitude on them.

Jack came into the living room with two plates of steaming food and set them down on the coffee table. He went back to the kitchen for orange juice and silverware. Maggie put her phone on speaker.

"I think we're in shock," Ann said slowly.

"Hi, Ann and Mark. I'm here too," Jack said when he returned.

"Bryan said you could explain what Cate is dealing with," Ann said.

Mark cleared his throat. Jack and Maggie looked at each other. The omelets would have to wait.

"We'll be over in a few minutes, if it works for you," Maggie said.

"Oh, thank you," Ann said.

Maggie quickly packed up the cinnamon roll pudding, setting it in a large basket. She and Jack drove the short distance to the Carlson's. Mark and Ann were waiting on their front porch. The four of them went into the house.

"This is for you," Maggie said. "It's something you can eat anytime you feel hungry."

"Thank you," said Ann. She was hungering for answers about her daughter, not food. She absently set the basket on the kitchen counter. "Let's sit down."

They sat around the Carlson's kitchen table, and Jack honestly answered every one of their questions.

"Right now is the hardest part," he concluded. "We just have to wait until we see how the treatment works. Cate is where she needs to be."

"No," Mark said, "she needs to be home, here in Cherish."

They all sat in heavy silence. There were no words, just the ache of parents unable to protect a child.

Finally, Maggie looked at them and said, "Waiting to hear more news is painful and debilitating. I know Bryan will let you know what is happening. The time difference makes it a little harder."

"We told him to call or WhatsApp anytime," Ann said quickly. "We want to know how she is immediately."

"We won't sleep anyway," Mark said. "We have nothing else to do. We'll be home every day, and we don't want to miss a call."

Ann nodded.

"Would a prayer be helpful or futile right now?" Maggie asked. She saw the mixed emotions on their faces. "Got it. I will just say this." Maggie looked into the eyes of the stricken parents. "Please, God, we want Cate healed and whole and home. That's it. Amen."

Maggie and Jack sat down to microwaved omelets and fresh toast.

Maggie pulled out her phone and wrote a text to her mom:

Hi, Mom and Dad. I know Bryan called you.
Jack and I have been with the Carlson's tonight.
We're all waiting to hear more.
Love you.

There was an immediate response:

All will be well. We love you too.
P.S. Get some rest. You've worked hard.

"How does she know just what to write?" Maggie asked as she spooned strawberry jam on her toast. Strawberry was her favorite jam, not raspberry.

"She's the Mighty Mimi. Small but fierce and fiery," Jack said. "I suspect God consults with her on many happenings in this world."

"My Grandma Elzinga would say you're sputtin' right now. You're pretty close to blasphemy. Which is pretty close to, you know, hell. Watch it, sir."

"I wish I could have met your grandma. She would have been fun to tease."

"She would have teased you right back. She was a lot of fun, and one of those women who never grew old—in spirit, that is. Her body betrayed her, but her big heart and her mind stayed young and winsome. I love the word 'winsome.' It's a word that dances."

"I think some of her genetics trickled into someone I know." Jack got up and cleared the plates. "I'll clean up, then we better try to get some rest before the next news from Ghana."

Maggie set out treats for the cats and climbed up the stairs. Every step was heavy. By the time Jack got upstairs and brushed his teeth, she was fast asleep.

Jack did not sleep. He replayed the day. Pentecost. Bryan's first call. The long wait for Cate to get to the hospital. He knew what the doctors were doing to save Cate's life. He knew how dangerous this disease was, especially because it was in Cate's brain. Then he pictured the stricken faces of Mark and Ann Carlson as he and Maggie left them earlier. The unknown was more painful than the known. At least with the known, there was a clear understanding of what they were up against. They could make emotional adjustments, figure out next steps, if they just knew the facts of Cate's medical situation. The emotion connected to the unknown was fear, and fear was an emotion that could not be marshaled or controlled. It ravaged.

Jack was still awake as the sun snuck over the eastern horizon and heralded a new day.

North of town, Cecelia Chance awoke with a splitting headache. Her back felt like it was in two separate pieces. She tried to remember what might have happened to cause such pain, then she moaned. The tears came instantly. She heard Jim snoring, and her stomach lurched. As she carefully got out of bed, her back caused her to yelp in pain, but Jim did not wake.

Cecelia walked to the bathroom. When she looked in the mirror, she stifled a gasp. Her eyes were both blackened. Dried blood rimmed her nostrils. Her head throbbed. So much damage to her body. Her back kept her from moving easily. She got out the bottle of acetaminophen and took three tablets with a few sips of water. Then she washed her face and began to apply makeup to hide her injuries from her children. Did it ever work? Naomi and Bobby were in high school. They weren't stupid. The injuries were becoming harder to cover up. She peered into the shower. The crime scene. She closed her eyes and remembered how he'd grabbed her by the hair and slammed her down.

Cecelia stared at herself and her half made-up face. *Who are you? Why are you allowing this to happen over and over? What would you tell Naomi if someone was doing this to her? You would tell her to get out!* The tears kept coming, and they turned her perfect makeup into a grotesque mask.

After making another attempt to cover her bruises, she'd put on her bathrobe and unplugged her phone on the bathroom counter. She thought about the previous night. How Jim attacked her, and she'd finally fought back. The ambulance and the trip to the hospital. All the care Jim had received from the doctor and nurses as she sat in agony, waiting. She'd told the lie to everyone. Jim slipped in the bathroom and fell, but that part wasn't really a lie. The lie was what she did not tell them. With her hair still damp, she'd waited. A doctor she didn't know had come out of the emergency room.

"Mrs. Chance? I'm Doctor Cocanour." He sat next to her. "I've been with Jim, and it looks like he hit his head pretty hard, but he doesn't have any indications of a concussion or other brain injuries. He's sitting up and talking. So the good news is, you can take him home tonight. He'll sleep better in his own bed. We'll watch him for a little while longer, but I'll begin the discharge papers now."

"But he was unconscious. Doesn't that mean something?" Cecelia had hoped Jim would have an overnight hospital stay so she could have a break.

"We have a series of tests for accidents like this." He hesitated. "You know, you look like you slipped too." Dr. Cocanour stared at Cecelia's darkening eyes and bloody nose.

She knew what to do. She was good at it. She'd already told the nurse. She began her lie again.

"I was actually in the shower when Jim came in and his crutches slipped on the floor. I stepped out to try and grab him, but the water was soapy, and I slipped on top of him. His head hit the toilet while I went face-first onto the floor. What luck, huh?" She tried to smile but couldn't make her mouth work.

Dr. Cocanour looked at her thoughtfully.

"Then I called 911 because Jim wasn't moving. I was conscious the entire time. I followed the ambulance over here. But my kids are home and, well, if you are not going to keep him overnight, I'll call and let them know we'll be home soon."

She pulled out her phone and called Naomi. Her action dismissed any more questions from Dr. Cocanour. He stood up and left the waiting room. He had five more patients to see.

Walking quietly out of her bathroom, she remembered the humiliation of the previous night—and wondering if the doctor had believed anything she'd said—she felt her face burn with embarrassment. The house was quiet when she walked into the living room. She pulled out her phone and made the call she should have made months ago. Pastor Maggie would help. After leaving a message, she felt the warmth of power. Her power.

Cecelia walked back into the bathroom with Clorox Clean-Up and some paper towels. Jim snored. Dried blood streaked the white fiberglass. Her blood. The floor was streaked as well, along with the toilet seat. She sprayed and wiped the mess away.

Today was the day to clean up the entire mess. All of it.

5

Jack tried to stifle a yawn. The early morning meeting to update plans for the new free clinic was wrapping up. He, Dr. Charlene Kessler, and their new partner, Dr. Alan Cocanour, sat in the hospital board room with the CEO of Heal Thyself Community Hospital Sylvester Fejokwu. Two other doctors joined them. Dr. Betsy Sneller was a psychologist who'd agreed to donate her time to help patients with counseling or mental health issues, and Dr. Aimee Van Dyke was a local dentist who was excited to assist with adult and children's dental needs. Both women had their own practices in Manchester, a city just south of Cherish. Betsy and Aimee had each decided to volunteer four hours a week at the clinic. Aimee was also bringing her dental hygienist to assist. Dr. Alan Cocanour would help staff the clinic, along with his new position in the Cherish Primary Care office. Other support staff would also be part of the clinic team, as well as an office administrator, who would oversee the schedules and order needed supplies. Because the clinic would only be open three half days and two evenings per week, the workload could be easily balanced by the small staff. Jack and Charlene were more than thrilled as their team took shape.

Sylvester looked around the table of his conference room. "I can't thank you enough for your willingness to staff the clinic. The needs are great in rural areas, as you already know. We hoped the clinic would be finished by November first, but unsurprisingly, there have been a few delays. They put a new building inspector on the site. Do any of you know a Fitch Dervish?"

Jack sighed. "Yes, he is the building inspector of Cherish. How did he get appointed to oversee the clinic? It's closer to Manchester. I thought their building inspector was doing the job and we could avoid Fitch."

"The Manchester inspector was on the job until last week when she gave birth to twins," Sylvester said. "She had the babies a month early, but another month would have gotten us past the physical building, maybe even the electricity. Now it looks like this Dervish character is holding up everything to reinspect."

"There has to be more than one building inspector in each city," Alan said. "Is it possible to request someone else?"

"They are all assigned. The one possibility is that Dervish will read the papers already filed by the Manchester inspector. She was on the ball with her paperwork. I'll let you know further updates, but we should be open before Christmas, at the latest."

"Until then, how are we marketing the clinic to surrounding communities?" Betsy asked.

Betsy Sneller was no-nonsense. Her beautiful green, cat-shaped eyes narrowed and widened with animation as she listened to her clients, coworkers, or anyone. She listened to people's words while reading body language and eye movement. Her astute psychological skills assisted her in perceiving hidden truths and blatant lies, and her helpful results with clients kept her appointment calendar full. Betsy knew once the truth was revealed, no matter how unwanted, her clients had the opportunity to begin a new road of self-awareness and hopefully positive life changes. Sylvester knew the sacrifices Betsy, as well as Aimee, were making to donate hours of their free time to the clinic.

"Our marketing team has been told to saturate local communities with information," Sylvester said. "Print media, social media, three billboards, flyers, and hopefully word of mouth."

"Are you including dentists' offices in the saturation?" Aimee asked. She was tall and thin, with shiny black fingernail polish and light-pink hair that looked chic (unlike Irena, who continually startled the world with her kitchen-sink-hair-dye disasters). "I realize people who regularly go to the dentist aren't necessarily in need of a free clinic, but they could spread the word. The fact this clinic will do more than just medical care is a bonus. Betsy and I make you all pretty legit." Aimee laughed and winked.

Jack smiled. Aimee was right. The clinic would be a haven of care for those without means to get the holistic healthcare they needed. Unfortunately, they now had Fitch to contend with.

"Maggie and I dealt with Fitch when he oversaw work on a handicap ramp being built at church," Jack said. "At the time, the church was thinking of turning the building, and then the parsonage, into a childcare center. Fitch made problems out of nothing. In truth, he *was* the problem in most circumstances due to his innate clumsiness. Maggie has cleaned up his messes and his blood on more than one occasion."

"How does someone like that get a job as a building inspector?" Betsy asked, perturbed.

"I have no idea. He tends to create more work for any project he oversees." Jack looked at Sylvester. "If anyone can handle him, I'm sure it's you, Sly." Jack knew Sly didn't suffer fools.

"We'll see about that. He might be beyond my amazing skills," Sly said jokingly. "Again, thanks for your time today, everyone. I know you are busy. I'll keep you informed of all progress made, and we will look toward December."

Sylvester rose to leave, and the boardroom door opened. Everyone stared as a heavyset woman with salt-and-pepper hair cut into a straight-edged bob entered the conference room and slammed the door behind her. She was out of breath before she began to speak.

"Hello . . . I'm late, but it couldn't be helped." *Huff, huff.* "I just interviewed for a new job. It went longer than expected. But don't worry, it won't interfere with my work at the clinic." *Deep breath.* "It's short-term. This new job, I mean, and I will be done before I begin work at the clinic, even though I know I'm expected to do preliminary work with you." *Exhale.* "They are both part-time, so, no worries! I can handle both jobs. I'm skilled and qualified for both jobs." *Gasp.* "I know how to balance my time. Nothing will slip through the cracks. This will be a piece of cake." *One more very deep breath.* "So, what did I miss?" *Exhale.*

"Ednah," Charlene said with consternation, "sit down." Charlene pointed to a rolling chair next to Aimee.

The woman sat.

Sylvester also sat, staring with disbelief and some amusement at this chattering creature.

"Everyone," Charlene said, "this is Ednah Lemmen. She is from Ann Arbor. Ednah will manage the clinic office."

Charlene was exasperated. She had interviewed Ednah three days earlier, and although Ednah was competent with computer skills, purchasing experience, and other administrative details of running an office, Ednah's personality was rough around the edges. Painfully sharp, in fact. During the interview, Charlene had been surprised to find herself on the receiving end of questions, and through this unpleasant experience discovered Ednah's inflated self-confidence. Still, she had been the most qualified candidate, and she did have a reference from a prior employer who acknowledged she had an eccentric personality but had developed into an excellent employee.

Ednah smiled at everyone around the table. "Yes, I'm Ednah Lemmen and happy to be here to help you with your clinic. I have worked in many offices and am well-versed in all computer programs, have done excessive supply purchasing, and can easily run a front desk and oversee other employees. You may be wondering about my name. I'm sure you are. It's always the first thing people want to know about me." She gave a little chuckle and shook her head in mock surprise, which made her eyes bulge. "My name is Ednah. E-D-N-A-H. My mother wanted my name to really stand out." Ednah tossed her head awkwardly and laughed a little too loudly. She sounded like a hungry goat.

"Hi, Ednah," Aimee said. "I'm Doctor Aimee Van Dyke. I'm a dentist. You have something green stuck in your teeth."

"What?" Ednah asked as she began to pick at her front teeth. Everyone stared. "Well, now. What could this be?"

She poked and prodded around her mouth until the offensive "something green" rested on the tip of her finger. She looked around for a tissue and discovered a box sitting on the windowsill. She got up, and her rolling chair flew into the wall behind her. She waddled over to the window, grabbed a tissue, cleaned the vegetation from her finger, and went back to her wayward chair, her neck and face bright red with embarrassment. She tried to sit, but her backside pushed the arm of the chair and it slammed into the wall again. Ednah's ample bottom landed on the carpeted floor.

"Oww!" she howled.

It took some maneuvering and many huffs and puffs to right herself and finally commandeer her chair. She carefully wriggled down in her seat. Everyone at the table stared at Ednah in dismay, not sure how to respond.

"Ednah, we just finished our meeting," Charlene said. "You have missed this planning session, but I expect you will not miss another. I will fill you in on the details we discussed later."

She looked back at Sylvester, who stifled a smile.

"Ednah, we're glad you will be part of the clinic staff. I'm Sylvester Fejokwu, the CEO of the hospital. Our next meeting is a week from today from eight to nine a.m. in this room. Please be on time. This meeting is adjourned." He stood and left the room.

Ednah's red faced deepened to crimson as she went from embarrassed to furious. She watched the others leave the room, remembering a time in seventh grade when some of the other girls had made fun of her. At lunch, spaghetti sauce had landed on the end of her nose, unbeknownst to her. She went to her last three classes with the offending sauce front and center. The other girls said nothing until the end of the day, when they surrounded her and laughed. She'd gone home humiliated, only to be laughed at by her mother. Embarrassment washed over Ednah the way it had so many years ago. Once again, she was the butt of a joke. Only she wasn't in middle school anymore.

∞

Maggie sat at a corner table in The Sugarplum Bakery. She speed-dialed Nora.

"Hi, Maggie!" Nora exclaimed.

"Is it too early to call?" Maggie asked.

"Fortunately for you, I've been up for two hours unpacking boxes."

Nora and her husband, Dan, were Maggie's best friends from seminary. They were the new co-pastors of the Glory to God Church in Lansing.

"How's the move going?"

"Great. The moving van got here yesterday, and I organized the kitchen until late into the night while Dan worked on our closet, bedroom, and bathroom. Now for the rest of the house. How is my pregnant friend?"

"Fine. Not fine. I need you and Dan to send some prayers up and around for Cate. Bryan brought her to the hospital in Accra. Cerebral malaria. Pray for Bryan too."

"Oh, no! Is she going to be okay?"

"We are waiting to hear more. It's kind of a nightmare right now. I'll keep you in the loop."

"Okay. I'm so sorry. Especially because they are so far away, or you are. How are things at church?"

"I think things are fine. I just interviewed someone to fill in for Hank while he's away. She's, I don't know, interesting, but I think she'll be fine for the short term. How about your new church? Are they excited for you to get started?"

"Yes. Wonderful people. A delicious dinner was dropped off last night, and another is scheduled for tonight. A welcome basket was waiting for us when we arrived, with cards and groceries. I can't wait to know them all."

"I'm happy for you, and I'm happy for them. I'm especially happy for me because they are willing to share you for a bit when the baby comes."

"I think it's the benefit of being co-pastors. Dan can handle things while I'm in and out."

"I can't make a prediction," Maggie said, "but I don't think I'll be down for too long. Even if I can't work full-time right away, I think I can get back to preaching in a month or so, and you wouldn't have to be here on too many Sundays."

"We'll play it by ear. You are fortunate to have a congregation who knows how to care for one another. Maggie, your congregation is re-markable. The work you all did to bring the Nasab family to Cherish, the childcare center, and soon, the free clinic. Your parishioners are doers."

"I'm sure yours are too. I can't wait for the stories. I'll let you get back to boxes. I'm at The Sugarplum for some treats."

"Yum. Listen, we'll be praying for Cate and Bryan. I'll ask our con-gregation to pray too. The more the better."

"Thanks, Nora. Bye."

Maggie stared at her phone. It was nice to have Nora and Dan clos-er to Cherish. She went to Mrs. Popkin's counter and placed an order. Then, with the pink bakery box in hand, she walked into her own love-ly church.

Red streamers still hung in all the doorways. The thought of yes-terday's service made her smile. It seemed like weeks since Bryan's call with the news about Cate and the long day she and Jack had endured as they waited for an update from Ghana. The red candles on the altar and the fans were still in place, and the red streamers hanging on the doorway to the offices brushed against her face as she stepped into Hank's office. Hank was her administrative assistant. She'd interviewed and hired him three years earlier. His wife, Pamela, was a hospital vol-unteer and a friend of Maggie's as well.

Maggie stopped once she stepped through the door at a familiar Monday morning sight: Hank removing bits of trash from his desk, which was carefully protected by a blue tarpaulin. She couldn't help laughing. *We're all so funny and predictable with our little habits.*

"Good morning, Pastor Maggie. I'm settling in for the day. What do you have there?"

Maggie looked at her hands, holding the pink bakery box from The Sugarplum Bakery across the street. She thought she would make it back to the office before Hank arrived. She laughed and quickly put the box in her own office.

"Oh, nothing," she chimed. "How are you this morning?" Maggie felt a small stab of pain as she thought about not seeing Hank and his tarpaulin for three months. She stepped back into his office. "Let me help you. Only a few stray coffee cups and dirty napkins. This is a record. Maybe people are finally learning."

Hank's tarpaulin had been instituted when he got sick and tired of having his desk used as a refuse station on Sunday mornings during coffee time.

"So, are you and Pamela packed and ready to go?" Maggie tried to sound cheerful, but the end of her sentence dragged off somewhat desolately.

Hank took the folded tarp from her. "Well, uh, yesireebob, Pastor Maggie. We are mostly packed because it's winter there, so our winter clothes are ready to go. But as you know, we don't leave until two weeks from today." Hank looked kindly at his boss.

"Well, we sure will miss you around here, but a trip to Australia. Wow . . . It's a trip of a lifetime." Her smile wavered on the corners of her lips and didn't quite make it up to her eyes.

"It certainly is." Doris Walters pushed her rolling trash can through the red streamers and into Hank's office. She was wearing lime-green rubber boots, her large yellow apron was stuffed with cleaning supplies, and her head was wrapped in a bright-orange bandana. She looked like a walking citrus bowl. "But we are going to miss you around here, Hank. Whose head am I going to dust?" She snorted with laughter.

Hank threw the stray cups and napkins into the rolling trash can.

"I don't know, Doris. You'd better leave Pastor Maggie's head alone. That's all I've got to say about it. Are you scrubbing floors today?" He looked down at her boots.

"Yes. It's the first Monday of the month, and those kids made a doozy of a mess downstairs yesterday during Sunday school. Red glitter and glue everywhere. Do we know who will take Hank's place yet?" Doris swung her orange head toward Maggie.

"Not 'take my place.' I'm coming back." Hank glared. "And we're not leaving for two weeks, Doris."

The trip-trap of stilettos could be heard in the church entryway. The other three remained silent and waited for the event of Irena. They were not disappointed. Irena burst into the office, swatting at the streamers while balancing a stack of music. Sitting precariously on top of the stack was a pink bakery box.

"Good moorrning!"

She plopped her music on Hank's desk, and the bakery box slid off the stack of music, landing upside down on the floor. Irena, Hank, and Doris all reached for it, but the flimsy lid of the box slid through their hands. Six of Mrs. Popkin's cream-and-berry-filled pastry horns plopped gracelessly to the floor.

Three gasps from Maggie, Hank, and Doris filled the room. Almost.

Irena let out a hysterical scream as the horns cracked, then oozed berries and cream all over one of her shoes.

"No! No! No! Stup eet! My shoe!"

Maggie grabbed the paper towels out of Doris's apron. "Here, I'll clean this up, Irena. It doesn't look like your shoe is ruined, just decorated a little."

"Pastor Maggie, don't you dare clean up that mess. You are too round," Doris said (even though she was rounder). "I will clean up. It's what I get paid for."

"Well, I brought dis cream horrns for Hunk. It is almost ourr last Munday togeterr. Now, ruined!"

Doris laughed and stepped out of the office. A minute later she came in with a pink bakery box.

"Never fear, you crazy little Romanian. I also bought donuts for today. Hank, I was pretty sure we might not see you next week. Australia is a big trip to prepare for, and you can be awful fussy. Have a donut."

Maggie hurried into her office and proffered her pink box with a smile. "Guilty of the same crime."

"What? But we are only going on vacation," Hank said, obviously touched by their thoughtfulness. He chose a large triple-chocolate muffin from Maggie's box.

"Three months is more than a vacation. Unless you are Bill and Melinda Gates," Doris said. She opened her box and took out a maple-frosted Long John.

"Dorrees is right. Also, I neverr been on vacation. Neverr," Irena chimed in.

She took Maggie's box from her and opened it. Her red-painted claws grabbed a huge lemon-cream-cheese Danish.

"It's as big as your face," Doris said, her mouth full.

Maggie moved the little party into her office. Hank dragged in his chair, while Doris and Irena each sat in one of the cream-colored visitor chairs.

"Okay, everyone, I would like to say a few things." Maggie lifted a cranberry bar. "To Hank and Pamela. May your three-month vacation be full of fun and adventure and romance. We will miss you terribly, but we will also look forward to the pictures you post on Facebook and the stories you will bring home to us."

"Hear! Hear!" Doris chimed in.

"I neverr been on vacation," Irena mumbled again. She held her remaining Danish in one hand and took another pastry out of the box with the other.

"Thank you, ladies. I will miss you, yesireebob, I will. Pamela's had a bee in her bonnet about going to Australia for about a hundred years now. So, here we go. I will be back at my desk before baby Elliot gets here, that's for sure." He stared at Maggie's bump. "I can't wait to see who's in there. Are you sure you can't tell me if it's a boy or a girl?"

"I am absolutely sure. Anyway, you will be back in time. In fact, you'll have almost a week to spare. I will be nice and cranky by then. Which leads me to my next toast. Congratulations, Irena." Maggie took a bite of her bar. "You and Keith surprised us all at the wedding. When is your baby due?"

"I dun't know. My Captain Crrunch and I will go to de doctorr next week on wendesday. Den I will tell you." She took a bite from a glazed apple fritter.

"Well, congratulations again. I can't believe we're both pregnant at the same time." Maggie could not have been more truthful. She was absolutely and completely shocked. "Lastly, I interviewed someone earlier this morning over at The Sugarplum. She's available to fill in for you while you're away, Hank. It was an interesting interview, but I think we can make it work. I will recommend to the council we hire her. She's from Ann Arbor and has worked as an administrative assistant in churches and even in some small businesses."

Hank's smile faded ever so slightly. "Well, now. This is good news," he said flatly. "But does she really know how a church works? Does she understand our copier? What about our computer system? The bulletin is complicated. Did you show her yesterday's? Is she a detail kind of person? If she isn't, she'll run into trouble, yesireebob, she will." He absently took a bite of his muffin.

Maggie smiled. "Hank, she will only fill in while you're gone. She knows it is part-time and short-term. Plus, it's summertime. Our services are more laid-back. I promise I will keep things simple for her. She will be in later this afternoon to see the church and meet all of you. You can instruct her in the ways of the Loving the Lord Community Church office. I have asked her to come in each morning this week for training. You will prepare her well, Hank, and next week you and Pamela can do all your last-minute preparations and not worry about being in the office. I have no doubt we will all survive the next three months."

Cecelia took her cell phone and went into the garage. Jim was watching his right-wing news show, occasionally pounding the arm of his

La-Z-Boy and yelling at the television. His voice was ugly and full of hate.

Cecelia dialed the number for Dr. Betsy Sneller.

"This is Doctor Sneller. How may I help you?"

"My name is Cecelia Chance. Pastor Maggie Elliot gave me your phone number. I'd like to make an appointment."

"Which days and times work for you?"

"I am free on Tuesday afternoons. Do you have any openings?"

Betsy could hear desperation and desolation in the woman's voice. "I do. Would next Tuesday work? Is there a specific time?"

"Two o'clock would be safe. I mean, would work."

"Cecelia, what's your phone number?"

Cecelia hesitated. "Do you need it?" She knew it was a stupid question.

"Yes. In case I need to change your appointment. When you come in, I will need other information from you, like your address, health insurance, place of employment."

"Of course. I'm sorry. It's just that my husband regularly checks my phone. He knows all my contacts. He might get suspicious."

Betsy thought for a moment. The fact that Maggie had directed this woman to her was significant, and words like "safe" and a suspicious, phone-checking husband were red flags.

"Why don't you put my name in your phone as Betsy. We are new friends. I believe we met through Pastor Maggie," Betsy said calmly.

"Yes. Thank you. Can you tell me your fee?" The thought that she had little access to money had suddenly popped into Cecelia's mind.

"The first session is no charge. We can talk about fees when you come in. I do work on a sliding scale."

Cecelia felt humiliated, then angry. Jim had taken every shred of independence away from her. He controlled the money. He controlled her time. He spied on her phone and computer. She lived under a magnifying glass.

"Thank you, Doctor Sneller. I will pay for your time."

"I have you down for Tuesday the 13th at two o'clock. I'll see you then. Goodbye, Cecelia."

Cecelia hung up just as Jim opened the side door to the garage. She quickly turned toward the lawn mower.

"What are you doing in here?" he said as she shoved her phone into her pocket.

"I'm going to mow the lawn. Bobby is at Jason's house, and Naomi is babysitting."

He stared at her, then silently walked out of the garage. He would check her phone later.

Cecelia waited. Finally, she pulled her phone back out and typed in the new contact: Betsy. When he asked later, after examining her phone, she would have an alibi all ready. Betsy was a new friend.

6

Maggie met Jack in the hospital cafeteria for lunch. They sat in a corner with their laden trays and quickly began to eat.

"I'm sorry for the short lunch," he said with a wink. "I only have twenty minutes for my repast today. I've got another meeting about the clinic after this, then patients all afternoon. I'm swamped. Have you heard anything from Bryan?"

"No. I would have called you if I had. He must not have any news yet. How long will it take to know if Cate is responding to the treatment?"

"The IV fluids and antibiotics should have kicked in within a few hours, but we don't know her exact medical condition when she arrived. How was your morning?"

Maggie took a forkful of chicken salad and held it in midair. "Well, I meant to have a celebratory morning for Hank, but it didn't exactly go the way I'd hoped." She ate the bite of salad.

"Let me guess. Irena did something to ruin it." Jack bit into his loaded grilled cheese sandwich.

"No, she actually was thoughtful for one single second and brought a box of cream horns from The Sugarplum. Doris also brought a box of donuts, so along with my box of pastries, we could have opened our own bakery in the church basement." She sipped her tea. "No, the problem happened when I mentioned I'd interviewed someone to fill in for Hank while he and Pamela are away. He knew I was going to find someone. I told him last month. But I think the reality of it all was unhappy news for him today. To be honest, the woman I hired is not ideal, but she has experience in church offices, and it's only for three months. She's well-qualified, and I didn't get many applications since it's a temporary job."

"What's she like?" Jack asked, wiping his mouth.

"It's hard to put my finger on it. She kept cutting me off before I could get a question out of my mouth. I finally asked her to please not interrupt. She did not like that one bit. She is older than I am but seems ancient and stuck in her opinions. It's apparent she needs to know more than anyone else about everything, even though it was evident her knowledge had limits. She tried to give me tips on how to be a more efficient pastor and offered to critique my sermons. Unpleasant. I don't want to be mean, but her condescension irked me. I hope I didn't make a mistake."

"I doubt that. We met our new office manager this morning. She'll be working at the clinic part-time, but for now we will set her up in our office so she can learn our computer system, including the EMR, order equipment and supplies for the clinic, and work a little with our marketing department. She won't really begin her regular hours until closer to December when the clinic should open, thanks to Fitch Dervish."

"Fitch? Oh dear."

"Yes, he's been assigned to inspect the clinic. It's Sly's problem now."

"I know it takes all kinds of people to make a world, but we could do without some of them." Maggie took another bite.

"Ednah showed up late to the meeting this morning, which upset Charlene. I think there might already be a conflict brewing between those two. It was kind of awkward. Ednah missed her chair and fell on the floor. She was flustered."

"Ednah?" Maggie set her fork down. "Ednah with an 'h'?"

"Yes. Ednah with an 'h.' She's got a lot of . . . self-confidence. Maybe not all warranted."

"Ednah Lemmen?" Maggie asked.

"Yes, Lemmen."

"Jack, we have both hired the same woman."

"Well, won't this be fun." He laughed.

Maggie's phone rang. "Oh! It's Bryan." She answered quickly. "Bryan, what's happening?"

"Hi, Maggie. Is Jack there by chance?" Bryan's voice was weighted with exhaustion.

"Yes, he's here. I'll put you on speaker." She pushed the speaker button and turned the volume down a little so other people wouldn't be bothered or enticed to eavesdrop.

"Hi, Bryan. It's Jack. How is Cate doing?"

"It's more complicated than we thought. Along with having cerebral malaria, Cate was seriously dehydrated when we got her here." His voice began to rise with emotion. "They are doing tests on her kidneys and a scan of her brain. No one is saying she will be fine. I am going out of my mind!" They heard him stifle a sob.

"Bryan, I'm sorry," Jack said. "I'm sorry you have to wait for answers without feeling reassured in any way."

"I should have brought her here sooner. Why did I wait?"

"You can't do that," Maggie said, trying to control her own emotions. "Don't replay the past. She is right where she needs to be, and the doctors are skilled in treating malaria and other diseases. Where's Pastor Elisha?" Maggie desperately wanted someone to take care of her brother.

"He's waiting with Cate before she goes in for the scan."

"Can you wait with them?"

"No. I have to stay in the waiting room at the end of her hallway. Elisha is going to meet me there when she goes in." There was a long pause before he spoke again. "Will you call the Carlsons? You can put it more carefully. I want to get back to the waiting room. Part of the problem is I am not related to her. Being her boyfriend doesn't count. Elisha is the one they talk to." There was another long pause. "But I'm the one who loves her. I've got to go." He hung up.

"What do you think?" Maggie asked Jack softly.

"Cate is a very sick young woman. If she has kidney failure, everything will be more complicated. But I'm not there, and even Bryan doesn't know what all is happening."

"Will you call Mark and Ann?" Maggie asked. "I'll go to their house this afternoon, right after I get Ednah and Hank settled. But I won't be able to help with any of their medical questions."

"Yes, I'll call them as soon as I get back to the office."

They quickly and quietly finished their lunches.

Afterward, Maggie sat in her car and texted Nora.

Please continue to pray for Cate and Bryan.
She's very sick. I'll let you know more when I do. Thanks, friend.

Maggie returned to church only to hear raised voices as she once again walked through the red streamers. They weren't so delightful this time. She sighed. As much as she wanted to run right out the double doors, she forced herself to walk into the fray. Ednah and Hank were standing over the computer.

"Now, Hank, you have no idea how many bulletins I've typed in my day. I think you have been a little simplistic in your design. I can take over from here." She tried to push him out of the way with her derriere. Hank did not budge.

"Miss Lemmen, I believe it is *you* who are supposed to learn how we do things around here at Loving the Lord. Which means *I* probably need to show *you* how we get the job done." He was trying to be patient, but Maggie could hear the frustration in his voice.

With an all-knowing and condescending smirk on her face, Ednah said, "I'll tell you what, Hank. Let me settle in here and show you how to do a first-class bulletin. No offense, but this bulletin is too plain. It could have been typed by a first grader. You just let Ednah teach you a thing or two. I will have this office whipped into shape before you get back from Austria. Where's the scanner?"

"Australia. We do not have a scanner. And the office is in fine shape." Hank's temper was rising.

"Ednah." Maggie's voice was harsher than she meant it to be.

Hank and Ednah looked up at once.

"Ednah, I think I made it clear Hank would be training you this week. It's important you understand how the office is run and how bulletins are designed. I know you have some experience—"

"Maggie, I don't have 'some experience.' I have *extensive* experience. I think Hank could benefit from my knowledge."

"Please call me *Pastor* Maggie." Maggie was not normally bothered by proper titles, but Ednah was getting under her skin. They had three months to go. Maggie needed to set the tone. "I would like you to listen to Hank and do as instructed. We want the next three months to be seamless while Hank is away. We do not need any changes."

Hank, who was over a foot taller than Ednah, looked at Maggie and rolled his eyes. Maggie was sure he was trying to figure out how he would tell Pamela the trip to Australia must be cancelled. Leaving the church office in the hands of Ednah Lemmen was dangerous.

Ednah looked at Maggie. "Oh, dear. I see how it is. Change is hard for some people. They need to keep things the same. I do understand. I've seen this time and time again. Let's just all calm down, and I'll let Hank show me his nice bulletin template. It's all going to be just fine." Her condescension dripped all over the room like warm, sticky molasses.

Maggie was at a loss. This woman was going to make things complicated.

"Hank, thank you for the work you are doing to get Ednah up to speed. Ednah, take notes if you need to."

Maggie went into her office and closed the door. Some of the red streamers got caught in the door and hung helplessly on Maggie's side. They looked strangled. She opened the door and let them dangle back on Hank's side.

She would wait a while and see if the ruckus in Hank's office settled down before she went to the Carlson's home. She heard Hank explain the schedule for each week. Ednah made small, patronizing utterances, but didn't challenge Hank.

Maggie opened her lectionary Bible and read through the passages for Sunday. The Sunday after Pentecost was Trinity Sunday. As if on cue, she heard Irena on the organ, playing loudly and joyfully.

Holy, holy, holy! Lord God Almighty!
Early in the morning our song shall rise to Thee;
Holy, holy, holy! Merciful and mighty!
God in three Persons, blessed Trinity!

She looked out her window as Irena played. Why do people make it so difficult to be merciful and kind? We can't seem to get out of each other's way.

Cecelia Chance watched Jim head out of the driveway. He would be gone for over an hour as he met with his lawyer in Ann Arbor to talk about the settlement from his accident. He'd broken his back on the job. He'd stopped allowing Cecelia to join him at these meetings months ago. She had no idea if he would get the settlement his lawyer was hopeful to win. She took a deep breath. Whenever he left the house, she could breathe. The night before, he'd found the new contact on her phone.

"Who is Betsy?"

Cecelia jumped. "I met her at church." Cecelia didn't offer any more information.

"What does she do?"

"I don't really know. I think she works in Manchester somewhere. Pastor Maggie introduced us."

Jim had no use for Pastor Maggie. To him she was simple-minded and too emotional. Her plan to welcome refugees into Cherish last year sent him straight out of the congregation. He vowed never to go back, but Cecelia brought Naomi and Bobby to Loving the Lord every Sunday. Jim had tried to stop her at first, but she let him know she would be taking the kids to church no matter what. Whether he sensed this was one thing he couldn't control—or he didn't want to enter the boxing ring with God—he said no more about it.

"Is she as stupid as Maggie?"

Cecelia didn't answer.

"Whatever." He'd walked out of the room.

Now, with Jim away for his meeting, Cecelia was anxiously waiting for her appointment with Betsy. It was time to get a real strategy. She needed help with a plan. One Jim couldn't destroy. She and the kids had to get out, but she didn't have a clue where to begin.

It was Wednesday morning, two days since Bryan last called. Ann Carlson sat at her sunny kitchen table and poured Maggie a cup of herbal tea. Maggie noticed a photo album was opened to a picture of Cate when she was in elementary school.

"How old is Cate here?" she asked.

"She was eight. She'd won a spelling bee. She's holding her blue ribbon."

Ann poured herself and Mark cups of tea. Maggie turned the page and saw Cate holding a blonde cocker spaniel puppy.

"What a cute puppy," Maggie said.

"Cate picked him out of the litter," Mark said. "His name was Rupert. He was a good pet for our girls."

She knew Cate was the youngest of four. They'd stayed involved in church when the girls were school-aged, but once there was no need to bring the children, Mark and Ann found it easier to sleep in on Sunday mornings and enjoy cups of coffee while reading the paper. They had slowly slipped away from church before Maggie arrived. Cate was off to college the first autumn Maggie was installed at Loving the Lord.

"Where are the other girls?" Maggie asked.

"They are waiting to hear from us," Ann said. "They all have families and jobs, so we told them there was no need to come home. Yet." She winced. "Jack was nice enough to call us and explain things in plain English. We must wait for Cate's body to respond to the treatment and hope there is no permanent damage to her brain or kidneys. Just those two tiny things."

"She's young, strong, and has had malaria more than once," Maggie said. "She also has Pastor Elisha breathing down the necks of the doctors. He is her best asset right now."

She smiled as she turned pages in the photo album and watched Cate grow up. The fact this beautiful, loving girl could be her sister-in-law caused a lump to rise in Maggie's throat. She coughed.

"Is there anything I can bring you? Dinner?"

"We're fine on food. We've been eating your cinnamon roll bread pudding. It's delicious." Ann took a sip of her tea.

"I know there's nothing anyone can do," Maggie said. "The only helpful thing will be when you hear her voice on the phone and know she's well."

"We need her to be well and be home," Mark said, not quite keeping the gruffness out of his voice. "This has been a good thing, this Ghana thing, but enough is enough. She needs to come home as soon as she can travel. If we could go to her, we would. But without the necessary vaccinations and malaria meds, along with visas from the Ghanaian Embassy, she'll be back before we'd get there."

"My passport isn't even up to date," Ann sighed. "This waiting is the worst."

Maggie wondered how much her own mother worried about Bryan in Ghana. What had begun as a short stay turned into over two years. Maggie had the careless way of believing nothing could harm her brother. She realized this was foolish.

Her phone dinged. WhatsApp. She looked at Mark and Ann. "It's Bryan."

7

Maggie answered her phone. "Bryan, hi. I'm here with Mark and Ann." She waited. She didn't want to pressure Bryan to be on speaker. Who knew what news he would share?

"Oh. You can put me on speaker, Maggie."

Maggie pushed the button, and Bryan's voice filled the room.

"Hi, everyone. We've got some good news."

Ann and Mark leaned into one another, both exhaling.

"Cate doesn't have brain damage from the malaria. Her kidneys also seem to be responding, not to where the doctors would like, but the antibiotics and fluids are working in her system. They are hopeful."

Maggie could tell Bryan was carefully controlling his own emotion. She suspected if Ann and Mark were not sitting there, he would have told this good news through tears.

"Bryan, have you seen her yet?" Ann asked.

"I might get to see her tomorrow, but Pastor Elisha has seen her and prayed with her. She was groggy and fell asleep in the middle of the prayer, but Elisha thinks it still took," Bryan said with a very small chuckle.

"How are you doing? You know we all wish you were the one sitting by her, don't you?" Mark said.

"Thanks, Mark. It means a lot. Being just a boyfriend sucks. I might need to figure out a new way to never be away from her again."

Ann covered her mouth with her hand, and her eyes crinkled at the edges.

"I'm sure you'll come up with an idea on how to make it happen," Mark said, his relief palpable. "Let us know if you think of anything we might find interesting."

"Will do. I believe my sister will be helpful in the execution of a certain plan." Bryan's relief turned into a tentative version of happiness.

"We'll pray that by the time you call us tomorrow, there will be some good news about Cate's kidneys and she won't fall asleep on you," Maggie said. "Are you going to call Mom and Dad?"

"Yes. I need to hear their voices," Bryan said.

Maggie winced. Bryan had Pastor Elisha, but he also needed his family.

"Thanks. More tomorrow. Bye, all." Bryan clicked off.

There was a long silence in the Carlson's kitchen. The swirl of emotions made minds and hearts careen, then search for which emotion to land on first.

"We have hope," Ann said finally.

"Yes, we do," Maggie said. "May I pray with you, or would you rather not?"

Mark's eyes were shining. In a low voice he said, "Pray."

The three held hands in a sacred circle and lifted petitions to God. And they were comforted.

Maggie drove the short distance home and sat on the porch with a glass of ice water. The day was hot, and carrying around another little human did not help. She felt like she should get back to the office and referee Hank and Ednah. The past two and a half days had been tense, to say the least. Ednah's presence had everyone on edge, especially Hank. Maggie rocked gently in her wooden rocking chair. A soft breeze blew, and she closed her eyes. Sleep came quickly.

Maggie was standing on top of a tall ladder inside the sanctuary. She was at the highest point of the ceiling, holding red streamers and ribbons.

"I've got to get these up. Church is going to start any minute."

"Maggie, what are you doing up there?" Jack sounded frantic.

"We have to be ready for Pentecost. I'm doing the entire service in Greek."

"Maggie, you're pregnant. Please come down from the ladder."

"I'm not pregnant. Don't be ridiculous. But I do have to preach in five minutes, and I don't have a sermon."

Then Bryan walked into the sanctuary. "What are you doing, Maggie?"

"I'm hanging red for Pentecost. Jack thinks I'm pregnant. Do you have my sermon?"

"No, but Cate is pregnant." Bryan laughed and slapped Jack on the back.

"No! No! No! I em prregnant!" Irena screeched as she crawled onto the organ bench and began angrily pounding on the keys and pedals.

"Now, now, now." Ednah's condescending voice shouted above the discordant noise. "Let's all just calm down. Irena, let me teach you how to play the organ. You haven't had much training, have you? And Maggie, have you never hung streamers before?"

Maggie looked down and saw Hank hiding behind the pulpit.

"Hank, how is Australia?" she asked.

"Maggie, get down!" Jack sounded angry. "You're going to get hurt. And the clinic is not open for business yet."

Ednah took Jack by the hand. "It doesn't matter, Jack. I'm also a doctor. I can take care of any medical problem. I went to medical school online. I know how to scan. You just sit here and get ahold of yourself." Ednah helped Jack sit down in a pew.

"Everybody, shut up!" Maggie screamed.

They all looked up. She watched them as she wavered slightly, reaching for the top of the ladder as her foot slipped. She let go of the streamers and ribbons, and they fell in a cloud of red onto the altar. Maggie looked at her free arm. She was holding a baby.

"Whose baby is this?"

She let go of the ladder to hold tightly to the baby with both arms and fell backward. Down, down, down she went with the baby crying in her arms.

Maggie startled herself awake, her heart pounding. She was grasping the sides of the rocker with both hands, but she was on her own front porch in her rocking chair. She heaved in a breath and tried to steady her heart, then shakily took a drink of water. *Good grief! Now what was that all about?*

Once her heart calmed down, she went inside and into the kitchen. *I really should get back to church. I can't leave Hank alone to deal with Ednah. It was a mistake to hire her. Maybe someone else could help around the church for a bit.* She kept talking to herself as she pulled out graham crackers, sugar, butter, cream cheese, and eggs. *I don't have time to bake right now. I should do this later. Oh dear.* She methodically mixed the ingredients for a pie-plate cheesecake. *I'll go straight to church right after this.* She poured a mixture of berries in a small saucepan with some sugar and made a berry sauce. Once the cheesecake was baking and the berry sauce was cooling, she picked up her phone and called the church. One ring, two rings, three rings.

"Hello, Loving the Lord Community Church. How may I help you?"

Maggie paused. "Ednah?"

"Yes. Who is this, please?"

"Pastor Maggie."

"Oh, hi, Maggie. What do you need?"

"Where is Hank?"

"I sent him home. He was getting into such a state, I thought it best he just go on home and get ready for his trip. There's no reason for him to be here. Now, when will you be back in the office? We have some things to go over." Maggie could hear shuffling papers and drawers being opened and closed.

"I'll be in tomorrow morning. Let's meet then and clarify some things about your position. Goodbye."

Maggie hung up. She quickly dialed Hank's cell phone.

"Hi, Pastor Maggie." Hank sounded beleaguered.

"What happened with Ednah?"

"Well, after I tried for the one hundredth time to explain our system at church, she told me she has a different way of doing things and it would be best if I went home. By then I could feel my blood pressure going sky-high, so I left."

"Hank, I'm so sorry. I had no idea she would be this difficult. Will you come back in the morning? I'll be in early. We'll set things straight."

"I'll be in. But don't get your hopes up about setting things straight. Ednah is all mouth and no ears."

After they hung up, Maggie decided she could handle this Ednah situation. Maggie knew other overbearing women with a lack of self-awareness. They stayed busy organizing and bossing other people around because they had no sense of how to organize themselves. Maggie would take Ednah in hand and set the boundaries for the next three months.

After a quiet dinner on their deck, Jack took a bite of cheesecake and stared out over the back field.

"Mmm . . . This is so good. Your habit of stress-baking benefits me greatly. What stressed you out today?"

"Besides Bryan and Cate, I think I might have to strangle Ednah tomorrow."

"How fun." Jack dipped his fork in the berry sauce and licked it off. He looked up. "Hey, what's that?"

"What?"

"It looks like an animal just ran toward the barn."

"A dog?" Maggie leaned forward and looked.

"More like a skunk. We don't need it in the barn." Jack set down his fork and stood.

"Oh, just leave it alone. It won't harm anything."

"It could quite easily harm our noses. The smell doesn't go away. I was skunked as a child. It wasn't pleasant."

"I'm sure it wasn't, but you survived. Sit down and eat your dessert. We can let one little creature just be."

He could hear the exhaustion in her voice. "Okay, honey," he said in a singsong voice. He kissed the top of her head and sat back down.

They watched the sunset and let God remind them who was in control. As they got ready for bed, she pictured the sun rising over Accra and shining down on Bryan, Cate, and Elisha. God would keep showing up.

Ednah had been in residence for almost two weeks. Hank was now "officially" home to pack and do the other necessary things to leave the country for three months. Ednah had full rein, and once she had her own set of keys, she was at church at all hours of the day and night.

Maggie walked into the church office at seven thirty a.m. on Ednah's second Thursday. They'd muddled through the previous week with outbursts here and there, but with Hank out of the way, Ednah had the air of complete control. Maggie was not prepared for what she saw when she walked through the door. Hank's office was "reshaped" with furniture and the copy machine moved against the back wall. Nothing was on his desk except a cup filled with pens and pencils. She had no idea where the blue tarp was or any other of the handy tools Hank always had available for her to use, like the stapler, sticky note dispenser, scotch tape, ruler, three-hole punch, the box of markers, and tissues. She realized she foraged around Hank's desk regularly as she made her plans for daily ministry. *For crying out loud!*

But even Hank's stark office could not have prepared her for what she saw next. She opened the door to her own office and gasped.

Her office furniture was also rearranged. Every book was removed from her bookshelves and stacked in rows on her worktable. Everything originally on her worktable—including boxes with her ideas for

Easter, Ascension, and Pentecost—were nowhere to be seen. Her desk looked as sparse as Hank's. Even her blotter was gone. She scribbled thoughts for future sermons on her blotter. Then she looked up and realized the curtains from her window were missing. *What in the world?*

While checking her closet, she heard a noise. It was the oak doors of the sanctuary. She stepped back into Hank's office and waited until Ednah walked through the door from the gathering area.

"Oh! Hello, Maggie. What are you doing here so early?"

Maggie felt her temper rise. "If I asked you the same question, what would you say?"

"I'm here to get back to work. I couldn't get everything finished yesterday, as I hoped, so I thought I'd get an early start this morning. I had to do the bulletin and write a new draft of next month's newsletter earlier in the week, but last night I was able to get some real changes made. There's so much to be done, Maggie."

Maggie took a deep breath. "Ednah, I'd appreciate being called *Pastor* Maggie. Please respect my title and position. Also, I don't think you understand your job here at church. Your job description is clearly outlined for you. This is part-time work answering the phone, printing the bulletin, and working on other administrative tasks as directed by me. Where are Hank's and my things? Where's Hank's blue tarpaulin?"

"In the dumpster out back. Along with many superfluous items. Has no one cleaned or organized this church in the last one hundred years? I've never seen such an unnecessary mess. I don't know how you ever worked a day in here, and I certainly cannot."

Maggie heard the oak doors open again. Then she heard two voices.

"I just wanted to make sure Pastor Maggie has everything she needs from me before we leave," Hank said. "I have some of our contact information for the different hotels we'll be staying at and my international phone number."

"Well, now," Doris said. "I wouldn't mind having your information. What if I need to call you in an emergency? What if Ednah burns down the place? Hahaha! Just kidding. Don't worry. Along with Pastor Maggie, you have me to keep another set of eyeballs on the place."

Her laughter stopped abruptly as she and Hank came through the office door. Doris used her eyeballs to assess the situation in Hank's unrecognizable office. She walked right past Maggie and Ednah and investigated Maggie's office.

"What in the world is going on here?" Doris asked, turning to face Ednah.

"I am. And it's about time someone cleaned up this place," Ednah condescended with a knowing look. "It's time to declutter and get this office up and running."

"We've been 'up and running' for one hundred and sixty-two years. Have you not seen the historical marker in front of the sanctuary?" Doris glared.

"Exactly. It's time to bring this church into the current century. We need new office equipment, new bathrooms—handicapped accessible—and I was down in the kitchen. What a calamity. When was the last time the place had a good look over? The plumbing around here is atrocious. I could barely get the water going in the sink. No pressure whatsoever. Just a drip, drip, drip. We need a plumber, a professional cleaning company to come in and wax the basement floors, an overhaul of the nursery. How old are those toys? Oh, my, my, my! It's hard to know where to begin, but I'm here now. I'll make the calls, and we'll be on our way."

Maggie looked at Hank and Doris. Hank was right in his first assessment; Ednah was all mouth and no ears. This was a disaster.

The trip-trap of stilettos could be heard coming through the oak doors.

Maggie waited.

They all heard a scream or a squawk—something unpleasant and guttural came from the sanctuary. There was a loud bang and then the sound of music pages scattering. Another screech. Maggie led the way to the organ.

"Irena, what's wrong?"

Irena turned her blazing eyes on Ednah, who waddled in behind Maggie, Hank, and Doris. Ednah once again wore her knowing smirk, her nose arrogantly lifted, but before she could get a smug word out, Irena attacked.

"What you do wit my museek books? Vere is my clock, my cup, my tissue box, my lotion, my makeup bag, my tiarra? Vere arre my tings??" Irena stormed right up to Ednah's face.

"Now, Irena, did you just hear yourself? This is a church organ, not your second apartment. I cannot abide this disorderly clutter and mess. Let's treat this grand instrument as it deserves to be treated, shall we? I have put your belongings in a box so you can bring them home where they belong."

It seemed like time stopped. There was absolute silence in the sanctuary. No one breathed. Except Irena, who took her stilettoed right foot and ground it into Ednah's left foot with all the vim and vigor she could muster.

Now it was Ednah's turn to yelp. The stiletto made a deep indentation in Ednah's practical rubber shoe. "Owwww! Get off my foot!"

Irena ground her foot one more time then stepped back before Ednah could shove her away.

"Vere's my tings?"

Ednah bent over, staring at her aching foot, her face reddening. All smugness and arrogance were erased.

"Your box is in the pew over there." Ednah pointed. "I put it there for your convenience."

Irena toddled over to the last pew and found her precious possessions. She lifted the box and carried it to the organ bench. She took each item out of the box and spread them around the top and sides of the organ where they belonged. With so many nooks and crannies, she was able to empty the box and restore orderly disorder to her world.

"Now, please, all you go. I must prractice for Sunday." Her clawed hands shooed them away.

"But this is not right," Ednah said with a pained, although regained, authoritative voice. "You can't have this mess in the House of the Lord. Oww!" She sat down in a pew and held her foot.

"Yes, Ednah, I can hev my tings vere I vant dem. No one touches dem. NO ONE! Now get out!" With a large flourish of her arm, Irena sent them away for good.

Maggie turned to leave, then remembered something. "Irena, didn't you have a doctor appointment yesterday?" *How did I forget that? I should have called her last night. Drat!*

Irena, now perched on the organ bench, grinned gleefully at her workmates—excluding Ednah, who was limping back to Hank's office.

"Yes. I did. My Captain Crrunch and I vent to de baby doctorr."

"And?" Maggie, Hank, and Doris asked in unison.

"Yes. Ve hearrd de svish, svish, svish ov de hearrtbeats." For just a moment, Irena looked dreamy.

"Beats?" Doris asked. "As in *plural*?"

"Did you find out what you're having?" Maggie persisted.

"Oh, yes. Ve did." Irena looked from Maggie to Doris to Hank. She had them in the palm of her hand and relished her power. She took a deep sigh to build to her announcement. Then . . .

"Doctor Jack told us about de trriplets."

For the second time in less than five minutes, it seemed like time stood still.

"What?" Maggie was not comprehending either "Doctor Jack" or "triplets."

"Okay. I talk slow, like to a baby. Doctorr Jack, you know heem? Yes. He says, 'You are heving de tree babies, trriplets.' So, we get de beeg surrprise."

"Well, by golly!" Hank let out a hoot. "Little Irena, you are going to have a litter. Yesireebob! This is great news. I can't wait to tell Pamela. Oh, may I tell Pamela?"

Irena looked like a devilish little queen on her organ bench throne. "Yes, yes, ov courrse. We not keep a secrret like de other dum-dums. Ve sharre ourr heppiness." She bestowed a regal nod to her three friends.

"When are you due?" Doris couldn't help looking at Irena's mid-section. There was a bit of a bulge. Irena wasn't wearing one of her painted-on miniskirts. She was wearing leather pants and a flowy silver blouse which was *not* tucked in.

Irena followed Doris's gaze and put her hands on her small stomach. "It look like dis three will be herre for Tanksgiving." She smiled and hugged herself. "Yes, dey vill come beforre dey are all de way done, but I'll go as long as I can to grow dem."

"You will grow them beautifully," Maggie said, wondering how long Irena's tiny body could hold three babies.

"Thanksgiving. What a way to ring in the holidays." Hank grinned. "Hey, Irena, will your kids call me Uncle Hank? I feel like we're all family around here." He whispered, "Except for you-know-who." He pointed to the office into which Ednah had disappeared.

"How did you choose Jack to be your doctor?" Maggie asked. "I thought you would go to one of the bigger hospitals in Ann Arbor."

"Vy? I luv my Cherrish. Ov courrse, I hev my babies in Ann Arbor. Doctorr Jack says eet's de best place for trriplets. He vill be dere too, so I said yes. Now, who vill go and get me some tea and donuts?"

Hank ran for the big oak doors. "I'm on it, Irena!"

"And Hunk, you vill definitely be de uncle to de leetle chicks."

8

"So, how was the appointment yesterday with Irena and her happy uterus?" Maggie asked as she and Jack watched the sun set again from their deck.

"I wanted to tell you last night, but she made me promise to let her tell you first. She is going to give me a run for my money. I don't think 'high maintenance' begins to describe the kind of patient she's going to be."

"How's Keith?"

"I can't figure out if he is in shock or in love, or both. He's very attentive to Irena and had more questions for me than she did. I think he was getting used to the idea of being a father, but to just one baby. The news of triplets seemed to numb him somewhat. I had to explain to them that we couldn't deliver triplets in our little hospital. She will have to deliver in Ann Arbor. I already contacted Doctor Cal Siegers. He'll take the lead for the C-section, and I'll assist. Irena threw a tiny fit at first, but I told her it was the only way."

"Have I met Doctor Siegers?" Maggie asked.

"Last Christmas, at the hospital fundraiser. He helps us with all the emergency or high-risk pregnancies. Irena is exactly his kind of patient. She's in her forties, first pregnancy, triplets. Bam."

"I'm so happy for them both. I remember when we found out they were dating, and we were shocked and grossed out. But slowly it became normal, 'Keith and Irena.' Then two weeks ago we found out they were expecting a baby. Once again, totally grossed out, but quickly the news settled into reality. Now, triplets! Life really showed up and turned their normal craziness into insanity."

"Do you think we will have playdates with the Crunch children?"

"Good grief. Can you imagine? Three little Irenas running circles around our precious baby?"

Hank and Pamela were sent off to Australia with much fanfare, both at church the day before and at the airport the day of. Loving the Lord, headed by Doris, put together a surprise party right after church on Sunday. Hank and Pamela were lured down to the basement, where tables and chairs were set with the wedding tablecloths and the church china. After a delicious potluck lunch and Mrs. Popkin's cakes and pies, Maggie, Doris, and Irena got up as the Mistresses of Ceremony and roasted Hank, while extolling Pamela as a saint to travel around the world with their hapless workmate.

"Have you packed your blue tarp?" Doris asked.

"Hank, did you learn your Australian? I hear it's a tricky language. I think they even have their own alphabet," Maggie chimed in.

"Hunk! Deed you put de Pepto-Dismal in yourr suitcase?" Irena asked sweetly.

"You mean 'Bismol,' Irena," Doris said on cue.

"No. I dunt. I mean DISMAL!" Irena bowed at the laughter from the congregation.

Finally, after more jokes at Hank's expense, Maggie invited Hank and Pamela to come forward.

"We know it's probably been hard to pack everything you might need to be gone for three months. So we have something to give you, in case you run out of Pepto-Dismal or anything else you might need." Maggie handed them an envelope.

Hank opened it and found a stack of Australian dollars in differing increments.

"We will miss you so much," Maggie said with a small catch in her throat. "We thought it would be good if you had currency you could use right away, like in the airport when you arrive. You might need a donut or something."

Hank smiled, then cleared his throat. "Pastor Maggie, Doris, and Irena, thank you for all your kind and loving words." The crowd laughed. "I will miss being here and working with you for the next three months. Pamela and I love this congregation more than anything." Pamela nodded and smiled. "We'll miss worship and meals like this one and being part of everyday life during your everyday lives. We will bring back many stories, yesireebob, we will, and we look forward to meeting the newest member of Loving the Lord." He looked at Maggie. "And we will await three more members along with you." He looked at Irena. "Doris, do you have anything you want to announce?" Laughter again.

"Just that I'll be ready and waiting to dust your head as soon as you get back." Doris quickly wiped away a rogue tear.

"We love you all so much," Pamela said, looking around the crowded basement. "I promise to send updates for the newsletter. We will miss you."

More tears were wiped away from many cheeks, and a long line of hugs and well-wishes enveloped Hank and Pamela.

The next day, a caravan of cars followed Maggie, who had the two travelers in her backseat. Once they all parked, a group of children and adults surprised other travelers in the parking garage by forming a large circle around Hank and Pamela and praying them on their way. From the youngest voice of Zoey Teater, to the shakier voice of Howard Baker, everyone made their requests known to God for Hank and Pamela's traveling mercies and a safe return in September. Then they watched Hank's cowboy hat and Pamela's straw gardening hat walk into the airport to begin their adventure.

It was three days later, as Maggie sat at her kitchen table eating her favorite oatmeal with banana and pure maple syrup, when she heard her phone ding. She smiled and read Hank and Pamela's WhatsApp message upon their arrival in Australia.

G'day, Pastor Maggie! We've arrived in the Land Down Under.
Haven't seen a kangaroo yet, but hope to soon, yesireebob! Got a
donut as soon as we landed. Good thing we had some Australian
currency at the ready.
Hope all is well at Loving the Lord. We'll check out some churches
down here and let you know what we find.
If we can understand them, that is. It's a strange language
they speak here. Good thing I took those lessons! ☺

Maggie could imagine Hank's laugh. He was so good at laughing at his own corny jokes.

Almost three weeks later, Maggie's phone dinged, but this time it was from Bryan.

Hello, Sister Margaret. Are you and your husband available for a call?

She quickly replied:

OF COURSE, YOU NITWIT!

"Jack!"
"I'm upstairs."
"Bryan's calling!"
Bryan had called intermittently in the prior weeks, but it had been slow progress for Cate. Jack, Maggie, Mark, and Ann heaved from

hope to despair more than once. Maggie held her breath. *What will this call bring?*

She heard Jack's footsteps running down the stairs to the kitchen just as the phone rang.

"Bryan! How's Cate? How are you?" Maggie waited breathlessly as she put her brother on speaker phone.

"Hi, Bryan," Jack said, a little breathless.

"Hey, Jack. Listen, it's good news. The drugs have worked. It looks like her kidneys are functioning normally. They moved her to the rehab wing of the hospital so she can gain back her strength. I've been able to see her, even though, at first, she often didn't know I was there. But today I finally got to see her, and she saw me back."

"Maggie registered the emotion in her brother's voice. "I bet she was so glad to see you too, Bry. She's been in the hospital for so long."

Bryan coughed. "Yes, she has. It's been a long haul. And it's not over. Her rehab will take at least two more weeks. I've been making the trip from Bawjiase to Accra this past week. I have work to do for our next building project. I feel torn. United Hearts is so important to both of us, but I realize Cate means more to me. Being away from her about killed me."

Jack looked at Maggie and mouthed the words, *I know the feeling.*

"Today was just . . . She was so . . ." Bryan's emotions couldn't be corralled anymore. "I . . . uh . . . I . . . asked her to marry me." A strange laugh-sob-hiccup noise came through the phone.

Maggie's eyes filled. Maybe she was just tired. Maybe it was the pregnancy. Maybe it was the stress of Ednah. Maybe it was the weeks of worry over Cate and Bryan. Whatever it was, tears streamed down her face. "Oh, Bryan!"

"Bryan, congratulations!" Jack said. "There's not a more romantic place to propose than at the side of a hospital bed in a foreign country." He laughed.

Bryan got ahold of his laughing/crying jag. "I thought so. It actually was amazing."

"How did you ask her?" Maggie wiped her eyes and nose with a kitchen towel.

"Well, they let me in to see her, and she was just finishing her supper. She looked so tired, but when she saw me, I got the smile . . . The beautiful Cate smile."

"And?" Maggie didn't have patience for this. "What did you say?"

"I sat down next to the bed and held her hand. But then she made a face."

"WHAT KIND OF FACE?"

"Like she was in pain or something. And then she threw up."

Maggie and Jack stared at each other. Maggie unknowingly reached up and held her nose.

"She just kept throwing up her whole supper. I tried to get a bowl or something, but there wasn't anything. So I held her tray, and she threw up all over the tray and all over me."

Maggie was speechless.

"Then what?" Jack asked.

"When she was empty, and I knew she was okay, I wiped her face with a towel, and I said, 'Cate Carlson, we have just shared a very intimate moment.' Then I got down on one knee, in a small puddle of vomit, took her hand, and asked, 'Will you please be my wife and let me be your husband?'"

"Ewww!" Maggie thought she might be sick herself. "This is your engagement story for all time?"

"Yeh. It was kind of gross, but she said yes!"

"Then what happened?" Jack was trying not to laugh.

"A nurse came in and was perturbed at the mess. She pushed me out of the room so she could clean Cate, the bed, and the floor. But Cate said yes, and I'm going to marry her."

"Congratulations!" Jack said. "I think it's great you proposed, despite such deterrents. I don't know if I could have hung in there." He winked at Maggie.

"Okay, okay, you two weirdos! Bryan, do the Carlsons know? Have you called Mom and Dad?" Maggie's romantic sensibilities were bruised by this most unromantic proposal.

"Let me finish. I found a bathroom and tried to clean myself up. Pastor Elisha brought an extra shirt and some shorts, so I changed my clothes. Then, when Cate was cleaned and the doctor gave her a checkup to make sure the vomiting wasn't a sign of something serious, I went back in, and we talked it all through. She's still very weak, but we called her parents and Mom and Dad and told them our news."

Maggie smiled. "Congratulations, Bryan. We're so happy for you."

"Thanks. We've decided once Cate is fully recovered and has her strength back, we will come home. I have an idea the two of us leaving Bawjiase might help Pastor Elisha and United Hearts more than the two of us staying. Cate won't be able to work for a while, and I can see everyone is functioning just fine without us around. The staff is really doing well and can hire people from the village to help with projects and planning. Unfortunately, I've discovered I'm not necessary." He laughed. "I've worked myself out of a job, which was the goal at the beginning of June. But that's for another phone call. It's after midnight here, and I've got to find Pastor and get some sleep."

"I'm glad you're coming back," Maggie said. "It's purely selfish. I miss you and want to see my new almost sister-in-law."

"I'll tell her."

"I hope you have the best sleep ever, even though you will be on the floor or in an uncomfortable chair."

"I'm going to sleep like the happiest man alive. Because I am. I'll call soon. Love you guys!"

"Love you too. Give Cate a hug from us," Maggie said.

"But not right after she's eaten anything," Jack cracked.

The call ended. Immediately, the phone rang again.

"Hi, Mom! Hi, Dad!" Maggie said. "I know . . . I know . . . Can you believe it? I know . . . And in a puddle of vomit! That's our Bry!"

After the phone call, she sent a text to Nora.

Good news! Cate is getting better.
She threw up on Bryan.
He proposed.
She said yes.

9

Dr. Betsy Sneller reread the notes from the most recent visit of her last client.

Irreparably broken relationship with spousal abuse. Two teenage children. Fear for the future. Anxiety. Ready to file charges and restraining order. Police will be contacted by client. Recommend a Lexapro script. Client will contact MD.

How many times had she written similar words in other files? Broken family, domestic abuse, police, anxiety. But who of her clients weren't riddled with fear and anxiety? She wrote a prescription for an antidepressant and set another appointment for the following week. It was weekly appointments from then on. The writing was on the wall for this client.

The country was torn in two since the last presidential election. The new administration had no knowledge of governance, but enjoyed turning the nation into one large *Jerry Springer Show*. Division and hatred were the tools of an emotionally and mentally deficient president and cabinet. Families were divided. Friendships took on enemy status. Worries about cruel immigration policies devastated some of her clients, and elated others. Hatred of "the other" fueled the fires of racism and white supremacy, which had been quietly simmering forever.

Betsy had seen an influx of marital issues among many of her clients. The woman she just counseled had decided to file for divorce. She'd said so the first time she came in. When Betsy knew she would be unable to bring resolution to the marriage, she'd moved into the practical steps to help end the relationship—things such as contacting a lawyer and ways to support the children through divorce proceedings. They'd strategized. Betsy was an expert in the nuances of abusive situations. Different realities required different plans of action. They talked about violent behavior, which had already ensued, and how to file for a restraining order. The husband had refused from the start to come in for counseling and had forbidden his wife to get help. She'd made appointments anyway and kept all but one—when he was home, and she could not leave undetected.

"That's when I realized I was acting like a crazy woman," her client had said at the last appointment. "He controls every minute of my day. He watches me like a hawk. He times my trips to the grocery store or to pick up the kids from school. I've made appointments with you when he is having physical therapy on Tuesday afternoons. I used to have to drive him there and wait for him to go through his therapy sessions. He can drive now, and his appointments are at St. Joseph Hospital in Ypsilanti, which gives me time to drive down here to see you and get back before he does. He also has occasional meetings with his lawyer. Thank you, Doctor Sneller, for seeing me while he's away."

"You are welcome. I agree, you have an untenable situation. From what you have told me, his violence has escalated since earlier in your marriage when he began by verbally abusing you. You and your children are not safe. It may be the hardest thing you ever do, but leaving him will bring emotional health to the three of you. You will have support during the bumps of reclaiming your lives. The decision is yours, of course, but the pattern is clear; his violence will only escalate further."

"I'm ready. I hate him, and I hate what he's doing to our children. I do not want to be afraid in my own home anymore. I don't want to live in fear of his attacks."

"You are ready. You have my number and can call anytime, day or night, if an emergency arises. You have your support people, as well."

Betsy finished her notes and sighed. Her intellect, training, and skills usually led people to emotional health—to healed minds, souls, and relationships. She knew the importance of relational peace through respect and dignity, but she was up against something different now. Hate and cruelty had a front-row seat in society and spilled into families and friendships. Middle ground and thoughtful understanding fell away on both sides of the issues. And it had only been six months. Could the country take four years of this?

Betsy pulled out another file. Her next client was waiting.

Cecelia Chance drove home from Manchester to Cherish with the strange sensations of dread and relief. *Drelief!* She laughed at her made-up word. *When was the last time I laughed? We've been living under a black cloud.* Her hands nervously gripped the steering wheel.

For over a year, she had watched her husband Jim change. It began when he was injured at work. A forklift accident had left him with a broken back. He went on short-term disability and hoped for an insurance settlement. At first, his determination to heal his broken back and return to work kept him motivated. As the weeks went on, and little physical progress was made, Jim began to slide into depression. He was supposed to move from wheelchair to walker to crutches to cane to his own two legs, but his back was not healing as it should. He could walk, but struggled with lack of strength and balance. On top of that, the insurance claim was held up and finally was settled at a much lower sum than his lawyer had predicted.

The first time he'd hit Cecelia, she was loading the dishwasher. He smashed her head down on the kitchen counter with one of his crutches, and the plate in her hand broke into the sink. This attack came after months of verbal fighting over politics and the wave of abuses coming from the White House. Cecelia didn't want her children—Naomi and Bobby—to hear the foul language coming from their father. His agreement with an inept and cruel president to treat immigrants with draconian brutality on the country's southern border, demean women, abuse media correspondents who dared to criticize him, and his basic animosity toward decency, filled Jim's mind and heart. Their small home became unsafe over time as Jim grew in his anger and need for someone to blame for his accident but also the loss of what he thought his life should be.

His wife was the perfect target because she did not agree with him on much of anything. In fact, she disagreed with him on every issue. Instead of silently sitting by, she became more vocal. His onslaught of verbal and emotional abuse was a constant and putrid drip, drip, drip on their splintered lives.

Cecelia herself was at a breaking point by the time her head was smashed on the counter. She'd started sleeping in her daughter's room when Jim began to punch the air in his sleep and yell obscenities. She'd woken him up and slid quickly out of bed to avoid his raging fists.

One night he cried out, "I'm going to kill you!"

She didn't know if he was dreaming or fully aware of his threat. The coming days and weeks revealed his brutality.

His tactics were surprising her with a hard slap, a push into the wall, or coming up behind her and holding his forearm around her throat, using her body as a crutch while cutting off her oxygen.

The violence had escalated.

The last time he struck her, she was in the shower. With shampoo dripping down her face, he reached into the shower, grabbed her soapy hair, and hurled her to the floor of the shower. Leaning on one crutch, he'd used the other to slam her spine.

"I'll break *your* goddamn back! I'll put you in a wheelchair, and you'll rot there, you stupid bitch!"

The pain from the blow took her breath away. Once she could inhale, she sensed he was going to hit her again. She reached out, grabbed the crutch he was leaning on, and yanked it from under him. As he slipped in the puddled water, his other crutch fell and missed Cecelia only by inches. Unable to gain purchase, he went down hard, hitting his head on the toilet.

Cecelia had crawled out of the bathroom and locked herself in the bedroom. She quickly used a T-shirt to wipe the shampoo from her face and hair, dressed, then listened for Jim's revenge.

There was only silence. She waited longer, her back and face aching. Was he waiting for her to open the door so he could hit her again?

When she finally unlocked the door, she peeked out and saw his legs sprawled on the bathroom floor. She touched his foot with her toe. No response. He was unconscious. Then she realized what she was hoping for.

She did not want him to wake up.

She wanted him to be dead.

But he wasn't. She could see him breathing, so Cecelia called an ambulance. She left him on the floor as she slowly and painfully tried to fix her face before the EMT arrived. She decided she would take her own car. Hopefully, they would keep him overnight. She took some acetaminophen. Then she went to the top of the basement stairs. The kids hadn't heard all the ruckus, apparently. Probably video game headphones protected them.

She shouted down, "Kids! Naomi! Bobby! Kids!"

Finally, Naomi answered, obviously annoyed. "What is it, Mom?"

"Dad slipped in the bathroom, and he's not moving." She waited.

Naomi and Bobby turned off their game and clattered up the stairs. They stared at their mother.

"What happened to you?" Bobby asked.

"I slipped too. Dad hit the back of his head, and I hit my face. An ambulance is coming. I will follow in the car because I think they'll want to keep him overnight. If we're there late, I want you in bed by ten o'clock. Okay?"

"Is it serious?" Naomi asked, trying to look around her mother and down the hallway.

"I don't know."

At the same time they heard the faint sound of a siren, they also heard Jim moan from the bathroom. All three walked down the hallway. Jim was on all fours, reaching for his crutches, but the floor was still wet, and his hands went out from under him. He began to swear. Cecelia pushed both kids away from the bathroom.

"Naomi, go answer the door for the ambulance attendants. Bobby, why don't you stay in the living room while they take Dad to the hospital. You don't need to worry. I'll call you from there."

Bobby's casual response surprised her. "I'm not worried. I'm going to go play my game."

Bobby disappeared back down to the basement. Had Naomi and Bobby been aware of the physical violence? She was so careful. She hid the evidence left on her face and her arms and legs. She smiled when it hurt and chatted gaily and acted like everything was normal. But acting wasn't reality. Everyone knew when they were watching a play.

Jim was now yelling profanities and hitting the bathroom cabinets with his fists as he sat in the bloodied water on the floor.

He was not going to change.

Things were not going to get better.

Cecelia felt a rod of steel slowly growing inside her battered and bruised spine. She was finished. She was not going to be the actress in this play anymore.

The shower incident had been her moment of clarity. Jim was home from the hospital, but he would not be staying. She'd had enough, and Dr. Sneller had helped her with the decision to remove Jim from their home. She would not be physically hit again. The verbal blows battered her soul to pulp. Today, after her most recent visit with Betsy Sneller, she finally had a plan.

She walked in the back door and saw Naomi in the laundry room, awkwardly sorting clothes into piles of whites, lights, and darks. She was crying, gasping, and holding in sobs until they erupted jaggedly. Her right arm was hanging limply at her side as she painstakingly dragged clothes with her left hand, one piece at a time, to the different piles.

"Naomi, what's the matter?" Cecelia asked, staring.

Naomi looked down at her dangling arm. The bruises were red and raw, but worse, the bones looked disconnected. There was a bright-red mark on her face. A slap.

"Your dad?"

Naomi nodded.

Cecelia gasped and rushed toward her daughter, gently wiping her tears. Then she had a moment's panic. "Where's Bobby?"

"He's at Jason Wiggins's house. He went after baseball practice." She robotically picked up a pair of jeans and dragged them to the darks pile.

"We've got to get you to the hospital. I'm so sorry," Cecelia whispered.

Naomi's eyes slowly rolled back in her head, her knees gave out, and she crumpled to the floor. Cecelia caught her and stopped her head from hitting the hard ground. She brushed her daughter's hair from her face and stroked her cheek. "Naomi?" Nothing. "Naomi?"

Cecelia gently laid Naomi's head down and quickly got a glass of water from the kitchen. Naomi's eyes were fluttering when she returned to the laundry room. Cecelia held her daughter, then held the glass of water to her lips.

"Take a little drink, sweetheart. Then we've got to get you in the car."

Cecelia felt a chill, not knowing where Jim was. He must be in the house somewhere. She had to get Naomi out. She gave her another sip of water.

"Do you think you can stand? Just lean on me, and we'll get to the car."

Naomi struggled to move, but the pain in her arm rushed in and she groaned. She rolled over to her knees, clinging to her mother with her left hand. Cecelia wrapped her arms around Naomi's waist and helped her up. They both began to cry as Naomi rested her head on her mother's shoulder. Cecelia had never experienced this kind of pain pulsing through her as she held her battered daughter.

Then she heard heavy footsteps coming up from the basement.

10

Cecelia grabbed her purse and half-carried, half-dragged Naomi out the back door.

"Naomi, can you lean against the car? I'll help you in, just lean here while I open the door."

"Naomi? Where are you? Naomi!"

It was Jim. He was in the kitchen. Something smashed on the counter or the floor. He banged cupboards and then went into the laundry room. Cecelia could see him through the window as she scrambled for the keys. First, he looked around the room, then moved toward the back door. She saw him go down. He must have tripped on the piles of dirty clothes.

"Damn it! Naomi! Get in here!"

Cecelia opened the car door and slid Naomi inside. She fastened the seat belt around her daughter, carefully but quickly moving her limp arm out of the way. By then, Jim was at the door. Cecelia ran around the back of the car and opened the driver's side as Jim came unsteadily down the steps. He stumbled toward her, tripped on the step, and fell face first next to the car, grabbing for her ankle as she crawled into the car and slammed the door, hitting the lock button.

"This will never happen again," she whispered, as much to herself as to Naomi.

She shakily put the keys in the ignition. Jim was up now and banging against her window. Naomi screamed.

Cecelia started the car and threw it into reverse. She wanted to run him over. The desire overwhelmed her. But she backed up, made a tight turn, and sped down the driveway. Something heavy landed on the roof of the car. It slid off onto the hood. It was a brick from the side of the house.

Cecelia's original plan was no longer the plan. Her escape with her children must be now.

Naomi began to cry again. "My arm hurts so bad." Now, with her mother in control, she couldn't hold back her pain or fear. "I can't move my arm," she sobbed.

"I know. I'm so sorry. We'll be at the hospital in just a few minutes."

"Do you think my arm is broken?" Naomi cried uncontrollably.

Cecelia didn't answer but nodded slightly. Once they reached the hospital, she helped Naomi out of the car, carefully led her into emergency, and helped her sit down near the front desk. Naomi closed her eyes while Cecelia checked them in.

"May I help you?" a young woman asked. Her name tag said Jenny M. She looked at Naomi slumped in the chair, her arm hanging limply, the red slap mark burning on the side of her face.

"I believe my daughter's arm is broken." Cecelia could barely say the words. It took all her strength not to scream or burst into tears.

"I'll need you to fill out some papers, show your personal ID, and do you have an insurance card?" Jenny M. was kind, but all business.

Cecelia opened her wallet and handed her driver's license and insurance card to Jenny M., who handed Cecelia a clipboard with forms attached.

"Just start on these. They don't need to be finished before your daughter is called back."

Cecelia looked around and was relieved to see only two other people waiting in the large room. She took the clipboard and sat down next to her daughter, but there was one more thing to do first. She sent a text to Bobby's cell phone.

Don't go home. Wait for me there. I'll come get you soon. Don't go home.

Fortunately, the response was quick.

Ok.

The fact that Bobby didn't question her at all made her suspect again that he knew exactly what was going on with his father. She made sure Naomi was as comfortable as she could be, then began filling out the paperwork.

Naomi stared at the wall as tears silently slid down her cheeks. All she could see was her father, his angry face. When she told him she didn't know where her mother was, he didn't even hesitate. He'd slapped her hard across the face. Naomi had never been hit before, not even a spanking as a child. The pain of the slap and the shock of being hit vied for her emotions. Before she knew it, he gripped her arm so tightly she couldn't move or twist out of it. Then the Slam! Slam! Slam! on the side of the washing machine until she felt something crack. The pain made her scream. He told her to shut up and used her broken arm to pull her to the floor.

"Don't you ever lie to me again. You're a goddamn liar, like your mother!"

He'd slammed the door as he left.

She'd leaned back on the dirty laundry, in so much pain she couldn't breathe. Nothing made sense. Pain made the room spin as her breaths finally came quickly and erratically. She didn't know how long she was on the floor, but she finally sat up, then slowly stood. All she could think to do was sort the laundry. She had to get the laundry done before Mom got home.

"Naomi Chance?"

Cecelia looked up from the forms, and Naomi came back from her harsh memory.

"Hi, Naomi." Ellen walked toward mother and daughter. She knelt down in front of Naomi and said quietly, "I know you from church. I'm Ellen."

"Of course," Cecelia said. "Hi, Ellen. It's so nice to see a familiar face." Cecelia thought she might cry, again. "Congratulations on your marriage."

"Thank you." Ellen touched Cecelia's hand kindly. "Let's go back and take care of Naomi."

Ellen stood up and led the way to an examination room. Once Naomi was seated on the exam table and Cecelia was in one of the extra chairs, Ellen opened her computer and began the preliminary exam.

"Naomi, can you tell me what happened?" Ellen asked.

"My dad got home from his physical therapy early. He was looking for my mom, but she was gone. I was doing some laundry when he got back. He asked me where Mom was, but I didn't know."

Cecelia shuddered. Her secret meetings with Dr. Sneller had put Naomi in harm's way.

"He said I *did* know, and I better tell him. But I really didn't." Naomi told the account flatly, as if it was just another story. "When I told him that again, he grabbed my hair and then he slapped my face. I yelled because it hurt. He told me to shut up. Then he pushed me into the washing machine. I tried to duck under his arm and get out, but he held my arm. Then he just began to smash it on the washing machine until it cracked. I screamed. It really hurt, and I couldn't bend my arm at all. He yanked me onto the laundry on the floor. Then he left to look for Mom."

Ellen took down the information of the abuse and trauma of the afternoon. Once she'd typed all the information into the computer, she took Naomi's vital signs and gently looked at her dangling arm. Ellen knew shock had set in and the reality and repercussions of this abuse would take hold soon enough.

"I am so sorry this happened to you, Naomi. Doctor Cocanour will be in, and he will be able to make his diagnosis and take care of your arm. I'll get you some pain medication." Ellen could see Naomi's face growing pale as she sat on the table. "Let's help you lie down for a minute."

Ellen put her hand behind Naomi's shoulders and carefully laid her back while stabilizing her injured arm. Naomi closed her eyes in pain. Cecelia put the clipboard on the chair and stood by her daughter. The room was filled with agony. All three women felt raw.

Ellen left to make the necessary call to the police department and then found Dr. Alan Cocanour.

"A young woman, a girl, from church is here. Her father beat her this afternoon and appears to have broken her arm. Her mother is with her."

Alan shook his head as he looked over Ellen's report on the computer screen. *I know this family.* "Let's see how bad it is. Please get X-ray ready for her."

Police Chief Charlotte Tuggle and Officer Bernie Bumble found Cecelia alone in a small waiting room, clenching her fists while Naomi was in X-ray.

"Cecelia," Charlotte said quietly.

Cecelia jumped, then turned to see who'd interrupted her trip to hell. "Oh! Chief Tuggle. You startled me." Cecelia rose and shakily shook both officers' hands.

"How are you doing?" Charlotte knew this was a ridiculous thing to ask, but she had to begin somewhere, and this usually broke the ice.

"Not well. I had a plan in place to leave my husband. Today, he accelerated my timeline. What do you need from me to arrest him and get him away from me and my children?"

Charlotte was taken aback by this frankness. She looked into Cecelia's eyes. "Good for you. We're here to help. We have read Naomi's statement of the abuse. Doctor Cocanour confirmed the injuries match her statement. We can move forward now with charges and the arrest of your husband. Will you give us your statement, please? Take your time."

Charlotte felt herself slipping into Cecelia's pain, but she set her emotions aside. It was a difficult thing for her to do. She didn't need any time to think about how to word her statement. She didn't need to have a good cry first or change her mind about speaking with the police. She spoke bluntly.

"Jim Chance slammed our daughter Naomi's arm repeatedly on the washing machine today. He broke her arm. He has abused me physically for more than a year, and emotionally for years prior. He drinks to excess every day. Yes, he's an alcoholic. I wish to press charges, and I want him to stay away from us. I want a restraining order. I want him arrested. I've wasted so much time, too many years."

"As I said, the doctor has confirmed the broken arm," Charlotte said. "It's enough to put him away. Do you know where he is right now, Cecelia?"

"I'd guess he's drunk and passed out at our home. He was probably drunk when we left and he tried to stop me from bringing Naomi here. He threw a brick at my car. My son, Bobby, is with Marla Wiggins, and I've told him to stay there. No one is home except . . . except the one who has caused all this pain."

"I will file this report and request a restraining order. Because of the child abuse, he will be in the county jail until he goes before a judge. Do you have a lawyer?"

"Yes. Harold Brinkmeyer. I already called his office earlier today and made an appointment for next week."

"You can take a deep breath, Cecelia. Jim will be behind bars and unable to hurt any of you." *How much hurt has he already caused? It will take quite a while to heal from the devastation.* Charlotte knew it was going to be a long process.

Marla Wiggins sat at the kitchen table with Addie. She gazed at her daughter as Addie described her course selection for the fall. She would be a Sophomore at Hope College in Holland, Michigan.

"I've heard she's an amazing professor, and I'm going to take everything she teaches," Addie oozed.

Once Marla had realized she could continue to breathe after she and Tom dropped Addie off at college last August, she'd continued forward with life and knew she was a lucky mother to have a daughter who checked in on FaceTime almost daily. The year had flown by, and Marla felt a part of Addie's new world, instead of sitting on the outside wondering. When Addie finished her final exams in April, Marla and Tom were ready to pack up her things and bring her back to Cherish. Marla suspected this would be the last summer she would have her daughter home. Addie would soon find jobs or internships in different places. But right that moment, Marla sat and watched her daughter, drinking in every word of Addie's plans for the fall. It was almost August, and even though it felt like Addie had been home for only a week, the summer was coming to an end. They would be packing her up and driving her back to Holland.

Marla's phone rang. She looked to see who it was, knowing she wouldn't answer unless it was from the childcare center. It was Cecelia.

"Oh, Addie, just a minute. I have to take this call." She quickly put the phone to her ear. "Cecelia, are you all right?"

"No. I'm at the hospital with Naomi. He broke her arm today. I just met with Chief Tuggle and Officer Bumble. I pressed charges and asked for a restraining order. Naomi is having her arm set now. Thank goodness she didn't have to have surgery. But I'm done, Marla. I didn't protect my own child. He's been abusive forever, and I let it go on!" Cecelia began to sob.

Marla could hear the anger in her tears. She quickly moved outside to the front porch.

"Cecelia, you are doing the work to end this violence and protect your kids. Hold tight. The police will take care of Jim. You just take care of Naomi and yourself for now. Will you let me know when you're home?"

"Yes. It's so surreal. This isn't how I thought it would happen." Cecelia felt dizzy, as if she'd been riding a tilt-a-whirl for the last several years and just now stepped off. "He got home before I did because his physical therapy time was shortened. He got mad at Naomi when she said she didn't know where I was. When Naomi told him that, he took her arm and slammed it against the washer several times." Cecelia let out a sob.

Marla closed her eyes with the vision of Naomi's slender arm snapping. She couldn't imagine anyone harming Addie, especially her own father. But Tom was a completely different kind of man.

"What's your new plan?"

"I'm relieved the police came here to the hospital. I've never been able to do it before, you know, press charges. There was always an excuse. There was the hope he wouldn't do it again. I didn't want to break up our family. What a fool I've been for all these years."

"No. You're moving forward. You are strong, and you refuse to be bullied and attacked. I know you can do this, Cecelia."

"I'll call you when we're on our way home. Is it okay if Bobby stays with you for now?"

"Of course. He and Jason are outside. Do you want me to tell him anything?"

"I already sent him a quick text. I'll call him on his cell once I know Naomi's okay." She took a breath. "Ellen Bright is here . . . I mean Brinkmeyer, and has been amazing. She walked us through everything, and she's so kind. I really don't know what I would do without people like you and Ellen and Pastor Maggie and Doctor Sneller in my life. There's no way I could have done what I did today without all of you. Thank you, Marla."

"You're welcome, Cecelia. We are with you and the kids through all of this. You're not alone. Let me know when the two of you are home. Bye."

Marla walked back into the kitchen. Addie looked at her mother.

"Is something wrong?" Addie asked.

"Yes. Let's make some more food, okay? I think we will be taking dinner over to the Chance house." Marla pulled out ingredients for a chicken, cheese, and broccoli casserole and began layering them in a baking dish. "Will you make a salad?"

"Yes. And I'll grab some cookies from the outdoor freezer."

As mother and daughter worked side by side, Marla told Addie about Cecelia.

"And so, Cecelia has been working to put a plan together and get Jim out of the house and out of their lives. It won't be easy."

"When did the two of you become friends?" Addie asked, surprised by the fact her mother was helping a woman who lived in an abusive situation and hadn't told her anything about it.

"Actually, it was after the election last fall. I bumped into Cecelia downtown. I'd seen her in church on Sunday mornings, so I asked if she wanted to get some coffee, and we did. We met on Thursday mornings during my lunch break from the childcare center. I didn't know it at the time, but Jim went to physical therapy on Tuesday afternoons and Thursday mornings, so she had some freedom to leave the house. One day she shared her story. I guess I've known her for about seven or eight months. I really like her. She's smart and funny—when she's given the opportunity to forget about her reality at home. She's living in hell."

"You were the right person for her to connect with," Addie said.

"I like her. And I'm glad we're friends."

"What will happen now? How do they keep him away?"

"I don't know, exactly. He hurt Naomi today. He broke her arm, so he's not only guilty of spousal abuse, but child abuse as well."

Addie winced. She couldn't imagine any man she knew intentionally hurting her like that.

"To be honest," Marla said, "I hope the child abuse charge will keep him from having any rights to see the kids, but I don't know the laws. Cecelia will do whatever it takes to keep him from them. She also mentioned getting both kids into therapy. They would have a chance to heal from the inside out."

"Do you think Bobby has ever been hurt?"

"I don't know. He's a quiet kid, but he and Jason have really hit it off. I think today is the first time Jim ever physically hurt Naomi. Cecelia has only told me stories about her abuse in the past. I guess we never know what goes on in another household. People are good at masking their embarrassments and pain."

Marla ran the Cherish Childcare Center. The center had grown in popularity, but Marla saw a few ugly secrets in her close work with families. She had called Charlotte twice, suspecting child abuse. Sadly, she had been right both times.

Addie impulsively turned and hugged her mother, even though she was slicing tomatoes and Marla ended up with tomato seeds and goo clinging to her hair.

"Thank you for taking care of her, Mom. She needed you to be there for her."

"I truly believe God puts us all in unexpected places to do good in this world. We must pay attention and take the opportunity to do something for someone else as often as we can. Living for our own pleasures is a shallow pool to swim in." Marla sprinkled panko crumbs on top of the casserole. "Into the oven with this."

I wish we could do more than make them dinner. But it's a good place to start.

11

As Maggie pulled into her long farm driveway, her phone rang. She stopped the car and quickly answered. "Cecelia, are you okay?"

"Yes. No. We will be."

"Where are you?" Maggie waited. "Cecelia! Where are you?"

"Pastor Maggie, I'm at the hospital with Naomi. Jim attacked her today and broke her arm."

After a long pause, as Maggie absorbed what Cecelia had said, she continued.

"I've pressed charges with the police. They came here once they knew it was child abuse." She paused again. "I've called Marla and Doctor Sneller. This wasn't the plan exactly, but he hurt my child today. The police are on their way to our house now. By the time I take Naomi home, the monster will be gone. I wanted you to know."

"Is Bobby safe?" Maggie asked.

"Yes, thank God for Marla. He's with Jason. I called him to let him know what happened. He didn't seem surprised. He'll stay at Marla's until I have Naomi settled back at home. I think the three of us have a lot of work to do."

"We are all here for you. Cecelia, you are one of the bravest women I know."

"I'm not brave. I should have taken care of this situation the first time he hit me. Now Naomi has a broken arm. A BROKEN ARM!"

Startled, Maggie said, "I'm sorry, Cecelia. Yes, you know how you feel. There's no way I can totally understand. I'm here for you and Naomi and Bobby anytime. May I come to the hospital?"

"No. That's not necessary. Ellen just told me Naomi's arm is set. Once the swelling goes down, she'll get a permanent cast. As soon as I sign papers or whatever, I'm taking her home. I'll be in touch, I promise. Bye."

After they hung up, Maggie bowed her head. When her prayer for Cecelia, Naomi, Bobby, and Jim was ended, she leaned her head on the steering wheel and began to cry. Tears came in a torrent—tears for Cecelia, Naomi, Bobby, for Jim, for Charlotte and Bernie, who were on their way to the Chance home.

She finally put her car in drive and pulled up to the barn. Through watery eyes, she thought she saw something black dash through the partially opened barn door and was quickly jarred out of her emotion. She wiped her eyes and blew her nose. Last month, Jack thought he'd seen a skunk going toward the barn. What if there was a whole skunk family hiding in there? But they both had been in the barn several times since then, and there was no evidence of sight or smell of a skunk and family.

She went to the barn door and slowly opened it wider, breathing in the smells—old, seasoned wood beams, random bales of hay leftover from the previous owners, the faint scent of oil and turpentine. The smells brought her back to her grandparents' farm, when she was a little girl. She would help her Grandpa Bootsma feed the cows and horses and then go with her grandma to gather eggs from the chicken coop. Each chicken had a name and a personality. Queen Victoria, who had a crown of goldish-brown feathers wreathed around her tiny head, was Maggie's favorite. Queen Victoria strutted and clucked the moment she saw Grandma Bootsma walking out the back door with her feed bowl, a sentinel for the rest of the less astute chickens who were too busy gossiping with one another.

Maggie let her memories run freely as she breathed in the solid, earthy scents of her own barn. Her grandparents had farmed for the enjoyment of farming. Their living expenses were covered by her grandpa's work driving a Standard Oil truck. He delivered gas and oil to the farmers all over West Michigan. Grandma and Grandpa lived on his deceased parents' farm early in their marriage. When he retired from Standard Oil, he enjoyed riding his tractor, growing a field of hay, and caring for his animals. Their twilight years were gentle years. Their animals were more like large pets than commodities of trade. No nameless herds but, rather, named friends. Maggie had a secret hope of someday gathering a few gentle "friends" for their farm. She looked at the roof of the barn and whispered, "Thank you, Grandma and Grandpa, for teaching me to love all creatures with care and respect and joy."

Then she saw it. Something black dashed behind a bale of hay. She caught sight of what looked like a striped tail. Maggie gasped. Was it a raccoon? It must be something wild.

"Well, hello there," she said, as if a small wild animal would respond. "Who are you?" She used her Snow-White voice, always reserved for animals and babies. There was a scuffling of claws and a disruption of hay.

"Okay, I'm going to leave now. You just calm down. Goodbye."

Maggie left the barn door cracked and walked toward the house. When she got to the porch, she turned and watched. Nothing. She waited a few more minutes, then went inside. She needed to bake something while she waited to hear from Cecelia. She reached for flour and sugar.

Charlotte Tuggle and Bernie Bumble pulled into the Chance driveway and shut off the siren, leaving the flashing lights on. Jim Chance was standing on his front porch.

"He's waiting for us. He heard the siren," Charlotte said.

She pulled the squad car as close to the porch as she could. Then, taking a deep breath, she slowly opened the door and got out. Bernie got out too and stood by the hood of the car. He waited for Charlotte's lead.

"Mr. Chance, is everything all right?" Charlotte asked, standing in front of the porch steps.

"What are you doing here? You have no right coming here to my house," Jim said in slurred words.

"We've been to the hospital. Naomi is being treated there. Her arm is broken, Jim." Charlotte kept her voice calm.

"She lied to me. She's a liar. Just like her mother. I had to teach her a lesson. Don't never lie to me!"

He tripped over a small wooden table and sent a potted geranium flying off the porch. The little plant landed on Charlotte's boot, scattering red petals. Charlotte slowly bent down and moved it to the side of the step.

"Damn it! What the hell's this doing here?" Jim kicked the table.

"So, Jim, you admit you broke Naomi's arm today in your home?"

"Yes. She's just like her mother. Lying bitch."

"Jim, we're going to need you to come with us." As Charlotte spoke, Bernie took a step closer. "We don't want any trouble, but we need to get some information from you down at the station."

"What information?" He stumbled slightly. "The fact that I have a lying bitch for a wife and lying daughter too? Take *them* to the station!" He tried to sit down but missed the chair and fell into the side of the house. "Damn it!"

Charlotte and Bernie moved as one. They stepped onto the porch and each took one of Jim's arms. Bernie read him his rights as they handcuffed him.

Jim pulled away at first, then resigned himself. Cecelia would pay for this.

Bernie led him to the car while Charlotte waited until Jim was in the backseat. The police car silently drove away.

An hour later, Cecelia and Naomi pulled into the driveway. The kitchen light was on. It gave Cecelia a chill, immediately thinking Jim was home even though Charlotte had called her and told her Jim was on his way to the county jail. Cecelia parked the car and helped Naomi get out. They walked slowly to the porch steps. Cecelia spotted the broken geranium and bent down to pick up the pot.

"Well, what happened to you?" Cecelia knew, all too well. "There, there, we'll get you back together again," she said softly as she pressed the plant back into the pot, then scooped up the spilled dirt with her hands and added it on top. "You will be okay. You'll grow and bloom again. I promise," she whispered.

Cecelia righted the overturned table and set down the small flowerpot. She was about to help Naomi inside when another car turned into their driveway. Cecelia recognized the car at once and smiled wearily.

Marla, Addie, Jason, and Bobby pulled up behind Cecelia's car and got out.

"Perfect timing. We didn't want you to miss dinner." Marla's smile was warm, even as she tried to read the scene before her. She stood still until Cecelia spoke.

Bobby loped up to his mother. "Is he gone?" His eyes darted around the porch and through the kitchen window.

"Yes. We just got here. The police have taken him away."

She put an arm around his shoulders and gave him a hug. Bobby stood by Naomi and stared at her sling-wrapped arm.

Marla and Addie got the food out of the car while Jason grabbed a cooler from the back.

"Tom's working at the hardware store tonight, so we hoped we could eat with you, unless you need some time alone." Marla spoke frankly. "Naomi, we're sorry for what happened. It must be confusing, or maybe it isn't. We want you to know we love you." She stopped there, knowing not to clutter the air with too many words. Silence was a necessary resting place.

Jason carried the cooler up the porch steps and stood by Bobby.

Addie looked at Naomi's arm. "Does it hurt?"

"Not too bad now. It was awful while Doctor Cocanour set it. He pulled so hard."

Addie, Jason, and Bobby groaned. Marla looked at Cecelia, who briefly closed her eyes.

"But they gave me some pain medicine," Naomi said. "I'm just kind of tired now."

"Let's get you inside," Cecelia said, "and make you more comfortable."

They entered the house, and the first thing Cecelia felt was relief. *He's not here. He won't be yelling or embarrassing us or ruining another evening. We can have friends over. We can watch what we want on TV.* Her thoughts raced.

"Are you hungry?" Marla asked. "Or do you want to wait?"

"Let's eat now," Cecelia said. "You must be as hungry as we are. Bobby, will you set the table, please?"

Cecelia settled Naomi on the couch with pillows to support her arm.

"It feels weird to be here, doesn't it?" Naomi said softly.

"Yes, but he's not here. He won't show up. Are you doing okay?"

"I'm all right. It sort of doesn't seem real, except for this sling on my arm."

"I'm so sorry. I don't think I can say it enough."

"It wasn't your fault. He did this all on his own." Naomi put her head back on a pillow and closed her eyes.

"You rest. I'll bring you some dinner."

Naomi's head flew up when they heard Bobby yell, "Whoa! Mom!"

Cecelia ran to the kitchen, followed by Marla, Addie, and Jason. She was faced with Jim's parting gift.

He had pulled pots and pans out of cupboards. They were scattered on the floor. He had left the refrigerator and freezer open, and something was dripping. But the worst sight was the cruelest: Cecelia's grandmother's china. It had been passed down to her from her own mother and only used on holidays. It was now smashed to pieces on the countertops and the floor. Not one piece remained intact or was reparable. This last act of abuse brought Cecelia to her knees.

Addie led Jason and Bobby into the living room.

"What happened?" Naomi asked.

"Great-Grandma's china," Bobby said. "It's all smashed. And something gross is dripping out of the freezer. It's wide open."

Marla knelt beside Cecelia and rested a supporting hand on her back. They grieved in silence.

"I should have been ready for this," Cecelia finally said, "but I wasn't. I thought he was gone, but he did this after I took Naomi away to the hospital. This china was very special to me."

"I'm so sorry." It was all too horrible. Marla knew there were no words to make it better.

"The kids are hungry," Cecelia said, lifting her head. "I'll clean this up."

"*We'll* clean this up. Where's your broom?"

Cecelia pointed to a closet, and Marla got up and found the broom and dustpan. Then she called, "Addie, can you come in here, please?" Addie did. "Cecelia, what if you go and sit with Naomi? This won't take us long, and it seems like you have been through enough today."

Cecelia nodded mutely, got to her feet, and left the kitchen.

Marla picked up a piece of the broken china. Small purple pansies danced with tiny yellow roses on the snowy-white background. Marla swept up the shattered pieces with care. Addie searched under the sink for some cleanser and a sponge.

"What should I do with this melted food?" she asked.

"Just a minute. Why don't you pick up the pots and pans, and then we can clean out the freezer."

Marla put her casserole in the oven and set the temperature to keep it warm. Addie matched lids to pans.

They swept, organized the pans, and finally emptied the freezer and some of the contents in the refrigerator into a large garbage bag. Marla found a sponge mop and a bucket. She quickly mopped the floor. Then she called for Jason and Bobby.

"Jason, please take this trash bag out to the bin by the garage. Bobby, will you help me in here?"

Bobby got plates and cups and six sets of silverware. Jason took out the trash, then brought the cooler into the kitchen. He helped Bobby set the table.

"Do you want to play a video game later?" Jason asked.

Bobby looked up with relief in his eyes. "Yeh. Portal?"

"Yeh."

Addie got drinks and salad out of the cooler, while Marla removed the large casserole from the oven and put French brioche rolls from The Sugarplum in a basket.

"Dinner's ready," she said as she stepped into the living room.

Both Cecelia and Naomi were asleep, but Cecelia's eyes opened when she heard Marla's voice.

"Naomi," she whispered, "are you hungry?"

Naomi came groggily out of her sleep. "I'm so hungry, Mom."

"I can bring you a plate."

Naomi shook her head as she slowly sat up. "I can sit at the table. Let's just be normal, like other people."

Cecelia wondered what their new normal would look like.

The meal commenced without forced conversation or small talk. The homey food and the presence of friends were a comforting balm on the fresh wounds of the day inflicted on Cecelia's little family. The healing would be unpredictable and different for each of them. Cecelia sighed.

"Are you all right, Mom?" Naomi asked.

"Yes. We have a lot to deal with right now, and I'm thankful for friends who care about us and feed us delicious food."

After the meal, the boys helped clear the table, then grabbed a bag of Marla's cookies and disappeared into the basement and a game of Portal. Addie loaded the dishwasher while Marla and Cecelia put the leftover food into the clean refrigerator. Then Addie sat on the couch with Naomi.

"What's it feel like?" Addie asked.

"My arm? It hurts. I have to go back in a few days to have it put in a cast."

"How do you feel about the whole day? Does it even seem real?"

"It's weird because he's my dad, but he's not like a dad. I knew he hurt my mom. Bobby did too." She paused and closed her eyes for a moment. "It's the worst to hear your mom cry. When he hurt me today, I thought maybe he wouldn't hit her tonight. Maybe I was saving her from him for a while. Does that make sense?"

"Everything you say makes sense. I'm sorry he hurt you and your mom." She paused. "I didn't even know our moms were friends. My mom really likes your mom. She says she's smart and easy to talk with."

"She is."

Addie took a breath, then dove in with another question. "Is it good your dad is going to jail?"

"Yes. He was getting worse." Naomi fidgeted with her hair. "My mom had to sneak out of the house to run errands. He timed how long she was gone and yelled at her if he thought she was gone too long. Once he started yelling, it only got worse. She couldn't calm him down. For a long time, she didn't think Bobby and I knew how he was hurting her. Dad didn't care if we knew because he blamed her for everything. I think he wanted us to know she deserved to be hit. But we knew she didn't. He used to be different, so it's hard because he wasn't always so mean. At least he didn't hit us. He's like two different people."

Addie thought of her own dad. Tom was a generous and other-focused man. He ran his business honestly, donated profits and items from the store to those in need, and he was attentive to his family. Addie couldn't imagine ever being afraid of her dad. He and her mother treated each other with respect and didn't hide their affection. Sometimes she would hear them at night, talking softly in bed or laughing. It grossed her out, but she knew those were the right sounds to hear.

"Do you think he'll come back?"

"I don't know. I don't think Mom will let him come back if he's going to be mean again."

"I wonder where he'll go?" Addie asked, more to herself than Naomi.

Cecelia and Marla moved out to the porch and sat on either side of the battered geranium. They sipped mugs of tea with their cookies.

"What's next?" Marla asked.

"I don't know all the details. Doctor Sneller is helping me with the next steps. I do know he will be in jail until he goes to court, which gives us time. Doctor Sneller is going to help me explain the process to the kids. I'm also going to set up some appointments for them each alone with her. The sooner we all get help unraveling this dysfunction, the better. I finally thought of it like this, if there was a man at church, or anywhere, who was rude to Naomi or Bobby, or hurt them in some way, I would tell them to stay far away from him. I would tell other adults he was inappropriate or dangerous. I would tell him to stay away from my children. Children do not have to be polite to rude or hurtful adults. I don't think we teach them well enough to speak up if an adult is unkind to them. Naomi and Bobby must get the message now, even though the person hurting them is their father. I never would have thought of telling anyone how abusive Jim is until I talked to Pastor Maggie and she directed me to Doctor Sneller and then you. You kept calling me, and you were always available, no matter when. Thank you, Marla."

"You're welcome. I am thankful for our friendship. It goes both ways. What else do you need?"

"A job." Cecelia smiled. "I have been thinking of this day for so long. The day he would be gone and I could make a life for Naomi, Bobby, and for myself. I won't keep Jim's secrets, and I won't be a victim. Doctor Sneller has shone a light on all the misconceptions of my situation. I never need to protect or defend Jim again. Ever."

"It makes things so hard. You want your kids to know and love their father," Marla said. But even as she spoke, the words sounded wrong.

"Not if he hurts them emotionally or physically. He's an abuser."

Cecelia's voice was calm, but Marla could sense the anger underneath. Good, productive anger.

"We are here for you all the way. Anything you need, anything the kids need. We are available. I'll also find out about job possibilities. What would you like to do?"

"Jim and I were married before I finished college. I always wanted to be an architect. My dad was an architect, and I loved going to his office and watching him design and draw plans on his drafting table."

"Well, now this is a surprise." Marla laughed. "How much schooling would it take to finish your degree?"

"One more year of classes for the degree, then one to two years of work experience to get licensed. It seems unattainable now. I need work to pay bills."

"I'll keep an eye out. Let's have coffee tomorrow, if it works for you. I can come here so Naomi will have you close by. How about ten a.m.?"

"Don't you have work?"

"Yes, but I can make time to stop over. One of the little perks of being the director," Marla said with a smile.

"Yes, I would appreciate it. Thank you for everything today, especially for keeping Bobby this afternoon and making us dinner. I hope this whole thing is handled quickly, but I suspect we may have some bumps along the way."

Maggie's phone rang, and she grabbed it quickly. "Hi, Cecelia. How are you?"

"I'm fine, and so are the kids. I wanted to let you know what happened tonight."

She sounds so tired. "Yes. I've been wondering and praying for all of you."

Cecelia recounted the day's and evening's events, including the destruction in her kitchen. "I'll see Harold Brinkmeyer next week. I don't know much more."

"Jim is in jail?"

"Yes. He will be held until he sees a judge."

"Will you be able to sleep tonight?"

"Yes, I think I'll be able to sleep well for the first time in quite a while. The kids are doing okay, but we will all have work to do. Naomi will get a permanent cast, and her arm should heal completely. Marla, Addie, and Jason all coming over with dinner tonight was just what we needed."

God bless Marla. "I'm so glad, Cecelia. Glad you were able to make such a hard decision, and glad you were surrounded by people who care for you and love you. We're all here for you."

"Thank you for the support. I'm going to check on the kids one more time and then go to bed. Good night."

"Good night, Cecelia."

Maggie's head whirled, and she began to jot down a list of things to do the next day to make sure Cecelia, Naomi, and Bobby were taken care of.

12

Maggie awoke at five in the morning with thoughts of Cecelia's situation flooding her mind. She remembered when the whole church came together for Julia Benson and her daughter, Hannah. Julia was married to Redford Johnson and lived with abuse until Hannah was born. Then she quickly fled to protect Hannah from being harmed. Maggie led the church to give Julia and Hannah a "homecoming shower." Through the generosity of a dying woman, Julia found herself the owner of a home for herself and her daughter, free and clear. The church then surprised her with furnishings, appliances, and home products, along with bags and bags of groceries. Maggie wanted to do something similar for Cecelia and her children. She would call Marla and begin the plans.

Her phone rang.

"Bryan!"

Jack rolled over and groggily opened his eyes. Maggie pushed the speaker button.

"Hi, Maggie. I know it's early, but I had to call."

"I was wide awake, so no problem."

"Is Jack there? Oh, um, yeah . . . I'm sure . . ."

"I'm here, Bryan. I wasn't awake. My wife is an insomniac. What's up?"

"We're coming home!" Bryan and Cate said together.

"Cate? Oh, Cate! How are you? How do you feel?" Maggie was thrown from worries over Cecelia to elation over hearing from Bryan and Cate.

"Hi, Maggie. I'm getting stronger every day." Her voice sounded far from strong.

"We're so glad you are healing. These have been some scary days, especially for you," Maggie said. "When are you coming home so we can see you with our own eyeballs?"

Bryan laughed. "We will be in Detroit on August twenty-fifth. All the parents know. We woke up everyone but you."

"Next month! It will be so good to hug you both. How long will you stay, do you think?"

"I think for quite a long time. We're still formulating our future, and we'll fill you in when we get back."

Bryan sounded so grown-up. *When did that happen?*

"Have fun planning. Cate, we're praying for you and your continued healing. Bry, take extra good care of her," Maggie bossed.

"It's easy to do. Did I mention she's going to be my wife?"

"Yes. We hope Cate knows what she's getting into."

"Oh, I do," Cate said with a quiet laugh.

"Well," Bryan said, "we wanted you to know about our homecoming so you will make us a pie or a cake or anything out of your oven."

"I will have a kitchen full of baked goods for you. Have you thought at all about where you'll live when you get back? Do you need to crash here?"

"We are just trying to put a plan together. Cate will go home, at least for a while, as she heals. I'd like to stay in Cherish to be near her."

"Ahem, we live in Cherish."

"Yep. But a long-term houseguest might be inconvenient as you bring my niece or nephew into the world."

"Do you want to sleep in the church basement or maybe our barn?" Maggie teased.

"As comfortable as those both sound, I have to say no."

"We have room and would love to have you here. Just put it in the back of your mind."

"Thanks to you both. I will keep it in mind. We'll call again before we leave."

"We love you," Cate said.

"We love you too! Bye-bye," Maggie and Jack said together.

Jack wrapped his arms around Maggie and pulled her close.

"What a great way to begin the day." Maggie sighed as she cuddled into his arms. "They'll be home when the baby is born. I'm so glad."

Jack held her and soon felt her gentle, steady breaths. He slipped into dreamland too. They didn't wake up until the alarm went off and three cats jumped on the bed to remind them it was time for breakfast.

Unfortunately, even after all the happy news from Bryan and Cate, Maggie faced another day of Ednah Lemmen. It had been over a month since the advent of Ednah's loud and overbearing presence. She managed to annoy, anger, or enrage the small staff of Loving the Lord on a daily basis. Maggie thought time would never pass until Hank and Pamela returned. She knew this morning would be contentious. Doris would be in to do her Friday cleaning, and Irena and Keith were scheduled to put the final touches on their wedding, which was only two weeks away.

"What are you thinking?" Jack yawned as he released his arm from under her back. It was still asleep.

"Oh, bits and bobs, odds and ends, this and that."

He kissed her shoulder. "Besides being awake at the crack of dawn, did you sleep last night?"

"I was up around two a.m. thanks to the baby bouncing on my bladder. Then I started thinking about Cecelia's family, Irena and Keith's wedding, and another day of Ednah. I took *A Demon Summer* with me to the guest room and let G.M. Malliet whisk me away to Monkbury Abbey and enjoy the terror of poisoned fruitcake for about an hour, then came back here. I'm glad I didn't wake you. You can blame Bryan for rousing you from your slumber." She kissed him.

"I think we—and by we, I mean you—need to begin to slow down a little."

"I still have two months before the baby is born and my maternity leave. And there is so much to do. I want things to be in tip-top shape when Nora steps in. Oh gosh! I have to text Nora and let her know Bryan and Cate are coming home."

She grabbed her phone and shot off a text. It almost immediately dinged back with Nora's thumbs-up emoji and a bright-red heart.

"The best thing is, Hank will be back by the time Nora settles into my office. No Ednah for Nora to deal with. She will be your problem by then."

"She'll be Sylvester's problem. Back to you slowing down, I know your work isn't physically taxing, but you do an incredible amount of emotional labor. No need to do it all. We have a very helpful congregation." He kissed her back.

"Emotional labor is at the top of any pastor's job description, or it should be. I like caring for people. I'm just feeling a little worn out. The most helpful thing would be for someone to put Ednah away somewhere until Hank gets back. Two more months of Ednah will be the end of me. Yesterday, she saw my sermon on my desk while I was in the sanctuary with Irena. She took it upon herself to sit down with a red pen and scratch out things she didn't think were necessary, and she even added her own comments. To my *sermon*!"

Jack stared.

"Yes, she really did. See what fun you'll have when she begins work at the free clinic? Is December still the grand opening?"

"I think I'll be able to answer you tonight. Sylvester is going to the site again today to meet with Fitch Dervish. Apparently, there have been some compliance issues, at least according to Fitch. They were not on the report from the original inspector, but she went and gave birth to a set of twins and isn't available to clarify her report."

"Women. Useless. Always having babies and messing things up for the menfolk." Maggie sadly shook her head, then giggled.

"In the good old days, a woman could have a baby and be back in the field by the next day. Things have gotten lax. Now you all expect to have six weeks to lie around and do nothing."

"You're an idiot, but I love you. I'll make sure not to waste too much time lying around after giving birth. I'll be in the pulpit within a week, I promise you, oh, master. Now, please rub my back. It aches."

Jack obeyed. "Tonight will be fun. I can't believe we haven't had Ellen and Harold over since their honeymoon."

"I know. I wonder if Sly and Sky will have any wedding plans to share with us? Their wedding is in October, but they haven't had time to meet for premarital counseling yet. Maybe we'll find out tonight."

By the time Jack and Maggie were dressed and fed, along with the felines, and ready to leave for their respective places of work, Maggie remembered she had left a fresh copy of her sermon in her home office printer tray.

"Give me a kiss. I forgot my sermon."

Jack kissed her and left. Maggie went back into the house to retrieve the sermon and pet the cats one last time, stalling going to church. As she headed out to the driveway, something caught the corner of her eye. She looked at the barn just as a fluffy dark tail ribboned its way through the crack in the door. Happy to have a reason to put off seeing Ednah, Maggie walked to the barn and slowly peeked inside the door. There he was, sitting right on top of a hay bale—a long, skinny black cat with a quite-dead bird hanging limply in his mouth. The cat saw Maggie at the same time Maggie saw him. He jumped down without dropping the bird and ran behind the riding lawn mower in the corner of the barn.

"Don't worry, my good sir, I won't hurt you," Maggie said quietly.

She went back to the house, opened a can of cat food, and dumped it into a bowl. Marmalade, Cheerio, and Fruit Loop all came running from their napping places because apparently breakfast was being served again. Maggie filled another bowl with fresh water and, with a chorus of meows following her, went out the door and back to the barn. She awkwardly bent down and put the food and water inside the barn door. The barn was silent, but Maggie was sure her scrawny intruder was not gone. She smiled to herself as she walked to church. Who was their little visitor?

The organ was blaring as Maggie walked up to the large oak doors. Irena was either gleeful or furious. Maggie took a deep breath and entered the church. Irena, perched on the organ bench, was playing a rousing rendition of "Hark! The Herald Angels Sing" but stopped as soon as she saw Maggie enter.

"Pastoorr Maggie! Vere you been? I've been vaiting forr you!"

Maggie heard a strange whirring noise.

"Good morning, Irena. It's nice to see you too." Maggie noticed Irena was dressed in a small fluorescent-pink muumuu. *Good grief.*

"Ve must talk about de Chrristmas Eve serrvice." Irena rolled off the organ bench and clutched Maggie's hand. "To de office!"

The whirring noise continued.

Maggie allowed herself to be led by little crazy Irena, who pushed through the door of Hank's office, dragging Maggie with her. They both stopped and stared. Ednah Lemmen's corpulent rear end was front and center. She was bent over a box of documents, which she picked up with a loud grunt and placed on Hank's desk. She then took a file from the top of the box, removed several sheets of paper, and shoved them into another box. The whirring sound commenced.

"Ednah!" Maggie yelled.

Ednah jumped ever so slightly and turned. She stood up straight and smoothed the front of her blouse over her overgenerous stomach.

"You scared me. What do you want, Maggie?"

The whirring stopped.

"What are you doing with those files?"

Maggie walked to the desk and picked up the next file in the box. It was labeled "Financial Records of Loving the Lord Community Church 1904-1914." Maggie then looked down and discovered the source of the whirring. It was a shredder.

"Calm down, Maggie. I found these old files in a closet in the basement. Not only are they a fire hazard, but they are financial records and are unnecessary for the functioning of this church. There are several more boxes down there. I'll have Doris bring them up when she gets here. I see she's late again. She should have cleaned out that closet a long time ago. I'm not sure she's right for her job. Not very clean, in my estimation. I think it might be time to let Doris go and let someone who knows how to *really* clean take over the position. I'll be happy to do the interviews and select a new janitor."

"Stop talking!" Maggie yelled, shaking with rage. "How many files have you shredded?"

"This is the fourth one. I only found these files last night, or I would have taken care of this issue much earlier in my tenure. What a musty, dusty waste of space. The closet could be used for necessary storage, not trash."

Maggie's head spun. "Don't touch another file. I can't believe you did this without asking. I can't believe you don't understand the meaning and significance of our church history. This is not *trash*. These documents are our heritage, everything the founders of our church did to establish a congregation, contract a building, make a charter. These files remind us of who we are. They remind us of God's faithfulness through the years of ministry. How could you be so ignorant? This is not your job! Your job is part-time and during the day. WHAT THE HELL WERE YOU DOING HERE LAST NIGHT?"

Silence.

Humiliation immediately washed over Maggie.

"Well. I never. How dare you speak to me with such foul language!?" *Snort*. Ednah's neck became blotchy and red. The redness began to creep up her face, and her eyes blazed. "I'm just sure the congregation of this place would be interested to know about your filthy mouth. What would your husband think, Maggie?"

At this outburst, Irena vaulted to life. She toddled over to Ednah and poked her with a long, black-painted fingernail.

"*Pastorr* Maggie! She ees our pastorr! And who carres vat her husband tinks?" She poked Ednah again. "Who carres vat dis congrregation tinks?"

Ednah stepped back. "Ow! Stop it."

Irena stepped forward and jabbed one more time. "You dun't fit herre. You dun't rrespect dis place or de people who love eet. I love eet. Pastorr Maggie loves eet. You dun't. You tink you know eet all, but you know noting. You arre so busy trrying to show off and be de boss. You arre nut de boss. You mek our jobs harrder. You dun't fit herre." Irena finally stepped back.

Maggie wanted to applaud but pulled herself together. The office door opened. Doris pushed her rolling trash can through, saw the occupants, and gave them a generous smile.

"Good morning, ladies. It's a beautiful July day outside. I think I'll weed the front flower beds after cleaning your offices. Why, Irena, can you believe you'll be a married woman in just about two weeks? Who would have guessed it?"

With her kerchief-wrapped head and large yellow apron, Doris pushed her trash can toward Maggie's office but stopped. She turned and looked at Hank's desk, then spotted a familiar box. She looked up at Ednah's red, blotchy face. She saw Irena's furious dark eyes boring holes into Ednah, and Pastor Maggie's pale, tired face.

"What's going on around here?"

Irena and Ednah both began shouting at once.

"She's burrning ourr historry!"

"I'm shredding old, useless documents and being assaulted by the pastor and the organist!"

"She's an idiotttt!"

"This church is filthy, and so is the pastor's mouth," Ednah spat.

"Quiet!" Doris grasped the lay of the land. "Pastor Maggie, you look like you need to sit down. Let's get you to your desk."

"I'm fine," Maggie said quietly. "Let's *all* go into my office and sit. I think it's time for a staff meeting."

Maggie sat down at her desk. Ednah waddled in and squeezed herself into one of the cream-colored visitor chairs. Doris dragged Hank's chair in so Irena could sit in the other visitor chair, which was much more comfortable for the pregnant organist. Once everyone was seated, Maggie took a deep breath. She noticed Ednah's mouth preparing to speak and quickly cut her off.

"Ednah, I apologize for yelling and swearing. I shouldn't have done either of those things. Please accept my apology. We must figure out how to function together for another eight weeks. It won't work if you continue to interfere with the way things are done here. You were hired to work part-time answering the phone, preparing bulletins, and doing the administrative tasks required of you *by me*. Nothing else. Your lack of understanding of the incredible significance of what is in the box you are shredding is shocking. Here is what I suggest. You, Ednah, will be on probation."

Ednah made a slight gasp.

"I would like to have your set of keys returned. Please leave them on the desk today. Doris or I will let you in the church when we arrive in the morning. You will leave between noon and one p.m. each afternoon on the days you are here. I should have done this from the beginning. It's my fault for letting things get so out of hand."

"Excuse me, I do not need to be on *probation*. I am not a criminal." Ednah's red face glowed. "You don't seem to understand the knowledge I bring with me to this job. This is old hat. I have done this work in—"

"Eef she dun't shut up, I vill slap herr silly," Irena growled.

"Irena, please stop. And please don't physically hurt people." Maggie listened to herself and almost laughed. This was the most ridiculous conversation. "Ednah, if you don't like or accept the new rules, feel free to resign."

"Wha . . . what?"

"You heard Pastor Maggie," Doris said plainly. "We have a way of doing things around here. We all know our part. I don't try to play the organ, and Irena doesn't mop floors. Pastor Maggie doesn't type bulletins, and Hank doesn't do baptisms. You don't go through closets, you don't move furniture, and you don't change the format of the bulletin. Just about everything you've done since you arrived is not what you're actually supposed to do. So, quit it. Or just quit. All your blustering proves nothing except you know how to bluster."

Ednah sat in her chair and felt like she was back in seventh grade, constantly surrounded by other girls who called her fat, made fun of her patchy and acned skin, and teased her when the teacher complimented her on a particularly well-done assignment. When they gathered around her at lunch, they shouted out, "Ed-NAH!"

Maggie watched as Ednah slowly deflated.

There was a knock on the door. Marla opened it and stuck her head in. "Oh, I see you're having a staff meeting. I'm sorry to interrupt. I'm taking a quick coffee break. Maggie, would you have time to meet later today?"

"Hi, Marla. Yes. I meant to call you first thing this morning. I can meet this afternoon. Would that work for you? You're off at one o'clock?"

"Yes, perfect. I'll see you a little after one. Bye, all."

Marla left, closing the door behind her, but only seconds passed before there was another knock. Verna Baker didn't wait for an answer. Her bunned head peered around the door. She was holding a large bouquet of her legendary zinnias.

"Pastor Maggie, where's that Ednah person?" Then she looked closely at who was in the office. "Oh, there you are. Ednah, I need the flower roster for September."

Ednah opened her mouth to answer, but Maggie cut her off.

"Verna, could it wait? We're in the middle of a meeting right now."

"Yes, fine. I'll be in the sanctuary arranging flowers for the next half hour or so. Will you be done by then?"

Again, Ednah opened her mouth.

Maggie said, "Yes, we will. Thank you, Verna."

Verna and her flowers departed.

Maggie thought for a moment, then said, "Doris and Irena, will you please excuse Ednah and me?"

Doris and Irena stared at her blankly.

"You mean you vant us to leave?" Irena finally asked, confused.

"But we're not done with our meeting, are we?" Doris questioned.

Ednah opened her mouth in vain.

"I think we are," Maggie said, "and I'd like to talk with Ednah privately."

Ednah sat stone-faced, staring at the picture of Jesus laughing behind Maggie's head. *Even Jesus laughs at me. Churches are poor people's country clubs. Why would anyone choose to attend a church like this? It's full of hypocritical people who are mean to strangers and to one another. They pretend they care but protect themselves by judging others.*

Irena stood up. "Vell, eef you dun't vant our help." She brushed her fingertips together, as if washing her hands of the whole affair. "But ve still hev to talk about Christmas."

Doris really wanted to stay and watch Ednah get fired, but she stood up and gave Maggie a knowing wink. The two women left.

"Ednah, let's try this again. Would you be willing to be the part-time administrative assistant of this church until Hank returns? I would appreciate you following your job description. Your hours would be from eight a.m. to noon, Monday through Friday. I'd like you to stay."

Ednah stared at Maggie, feeling a loathing for Maggie's "perfect" life.

"Yes. I'll stay. I think you are under-utilizing me, but it's your decision. I'll return the box of files in my office to the basement." Ednah stood and went to the door. "I wish you understood, I really do know what I'm doing."

She huffed out of the office, closing the door a little too loudly. Then Maggie heard drawers slam and a loud thump.

"Ow!" Ednah screeched.

She seemed to be having a full-blown tantrum.

13

Maggie sighed, stood up, and walked to her window overlooking the lawn between the church and parsonage while holding her aching lower back. She watched as the Nasab children played with several of the other little ones from the congregation, jumping in and out of two sprinklers. They were all ready to begin a new school year.

The first-year anniversary of the Nasab family living in Cherish was coming up on October third. What a difference since the day church members picked them up from the Detroit Airport. The children were now fluent in English and taught their Sunday school friends how to speak Arabic. Sabeen, the children's grandmother, kept the house. Amira, their mother, worked at the childcare center, and Mahdi, their father, worked at Fred Tuggle's quarry just north of town. In one way, it felt like the family had been part of the church forever.

Maggie walked past Ednah, who was huffing and puffing in Hank's office as she prepared to carry the box of files down to the basement. Maggie walked past Verna, who was busy making several zinnia bouquets, and Irena, who was playing "O Come, All Ye Faithful" with much fanfare. Maggie continued out the large oak doors and stopped to watch the sprinkled children. Carrie and Carl Moffet, Hannah Benson, Ryleigh and Zoey Teater, and Iman, Jamal, Karam, and Samir Nasab were playing together. They all came running to her with joyous squeals and threw their arms around her legs and baby bump. Maggie stumbled backward, laughing.

"Pastor Maggie!"

"We're in the water!"

"It's cold!"

Maggie could see it was cold by their little blue lips.

"This looks like a fun play day." Maggie tried to get down on her knees but ended up on her bottom as the children swarmed around her.

"Pastor Maggie, look at your tummy," Ryleigh said. "You have a baby in there."

Zoey crawled into Maggie's almost non-existent lap. "Can I pet the baby?"

Maggie laughed. "Yes, when the baby gets here, you can pet . . . it." Maggie almost revealed the gender.

"Can the baby play in the sprinklers with us?" Samir asked. As the youngest in his family, he knew little about babies.

"Probably not this summer, but maybe next summer a little bit."

Carrie looked at Samir and said with all the wisdom of an almost third grader, "Babies can't play in sprinklers because their legs don't work yet." She looked at Maggie. "How long does it take for their legs to work, Pastor Maggie?"

"I think it takes about a year for the baby to walk. They have to learn to roll over and sit up and then crawl before they can walk."

Carrie looked at Samir again. "It takes about a year for the legs to work."

"Pasto Maggie," Carl said. He had almost overcome missing his "r"s but occasionally slipped back into his little impediment. "What is the baby's name?"

"We don't know yet. Do you have some names you like?"

Carl thought about this. "Yes, I like Spider-Man and Olaf."

"What about Anna and Elsa? How many babies are in there?" Hannah asked, staring at Maggie's bump.

"Just one."

Iman gave Maggie a shy, beautiful smile. "Miss Irena has three."

"Yes, she does. She might need help with names too." *Triplets! Still unbelievable.*

"What are the names of the three little pigs or the three blind mice?" Ryleigh asked in all seriousness. Why expend energy making up three names when a fairy tale or catchy children's song could easily provide them?

"I have no idea," Maggie admitted. "So, Ryleigh, Zoey, and Hannah, are you ready for Sunday?"

"Yes. We are going to be baptismed," Hannah said.

"Baptized, yes. It will be a special day."

"You sprinkle us," Zoey said with big eyes.

"But we're all sprinkled right now," said practical Carrie. "Aren't we all baptismed right now?"

"You remember when I baptized you, Carrie?"

"And me!" Carl piped up.

"Yes, and you, Carl. It was a very special Easter Sunday."

"We got Easter candy after you sprinkled us, and God made promises. And Mommy and Daddy watched from heaven."

As always, when children spoke the truth so plainly, Maggie felt a lump in her throat. Carrie and Carl's baptisms happened when Mary and William Ellington, their adoptive parents, made the request to have them baptized.

Carrie turned her attention to Ryleigh and Zoey. "Pastor Maggie will say a prayer, then she will sprinkle water on your face, then you get to walk around the church with her and she talks about what your name means, then we get to eat special cookies." She looked at Maggie. "Do they get Easter candy or Halloween candy? And, hey, Pastor Maggie, why don't you baptism people out here in the big sprinklers? It would be way more fun. Or at least why don't you use a squirt gun, if we all have to actually be inside church?" Carrie looked back at the other children. "Anyway, it's not scary, and you get some candy *and* cookies, and you are also part of the oven mitt."

"The what?" Maggie studied Carrie's serious little face.

"You know, the oven mitt. All of us together. You know, God's oven mitt." Carrie was a little surprised Maggie didn't remember. Maybe it was because she was going to have a baby.

"Do you mean the 'covenant'?" Maggie asked gently.

"Well, I guess so. I thought you said oven mitt. You know, like God wears oven mitts and holds us in his hands. It's softer that way." This all made perfect sense to Carrie.

"Hey, we already know," Ryleigh said, who'd had enough of Carrie always knowing everything. "We practiced after church last Sunday. Didn't we, Pastor Maggie."

"Yes, along with little Maggie Barnes."

Just then, Sabeen came out of the parsonage. The matriarch of the Nasab family smiled broadly and clapped her hands as she walked toward Maggie and the children. She patted each child on the head, then bent down to pat Maggie's baby bump too.

"Bread?" she asked Maggie.

"Yes, please. Two breads?"

Sabeen nodded her head. "Just made breads in morning."

Sabeen made Syrian bread for the family, but also for church on Sunday and for Maggie anytime. The small, round breads were fried and a huge hit with the congregants at Loving the Lord. Everyone, especially Mrs. Popkin, didn't think the loaves were going out far enough into the world. Plans were being hatched.

There was a tiny squeal, but it came too late. Carl was surprised by the sprinkler after his big sister moved it closer to him as a tease. Unfortunately, it was positioned perfectly to rain down on Sabeen and Maggie a second after Carl received the first cold drops.

"Look! Look! Pastor Maggie and Mrs. Nasab are getting baptismed!" Hannah laughed.

The rest of the children began jumping back into the water as Maggie stood up awkwardly and led Sabeen out of water range.

"Thank you, Sabeen. I will pick up the breads on my way home." Maggie used her hands to describe walking, then pointed in the direction of the farm.

Sabeen wiped the water from her face and nodded her head. "Good, yes."

She indulged in a few moments to watch the children play. Her own grandchildren laughed and squealed along with the others. She'd never imagined she would hear them laughing or playing so free of care when they lived in the refugee camp in Turkey. As the one with the longest memory, Sabeen carried the history of the family in her heart and mind. This present chapter in their lives could never have been anticipated by the matriarch. It still startled her at times. She slipped her arm around Maggie's waist and gave her a squeeze.

"Good, yes. It is good."

When Maggie walked back into the church, it was surprisingly quiet. She expected to hear someone yelling at someone else or the organ blasting or the vacuum roaring. But no.

But yes. Maggie jumped when she heard "Vat you doing?" Irena was perched on her organ bench.

"Oh, Irena, you scared me."

"I did nut scarre you. Dis is vere I alvays am." She moved a piece of music from one side of the organ bench to the other. "So, did you fire Ednah?"

Maggie didn't want to get into this little discussion. "No, Irena. I decided to give Ednah another chance. I think you and Doris can give her another chance too. Isn't this what the church should be about? Figuring out how to get along with one another?"

"Nut with herr! She mek trouble. Nut so good for de rest of us."

"I think she understands now she has a certain job to do and she doesn't need to do anyone else's."

"Nope. People like dis, dey hev to always proof dey know morre. You watch. She will do someting you can't fix. She will do damage." Irena looked loftily at Maggie.

"I'm willing to bet she won't. She just needed some parameters and a quick reminder it's okay not to know everything about everything."

Maggie tried to look loftily back at Irena, but it didn't work. She really didn't know if it was the right thing or not to give Ednah another chance, but it was only until Hank and Pamela came back. They could all manage a few more weeks. Maybe.

The secret door opened, and Verna walk through with a huge bouquet of orange zinnias. She placed them on the altar table and began to fuss with the stems.

"Hey, Verna, did you get the flower schedule from Ednah?"

Verna jumped at Maggie's voice. "Oh, you startled me. I found the chart on her desk while you were talking in your office. She seems to make simple tasks more complicated."

"Where is she?" Maggie scream-whispered as she looked toward Hank's door. It would always be *Hank's* door.

"She's in the office now, pouting. Do you have a moment?"

"Of course, but hang on for a second."

She hoped Ednah wasn't pouting too much. Maggie went to the office door and overheard Ednah on the phone.

"I know! I'm so over-qualified for this job. Maggie couldn't run a picnic if she had to. But let her keep bumbling along—" Ednah looked up as Maggie walked through the door. "I've got to go now." Ednah plunked down the phone.

"Ednah, who were you talking to?"

"Is it any of your business?"

"Yes. When you make derogatory statements about me, I'd like to know who you're making them to."

Ednah's neck began its blotchy climb. As it spread north to her face, she looked down from Maggie's stare.

"I'd hoped this morning was a fresh start for you working here. If you don't think so, maybe there's another job better suited for you outside the church."

Ednah sat silently.

"Pastor Maggie, is now a good time?" Verna came from the secret entrance and waited to enter Maggie's office.

"Yes, it is." Maggie led Verna into her office and shut the door behind them.

"She really is abominable, isn't she?" Verna said as she sat in one of the visitor chairs.

Maggie sat in the other cream-colored chair and nodded. "She can't get out of her own way."

Verna nodded. "I suspect she's been a misfit her whole life. It might be why she's so insistent in her pretense to know more than anyone about everything. She's very disagreeable."

"Yes, but what can I do for you, Verna? Please don't ask me to arrange a picnic, because apparently I can't run one."

"I heard her say that too. What a sad creature. I'm here on a totally different matter. This is personal, and I would appreciate your discretion."

"Of course." Maggie sensed something heavy in Verna's voice.

"I have just been diagnosed with breast cancer." She brushed a small zinnia pedal from her cotton dress. "It was a suspicion in my yearly mammogram and confirmed in a lumpectomy."

Maggie took Verna's hand and waited.

"I found out yesterday. It's not related to the skin cancer I had when you first came here to Cherish. I asked the doctor, but he said they are different. So, I have a different kind of cancer." Verna's lip quivered slightly. She squeezed Maggie's hand to gain control of her lip.

Maggie hesitated, then said quietly, "What else did the doctor say?"

"I will have surgery and begin treatments of chemotherapy and radiation. I have heard these words so many times from other women. I never thought I would say them about myself."

"What can I do?"

"Howard is taking it badly. He will need some extra support. I have transferred my records to Jack. I didn't want to drive to Ann Arbor for treatment. I'll make an appointment with Jack as soon as he has an opening."

He'll have an opening this afternoon if I have anything to say about it.

"How are you taking it?" Maggie asked.

"I'm stunned, so I'm doing all the practical things I can in order to not think about dying."

"I'm going to not think about you dying either."

"I know the verse: 'The Lord giveth, and the Lord taketh away; blessed be the name of the Lord.'"

"I've never really liked that verse," Maggie admitted. "It makes God sound punitive or random or far too distant. I think God is right here. God is with you."

Verna sighed deeply, as if she hadn't breathed since she heard the diagnosis until that moment. "Thank you. I needed the reminder. I might need it again, now and then."

"Got it."

"I don't want this on the prayer chain or in an email. Not yet, anyway. Howard and I need to spend some time with this news first. Then prayers from our church family will be welcome." She took Maggie's other hand and held the two young hands in her older ones. "I want you to pray for me. Will you?"

Maggie stared into Verna's eyes and prayed. "God, thank you for being with us always, especially for being with Verna in this moment. Continue to make your presence known in the days to come. May she feel your peace and comfort stitched around her like the softest of blankets. Set practical tasks before her, and occupy her mind with healing thoughts. Howard needs you too, but you already know this. May Howard and Verna walk through these new kinds of days without fear, but with hope. Guide the rest of us to be helpful. Keep us from being nosy, giving unsolicited advice, or inundating them with casseroles. May we be kind comrades to these two people we love so much. Bless her doctors and nurses and other caregivers with wisdom, healing treatments, and compassion. You are the healer of our ills. Thank you. Amen."

One small tear escaped from Verna's eye and slid down her cheek. Maggie took a tissue and wiped it away.

"May I stop over this weekend?" Maggie asked.

"I'll let you know. Let me see how Howard is doing. He's very emotional, you know." She gave a thin smile.

"Got it," Maggie said again.

Verna stood to leave, and Maggie pulled herself out of her own chair.

"Thank you, Pastor Maggie." She surprised Maggie by reaching over and giving her a stronger than expected embrace.

As Verna turned, she and Maggie both saw the door quickly close, like it had been open a crack. Verna looked at Maggie mutely.

Maggie hurried to the door and opened it. No one was there. Hank's chair was empty, as was the entire office. She looked at the door to the gathering area, also closed. Then she looked in the small hallway to the secret entrance into the sanctuary. The door was open. But no one was in the sanctuary, and Irena was not at the organ. Who could have been on the other side of her office door?

"I need to get home now," Verna said, walking to the large oak doors. "It looks like we have a ghost around here."

Once Verna was gone, Maggie went back into her office and closed her door, making double-sure it was shut. She sat for a moment, wishing Ednah Lemmen into a different universe.

She pulled out her cell phone and called Jack. As she explained her meeting with Verna and implored him to see her today, she watched her door and listened for any noises on the other side of it. Nothing.

"I'll have Ellen call Verna and see if she can come in at the end of the day," Jack said. "Thanks for letting me know. I can also call her doctor in Ann Arbor after I read her test results. On a different subject, are you all set for dinner tonight? Do you need me to pick up anything?"

"I'm ready. I just want to have a nice evening with friends and forget about Ednah and cancer and whatever else is harming people out there."

"You sound defeated."

"It's been a day. And it's only lunchtime. But this afternoon I meet with Keith and Irena for their final wedding plans. It should be fun."

"Good. Love you."

"I love and adore you. I'll be much happier when you see me tonight."

14

Maggie walked into The Page Turner Bookshop and took a deep breath. *Books.* Real books made of paper and ink and binding. She was greeted by the two smiling faces of Jennifer and Beth Becker.

"Good . . . um . . . lunchtime, you two."

"Pastor Maggie, it's good to see you. We have your order all ready." Jennifer walked behind the counter and pulled out four identical packages wrapped in pale-green tissue paper and tied with straw-colored twine. "Here we go. Just in time for Sunday." She handed Maggie the books.

Maggie pulled out her credit card to make payment, then looked at both sisters.

"So, any updates for me? About any important events? On your calendars? Events that should be on my calendar?"

"As a matter of fact, we do." Beth giggled.

It had been a memorable coffee time when Max Solomon proposed to Beth Becker. Max always sat in the last pew of the church on Sunday mornings and only became a churchgoer after Maggie buried his father three years earlier. After the funeral, Beth and Jennifer had noticed Max sitting alone in the back of the church and decided to sit with him so he wouldn't be lonely. Once Jennifer found herself happily falling in love with her old beau from high school, Darcy Keller, Beth kept Max company on Sunday mornings. But it seemed Max wanted her to keep him company for more than an hour a week. Earlier in the spring, Max had stepped out of his shyness and, in the middle of coffee time after church one Sunday, got down on one old knee and asked Beth to marry him in front of the entire congregation. She said "Yes." Then Jack and Harold Brinkmeyer were required to help the older fellow get back on his feet again. The two sisters had both found love, and two weddings were being planned.

"At first," Beth said, "we thought we would have a double wedding. Less work for us and for our guests. They would only have to come to one wedding instead of two. But, of course, my sister's fiancé has his own plans."

"Yes, he does," Jennifer said. "He's a bit of a showman, if you haven't noticed. He wants all the pomp, no matter the circumstance."

"My dear Max would rather walk to Mars than have all that attention heaped on him, even though he did make quite a spectacle of himself at coffee time." She looked down at the pretty ring on her finger. "He doesn't want to make a fuss," she said dreamily.

"So, do you have any news for me or not?" Maggie loved romance more than most people, but her back hurt, and she was hungry, *and* she had to work with Ednah.

"There will be two weddings," Jennifer said decisively.

"I got that part. Do you know when and where?" Maggie smiled a little too broadly.

"Not quite yet, but you will be the first to know," Beth said enthusiastically.

Maggie took her receipt and the books. "I look forward to it. See you on Sunday."

She left the bookshop—with the owners all aflutter over their own personal happiness—and headed to The Sugarplum, hungry for some soup and maybe a donut. She opened the door of the bakery to the sound of fairy bells and was immediately hit by savory spices. Normally, Mrs. Popkin's homemade concoctions were a delight to Maggie's nose and a greater delight to her taste buds, but not today. Maggie felt her stomach twist slightly. She tried not to breathe. The spices were overpowering. Even with her mouth open and gasping, she couldn't avoid the smell.

"Well, hokey tooters! How's my favorite pastor in the whole world? Of course, you're my only pastor." She laughed heartily at herself. "What can I get for you?"

"What am I smelling?" Maggie tried not to gasp. Or throw up.

"It's potato eggplant stew. I'm learning a lot about new spices and recipes from Sabeen and Amira. They are great cooks. So many things I've never heard of in my lifetime. Hokey tooters! I'm going to pay them to make Syrian pastries, bread, and stews here in the bakery. We'll sell them to the world of Cherish, and they can do what they're good at and oversee the cooking and baking. I don't mind stepping back a little and letting them share their talents. Surprisingly, I'm not as young as I was thirty years ago. Hokey tooters! You know, this potato eggplant stew is full of deliciousness. You see, I begin with onions and garlic. I soften them up and add piles of diced potatoes and eggplant. Tomatoes finish off the dish. The spices are a mixture, including coriander, cardamom, sumac, and turmeric. Now whoever in the world heard of "sumac"? Next, I serve it with—"

"Thank you, I'm so sorry, I forgot I have a meeting I'm late for. Got to go. Bye, Mrs. Popkin. See you Sunday."

Maggie fled the bakery. She escaped across the street to her office, having kept her breakfast intact, but just barely. She set the four books on her worktable and dug through a drawer in her desk for a granola bar. Lunch. She'd just finished her meager meal when Irena burst into the office with Keith in tow.

"Ve arre herre! It's time to mek sure de wedding is ready."

When Irena got excited, her accent was much more pronounced. Maggie thought Irena could speak English better than she let on.

She shut the door none too softly and settled herself in one of the visitor chairs while Keith, grinning all the way, sat in the other.

"Good afternoon, Pastor Maggie," he said.

"Good afternoon. How are you, Keith?"

"I'm dandy. Two weeks from tomorrow, I'll be a married man, and I can't wait."

"It's so much better than the alternative." Maggie laughed.

Irena arranged her muumuu around her belly. Maggie opened her wedding notebook and looked over the pages she'd typed the week before.

"I think the service is in good shape. Just a couple of questions. Have you decided to use the traditional vows, or do you want to write your own?"

"Write our own," Keith said.

"Ov courrse we vill make de vows in our own worrds," Irena said condescendingly

"Great." Maggie jotted it down in the notebook. "Have you applied for your marriage license?"

"Yes, last week," Keith said.

Irena nodded. "Ve vill pick eet up next veek."

Maggie checked "license" off her list. This was easy.

"And have you figured out music?"

Irena was the music czar of the church, so Maggie wouldn't have been surprised if Irena planned to play the music and then trip-trap down the aisle for the ceremony, only to make it back to the organ for the recessional.

"Ov course. I will tape de museek ahead of time. It will be played on de machine."

"Through the sound system," Keith clarified.

Maggie smiled as she wrote this down. Irena was still in control.

"Let's go into the sanctuary for a bit and talk about the logistics." Maggie stood and walked to her door, followed by the couple. When Maggie opened the door, she was surprised to see Ednah standing on the other side of it.

"Ednah, what are you doing here?"

"I'm . . . uh . . . working. What else would I be doing?"

"But you only work in the mornings." Maggie couldn't keep the anger out of her voice.

"I had a few things to finish up," Ednah said with insolence. "This morning in your office wasted a good deal of my time."

Maggie wanted to tell the annoying woman to go home. She was an intrusive and unwanted presence.

"Please excuse us," Maggie said instead and walked past Ednah.

Keith followed, but Irena paused to glare.

Once they were through the secret door and in the sanctuary, Maggie stood on the altar and directed Irena and Keith to stand facing her.

"I'd like to begin at the end of the service. I will now pronounce you husband and wife, and then you will kiss, and then turn to the congregation. I will introduce you as Keith and Irena Crunch. Is this what you would like?"

"No. I keep my own name. Dalca," Irena said decisively. "Eet's my herritage."

"Okay, 'Mr. and Mrs. Keith Crunch and Irena Dalca.'"

They both nodded.

"Then the recessional will begin, and you will walk down the aisle to wild applause."

"I like dat." Irena looked enthralled as she imagined all the attention and acclaim she would receive on her wedding day.

"Go ahead and walk to the back of the church," Maggie said.

"Don't I get to kiss her first?" Keith was ready to pucker up.

"No. No kees until de vedding!" Irena barked.

"It seems a bit late for that," Keith said, smiling, and kissed her anyway. Then he put his hand on her burgeoning midsection.

"Okay. Down the aisle with you." Maggie practically pushed them down the altar steps. *How much sex do they have? Ick.* She shook off the thought.

Irena and Keith walked down the aisle. Irena nodded and waved like Queen Elizabeth to her imagined fans.

"Now, Keith, before the wedding, you and I will be behind the secret door." Maggie pointed to the door and waved Keith back down the aisle to his hiding place. "Irena, are you walking yourself down the aisle or . . . ?" Maggie knew Irena had no one in her life to walk her down the aisle on her special day.

"Ov courrse I hev someone."

"Oh! Wonderful. Who is it?"

"How could you nut know?"

"I don't know. Is it someone from the choir?"

The choir was made up of four to six people, depending on the Sunday. They only sang once a month, mainly due to the way they were treated at choir practice by Irena. Someone always left with hurt feelings. Perhaps Irena asked Howard Baker? Winston Chatsworth? Verna?

"Pastorr Maggie, eet ees Doctorr Jack, ov courrse."

Maggie stared. "Really?"

Irena nodded her head enthusiastically.

"Does he know?" If Jack forgot to tell her this little tidbit of news . . .

"No. You will ask him. But he will say yes. He is de only person who can do it. He is my frriend."

Maggie smiled. "He will be honored, I'm sure."

They continued their little rehearsal, with Irena shouting directions intermittently. All in all, the three participants felt a moment of anticipation for the wedding day.

The moment ended when Maggie went back to her office and found Ednah standing at her worktable, unwrapping one of the four books Maggie had bought from The Page Turner.

"Ednah! What are you doing?"

Ednah jumped, then turned and looked at Maggie unblinkingly. "I was looking for a hymnal to put the page numbers of the hymns in the bulletin."

"There is a hymnal in Hank's office," Maggie said purposefully. *How does she come up with so many lies so quickly?*

"I couldn't find it."

Maggie walked out and plucked the hymnal off a low bookshelf behind the desk.

"It's right here, and you know it. You've typed several bulletins since Hank and Pamela left. Please don't go into my office anymore unless asked. I thought we were going to have a second go at this working relationship?"

"I don't know what you're so upset about." Ednah scowled.

"I'm upset because you were unwrapping one of the books on my worktable, which is none of your business. Just stick to your job description, please."

Ednah took the hymnal from Maggie and sat at the desk. Maggie turned toward her office, but she spotted the stack of bulletins sitting on a small stand near the door.

"Ednah, the bulletins are right here. You didn't need to add the hymn numbers. Why did you lie?"

Ednah sat stock-still, like an animal deciding if it was going to fight or take flight. Then she pulled herself together.

"I meant for next week's bulletin. I wanted to get an early start."

Maggie couldn't argue. Over the past three years she'd learned to be at least four weeks ahead of herself as far as worship services were concerned. She and Irena met each week to choose hymns (Irena always chose the hymns, no matter what Maggie requested), and Maggie prepared liturgy and working sermon titles weeks in advance. But Maggie didn't believe Ednah was really working on the next week's bulletin.

"Why don't you go ahead and finish the bulletin for next week and give me a copy to proofread before you go home."

Maggie wasn't looking for a reason to keep Ednah in the church for another minute, but making her do the bulletin would put an exclamation point on who was working for whom.

Ednah slouched in her chair. She hadn't even looked at the bulletin for next week. She turned on the computer, pulled up the liturgy, and got started.

The office door opened, and Marla stepped in and smiled at Maggie.

"Pastor Maggie, I was hoping you would still be here. Hi, Ednah."

Ednah nodded without looking up.

"Come on in, Marla."

Maggie led Marla into her office and closed the door until it clicked. They sat down in the visitor chairs.

"I wanted to give you an update on Cecelia, Naomi, and Bobby," Marla began.

"Yes, how are they?"

"I was there this morning, and we are taking the three of them dinner tonight. Naomi is in some pain, but she has medicine to help. Cecelia seems to be fine. Not regretting her decision to have Jim arrested. I didn't know how she would feel today, but I think it's been on her mind for some time. She told me she knew when she saw Naomi's arm. Something clicked, and she was ready to 'cut the cancer out' of her home and protect her children's lives, and her own life. Those were her words. She did make an unnerving discovery, however. Jim has a gun safe with two hunting rifles and a handgun. For some reason, she wanted to check the safe late last night. When she opened the lock, the three guns were gone. There's no way he had them on him when he was arrested, of course, but they are gone."

Maggie's eyes widened. "That's strange. Why would he have taken them out?"

"She doesn't know. They aren't anywhere in the house. She searched this morning. They aren't in the garage or the shed they have behind the house either. They're just gone."

"Well, we know he can't get his hands on them. But it's weird. Like he knew he was going to be leaving. Does Charlotte know?"

"Good question. I'll ask Cecelia. It would be good for her to make a formal report."

"What else have you noticed?"

"All three of them are handling the situation differently. Not the guns, but the arrest. Bobby is not talking much, but last night when Jason was playing video games with him, he opened up a little. Naomi seems to be in some shock. I can't imagine what she is remembering from yesterday." Marla shuddered. "Cecelia is moving forward. Mentally, she'd prepared herself for quite a while. Naomi and Bobby need a chance to catch up. Even though they knew Jim was abusive to their mother, they hadn't imagined his arrest or their mother's plan to divorce so quickly. I know the word will get out soon. With Martha Babcock on the police radio, the gossip-fest will begin. But Cecelia is hoping some of the details can remain private. Jim's brutality toward

Cecelia is one thing, but breaking Naomi's arm doesn't need to be public consumption. Cecelia does not want Naomi pitied through the salaciousness of gossip."

"Right. I don't know what Martha would have heard or what Charlotte warned her not to share. Are they getting any other help?"

"Cecelia told me she's taking the kids to Doctor Sneller to talk things through. I think it's an excellent idea, especially since her office is in Manchester and not Cherish. No one will see them. She has already called Harold. It sounds like he will help her pro bono. He sure is a good man. I brought groceries to them this morning that should last quite a while. And we, as a family, are going to help her clean the whole house and yard tomorrow."

Maggie marveled at her friend. "I hope you will take me seriously when I say this: Thank you for being Jesus to Cecelia, Naomi, and Bobby. You are literally helping to heal their souls."

"It's easy to do. I just thought, what would I need most if I were in her shoes? I would need a trustworthy friend and not to have to fix dinner."

"Thank you, Marla. How can we help with friendship or dinner or anything?"

"I think it would be helpful to pay Doctor Sneller's bill. It would be one less thing to worry about. Maybe we could make a list of people who would also be willing to donate money for groceries and bills. Cecelia will land on her feet, but if she didn't have to worry about this month's bills, it would give her time to get things in order."

"Jack and I will pay Doctor Sneller. I will also ask some discreet folks if they will help with the bills and food. I know we can make this work."

"I also have another idea, something special for Cecelia."

There was a loud clattering noise against Maggie's door. Both women looked over. Maggie got up and whipped the door open. Ednah was standing there, not suspecting Maggie would appear. The small stand with that week's bulletins had fallen against the door, and bulletins were scattered everywhere.

"Ednah! What are you doing?"

"I was trying to—"

"Go home. Please leave the church now, and we'll talk about this on Monday."

Ednah bent over and picked up a bulletin.

"Just go. I will deal with the bulletins and put them out for the ushers."

Ednah, neck reddening by the second, took her purse from the desk drawer and left the office without a word. Maggie spotted the church keys on Hank's desk and breathed a sigh of relief. Marla got up and helped Maggie collect the bulletins.

"We'll talk more later," Marla said. "Ednah doesn't seem to be fitting in yet."

"I don't think she's ever fit in anywhere. I don't think we will survive until September."

Maggie said goodbye to Marla, set the bulletins out for the ushers, locked the big oak doors, and walked home with a heavy heart.

15

Maggie meandered down the driveway toward the farmhouse. She made a detour to the barn and checked the cat food and water dishes she'd set out earlier. Empty. Some little critter, hopefully the black cat, had a snack. She picked up the dishes and went into the house. She almost sat down, but thought better of it. *I'll fall asleep in two seconds.* Instead, she put her work bag in her home office, then indulged in petting her elated felines.

"I saw someone new in the barn this morning, babies. What would you think of a brand- new friend?"

Oblivious to this brand-new threat, Marmalade, Cheerio, and Fruit Loop writhed around on their backs, enjoying belly rubs and ear scratches.

"I'll keep you posted on his whereabouts."

She stood up with the help of her desk and went into the kitchen, took dishes out of the cupboards, and set them out buffet-style on the island. After the uncomfortable ending to her day at church, she looked forward to having friends over for the evening.

Jack walked in the back door. "Honey, I'm home."

"Honey, I'm glad!"

He was carrying an overly large vase full of bright-red carnations. He kissed the top of her head.

"These are for you, wife. Now, what needs to be done?"

He put the vase on the island next to the dishes, then headed toward the stairs to change his clothes and dump his day planner in his office.

"Thank you! These are beautiful and brighten up the whole room. As for what needs to be done, all things regarding the grill, please."

"The grill master shall return." He ran up the stairs.

Maggie created a cheese board with cheeses, grapes, cherries, crackers, and cashews for a tasty appetizer. Jack came in wearing shorts and a pastel short-sleeved shirt. He grabbed some cheese and a savory cracker and popped them into his mouth.

"How was your afternoon?" he asked with his mouth full.

"First of all, you look great in that shirt. Second, about my day, I'm glad it's over. This evening is just what I need."

"Let me guess. Ednah?"

"Ednah, yes. But also Verna and her cancer diagnosis. How was your visit with her? Can you tell me?"

"She and Howard are both in some shock. Howard is really having a tough time. I'll be talking with her oncologist on Monday. She has scheduled Verna's chemo to begin next Friday. Thankfully, she can have the treatments here in Cherish and doesn't need to drive to Ann Arbor. For now, Verna and Howard need to wrap their heads around what it means to live with cancer and its treatment."

"Will the chemo work?" Maggie knew she was asking a ridiculous question Jack couldn't know the answer to.

"Time will tell. Let's hope the cancer hasn't spread."

Jack pulled covered bowls of marinated meat from the refrigerator.

"I'll make potato and vegetable packets as soon as I'm done with this," Maggie said, putting the finishing touches on her cheese table. "The corn soaked all day. It's still in the bucket by the sliding door."

An hour later, the doorbell rang. Maggie welcomed Sylvester Fejokwu and Skyler Breese. Ellen and Harold were right behind them.

"Come in! We've been waiting for you."

Before she shut the door, Lacey and Lydia drove up. The party was complete. Everyone made their way into the kitchen and began enjoying plates of the cheese table nibbles and happy drinks—except for Maggie, who stuck with water.

"So, tell us about married life and if you think we should still have Pastor Maggie officiate our wedding," Lacey said with a wink to her pastor.

Harold raised his glass. "Marriage is, shall I say, extraordinary. As for the ceremony, I don't remember any of it."

"You were crying too hard," Jack chimed in.

"We loved our ceremony, our honeymoon, and now, our new life here in Cherish," Ellen said. "Maggie made the wedding meaningful, even though my husband seemed to be under great duress about having to marry me." Ellen clinked her glass against Harold's. "Lacey and Lydia, when is your wedding?"

The two women looked at each other. Lydia said, "Our plan is November fourth." She paused for a moment. "I hope there's a chance to have Lacey's family be part of our day."

Maggie's eyebrows raised. "Is it possible, Lacey?"

"I don't think so, but my fiancée seems to think the greatest miracle of all time can happen."

"I think there is always hope," Lydia said. "I might be too much of a Pollyanna, but I don't understand how a parent can completely cut off a child because they are gay. It makes no sense."

"Lydia and I have opposite experiences with family and the acceptance of who we are. Lydia is loved by her family one hundred percent for who she is. I am not. But I don't want to be a big downer. Tonight is meant to celebrate weddings and marriage and love. I'm surprised Irena and Keith aren't here."

"I met with them today. I think Irena and her burgeoning belly need more rest than she expected. Keith loves to hover. Their wedding will be . . ." Maggie thought a moment. "Entertaining." *I must remember to tell Jack he's walking Irena down the aisle.*

"What about you, Sly and Sky?" Jack asked. "You have about two and a half months before D-day."

"Well . . ." Sky said, "we're almost done with our to-do list . . . mmm . . . aren't we?" Sky looked at Sly, who settled his hand on her derriere. "Sly is . . . quite a fancy man and very particular about the details." Sky's dreamy voice trailed off, as it frequently did.

"I know what I like," Sly said plainly.

"Who's doing your flowers?" Ellen asked with a grin.

"Fortunately, I've just hired my first employee at Pretty, Pretty Petals . . . mmm . . . I'm an actual boss. He will be doing the flowers with . . . mmm . . . my oversight, of course."

Sky looked over at the beautiful bouquet of red carnations she'd created earlier in the day. Maggie's eyes followed Sky's, and she gave the tall goddess's hand a squeeze.

"They're lovely, Sky."

"Are you doing Irena and Keith's flowers?" Ellen asked.

"Yes. But they don't want traditional flowers. Irena wants trees. I have several . . . mmm . . . potted young apple trees. I'll decorate them for the big day. I actually love the idea. Mmmm . . . Trees."

"Leave it to Irena to do something completely unexpected," Lacey said. "I wish I could get my hands on her hair. Her home-dyed disasters will not do for her wedding."

"Have you asked her?" Maggie looked at Lacey.

"I haven't. She's so . . . What's the word? Scary? Unpredictable?"

"Tell her you would like to give her a gift," Sky said. "Yes . . . a gift of hair, a manicure, and a pedicure. She may not know you have your sights on her head . . . Mmm." Sky shook her own waterfall of blonde locks.

"I'll do it," Lacey said. "She won't even know what's happening, but I'll finally make her hair look like something that belongs on a human instead of a circus clown."

Jack looked at Sly. "How did it go with Fitch today?"

Sly rolled his eyes. "He's interesting. I immediately understood what you told me about your encounters with him."

"Did you have to wipe up any of his blood from the floor or wall?" Maggie asked with a laugh, remembering the times she'd had to do Fitch cleanup.

"When I got there," Sly said, looking perturbed, "he was on the floor. He was caught in an extension cord. Both feet were tied together. He unraveled himself, stood up, and hit his arm on a ladder, which went flying. How does that man keep a job?"

"But he wasn't bleeding. That's good," Maggie said.

"Not yet. We walked through the clinic so he could attempt to explain his findings to me. We were in Doctor Van Dyke's dental space, where much of the furniture and some equipment for the clinic are being stored. He was telling me about his construction concerns, all of which are unfounded, when he tripped over a rolling stool and slammed his head into the side of an X-ray machine. Yeah, then there was blood." Sly looked disgusted.

Jack laughed. "There it is. The man is in the wrong job."

"What happened next?" Ellen asked.

"It was obvious to me he needed some medical care. I found a case of toilet paper in the office, so I took a roll and told him to hold it against his head. I got him into my car," Sly shuddered, "and drove him up here to the hospital. He has fourteen stitches in his forehead."

"Fourteen?" Ellen said. "The man needs to be tied to a chair."

"But the best part is this." Sly was ready for the grand finale of his story. "I got the final report from the previous inspector. She signed off on everything, even filling out the final form while she was in labor. She just didn't remember to file it. Totally understandable. After Fitch got his stitches today, I drove him back to Manchester so he could get his truck. I gave him the final sign-off of the inspection and told him we are going to move forward because the building was completed to code."

"I can't imagine he agreed to it," Maggie said.

"He didn't have a choice. With the previous inspector's sign-off on the project, Fitch is out of a job. At least with our clinic. He can ruin someone else's life now."

"But how did you get the signed final copy?" Jack asked, looking frustrated. "We were originally told she didn't finish her paperwork before she had her twins."

"I called her," Sly said. "It's been seven weeks of nothing but delays. I figured it was long enough for the other inspector to be able to sign a piece of paper. When I was at the clinic last week, I knew it was time to get rid of Fitch. He's been wasting our time."

"I think we have just heard how the powerful CEO of a hospital can get things done," Maggie said, "when a lowly pastor just has to keep wiping up the blood. Cheers to you, Sly!"

"So, what's the timeline now?" Ellen asked eagerly. "When can we open the clinic?"

"I've handed things back to our director of facilities. She's trying to get the interior people rebooked to begin their work with paint and carpet, et cetera. Their timing will determine our opening day. I think we'll make the original date of November first, for sure." Sly took a drink of his beer, a look of satisfaction on his face.

Maggie noticed Lydia looking down at her phone with wide eyes.

"Is everything okay, Lydia?" Maggie asked.

"I don't know. Did you send out an all-church email this afternoon?"

"No, why?"

Lydia held up her phone. "There is an all-church email from you."

Maggie took the phone. Everyone else pulled theirs out of their pockets and read the all-church prayer concerns.

Dear Loving the Lord Congregation,

I'd like to share a list of prayer concerns with you.

First, the Chance family. Jim has been arrested for child abuse. He broke his daughter Naomi's arm. Cecelia, Naomi, and Bobby are still in the family home. They are all going to Dr. Sneller for help. Dr. Jack and I will pay the bill.

Second, Verna Baker has received a breast cancer diagnosis. She and Howard are taking it badly. Maybe you didn't know, but Verna had cancer of a different variety a few years ago.

The last thing is, Dr. Jack will be walking Irena down the aisle for her wedding to Detective Crunch next week because she doesn't have any family member to do so. Of course, since Irena is pregnant with triplets, the wedding itself is a bit of an afterthought.

Keep these people in your prayers,
Pastor Maggie

Maggie reached for her own phone on the counter, her stomach churning. She sat down hard on a chair and reread the notice. Then she looked up at Jack.

"Ednah. Ednah did this. She was eavesdropping all day. I caught her at it. She was talking to someone on the phone, saying unkind things about me. I let her know I heard what she said. This is her payback. I've got to call Verna, Cecelia, and Irena. This is just terrible."

Jack knew she was weighing the damage of this bombshell and felt his own anger rise. Maggie's name was attached to personal and confidential issues affecting members of Loving the Lord. Maggie would never have shared these private matters.

"Maggie, do whatever you need to do," Ellen said firmly. "We'll take care of everything out here, or would it be better if we postponed this evening?"

"No. Please stay. Excuse me." Maggie stood up. "I've got to explain."

She went into her office and closed the door. Her phone shook in her hand while her head swirled with humiliation and anger. But more than that, she felt the stomach-wrenching pain her dear parishioners would experience when they read this horrific email. She jumped as her phone rang in her hand. Marla.

"Hello, Marla. I just read it."

"Pastor Maggie." Marla's voice was shaking.

"I didn't write the email."

"Who would do this?" Marla could hardly speak.

"Ednah. It has to have been her. I must call the people mentioned in the email. I just don't know what to do about everyone else. The entire congregation received this."

"We're on our way to Cecelia's with dinner. We are leaving right now. I will let her know you did not write this. Why don't you call Verna and Irena," Marla said, getting ahold of her emotions.

"Yes, good idea. I will call Verna and Irena." *Oh gosh! Irena!* "Then I will circle back with Cecelia too. I can't believe this has happened."

"Ednah has caused horrible pain to some of our most vulnerable friends, but we will get through this," Marla said meekly.

"After the phone calls, I will write another church email and send it out. I just hope we can stop some of the damage." But Maggie knew she couldn't. Such personal stories of pain were now laid bare for all to know.

"Okay, sounds good." Marla didn't know what to say. Nothing was good.

Maggie hung up, and her phone immediately rang again. Howard Baker.

"Hello, Howard. I think I know why you're calling."

Maggie heard a heavy sigh.

"Pastor Maggie, we're in shock over here. We can barely accept Verna's diagnosis ourselves. Why does the whole church have to know? We need some privacy right now, not a lot of people involved in our pain."

"Howard, I know, I know. I am so sorry your pain is compounded now by the email."

"Did you . . . um . . . why?"

"I didn't. I did *not* write the email. I believe it was written by someone else in the office who overheard three private conversations I had today. My name was attached to it without my knowledge. I would never, ever, share such personal stories with the congregation." Maggie heard another voice on the phone.

"I hoped it wasn't you." Verna's voice was soft.

"Oh, Verna." Maggie bit hard on her lip. She could cry later, but not now. "Verna, I'm so sorry. You shared your story in confidence today, and I have kept your confidence."

"Yes, of course. It must have been that Ednah person. Is she who you think did this?"

"Yes. I do. I will take care of this situation. But I do apologize if you get bombarded with phone calls or emails tonight and tomorrow. I will try to minimize the response. Would it be okay for me to stop over tomorrow morning? I'd like to spend a little time with you both."

"Yes, please feel free to come by," Howard said.

"Let's say around ten a.m.," Maggie said. "We'll just focus on how you two are doing with the diagnosis. I'm praying for both of you."

The moment the call was finished, Maggie's phone rang. Irena.

"Hello, Irena. I just saw the email."

"It was Ednahhh!" Irena screeched. "I know de second I read it. It is nut from Pastorr Maggie. She doesn't write dis way. Dat Bitch!"

"Irena, I'm so sorry. Ednah was obviously out to hurt as many people as she could with her eavesdropping, and I'm sorry she hurt you and Keith."

"What you talking about? Ednah nut hurt me. She hurt Ednah. I am getting married to my Captain Crrunch. I am going to be a mama of tree leetle chicks. I am a heppy voman. No one in de worrld can stamp on my parrade. As Doris says, onvards and forwards!"

Maggie took a deep breath. Irena was fine.

"Yes, onwards and forwards. Thanks for understanding, Irena. Please apologize to Keith, and I'll see you soon."

Maggie turned on her computer and signed into the church's email account. There were already several email responses attached to Ednah's little disaster. Before she opened them, she dialed Cecelia's number on her phone. It rang several times, but Cecelia didn't answer. In Maggie's mind, this betrayal of the Chance family was by far the worst thing Ednah had made public. People, even—and sometimes especially—Christians, were quick to form opinions and judge others with very little information. Christians had the potential to be quite cruel. Loving one another could quickly turn into condemning one another. Maggie knew the last thing Cecelia needed was this kind of judgment and condemnation, and her children must be spared at all costs. They had enough to deal with.

When she couldn't reach Cecelia, Maggie took a moment to change the email password, in case Ednah was plotting more revenge.

Maggie's phone rang. Betsy Sneller.

"Hi, Betsy. You've seen the email."

"I have. I know you didn't write it. The language isn't yours. How are you?"

That did it. Maggie was so worried about her parishioners, but the fact Betsy added Maggie to her own list of concerns gave Maggie permission to feel the pain of her church family.

"I'm not okay. This is a terrible thing to happen to people who are already in a great deal of pain or trauma. I should have fired Ednah the first day she came to work. She has done nothing but cause discord and hurt feelings and damage to our staff and now our congregation. I need to get another email out, but the damage has been done. The things she wrote are all true. This is the worst."

"Maggie, do have just a minute? I'd like to bring a little perspective. May I tell you a story?"

Maggie wanted to get to her computer and write another email, but something in Betsy's voice made her stop. She was going to learn something from Betsy, and it would be worth her time. She took a deep breath and turned away from her computer.

"Yes, I need some perspective right now."

"I've come up with a version of a story by an unknown author. I use it in certain therapy situations where clients believe they have experienced the worst in life."

The Angel of Death felt overworked and decided he needed an assistant to help him. So he and the assistant went to earth for the assistant's training and visited a small, broken-down hut in the middle of a sparsely green field.

The Angel of Death and the trainee knocked on the door of the hut, and a little old man answered. He was bent over and dressed in rags. The Angel of Death said to the old man, "My companion and I have been traveling for days, and we saw your hut and wondered if you could take us in for the night. We have had very little to eat and have been sleeping on the hard ground, so we wondered if you could provide us with food and a place to sleep."

The old man asked them to wait, and he called to his wife. She was also dressed in rags and hobbled to the door to speak with him in whispers.

After a couple of minutes, the old man said, "My wife and I welcome you into our home. As you can see outside, we do not have good soil for a garden, but we have a good cow. She gives us milk, and we sell the extra in town so we can buy some fruits, vegetables, and occasionally some meat. We can have good meals. My wife and I have eaten today already, so we will give you our dinner, and we will eat again tomorrow. She and I will sleep on mats on the floor so you two can have beds for a night. You will be our guests."

The Angel of Death thanked the old man. He and the trainee entered the house, talked with the couple, ate their food, and slept in their beds. In the morning, the trainee woke to the sound of screaming. When he went into the other room, he saw the old man bent over the old woman. Her head was in her hands, and she was sobbing. The old man had tears running down his cheeks. The trainee asked what happened.

The old man replied, "We don't understand what happened. When we went to bed, our cow seemed healthy. But when we woke up this morning, she was dead in the field. We don't know how we are going to survive without her. She was our only source of food."

The trainee became distressed and responded, "This is horrible." He went back into the other room to talk to the Angel of Death.

The trainee was angry and said, "I do not understand how you could do this to the couple. They were very gracious hosts and gave us their beds to sleep in and the food off their plates. How could you respond by killing their cow, their only source of food?"

The Angel of Death looked the trainee in the eye and replied, "I came for the wife."

Maggie realized she was holding her breath. Finally, she breathed out, "Oh, dear God."

"I know you don't trade in the Angel of Death lore, Maggie. I don't either, actually. This story is a reminder that when we think we've seen the worst, it might only be the cow. There is often something worse. Our perspective can guide us to find the good in what we have."

Maggie felt hot tears sting her eyes before they slid down her cheeks.

"Betsy, thank you. You have certainly changed my perspective."

"Good. I'm going to call Cecelia. Have you already talked with her?"

"I tried calling, but no one picked up. Marla and her family are with Cecelia and Naomi and Bobby right now. I'll keep trying. My intention is to visit all three of them tomorrow and see how they are doing. For now, I have an email to write and send."

"Good. You will handle it with grace. I'll see you Sunday, if we don't talk before then. Goodbye."

Maggie turned to her computer. *It's only the cow.* She addressed the brief letter to herself and added the list of congregants to the Bcc line.

My Dear Congregation,

You received an email tonight. It appeared to be sent from me, but it was not. The email shared personal information about three of our families, information

IN sickness & IN health

that was private and confidential. I would never send you an email with such information.

For now, please show the greatest kindness and respect to those who are dealing with difficult situations. Please do not call them or write to them at this time. Please refrain from the temptation to gossip with others about our sisters and brothers in Christ. Please pray for them.

Let's choose to protect them with love. We, as their church family, will be the ones to guard their hearts and bind their wounds. This is our holy privilege and solemn obligation.

See you on Sunday.
Peace to all,
Pastor Maggie

She didn't need to write anything else. Her people knew her voice, even when her words came through an email. She hit "send."

Her phone lit up. WhatsApp.

G'day, Pastor Maggie!
M'lady and I send you greetings from Brisbane.
We have been here for a week now and have toured the National Gallery of Victoria (it took three days to see it all), the Royal Botanic Gardens (also three days because we chose to), and today the Queen Victoria Market.
We ate at the Café Verona. Multiple Nutella doughnuts. They are our new favorite food in the world. Can you believe it? Eating Italian in Australia! Yesireebob!
Hope you are doing well and Ednah is doing her job.

I mean, MY job. We miss you all and talk about you all
the time.

Oh, Hank. How I wish you were here. I won't tell you anything about
Ednah until you get back. I hope you aren't bothering with emails.

She took her phone and tried Cecelia's number again.

"Hello?"

"Cecelia, it's Pastor Maggie. How are you?"

"We're coping. We're just getting ready to eat with Marla and her
family."

"May I stop by your house tomorrow? I'm so sorry about the fake
email that went out tonight. I'd like to spend some time with you, Naomi, and Bobby."

"Yes, it would be helpful. Doctor Sneller has called too. We'll get
beyond this . . . She told me a story."

Maggie paused. Silence hung on the phone. "It's only the cow."

Cecelia let out a long, deep breath. "Yes, it's only the cow. Come over
anytime tomorrow."

"I'll see you around eleven thirty then. Bless you, Cecelia. You're
one of the strongest women I know."

"Thank you. See you tomorrow."

16

Maggie finally joined her dinner guests, emotionally beleaguered and emboldened all at the same time. Jack hugged her, then whispered, "I just read your email. It's perfect. How do you feel?"

"Like I'm on cleanup duty. At the same time, I won't let Ednah harm our congregation anymore. She's got to go. It was one thing to annoy the staff, but she stepped over the line by eavesdropping and purposefully sending the email."

"You've done what you can for now," Jack said. "The church will understand. You would never hurt people like this. They know it wasn't you. By the way, I guess I'm walking Irena down the aisle. That should be fun."

Ellen walked over. "Love the email. The truth is out there now. How are the Chance family and Verna?"

"The Wiggins are with Cecelia, Naomi, and Bobby. Howard and Verna know the truth now and will have to cope with people knowing something that was meant to be private. I was just telling Jack that Ednah has to go now. I can't keep trying to help her when she wants to hurt people."

Ellen looked at Jack. "What are we going to do with Ednah when she gets to the clinic?"

"I don't know if she's going to get to the clinic," Jack said just as Sly walked over.

"We can't have someone in the clinic who will have access to our patients' personal information and has shown she can't be trusted. The end." Sly took a sip of his beer. "I understand the church is a different kind of animal, lots of trust and forgiveness. It won't work for us. It's why we have an entire legal team at the hospital. Can you imagine if something like this happened at the clinic or hospital? We'd all be out of a job, just for starters."

Maggie thought to herself, *The church is a different animal. Lots of trust and forgiveness. Cecelia and Verna would never think of suing the church because their private information was openly shared. It would be different in a hospital situation or other business. But how do we hold each other accountable in the church? Trust and forgiveness can't mean we shrug our shoulders and say a prayer.*

"What are you thinking?" Jack asked.

"Right now, I wish we had a better way to care for each other. Ednah has made our church unsafe and unhealthy. Sly is right. Out there in the real world, there are legal checks and balances. You can decide to fire Ednah before she's even worked a day for you. If I did that, I'd be accused of lacking Christian kindness and understanding."

Ellen looked thoughtful. "I wonder which world is real. Inside the church, or outside? It might be simple and easy to say both are real, but they certainly don't always mingle well."

Harold opened the sliding glass door from the deck. "Well, friends, since Jack wimped out on grilling, I have saved the day and the dinner. Help yourselves to this only slightly burned offering of dinner meats." He set down a platter of charred burgers and chicken pieces.

"What about the corn and vegetable packets?" Jack asked.

Harold looked at the kitchen counter, where a tray sat piled with neatly folded aluminum foil packets. Then he spotted the bucket of corn soaking in water. "Oops."

Maggie put the oven on warm and popped in the platter of meat. Jack picked up the tray of packets.

"Harold, grab the corn bucket, if you please."

When the entire meal was finished on the grill, everyone filled their plates and went out onto the deck. The sun was still high and the dinner delicious, but Maggie was distracted by the events of the evening. She tried to pay attention to the conversation around her but found herself staring out into the field behind them and pondering how to lead her church with grace and fortitude.

It sounds so noble. But it's a lot messier with actual people involved. Ednah knows too much. It's obvious she has been eavesdropping ever since she began. And who was she talking with on the phone? She's got to go before she causes any more harm.

"What do you think, Maggie?" Lacey asked.

Maggie looked up, startled back to the dinner party. "I'm sorry, what are you talking about?"

"Our wedding. What if Lydia and I got married right here on your deck? It's beautiful, and it's big enough for the guests we want to invite. It won't be a big crowd, by any means."

Maggie absorbed this information. "Well, if it's what you would like." She looked over at Jack. "I do think there might be more people wanting to celebrate your marriage than you think."

"Really?" Lacey asked. "This doesn't seem like a pro-lesbian kind of town. It's cute and charming, but a tiny bit like something out of the past. Don't you ever feel like you are waking up in the middle of an episode of *Ozzie and Harriet*?" She continued, "I mean, no offense, Sly, but you and Doctor Drake at the veterinary clinic are the only two African Americans in this city. Lydia and I are the only two lesbians I'm aware of. Now, homosexuals can hide a little easier than you and Dana can, no doubt about it, but Cherish really isn't what I would call 'brimming with diversity.' Of course, we have the Gutierrez family, and our token Syrian refugees, the Nasab family. And let's not forget Irena, the Romanian contingency." Lacey's voice had a slight edge. "Logically, there is a much larger homosexual population in Cherish than just Lydia and me, but the color of our skin doesn't give us away. Yours does."

Maggie blinked. She felt slapped by Lacey's words.

"You're right, Lacey," Sly said slowly. "It's something I seriously thought about before I accepted the position at the hospital. Since the last election, we have a president and others in power who are doing their best to make sure divisions between us are stoked, not healed. From what you've said, you feel it too. Gay rights are at risk. Black and Brown lives are at risk. But we, and you, always have been at risk. This is where our country is today. And this is the history of our country from its beginning."

Maggie noticed Sly did not have a fix for the national situation, just an acute understanding of the reality in which he and they all lived. The fix would be complicated and a long time coming.

"Here's a question for you, Lacey," Sly said. "Why do you stay here in Cherish? You could go to a more open community and feel accepted. Actually, you could feel normal."

Lacey looked at Maggie, then paused. "Because I do feel accepted here. And normal. At least by the people who count."

"Who?" Sly asked.

Lacey thought back to when she'd told Maggie she was a lesbian. They were in Ghana on a mission trip. Lacey went on the trip as a kind of self-imposed "penance to God." Her embarrassment and self-ridicule for being a lesbian hung on her like a shroud. But when she finally told Maggie, as they sat in the dark during one of the many "light out" moments of no electricity, Lacey had felt the light go on inside when Maggie heard the words "I am a lesbian" in the same manner she would have heard "I have brown eyes." No funny look. No judgment. No sitting back slightly in her chair. Maggie had reached out and hugged her—the first person in Lacey's life who'd hugged and accepted her in her entirety. The remembrance washed over her.

"Maggie. Maggie was the first person who knew, outside my family, but she accepted me."

"It's how I grew up," Maggie said. "My parents never singled out people as 'other.' But . . . I think it takes more than that. If I don't understand how you live in and experience our culture, I'm still part of the problem."

"We all saw the reaction of the church when Darcy Keller fought to bring the Nasab family here from Syria," Sly said. "We saw how people reacted to starting a free childcare center for low-income people. Even our free health clinic caused ignorant judgment from some. Racism, bigotry, and a need to blame someone else out of fear or hatred has always been with us. Now we have a president who encourages it. I think we will see worse acts of division and cruelty as this administration moves forward." He reflected for a moment. "There is no easy answer."

Maggie opened her mouth to speak, then stopped. She had nothing to offer. It dawned on her that her own comfortable complacency made her complicit.

"We need more education . . . mmm . . . Yes. We can't continue to drift around these issues," said Sky, the woman who seemed to drift everywhere.

"But who does the educating?" Ellen asked. "Why would we put the burden of educating white people about racism on the African American community? Or the Native American community? Or the Latinx community? How could we possibly expect the Nasab family to teach us about what it feels like to be Muslim in America? Or tell Lacey and Lydia to enlighten us about the LGBTQI community? Then again, what can any straight white person teach about these things? It seems arrogant."

Silence hung in the air.

Lydia said, "We have to begin by listening to one another. People must be allowed to be individuals with personal stories and experiences, not lumped in with an 'unacceptable' group. I think a lot of judgmental people might be surprised how the things that affect their lives, cause them pain, bring them joy, and relieve their sorrow are like what brings most people pain and joy and relief. But if certain people are written off because of their skin color, religion, or sexuality, there isn't space for a conversation. I think it's easier for some people to make their world very small so they can avoid understanding those who are different."

"Why don't we start at church?" Harold asked. "Have a Listening Night, or, I don't know, you could come up with a better name." He looked around the deck. "The burden doesn't have to be on a particular person or persons. We all have something to say about living within diversity."

"Or living without it," Lacey said.

"The point is," Harold said, "if we begin to listen to each other, we'll not only learn about others, but I also think we'll learn a whole lot about ourselves and our own prejudices. The danger comes when we think we are free of all bigotries. We just aren't." Harold took a gulp of his beer.

Maggie's mind began to soar. She pictured small groups of church members . . . no . . . the whole congregation together. Maybe some of both. Should they have a dinner and conversation night? Should they have a question box? Is there a book they could discuss? What if nobody came? What if the whole congregation came?

Jack leaned over and kissed her cheek. "Come back, Maggie. I can tell from your face you have the whole event planned already."

"Not just one event, Jack, a series." She smiled. "Let's see how much good we can do in our little town. Education is the best antidote to bigotry. Let's learn."

The sun began to set as the conversation spun off more ideas for the church gatherings. When the discussion first began, Maggie had felt helpless rather than hopeful, but now there was a viable plan, and she was all in.

Once their guests left and the dishes were done, Maggie went out to the barn with bowls of cat food and fresh water. The moon lent just enough light for Maggie to see the empty bowls she last put out. As she bent down, she heard the rustle of loose hay. Then a black streak raced toward her. Before she could move or scream, the cat ran between her legs and was gone into the night. Maggie balanced herself against the barn door and caught her breath. She put the food down and what was left of the water, which had spilled during the cat chaos, and picked up the empty dishes.

You'll be back. I'm going to win you over yet.

When she walked back into the house, she heard Jack talking.

"I know someone who will love to hear this," Jack said with a laugh. "Here she is. Just a second, I'll put you on speaker." Jack hit the button.

"Sister Margaret?"

"Bryan!"

"Yes, it's me, your soon-to-be-homeless brother."

Maggie looked at Jack, her eyes widening. "Yes, I've heard. It's too bad." She winked.

"I was wondering if you might be willing to take in your mongrel brother. Jack was just telling me you feed a stray cat in your barn. If I could have a little kibble and some water, I'd be grateful to live in the barn with your cat."

"Done. We'll even give you a few bales of hay to make a bed."

"Okay, but seriously, I realize you're going to drop a baby soon after we get back. I will probably still be in your house at this miracle moment. Do you want me hanging around while the two of you try to become parents?"

"Of course. You can change the diapers. Hah!"

She looked at Jack and questioned him with her eyes. He mouthed back to her, *It's fine with me.*

"Cate and I are still taking things slowly. She'll recuperate at her parents' house this fall and be back in school in January, we hope."

"What about you?" Maggie asked.

"I've got a surprise for you. I've been in contact with the Ann Arbor Refugee Support Services office. It's a different kind of work than what we've been doing here, but I'm willing to learn how to welcome those from other countries into ours. They have a position opening in October, but I will volunteer for the month of September to learn the practical and legal issues. I checked it out because of what you and the church did for the Nasab family."

"You did?" Maggie asked.

"That's great, Bryan," Jack said.

"Thanks. I hope I can do some good once I learn everything. Anyway, I need a place to stay until I find my own place, which I can't do until I have a paycheck. If you have room in the barn, I'll take it."

"This is the best news at the end of a tiring day," Maggie said, not wanting to dump the cold water of Ednah's offenses on Bryan's bright future.

"Maybe your husband should rub your feet. Isn't that what soon-to-be fathers are supposed to do?"

"Great idea. Thanks for the call, Bry. I feel better just knowing you'll be here. It won't hurt you to learn how to change a diaper or two."

They chatted a few minutes more, then happily said goodbye with anticipation for the months ahead. Maggie fell asleep that night as Jack rubbed her swollen feet.

The next morning, Maggie was surprised to see eight thirty on her clock when she finally woke up. She couldn't remember the last time she'd slept so late. Then the happenings of the previous night came rushing to her mind. Ednah's email. The calls from Howard and Irena, and her call to Cecelia. The dinner party and exciting discussion about what Loving the Lord could do to combat the negative issue, and Bryan's phone call happily bubbled up around the negativity of Ednah. Maggie knew today she would visit Howard and Verna Baker and the Chance family. She needed to spend some more time with her sermon and fill out the baptismal certificates for the following morning. She'd chosen a special Bible verse for each child and would add these to the bottom of each certificate. Then she noticed Jack wasn't there. She was just about to roll herself out of bed when she heard his familiar footsteps on the stairs, along with a rattling noise. Jack walked in holding a tray. Three felines followed, hoping for a nibble or two.

"Good morning. I have brought you foodstuffs." He put the tray on the nightstand and gave Maggie a kiss.

"Is it my birthday? Our anniversary?"

"No, your birthday is in January, and our anniversary is in October. You're confused because you're pregnant." He quickly stepped back before she could swat him. "I thought you might like breakfast in bed before you go out on your cleanup-after-Ednah visits."

She sat back against her pillow. Jack's signature omelet, along with toast and jam, was steaming on a plate. A glass of orange juice and a cup of herbal tea, along with one of the red carnations in a small vase, filled the tray.

"Thank you, husband. With this sustenance I can only succeed in my day's endeavors." She took a sip of juice.

"You will succeed no matter what. Your email last night set things straight."

"Yes, but it will be good to see Verna and Cecelia in person." She took a bite of her omelet, cheddar cheese oozing out onto the plate. "Gosh, this is good."

"I noticed you didn't eat much dinner last night. You and baby Elliot must be fed."

"Thank you. I am starving. What are you going to do today?"

"I'm going to mow the front yard. I guess it's more like a small pasture than a yard. It should take up a couple of hours or so. Then I'll have to see. I could either watch some golf or paint more of the fence." Jack was slowly painting the fencing around the farm.

"It will be awfully hot to paint today. You better watch golf."

She gobbled down more omelet. Maggie knew how much Jack needed projects on the weekends. His work during the week took all his medical knowledge and empathy skills. From one patient to another, he never knew what the day would hold. Seeing Irena for a prenatal check was a very different appointment from sitting with Verna to discuss her breast cancer. When the weekends arrived, Jack needed projects he could start and complete that didn't involve too much emotional output.

"You never rest on the weekends. The only time you sit down is when you're in church. Maybe I need to expand my sermons to two hours, so you can sit longer."

"Yes," Jack said, "why don't you try that sometime. A two-hour-long church service."

"Maybe I will. Whatever you do today, enjoy it. I'll be back after my visits."

She finished her breakfast, cleaned up, and arranged monster cookies from the freezer on two red paper plates, which she slid into Ziploc bags. She grabbed some cat food and water and walked to the barn.

The bowls from the night before were empty. She heard a rustle and looked up. Two bright-green eyes shone out from a hay bale. The eyes seemed to be surrounded by a big, black blotch. Maggie slowly knelt, not knowing if the blotch would turn into another feline torpedo. It didn't. She put down the fresh food and water and picked up the dirty bowls. The cat stayed put. She stood up. The cat didn't move. The eyes didn't even blink. Maggie backed out of the barn.

Well, now. I call this an inch of progress. You just eat your breakfast in peace.

She stepped into the sunlight and saw Jack, wearing jeans, a T-shirt, and a baseball cap. His long legs were striding toward the barn.

"Turn around," Maggie said softly.

"But I'm going to mow. I need my mower."

"My feline friend is just about to eat his breakfast. You have to wait."

Jack rolled his eyes.

"Give him ten minutes. That should be long enough for him to eat and wash his face and paws. Then you can mow all the livelong day."

"So, now my days are dictated by a feral cat?"

"He won't be feral for long. I'm taming him. Remember? That's what we do. We love all God's creatures and adopt some of them along the way."

She took his arm and kissed his shoulder. They walked toward the porch.

"So, have you named your new beast?"

"Yes, of course. His name is Smudge."

17

Maggie stared into Howard Baker's watery blue eyes.

"I can't lose her," he rasped.

Verna was in the kitchen, making tea to go with Maggie's cookies.

"I know."

"She's my light."

"I know."

Maggie never would have thought that serious, sometimes dour Verna Baker could be a light to anyone, but apparently light was in the eye of the beholder.

"She has to go through chemotherapy. Chemical therapy, that's what it is. Poison."

"To get rid of the cancer, Howard. Then her body has a chance to heal. Would you want the alternative?"

He shook his head frantically, then pulled out a handkerchief and blew his nose.

Verna came in with a bone china tea service on an antique tray. The teapot and cups were delicately painted with cheerful pink and yellow roses. Caroline the cat followed, hoping for some tidbit from the tray. Maggie picked up the cat, who looked so much like her sister Cheerio.

"Howard, dear, are you crying again?" Verna set down the tray and gently put her hand on Howard's shoulder. "We'll get through this together, dear."

Maggie noticed the weariness in Verna's eyes. The patient was also the caregiver. Verna sat next to Howard. She poured and passed cups of tea and the plate of cookies. She had discarded Maggie's paper plate for one that matched the tea set. Once they each had their refreshments, she put her hand around Howard's.

"Has anyone called you about the false email?" Maggie asked, petting the sleek Caroline, who'd wedged herself between Maggie and the arm of the chair.

"I've received a few texts, but only from well-wishers. Our congregation is very kind. Have you spoken with Ednah?"

"I want to speak to her face-to-face. I'll stop by her apartment later today."

"How could anyone be so cruel?" Howard said. "The email seemed to drip with meanness."

He had cookie crumbs on his bottom lip. Verna carefully wiped them away with her napkin.

"It was cruel," Maggie agreed. "I think Ednah thought she could really hurt me, you, Irena, and the Chance family by sharing your private news. It's because she doesn't understand the church. She doesn't understand we are a family, and we care for one another. We *protect* each other. Now, how can our family help you while you go through your treatments?"

Caroline began to purr. Howard sniffed.

"I don't know how I'll be feeling," Verna said, "but I suspect not well. I've heard from my oncologist, and my first chemo treatment will be next Friday. I will go in once a week for eight weeks. Jack will receive all the information connected with my treatment. I'm glad he will be my primary care physician." She paused, then quickly changed the subject. "I'm making and freezing some casseroles and other meals for Howard, but maybe an occasional meal for variety?"

"Meals are a given," Maggie said. "I suspect I will have to ask people to stop bringing you food at some point. Would you like help with your gardening and lawn mowing? Housecleaning? Rides to and from your chemo?"

Howard sniffed again.

"Howard," Verna said, "please contain yourself. I have no intention of dying. I think there may be a time or two when Howard will need a break from all of this. If someone would be willing to take me to my treatments occasionally, it will give both of us a break. Let's see how it goes."

Howard took another bite of his cookie. Maggie thought how lost and childlike he looked. He couldn't take his eyes off Verna.

"Howard," Maggie said, "everything will be done to heal Verna and to care for you both. You aren't alone in this, but I bet it feels like it. May I say a prayer?"

Howard nodded his head slowly. Teacups and cookies were set down on the tray, and their held hands encircled the small feast.

Dear God, thank you for the communion of these cups of tea and monster cookies. We know where two or three are gathered, you are in their midst. So, you are here with us now, and we are comforted. We pray for the weeks ahead and for Verna's health. Thank you for medicine and therapies to treat cancer. Thank you for doctors and nurses who know how to care for our physical bodies. Thank you for a church family who knows how to love with great care. Protect Verna as she receives her treatments. Heal her and give her strength. Protect Howard as he cares for his wife. Watching those we love experience challenging times is difficult. So, please, shower them with your grace and guide all of us as we follow Jesus' command to love one another. Amen.

They finished their small communion. Caroline remained squashed next to Maggie for the entire visit, even the prayer.

"She's much better behaved than her sister," Maggie said with a smile at Verna.

They said their goodbyes, and Maggie got in her car. The next visit might not be as easy.

Maggie drove north of town until she turned into the Chance's neighborhood. She pulled into their driveway and saw Cecelia sitting on the front porch. She parked and clumsily got out of her car.

"Hi, Cecelia. How are you doing?"

Maggie handed Cecelia the red paper plate of monster cookies, then settled into one of the other chairs on the porch.

"Pastor Maggie, how are *you* doing? Are you feeling okay? I remember those days when babies made it impossible to do most things with any kind of grace." She smiled. "Thank you for the cookies. We will enjoy them." She set the plate on the small wooden table next to the potted geranium.

"You're welcome. And yes, I feel less and less in control of myself. I don't know how I can get any rounder, but I have several weeks to go."

"I'm happy for you. You and Doctor Jack will be amazing parents."

"Thank you. We're clueless, but willing. Now tell me how you are."

"I think we're doing okay. I have to admit, it's been a wild forty-eight hours."

Only two days ago, Jim Chance was arrested after breaking Naomi's arm. Last night, the wretched email went out blaring this incredibly private information. And now, Cecelia was holding her family together, battered in body and soul, but Maggie could see she was not broken.

"How are Naomi and Bobby holding up?"

"Naomi is dealing with the pain of her arm and, of course, how it happened. Bobby is processing everything. I have to say, Marla and her family have been living balms for me and for my kids. Addie and Jason can talk to Naomi and Bobby in a way no adult can. They ask questions, and my kids answer them. Doctor Sneller will meet with all of us next week, and then we will set up individual appointments for as long as needed. She is amazing."

"She is, and so is Marla. What else do you need?"

"I need Jim to be locked up for a long, long time, but that won't happen. I called Harold this morning, and he said Jim would probably only face six to eighteen months in jail. I don't understand it. He broke his daughter's arm! The thought of him getting out and coming around here in a year or so scares me worse than anything. I'll have a restraining order, but that won't stop Jim. He will be out for revenge."

The front door opened, and Naomi and Bobby came out onto the porch.

"Hey, Pastor Maggie," Naomi said.

"Hi, guys. Your mom is just catching me up on things. How are you doing with everything?"

Bobby slumped into a chair, and Naomi sat a little more carefully, adjusting her arm.

"It pretty much sucks," Naomi said. "But Addie has been over, and she's awesome."

"She is," Maggie agreed. "She's one of my favorite people."

"I was just telling Pastor Maggie about the last couple of days," Cecelia said. "Marla, Addie, and Jason have been good friends to us."

Both kids nodded.

Maggie hesitated before asking her next question. "Do you feel safe now?"

Cecelia's eyebrows raised. She looked at Maggie, then at her children.

"Everything happened so fast," Naomi began.

"I guess we're safe because Dad is in jail," Bobby said simply.

"Is that good?" Maggie asked. She didn't know how far she could go with this line of questioning. Betsy Sneller was the one who knew what questions to ask. This was not Maggie's expertise. She was going on intuition.

"I think it's good because he was mean to Mom, and he broke my arm. Dad's aren't supposed to do that kind of stuff." Naomi looked at her mother.

"No, they're not," Maggie agreed.

"It seemed like he didn't even want us as a family. He was always mad about something," Bobby said.

"I want to apologize to all three of you for the email sent out in my name last night. It was a huge breach of your privacy, and it sickens me that your private pain was made so public."

Maggie exhaled. She hadn't realized how much she needed to apologize in person. Verna and Howard understood what had happened. Irena did too. But Cecelia, Naomi, and Bobby were so new to the church.

"The church doesn't usually behave like this," Maggie said. "We don't intentionally hurt each other. The woman who sent the email is not a member of our church."

"Why did she do it?" Naomi asked.

"I think she mainly wanted to hurt me, so she listened in on three private conversations and decided an email from me to the entire congregation disclosing these personal details would make people mad at me. I'll be talking to her later today."

"What are you going to say?" Bobby asked. This sounded pretty good. Pastor Maggie was going to kick some butt.

"I don't know exactly, but I will ask her to explain why she did so much harm to you."

"Yeah, like Dad." Bobby ran his hand through his shaggy hair.

"The difference is, Dad is your dad," Cecelia said. "The woman from church is a stranger. She was trying to hurt Pastor Maggie by hurting a lot of other people in the process. People she doesn't even know." Cecelia kept the anger out of her voice, but Maggie could see it in her eyes.

"The main thing is this," Maggie said, "the three of you have been through some terrible trauma. I want you to know the good people of Loving the Lord, including me, are here to help with anything you need. I mean anything."

Cecelia's face softened. "I remember when Hank and Chester first came to our house almost two years ago. They brought a Thanksgiving box and other bags of groceries. A turkey and everything to go with it. I didn't know what I was going to do for the holiday that year. Jim was out of work, and money was tight. Then they walked in and filled our kitchen. We not only had a feast for Thanksgiving, we had food for over two weeks. It was a miracle for us. They told us the youth group at church came up with the idea. That's when I knew it was time to get to church and get these two involved." She looked at her children. "The Thanksgiving gift of food put us on a whole new trajectory. I think I can say being part of Loving the Lord has given me the support I've needed."

"I'm glad," Maggie said. "You made a difficult decision."

"Yes." Cecelia's face hardened slightly. "It should have been sooner." She stood up and forced a smile. "Thank you, Pastor Maggie. We appreciate your visit, and don't worry about the email. The news is out. It's time for the three of us to learn we don't have to live with secrets anymore. Maybe the email was a gift in disguise."

"Only the cow," Maggie said as she awkwardly stood.

"Only the cow."

Cecelia walked Maggie to her car.

Maggie drove back into town. She parked on Main Street in front of Pretty, Pretty Petals Flower Shop and got out. She could see Skylar in the front window, arranging planters filled with black-eyed Susan, dianthus, hibiscus, blanket flower, and Shasta daisies. The window was a riot of color. Maggie walked into the shop and breathed in the heady scents.

"Pastor Maggie," Sky said, "long time no see . . . mmm."

"Hi, Sky. Your window is gorgeous. You certainly know how to lure customers into your shop. I think I could live here."

"You're more than welcome. May I help you with something?"

Sky brushed her slender hands on her apron. Her engagement ring flashed in the light.

"Your ring is gorgeous," Maggie said with a smile. "Sylvester knows how to pick them, and by them, I mean fiancées."

Sky stared at her ring. "It's very beautiful. He is a man of great taste. Mmm . . . And by taste, I mean diamond rings." She laughed.

"I need you to help me with two different orders, please," Maggie said.

Sky moved with the elegance of a ballet dancer. Maggie followed, feeling like a stodgy lump of bread dough.

"Okay . . . mmm . . . What can I do for you?" Sky's long fingers picked up a pen and poised it over an order pad.

"First, I need four white roses with baby's breath and greenery in four separate vases, each tied with a pink bow."

"Ohhhh . . . For the baptisms tomorrow. Mmmm . . . Lovely." She wrote this down on her pad.

"Then, I need one white rose to be delivered to Verna Baker, beginning next Friday and continuing for a total of eight weeks." Maggie reached into her purse and pulled out a small sheet of paper. "I would like these words used on the card, one each week."

Sky read the list. "What hopeful words," she said quietly. "What a beautiful idea."

"Thank you."

Maggie pulled out her debit card and paid for the order. Then she waited as Sky put the four vases together. Maggie wanted to drop them off at church so they would be ready for the morning. Sky spun her magic and created four white rose creations, each delicate and ethereal. She handed Maggie the cardboard box with the four slim vases.

"Sky, these are perfect."

"Thank you. Mmmm . . . It will be special to see those little ones baptized tomorrow. Can I do anything else for you?"

"No, thank you. These are exactly . . . Wait! Yes," Maggie said, her eyes lighting up. "I have one more order to place."

Sky took down the details for Maggie's third order of white roses.

Maggie thanked Sky and left with her four vases. She drove to church and heard the organ playing. She was glad. Irena was there. Maggie brought the roses to the altar table and took them out of the box. Irena stopped playing.

"Pastorr Maggie! You come to me now!"

Maggie smiled. "I will come to you right now, Irena. Get ready!" Maggie hurried to the small organist and threw her arms around her.

"Vat arre you doing?" Irena's voice was smothered by Maggie's shoulder.

"I'm giving you a hug. You have been so understanding after the Ednah fiasco yesterday. Thank you for not being upset."

"Oh. I am upset, yes, I am. But nut at you. When I see Ednah, she will know de wrrath of Irrena!"

"I almost feel sorry for her," Maggie laughed. "Almost."

"Now, about tomorrow. De museek is rready, for de leetle chicks and de baptism. What you going to do when my Captain Crrunch and I bring our trree leetle chicks to you for de baptism?" Irena smiled maniacally.

"I can't wait for that day. Maybe your three and our one should all be baptized together? The Loving the Lord Staff Baptism Sunday."

"Yes. Okay. I like eet." Irena nodded her head. "Now, go please. I must prractice my postlude." She quickly changed the organ stops, then raised her hands in the air and came down with dancing fingers as Charles-Marie Widor's "Toccata" filled the sanctuary with joy.

Maggie felt like dancing out of the church to the celebratory music, but her roundness prohibited such an exhibition. She walked over to The Sugarplum, hoping Mrs. Popkin was not cooking curried anything. Thankfully, when she pushed open the door to the sound of fairy bells, she got a whiff of old-fashioned chicken noodle soup and undertones of vanilla and cinnamon. *Delicious.* Mrs. Popkin was behind the counter with her large white apron and her chef's hat. She looked like one of her own meringue pastries.

"Hello, Pastor Maggie. Hokey tooters, it's nice to see you."

"Hello, Mrs. Popkin, likewise. It smells like heaven in here." Maggie peered into the pastry case. "I've decided not to cook dinner tonight. I thought you could help me out."

"Oh, yes, I certainly can. Soups, salads, sandwiches, treats, what can I do for you?"

"Hmm . . . It's hard to decide. I just want a bite out of everything in this case. But I'll take two chicken noodle soups, two apple pecan salads, and a blueberry pie. Jack will go out of his mind."

As Mrs. Popkin bustled the order together, Maggie stood up and looked around, relieved to have done her work for the day. The meetings with the "victims" of the email had gone smoothly, Irena was going to make tomorrow's service extra-special, and she didn't have to cook dinner tonight. *Splendid.*

Several tables were occupied by late lunchtime clients, but when she looked to the back corner, she gasped and stared. Sitting at the small table were Martha Babcock and Ednah Lemmen. The two women were eating sandwiches and in deep conversation. Maggie had one of those moments when the context was all wrong, like when a child saw her teacher in the grocery store. The teacher only belonged at school. Martha and Ednah sitting together made no sense.

Martha and Ednah know each other? Martha and Ednah are friends?

18

Maggie strode—as much as she could stride—over to the table. The two women, who were in deep conversation, looked up when they felt her presence. Martha remained stone-faced, but Ednah looked sheepish as red blotches began to creep up her neck to her face.

"Hello, ladies," Maggie said. "This is a surprise. I had no idea you two knew each other. Ednah, I believe you and I need to have a conversation about the email you sent yesterday."

Ednah opened her mouth to speak, but Martha beat her to it.

"We're eating now."

Maggie kept her eyes on Ednah, ignoring Martha. "When will it work for you?"

Ednah tried to make her face look indignant, but the redness crept up completely now, making her look like a lobster.

"As Martha said, we're having a private lunch." She couldn't hold Maggie's gaze and looked away.

"When will it work for you?" Maggie repeated.

Ednah gave Martha a "the jig is up" look. "I can meet with you when we're done eating."

"You look done now." Maggie stared at the two empty plates on the table.

"Pastor Maggie, here's your order." Mrs. Popkin's cheerful voice across the room broke the tension.

"I'll wait for you by the door."

Maggie turned and walked to the counter. After she paid for the food, she almost backed into Ednah, who was standing right behind her.

"Ednah, I didn't see you there," Maggie said, perturbed.

They went outside. Maggie could hear the organ music coming through the open windows of the sanctuary and knew it wouldn't work to bring Ednah into Irena's lair.

"Let's go for a walk."

Maggie headed toward the cemetery, carrying her bag of food. Ednah, not a fan of any kind of exercise, almost said no, but thought better of it. She got herself next to Maggie and walked.

"Ednah, what is your problem?" Maggie pictured the faces she had spent time with earlier in the day. Her fury rose.

"I thought it would be good if—"

"No!" Maggie stopped and turned to the other woman. "You didn't think it would be *good if*! Nothing was good about what you did. You hurt perfectly wonderful people who are going through difficult personal events, and you betrayed them to get some kind of revenge on me. There is nothing good about it."

Ednah visibly cringed, all the arrogance and impudence gone.

"And how do you know Martha Babcock?"

Maggie was curious about this sordid connection. Martha worked the radio at the Cherish Police Department. She'd attended Loving the Lord for a short period of time, but her blatant, malicious racism and gossipy troublemaking were well known in town. For some unknown reason, Officer Tuggle kept Martha in her job at the police station.

"I . . . uh . . . I met her when I went to the police station to have my fingerprints taken. You know, for the background check to work at the new health clinic. It was one of the first things I did once I applied for the job. She asked me where I was from and where I worked. I told her I had interviewed with you and the clinic staff. She said she knew about both places—church and clinic. She offered to show me around town."

"Then what?"

"She began to tell me things about the church . . . and about you. She seemed to know what she was talking about." A bit of Ednah's faux self-esteem showed itself. "She thought it would be good to take you down a peg or two. She said you were just a silly girl pretending to have more power than you actually had. That you were rude to her and to Officer Tuggle and her family."

Maggie took this in. "So, you two made your lofty plan to do what? Take down the pastor, or harm as many innocent church members as possible? Which one? Or both?"

Ednah dropped her gaze.

"You realize you can't work for us anymore, right? And you won't have a job at the free clinic either. Since they are church members, that email went out to most of the medical staff. They know all about it." Maggie stopped, her anger rising to a boiling point. She wanted to hurt Ednah with her words, but she paused and took a deep breath. "What made you listen to her?"

"She liked me. She was interested in me."

"You think she *liked* you? No, Ednah, she *used* you."

"She said it wouldn't hurt to play a few pranks. She said you were in over your head at the church. She said you were too political for a pastor and caused a lot of problems in town. She said the church was unhappy with you and you would be leaving soon."

Maggie stared, unbelieving.

"You seemed too young and inexperienced, so it made sense. She said you hurt a lot of people. Then she said if I got the job working at church, Hank would be fired too. The job would be mine permanently."

Maggie tried to process this new information. The shock of the lies said about her and Hank hit her like a sharp slap across the face.

Ednah's confession picked up steam. "I actually am capable of running an office. You saw my resume. But I believed Martha. No, I chose to believe Martha. That's the truth. Her ideas to sabotage you turned into a game I willingly played."

"It wasn't just a game. You terrorized Hank, Doris, and Irena. You shredded important historical documents. You eavesdropped. You condescended to me. You sent out one of the cruelest emails I can imagine. Those aren't pranks."

They walked into the cemetery. Maggie followed the familiar path in silence without really noticing where she was. Ednah knew exactly where she was and didn't like it. She was afraid of cemeteries.

"Can we turn around now?" Ednah said with a failed attempt at superiority.

"What?"

"I'd like to go back." Ednah turned around toward Middle Street.

"Why?"

"I hate graveyards." Ednah began to walk away.

"Ednah, stop. I would like to understand how you could do such heartless things to good and decent people."

Ednah looked at Maggie. "It was easy. I had access to everything. Once Hank was gone, I could go through files and cupboards and drawers anytime I wanted. Until you took my keys away." Ednah's mouth tightened. "Martha came with me sometimes at night. She's the one who found the files in the basement and thought I should shred them." Ednah stared insolently at Maggie. "When I didn't have access to the building anymore, Martha was furious. She told me to eavesdrop on your conversations with church members and staff."

Maggie felt sick. For weeks, Ednah and Martha had been creeping around the church, pawing through documents, drawers, and who knew what else. Then the eavesdropping. What made people act this way?

"Your cruelty is unbelievable and unacceptable," Maggie said, her voice raised. "I could call the police and have you arrested for destroying church property. You *and* Martha! You did it knowingly. Just because we are a church, and just because we are Christians, doesn't mean we will allow ourselves to be abused by people like you. You should be charged!"

170

Ednah stumbled back, shocked by Maggie's anger. She almost tripped over a gravestone but caught herself just in time. "I-I am . . . sorry."

"Are you? Those are easy words to say when you get caught. But it appears you and Martha were busy making new plans just now in The Sugarplum. What is *wrong* with you?"

Maggie's words, and possibly her tone of voice, took Ednah aback. The truth of what she had done at the church became clear. She had vandalized documents and harmed people. Who was she? She felt herself thrown back to middle school. Laughed at. Teased. Longing for a friend. But she wasn't in middle school. She was a grown woman who could be easily swayed, even to the point of vandalism and cruelty.

"Martha sought me out," Ednah said. "She took an interest in me. I thought she wanted to be friends. I'm so sorry. I truly am. I shouldn't have gone along with her. I was caught up in this . . . I don't know . . . revenge. But you aren't disliked by the congregation. They aren't going to fire you. They obviously love you. There's no way they're going to fire Hank either. I believed Martha until I saw with my own eyes what really happened in the church. I should have stopped the whole scheme, but then I hated how happy and above it all you were. You really do need my help!" Ednah looked miserable. "I will take the blame for what I have done. Martha is a force to be reckoned with, but I chose to go along with her." Ednah's neck and face grew red and blotchy again, and she bit back tears.

"I'll tell you what we're going to do, Ednah," Maggie said, walking her farther into the cemetery. "Come to my house. We won't be in the cemetery for long."

Ednah meekly followed. They exited the cemetery onto Dexter-Cherish Road, much to Ednah's relief, then walked down the long driveway to the farmhouse. Maggie opened the kitchen door.

Jack went in to greet his wife, curious about her morning visitations. He was not expecting to see Maggie walk in with Ednah Lemmen.

"Hi," Maggie said. "I believe you know Ednah."

Jack tried to rearrange his face into something more pleasant than the anger and disgust he felt at seeing Maggie's companion.

"Uh . . . yes. Hello, Ednah."

"Hello, Doctor Elliot," Ednah said, then looked down at the kitchen tile.

Maggie put the bag of food in the refrigerator.

"Ednah and I have been chatting. It looks like we have some work to do together." She gave Jack a thin smile. "Ednah, let's go into my study." She led Ednah through the kitchen and into her office, closing the door behind them.

"Okay." Maggie dove in as soon as they were both seated. "Your email hurt a lot of people. How should we fix it?"

"Would you like me to call the people mentioned in the email?"

"No. It's not just the ones you named, it's everyone who read the email. The rest of the congregation feels terrible for their friends."

"Should I write another email?"

"I don't think so. I have an idea, but it's up to you."

"What is it?"

"Come to church tomorrow. Sit with the congregation. During coffee time, you will have a chance to visit with the people you need to talk with and others." Maggie purposely didn't say "apologize to." She didn't see the need to rub it in. "It would be good to be visible."

Ednah looked uncomfortable. "I guess I can. Just tomorrow, though. I'm not interested in attending a church, any church. But if you think it's the best way to make amends, I can give it a try."

"Yes. I do. A phone call or an email isn't enough. Why don't you meet me in my office before worship begins, at nine forty-five?"

"Okay, I'll do it. What . . . uh . . . What about my . . . job?"

Maggie swallowed hard. "Ednah, I need to know you won't do another thing to harm anyone or anything in our church. I don't know if I can trust you. What about Martha?"

"I . . . uh, will tell Martha I'm not willing to cause any more trouble. I need this job."

Maggie wondered how that conversation with Martha would go. She knew she was in a bind. Hank and Pamela wouldn't be back from

Australia for another eight weeks. She needed the help in the office, though keeping Ednah wasn't going to go over well with many church members. If Ednah made one more bad move, she would fire her on the spot.

"I will give you one last chance."

"Thank you."

"I'll take you back to your car. Where are you parked?" Maggie asked, standing.

"Behind The Sugarplum." Ednah was dreading the confrontation with Martha, who would be waiting for a report about her talk with the pastor.

Maggie grabbed Jack's keys and shouted up the stairs, "I'll be right back. I'm taking Ednah to her car."

"What about your car?" Jack asked sensibly.

"Oh, right."

"I'll take you both over, and you can drive your car home."

Ednah was silent in the backseat of Jack's Jeep. Jack stopped in front of the church, and Ednah got out.

"Thank you, Doctor Elliot. I'll see you tomorrow." Ednah walked to the alley by The Sugarplum.

Jack stared at Maggie. "I can't wait to hear this one. I was thinking we need to find someone else to run the clinic office, but it looks like Ednah is still around. *Is* Ednah still around?"

"I'll meet you at home and tell you every little detail. I made a decision in the cemetery. I hope I haven't made a mistake. Again."

"I doubt it."

As she got into her car, Maggie heard Irena on the organ. *Irena. The Chance family. Verna and Howard. The entire congregation of Loving the Lord.* What would tomorrow bring?

Ednah walked down the alley to the back of the bakery. She pulled out her keys to open the car door, but she heard a voice behind her.

"So, what did Miss Goody Two-shoes have to say?"

Ednah turned and saw Martha Babcock sitting in her own car with the window down.

"What are you doing here?" Ednah asked, trying to keep her voice steady.

"I'm waiting for you, of course. I figured she was going to fire your ass. I hope you let her have it."

Ednah hesitated.

"So, what did she want?"

"Martha, I've got to go. Pastor Maggie and I have come to an understanding. I'm not going to cause any more trouble."

She quickly got into her car and started the engine. Peripherally, she saw Martha get out of her own car and begin to walk over. She backed out, and Martha stepped aside. The last thing Ednah saw was Martha with her fist in the air. She was yelling something Ednah couldn't hear.

This won't be as easy as I thought.

Maggie followed Jack up the driveway and parked her car next to his. Before she went into the house, she took a quick peek in the barn. Empty dishes. She smiled.

"Smudge? Are you in here?" She just heard the normal barn creaks. "I'll bring your dinner out later."

"Who are you talking to?" Jack asked, laughing.

"Smudge. He ate his breakfast like a good boy. I just wanted to see if he was still in the barn."

"I'm sure he's not far. Now, don't make me wait any longer. What's up with Ednah?"

"Let's sit on the deck. It's so beautiful out here."

They settled into chairs in the shade, and Maggie sighed.

"I saw Ednah in The Sugarplum. She was eating lunch with Martha Babcock." She looked at Jack, who gave the appropriate response.

"What?"

"Yep. Martha befriended Ednah in the police station when Ednah went in for fingerprints. Anyway, this whole mess was Martha's big scheme. I really think Ednah got sucked into this because Martha seemed to be interested in her. Then she told her a lot of lies about everyone. Anyway, as we were talking, I could tell Ednah was duped. I also saw a glimpse of the real Ednah. She's not the arrogant, know-it-all, condescending, annoying person I've come to believe her to be. It's all a front because she's probably the most insecure person I've met in a long time."

"But she *is* an arrogant, know-it-all, condescending, annoying person. I saw it myself with the rest of the medical staff. She knows more about running an office than anyone in the whole world. She practically thinks she's a doctor, according to Charlene, after they met earlier this week to go over the clinic updates."

"Jack, I think she's a person who has always been on the outside, hungrily looking in. She might even have been bullied and made fun of. You know how kids are. Instead of becoming more of an introvert, or acting out in negative ways, she created a persona of being the most knowledgeable person about all things great and small. Even when she didn't know something, she pretended she did. We both know how irritating that is. She did do terrible things at church and hurt our friends, but I don't think she's a bad person. I do, however, think Martha Babcock is one of the most wretched human beings I've ever known. I'm going to talk to Charlotte." Maggie huffed.

"So, how did you end things with Ednah?" Jack was not convinced Ednah was the victim, or that she should continue at the clinic with access to private information.

"She's coming to church tomorrow."

"She is?"

"Yes. I invited her, rather strongly, and told her it would be a time for her to be in the midst of our congregation and also have a chance to speak directly to the people she hurt in the email. She wasn't thrilled about the idea and told me she isn't a 'churchy' kind of person. But in the end, she agreed to come. I hope the congregation responds positively. She doesn't need to be on the outside anymore."

"Well, I didn't see this coming. I hope you're right. What if it doesn't work the way you're hoping it will? She has done some significant damage. No one else knows Martha is involved. It looks like Ednah did this on her own."

"I know, but I trust our congregation. We've been through harder things than this as a church family. I expect good to win out. The end."

"Okay. I love your enthusiasm. Now, what was in the bag you brought home earlier?"

Ednah's cell phone startled her awake. She looked at the time: three a.m. She hit the button and groggily said, "Hello?"

"So, you've been brainwashed by the idiot pastor. You are so weak and pitiful. I thought you had a backbone, but you're just a great big nothing. Call me when you're ready to finish our plan. If I don't hear from you soon, I'll be back in touch. Ednah, you're pathetic."

Click.

Ednah turned off her phone. Then she pulled the covers over her head and remembered all the times in her life she was called pathetic, stupid, ugly, fat, disgusting, and worthless.

Ednah's neck and face felt hot with embarrassment and self-loathing.

She pushed her face into the pillow and began to sob.

19

Despite the congregational email and the surprising news of Ednah's connection with Martha Babcock, Maggie woke up on Sunday morning with happy anticipation. She rolled over and kissed Jack on the nose.

"Good morning, husband."

Jack sleepily opened his eyes. "Good morning, wife. Come here." He awkwardly wrapped his arms around her. Then he closed his eyes for a little more snooze time.

"I'm so excited for today. The baptisms will be special, and our Ednah issue may no longer be an issue. Such a relief. Are you hungry? I'm hungry. Would you like some coffee? I'll make you some when I make my tea and bring it up here. Does that sound good?"

"Shhh . . . sleep time now," he whispered. "You're chattering."

She put her face next to his ear and whispered, "Wake up. It's a glorious day. I'll be right back with your coffee."

She trundled out of bed, put on her robe, which was growing increasingly too small, was greeted by a chorus of meows, and began her day. Jack rolled over and continued his slumber.

A few hours later, the church buzzed with greetings and conversation as Irena played her prelude and shushed as many people as she possibly could.

"You! Sit down! Shush . . . no talking! Listen to de museek!"

She wasn't quite as harsh as usual, and she was smiling while she was shushing. Her wedding was less than a week away, and she was living with the anticipation of the Israelites waiting for a Savior. Her big day was almost nigh!

Maggie organized her sermon pages in her office, then checked her watch. Nine forty-five. Ednah should be there any minute. Maggie put on her robe and adjusted her green stole, making sure the sides were even in her mirror, then clipped the small microphone to the neckline of the robe and double-checked the batteries with the "on" and "off" switch. The little green light blinked on and off. She put the control in her robe pocket. She looked at her watch again. Nine-forty-eight. There was a knock on the door.

"Come in."

"How are you?" Jack said as entered and closed the door.

"Have you seen Ednah?"

"No. I thought she was meeting you here."

"She's supposed to."

"She's probably running late."

"Maybe she's not coming at all." Maggie hadn't considered the possibility until right that moment.

There was a knock on the door.

"Come in."

It was Charlie and Kali Teater with Ryleigh and Zoey.

"Hi, Pastor Maggie, oh, and Doctor Jack. I hope we aren't interrupting anything," Charlie said.

"No, not at all. How are all the Teaters?" Maggie asked.

"We're getting baptismed today," Ryleigh declared.

"Yes, you are." Maggie knelt clumsily and caught herself with her hands. "Oops, I'm a little off-balance. Zoey, are ready to be baptized too?"

"Yes. Can we go outside in the sprinkler?"

Kali smiled. "Maybe when we get home. We'll stay in church for the baptisms."

"We just wanted you to know we're here," Charlie said, "and about twenty of our family members. The four of us will sit in the front pew, the way we practiced last week. We just wanted to let you know there are a lot of new faces out there."

"Great! The more the merrier."

The Teaters turned to leave as the door opened.

"Well, hi there and hello!" It was Jasper and Myrna Barnes. Jasper was holding little Maggie, who was wearing a lacy white dress. The other "M" children were jammed in Hank's office.

"We just wanted to let you know the gang's all here," Myrna said. "Mom is holding one of the front pews for us. Of course, we take up an entire pew with just our family."

"We should probably all get seated," Maggie said, discreetly looking at her watch.

She and Jack followed the two families out of the office. Then Maggie went to the secret door and took a deep breath before going out.

"Pastor Maggie?" a voice whispered just as she was turning the doorknob.

Maggie stopped and saw Ednah.

"Ednah."

"Yes, I know I'm late. I'll just go sit somewhere." She turned toward the gathering area.

"I'm glad you're here, Ednah."

Ednah looked at Maggie, and her face softened the tiniest bit. "Thank you."

Irena's prelude ended, and the service began. Maggie was relieved and elated when she walked out and saw the sanctuary completely full—so full the ushers and deacons were all standing in the back. Maggie spotted Ednah sitting with Jack, and she smiled at them both.

By the time Ryleigh and Zoey Teater, Maggie Barnes (held by her mother), and Hannah Benson were standing up front with their families, the whole congregation was watching with anticipation. Maggie invited the other children in the sanctuary to come forward and stand with their friends. Carrie Moffet went right to Ryleigh and Hannah and held their hands. Carl went to Zoey and did the same. Maggie read the beautiful liturgy of God's promises, then dipped her hand in the baptismal font of warm water. She sprinkled the water and made signs of the cross on the four small foreheads.

"I baptize you in the name of the Father, the Son, and the Holy Spirit."

Then she invited all the children to dip their hands in the font and to know how much God loves them. Once the other children went back to their section in the church, Maggie took little Maggie Barnes in her right arm and held her close to her own baby bump, while the other three small ladies held onto her robe and followed her up and down the aisles of the sanctuary.

"Hannah, your name means 'gracious' in Hebrew. Gracious means 'courteous, kind, and pleasant.'" She squeezed Hannah's hand. "Hannah, may you live graciously in the love of God.

"Ryleigh, your name means 'valiant' in Irish. Valiant means 'possessing or showing courage or determination.'" She squeezed Ryleigh's hand. "Ryleigh, may you live courageously in the love of God.

"Zoey, your name means 'life' in Greek." She squeezed Zoey's hand. "May you live fully in the love of God.

"Maggie." She looked into Maggie's little eyes. "Your name means 'pearl' in Greek. Pearl means a person or thing of great rarity and worth." She squeezed Maggie's little body. "May you live your life knowing you are of great worth in the eyes of God."

When the tiny parade had made its way back to the altar, Maggie gave little Maggie back to her parents and handed out the white roses and baptismal certificates to each of the older girls and to baby Maggie's mother. A gentle silence fell on the congregation as Hannah, Ryleigh, and Zoey held their roses.

"Sisters and brothers in Christ, please welcome these new little ones into God's Covenant." Then she looked at Carrie and mouthed *Oven Mitt*.

The celebration after worship was long and lively. The children grabbed as many cookies as possible and ran straight outside to play on the lawn. Maggie welcomed the visiting family members and invited them to come back to Loving the Lord anytime. Finally, she broke away, removed her robe, which made her feel like she was inside an actual oven mitt, and found Ednah with Jack.

"Ednah, I'm so glad you made it. How do you feel?"

"Perfectly fine," Ednah clipped.

That took Maggie by surprise.

"I was nervous at first. Irena gave me a few death stares, and Doris just looked shocked when I entered the church on a Sunday. But I've had a chance to speak to both of them and apologized to Irena for the email. I still need to speak to Mrs. Baker and Mrs. Chance."

"I'll go with you. Verna's right over there by the flowers."

They walked together.

"Verna, how are you today?" Maggie asked.

"I'm fine, thank you." She turned toward Ednah. "Good morning, Ednah. It's nice to see you in worship today."

"Thank you, Mrs. Baker. I'm glad you're here and feeling well. I would like to apologize for writing the email and disclosing your cancer diagnosis. It was wrong and hurtful. Will you forgive me?"

Verna stared at Ednah. When she discerned Ednah's sincerity, she said, "Yes, I forgive you. I hope you forgive yourself. Let's begin again. We are glad to have you here as part of our church staff. It's very nice to have you here on a Sunday. Please come again."

"Thank you. I appreciate your kindness. I actually enjoyed the service." A bit of Ednah's bravado returned. "The sermon was good, and the baptisms were sweet."

Maggie didn't take either of those statements as compliments. "Good" meant ordinary, and she was tired of the word "sweet" being slapped on everything and overused ad nauseam. She saw Cecelia and motioned her over. Cecelia made her way through the throng of people, and Maggie led her and Ednah into her office.

"Cecelia, this is Ednah Lemmen."

"Yes, I know."

Cecelia looked down at the ground, and Maggie felt Cecelia's discomfort. Ednah harmed this family, a family who was already in so much pain. Maggie wanted to fill the silent space with words but held her tongue. Ednah nervously rocked from side to side.

What is she waiting for?

"Mrs. Chance, I can't apologize in any way that would lessen the pain I have caused you and . . . your children. I am so sorry. I would give anything to have never written the email, especially for you." Ednah's neck and face were blazing crimson.

"I don't understand why my family was in your sights or made it into your email, but I have learned there are worse things to endure than this. Thank you for your apology. Now I must find Naomi and Bobby." Cecelia walked out of the office.

Ednah's eyes filled with tears. "I never wanted to hurt anybody. I'm not a mean person."

"Ednah, I don't think you are a naturally mean person. I think Martha made being mean attractive to you. Hurting others is never attractive. I also think it might be a relief for you to let go of needing to know everything about everything. You are an intelligent woman. Personally, I find it more important to discover what I *don't* know. I want to keep learning. Ednah, you have a chance to do good. You can gain people's trust again and do things that are positive instead of negative. So, let's get started on all the right feet, shall we?"

Ednah looked at Maggie. "I don't know what to do."

"Come in to work tomorrow, and we'll get organized. And remember, it's okay to say, 'I don't know how to do this' or 'I need some help.' You already know how to say 'I'm sorry,' and that's most important."

The next morning, Maggie found Ednah waiting on the steps of the church. Out of habit, Maggie felt herself tense up, then reminded herself to be patient.

"Good morning, Ednah."

"Good morning, Mag . . . Pastor Maggie."

"Let's get started." Maggie opened the large oak doors and led Ednah through the sanctuary. "Why don't you come into my office and we'll put a schedule together of what needs to be done each morning you're here."

Ednah grabbed a pad of paper and a pen and settled herself in one of the creamy visitor chairs in Maggie's office. As soon as she was seated, her cell phone rang in her pants pocket. Ednah maneuvered her roundness to extract the phone, quickly clicking the sound off.

"I'm ready to work," she said, looking at Maggie.

As they went through the daily lists of tasks, Ednah's phone buzzed several more times. She ignored it and kept writing.

"Do you need to get that?" Maggie finally asked.

"No."

Maggie was curious about the calls but went back to the meeting at hand. "Fridays are a catch-up day. If there is filing to be done, or last-minute messages or prayer requests before Sunday—"

Buzz. Buzz. Buzz. Buzz. Ednah shoved the phone under her leg.

"Okay, I think I have it. I'll get to today's work." Ednah got up, grabbed her phone, and walked into Hank's office, closing Maggie's door on the way out.

Maggie wondered about Ednah's phone for a moment, then turned her attention to Keith and Irena's wedding ceremony.

There was a knock on Maggie's door. Doris came in with her rolling trash can and cleaning supplies, then shut the door.

"What's she still doing here?" she whispered to Maggie, pointing her finger at the door.

"We're giving it another try."

"What about the email she sent and signed from you? We all knew you couldn't have written such an email. You would never."

"We talked it over and decided to move on from the email and make this work until Hank gets back. I think things will be better."

"I saw her in church yesterday. Was that part of the new plan?"

"Doris, you're being nosy. Let's just all go forward. Again."

Doris emptied Maggie's practically empty trash can into her big one and lightly dusted around the office. She was dying to know the details of the email, the fallout, and the reason Ednah was still employed but could tell Maggie was not going to reveal any more. Finally, she left and went down to the basement to put the kitchen to rights after yesterday's celebratory coffee time.

Maggie sighed. *People are exhausting. Gossip is a plague. I need a nap.*

It was Friday, the day of Verna's first chemotherapy. Howard sat with her and held her hand. A tube was inserted in her arm, and a red liquid was slowly pumped into her body. A nurse came in to check on the progress.

"Mrs. Baker, may I get you anything? Would you like something to drink or a snack? It looks like you have another hour, and then you'll be ready to go home."

They had already been there two and a half hours.

"No, thank you. Well, yes. I would like some ice water, please."

"Mr. Baker, may I bring you anything? Some coffee or a cookie?"

Howard looked up. "Yes, I'll have both."

Verna smiled at her husband. "You've got to keep up your strength."

"Yes, I do." He leaned over and kissed her soft cheek.

They had only been home from the infusion center for a short time when the doorbell rang. Verna got up to answer. A young man stood on the step wearing a Pretty, Pretty Petals T-shirt and holding a slender vase with a single white rose.

"Are you Verna Baker?"

"I am."

"This is for you. Have a great day." He handed her the rose and turned toward his car. He obviously didn't know she had just returned from her first chemotherapy treatment.

"Thank you," Verna said.

She brought the rose to the living room, opened the attached card, and read a single word.

"What do you have there?" Howard came in with two cups of tea.

"A rose."

"Who is it from?"

"I'm not sure."

Howard set down the tea. "Well, what does the card say?"

"Hope."

The young man from Pretty, Pretty Petals pulled into Cecelia Chance's driveway. He took another vase with a single white rose, brought it to the front door, and rang the bell. Cecelia opened the door.

"Cecelia Chance?"

"Yes."

"This is for you. Have a great day."

Cecelia took the rose and went into the kitchen. She opened the card. It said, "Strength." She turned the small envelope over. Nothing. She looked for any other sign of the sender. Then she looked once again at the card and the single white rose. It was so delicate, but with a solid, sturdy stem.

Someone knew I needed to remember this today.

Exactly one week later, the day before her wedding, Irena settled into the salon chair at the We Work Miracles Beauty Salon. Irena was ready to receive her wedding gift from Lacey.

"Now you just relax, Irena, and let me take care of everything."

"Yes. But what colorr are you put in my hair?"

"Will you trust me?"

"Eet's my wedding!"

"Yes. And no one wants you to look more beautiful than I do." *And semi-normal.*

185

"So, rred?"

"Just wait and see. If you don't like it, I'll change it."

Lacey turned Irena away from the mirror and stirred the hair color in her bowl. She divided Irena's hair into sections and pinned up all but one. Then she began to administer the color onto small strands and fold them in strips of aluminum foil. Soon, Irena's whole head looked like a funky space satellite.

"Now we'll let your hair do its thing while I give you a pedicure."

"You paint my toes?"

"Oh, much, much better than that. Wait until you feel this."

Irena's feet slipped into the warm, bubbly water. She closed her eyes and let out a happy sigh. She hated to admit it, but her stilettos had grown too small for her swollen feet. The massage, warm oil, and lotion, along with the vibrant turquoise polish, delighted Irena.

"I didn't know dis could be. I hev new feet."

"Let's get those foils out of your hair," Lacey said.

She led Irena over to the shampoo chair. The foils crinkled in the sink as Lacey removed them and then scrunched them into a ball. She laid Irena's head back and rinsed, washed, and conditioned her hair. Then she wrapped Irena's wet head in a heated towel and let her revel in the warmth for a few minutes.

"Dis is what heaven vill be," Irena said dreamily.

"Now, time to style," Lacey said, leading Irena to another chair. "And tomorrow before the wedding, I will restyle and help you with your headpiece."

"My tiarrra."

"Yes, your tiara." Lacey smiled to herself.

After a haircut, a blowout, and an encounter with a curling iron, Lacey turned Irena toward the mirror and held her breath. Irena's red-lipped mouth popped open. Rich auburn waves surrounded her face, looking wind-tousled—thanks to Lacey's curling iron—with chic straight ends.

"I look . . . I look like de model," Irena said. "I am gorgeous!"

"Yes, Irena. You are gorgeous. I'm so glad you like it. Tomorrow, I'll do the same. And how about you trust me with your makeup? I won't let you down."

Irena nodded her head. She couldn't take her eyes off herself.

Verna's second chemotherapy treatment took less time than the first. She and Howard sat together once again as the infusion of cancer-killing chemicals flowed into her arm.

"How are you doing, Mrs. Baker? Can I get either of you anything?" the nurse asked.

"I'm feeling a little chilled," Verna said. "May I have a blanket?"

"Of course. I have heated blankets to warm you up," the nurse said kindly. "Mr. Baker?"

"No, thank you. I have everything I need right here." He took Verna's hand and kissed it gently.

When they arrived home, the Pretty, Pretty Petals delivery car pulled in behind them. The same pleasant young man got out of the car with a slim vase and a single white rose.

"Mrs. Baker? Hello again. This is for you." He handed her the rose with a smile. "Have a nice day."

"Thank you. You also."

Verna took the rose into the house and set it next to the first rose, which had lost some of its petals. She opened the card as Howard peered over her shoulder. There was one word: "Perseverance."

20

Irena's wedding day dawned with a spectacular orange sunrise in a cloudless azure sky. She woke up in her small apartment alone. She'd told her groom he must stay in his own house the night before the wedding. Keith didn't understand this ridiculousness but acquiesced without argument. They had already moved most of Irena's possessions to his home, but she wanted to be in her own apartment to get ready for her wedding day. Then she would settle into her new home with her new husband.

Keith had driven to Ann Arbor for his last night of bachelorhood. He made a huge plate of nachos with extra onion, drank three beers, and watched the Minnesota Twins beat the Detroit Tigers nine to four. He awoke the morning of his wedding day and knew he was the luckiest man alive. He wandered through his "bachelor pad" and grinned at Irena's few pieces of furniture and three boxes of books and music. He couldn't wait to give her the world. She had lived on so little for so long. He wanted to give her every comfort he could.

She'll be my wife tonight. It's a wonderful world.

He set out his wedding clothes, made some coffee, and fried up a large plate of eggs and pancakes. A suitcase packed with clothes sat next to his nightstand. He almost laughed out loud when he thought of his secret plan.

Back in Cherish, Irena went to her small kitchen, made a cup of tea, and boiled an egg. She toasted a slice of Romanian *tara paine* and buttered it thickly. She didn't cook or bake too many things, but her mother had taught her a few recipes from the motherland. *Tara paine* was easy to make and reminded Irena of being in the kitchen with her mother as a little girl. She patted her expanding bump.

"I vill teach you to bake dis countrry brread, my leetle chicks."

Dr. Betsy Sneller surveyed the body language of Cecelia, Naomi, and Bobby Chance. They sat in her Manchester office to begin dealing with their new reality. Bobby yawned. It was Saturday morning at nine a.m., and he wasn't used to being vertical before ten during the summer. Naomi sat rigidly in her chair, trying to adjust her cast. Cecelia looked more relaxed but betrayed herself with a subtle and slow wringing of her hands.

"How have you been since our last visit?" Betsy asked.

Cecelia looked at her children.

"Things have been quiet," Naomi said.

"How does it feel in your house?" Betsy asked.

There was a long pause. Bobby yawned again.

"Is it different with your dad gone?"

"Yes," Naomi said, "but sometimes I forget he's gone. I listen before I come out of my room in the morning to figure out where he is in the house. Then I remind myself he's in jail."

"Bobby, what's it like for you?" Betsy pushed.

"Well, it's weird he's not around, but it's also good," Bobby said, clawing his fingers through his shaggy hair.

"What's the good part?"

"I don't feel like I have to hide," Bobby said.

Cecelia winced.

"Cecelia, what is it like for you?" Betsy asked in a softer tone.

"I think I feel like the kids. I didn't realize how much I . . . we three tiptoed around the house trying to avoid contact. Since his accident at work, his drinking became worse and worse. The political climate poured more fuel on the fire. He became so hateful and critical. It was a perfect storm for . . . for . . ."

"For violence," Betsy said bluntly. "Abuse might begin with verbal or emotional abuse. Often, we explain it away as someone just having a bad day, or we take the blame and think we've done something to upset the abuser, even though we don't use that word—abuser. Unfortunately, circumstances and tendencies to abuse can escalate from verbal and emotional abuse to physical abuse, the kind people recognize because it leaves a mark."

Naomi's arm twitched. She held the cast with her other hand.

"His abuse definitely grew," Cecelia said. "He was always sarcastic, even when we were dating. He put down people who were different. He was rude. But then he could be so charming."

"All sarcasm is repressed anger," Betsy said. "It's not humorous, it's hatred. The fact he could turn on the charm is not uncommon. It's how he manipulated others."

"I don't want him to come back," Naomi said.

"I will never let him come back," Cecelia said emotionally.

"What do we do if he does?" Bobby asked.

"We're going to get the facts first," Betsy said. "We'll find out how long he'll be in prison. We'll also find out what his restrictions are once he's released. We will talk through what you want, as far as contact with him. We will make a game plan, and the three of you will come through this in control and living in a healthy way. You no longer have to be victims. You have new strength."

Betsy didn't smile. She knew how hard this work would be. She'd seen it fail too many times in the past. She wanted this family to be free of the chains of abuse. She wanted them to thrive and not carry their visible and invisible scars into other relationships.

"I'd like to meet with you individually. Would this work for you?"

Cecelia again looked at her children. *We have new strength.*

"Yes," Naomi said.

"Does it have to be this early?" Bobby asked.

"No, we'll make sure to set your meeting for the afternoons."

Now Betsy did smile. She pulled out her appointment book. The plan had begun.

∞

Irena answered her ringing phone. "Hello?"

"Good morning, Irena. Happy wedding day to you!" Lacey's cheery voice rang through the phone.

"Yes, hello, Lacey. Tank you. I am verry happy today."

"Good. I thought I'd come over around two o'clock to spruce you up for your big day."

"Yes, dat would be a good time to spruce. I vill be here."

As soon as they hung up, the doorbell rang. Irena was in her negligee with a feathered neck and wrists. It had enough flowy space for her burgeoning belly and full breasts. She opened the door.

"Good morning, Irena. Congratulations on your . . . mmm . . . wedding day." Skylar's silky voice bubbled up in a breathy, gleeful chortle. Then she looked down—she was over a foot taller than the small organist—and her eyes widened. "Mmm . . . Irena, may I come in?"

"Ov courrse." Irena stepped aside.

Sky entered carrying a large square box, which she set down on the kitchen table.

"Irena, I can see . . . mmm . . . well . . . *all* of you," Sky said.

Irena looked down and realized what she was wearing. It was made to be see-through, and it was made well.

"Yes. Dis is my body."

"Yes, it is. You may want to change into something . . . more suitable . . . mmm . . . for visitors." Sky smiled. "Your body is beautiful, Irena . . . You look like a tiny . . . mmm . . . goddess of all life." Her fairy laughter gurgled out again. "I have brought your bouquet. Since you are getting ready here, I wanted to make sure you had it for the drive to church."

Irena ripped off the top the flower box. The bouquet was exquisite. Skylar had woven tiny pink and white rosebuds together with baby's breath and lily of the valley. It was made perfectly, just for Irena—not to overwhelm her small stature, but to enhance it.

Irena tipped her head back to look up at Skylar. "Dis is for me. Eet is for my hands. Eet smells like heaven to my nose. Tank you, Skylarr." Irena felt her bottom lip wobble ever-so-slightly.

"Irena, I'm so happy for you today. You . . . mmm . . . deserve all the happiness in the world." She bent down and hugged Irena, skimpy negligee and all.

"I dun't know why I'm emotional. Eet's de best day of my whole lifelong." Irena quickly brushed away a tear.

"But that's why, Irena. I think sometimes we can cry harder . . . mmm . . . on the happy days . . . than the sad ones. Your heart is full of . . . joy, and it must escape from somewhere."

Skylar squeezed Irena again, and Irena let her.

"I wanted you to know the trees are in place in the sanctuary . . . just as you wanted them. Five small apple trees down each side of the aisle. They are decorated with starry fairy lights. I hope you . . . love them."

"I know I love dem already. Tank you for de trees. I vill be at your nuptuals to mek de museek de best for your joyful eyes and your ears!"

"I'm so glad you will," Skylar said, and her mind wandered to Sylvester, their beautiful day, and the life they would share. "What will you do with the trees after the wedding?"

"Ve give dem to Pastor Maggie and Jack. Dey have all de land for an orchard."

"Just think," Sky said dreamily, "we'll watch those trees grow and count our anniversaries together over the years . . . mmm . . . So much happiness awaits."

Cecelia, Naomi, and Bobby drove north from Manchester. They each sat with their own thoughts of the session with Dr. Sneller.

"What can we do today for someone else?" Cecelia finally asked.

"What do you mean?" Naomi asked. "I just want to go home."

"Yeah, me too," Bobby mumbled.

"People have been so kind to us over these past two weeks. I know we have gone through some trauma, but I wonder if we come up with something else to focus on, we could forget about ourselves for a little while. What do you think?"

Silence.

"C'mon," Cecelia said. "Doctor Betsy was right. We have strength. We have control over our lives. And right now, we are going to decide to do something kind for someone else."

"Well, Marla, Tom, Addie, and Jason have done the most for us," Naomi said. "If we're going to do something, it should be for them."

"Like what?" her mother asked.

"They brought us dinners. Should we bring them a dinner?"

"What would we bring? Let's be creative."

Bobby perked up. "They have a firepit way back in their yard. What if we brought stuff to eat around a fire?"

Cecelia smiled. "Perfect. You guys start making a list on one of your phones. When we get into town, I'll call Marla and see which night works for dinner around the fire."

We are not going to be victims anymore. Everything Jim said "no" to, I want to shout "Yes!" We can be happy and spontaneous. We can laugh and mess up and try again. Cecelia's mind raced with new hopes. They could shut out the fears that had lurked. With more practice in thinking of others, they would eventually banish their fears. She wanted nothing more for herself and her children.

Irena sat at her kitchen table while Lacey and Lydia fussed over her. Lacey re-coiled the bride's hair with a curling iron, while Lydia soaked Irena's small hands and then applied the same vibrant turquoise polish to match her toes.

"This is your something blue," Lydia said, admiring her handiwork.

"Vat do you mean?"

"You know, the old saying for what the bride wears on her wedding day. 'Something old, something new, something borrowed, something blue.'"

"Vy must dis be?"

"Uh, I don't actually know," Lydia admitted. She pulled out her phone and googled it. "Okay, here it is. It's British. The British hold all the cool history." Lydia read the list silently.

"Vat?" Irena cried. "Tell me!"

"Here we go." Lydia decided to simplify things for Irena. "For the something *old,* you need an item that represents the tie between the bride's past and her family. Something like a locket with a picture of a loved one inside or a small article of clothing belonging to a loved one or relative, cut into the shape of a heart and sewn into the dress. For something *new,* you need an item that looks to the future. This is easy. It can be your wedding dress, or the wedding rings you will exchange with Keith today. Something *borrowed* should come from a friend who is happily married. It can be jewelry, or a shared wedding dress, or any small item that you wear or carry."

Irena nodded her head as she took in the information.

Lydia continue. "Next, something *blue.* Blue is the color of love, purity, faithfulness, and modesty."

Lydia and Lacey looked at each other. Modesty wasn't really Irena's modus operandi.

"It can be a blue piece of jewelry," Lydia said, "a hankie, or even a blue heart or love note written on the bottom of your shoe. That's kind of fun." Lydia scrolled down her phone. "There is one more thing, but we don't do this here in America, at least I've never heard of it. You must have a sixpence in your shoe."

"Why?" Lacey and Irena asked at the same time.

"It represents lasting wealth for the couple." Lydia looked at Irena. "Well, there you have it."

"Vait just a minute!" Irena screeched. "I dun't hev all de tings."

Lacey looked at Lydia as if to say, *now you've done it. You're going to have to go find all "de tings."*

Lydia smiled. "Irena, we're going to make all these things happen. Let's begin with something old. Do you have anything from your mother? A piece of jewelry or a special piece of clothing?"

Irena quickly settled down. "Yes. I hev my mother's wedding dress. I cannot wear eet because of de leetle chicks." She patted her bump.

"Perfect. Where is it?"

"De top of de closet." Irena waved her hand toward the bedroom.

Lydia trotted off to the bedroom and came back into the kitchen carrying a long yellowed box. The lid was torn in one of the corners, but underneath lay sheets of stiff, browned tissue paper. All three women peered into the box as the tissue crumpled in Lydia's hands. The once-white dress was as yellowed as the box. Lydia carefully pulled it out and held it up.

Irena took a deep breath. "Yes, eet's lovely."

Lydia looked back into the box. "Wait, there's something else in here."

She gently laid the dress on the back of a kitchen chair and lifted more of the decomposing tissue paper.

"Oh!" She carefully held up a lace veil. It was as tall as she was. "Irena, did you know this was in the box?"

"I did nut." Irena looked cross. "I only saw de drress when my mama showed eet to me. I was leetle."

"This is just the thing," Lydia said gleefully. "You can wear your mother's veil for your 'something old.'"

Lydia quickly pulled out her phone again. Her thumbs moved rapidly. "Got it. I'll be right back. We don't have a lot of time." Lydia looked at Lacey, then down at her phone again. "Lacey, here's the link to the bride's poem. Keep working on it." Lydia was out the door.

Lacey opened the link and read the next stanza in the poem: something new. She smiled.

"Irena, are you and Keith exchanging rings today?"

"Ov courrse. Vat you ask dis forr?"

"It says your ring can be your something new."

"Goot. Done and done." Irena almost rubbed her little hands together but caught herself just in time. No need to mess up the something blue.

"Okay, now we need the something borrowed. We need a happily married person to give you something to wear today. Who is the happiest married person you know?"

"Ov courrse, Pastorr Maggie. De end."

Lacey got on her phone. "PM, this is Lacey. We have a wedding request for you. Yes, I'm at Irena's. Lydia and I came to do some primping, but Lydia has taken the wedding thing to a whole new level. We need you to bring over something which is special to you, maybe something from your own wedding. Yes . . . I know . . . You must provide the something borrowed." She listened. "Perfect. Hurry."

Lydia and Maggie arrived at Irena's door together.

"This is so fun," Maggie said, squeezing Lydia's hand. "What a great idea."

Lydia looked at Maggie and said quietly, "We are Irena's people. She doesn't have one single familial soul on this earth to be with her today. We're going to smother her with love."

"Lydia, I just *love* you!"

They opened the door and went inside.

"I'm back," Lydia said. "And I caught a pastor."

Lydia headed over to the yellowed box and carefully removed the veil again. She took it to the kitchen sink and ran lukewarm water halfway up. Then she opened a grocery bag and pulled out a box of Borax.

"Irena, where is your laundry soap?"

"De seenk, below."

Lydia pulled out the small bottle of Tide. She mixed in a handful of Borax and a few drops of the detergent into the sink water. Then she carefully pushed the entire veil under the soapy water.

"Now we'll let that soak."

Maggie stepped forward and put her arms around Irena.

"Happy wedding day to you, my dear Irena! I think I have something perfect for your 'something borrowed.'"

She reached into her purse, pulled out a small fabric bag, and handed it to Irena. Irena opened the bag and removed two pearl-encrusted hair clasps. Her eyes widened with delight.

"Lacey gave these to me on my wedding day when she came to the parsonage and did my hair, just like she's doing today with you," Maggie said. "Aren't they beautiful?"

"Yes, dey arre beautiful," Irena said softly. She looked up at the three faces surrounding her. "You hev given me so much love and much kindness. Sky came herre today too, yeh. With de flowerrs. Dey are in de refrigeratorr. Why?"

Lydia opened the refrigerator and took out the flower box as she said, "Irena, we're family. We're sisters. This is what sisters do for each other on wedding days and every day."

The matter-of-fact way she spoke settled on the other three women. Without conscious thought on anyone's part, Irena's kitchen became a happy, holy space—a sanctified place. Love made it so.

Lacey broke the silence. "Okay, but we're not done." She thought for a moment. "Irena, do you have any coins from Romania?"

"Ov courrse. What you tink? Dun't be daft." Irena toddled into her bedroom and came back with a handful of Romanian leu. "See? Yes, I hev de leu." She pronounced it *lay-u.*

"Great. We must put one in your shoe. I think a leu is more appropriate for you than a sixpence."

Lacey slowly moved the veil around in the lukewarm soapy water. She went in the bathroom and grabbed a towel, which she laid out on Irena's counter. Then she carefully let the veil drain through her fingertips. After a gentle rinse, she laid the veil on half the towel and folded the other half on top.

"Now, fingers crossed it dries in time."

"I must take my leave," Maggie said, "but Irena, I need just a few minutes alone with you."

"Yes, okey. I know vat dis vill be. You ask me de questions."

Irena had watched Maggie in wedding-mode many times and knew how she asked each bride and groom to tell her why they were getting married, what they loved about their future spouse, and what they looked forward to in the years to come. Maggie and Irena went into the bedroom, and Irena gave Maggie her answers. Maggie wrote quickly so she wouldn't miss a single word.

When they were done, Maggie said, "I'm so happy for you, Irena. You deserve all good days with your Captain Crunch."

She gave the organist a hug, and they went back into the kitchen. Maggie opened the front door to leave.

"I will see you at church!"

21

Cecelia placed a call and heard Marla's cheerful voice. "Hello, Cecelia. How did the appointment go this morning?"

"It was a start. I think we have a lot of work to do individually and as a family. But I have something to ask you. Are you free tonight?"

"We are going to Irena's and Keith's wedding. Are you going?" Marla asked.

"I don't think we were invited."

"Yes, you were." Marla laughed. "Irena invited the whole congregation."

"What time is it?"

"Five o'clock. Why don't you come? It will be fun, and we all love Irena and Keith."

Cecelia thought a moment. "Okay. We'll meet you there. Thanks, Marla." She hung up. "Naomi! Bobby! Come here a minute."

They both came, but not happily.

"What do you want?" Bobby asked. "I'm in the middle of a game."

"We're going to a wedding. Irena and Keith's."

"Nooo . . . Mom!" Naomi shook her head. "That would be so boring. I thought we were doing a bonfire night at the Wiggins' house."

"We'll do the bonfire another night. Marla is the one who mentioned the wedding to me. Addie and Jason are going too. So, we'll sort of be together."

Both Naomi and Bobby softened their cranky faces.

"You'll need to wear something nice, and quite possibly take a shower." She perused her children. They were coming out of a personal war zone. She didn't want to pretend otherwise. But there had to be a way to bring back some normalcy as they healed. "We're going to have a great night. Get ready."

Lacey and Lydia were silently curious about what Irena was going to wear on her wedding day. Before doing her makeup and connecting her tiara to her head with the drying veil and pearled clasps, Irena had to get dressed.

"Do you need any help?" Lacey called to Irena, who was in her bedroom.

"Maybe, but vait."

They waited.

"We're happy to help button or zip," Lydia said loudly.

"Hold eet. Just a minute."

Lydia went over to the veil and pressed the towel down. Then she lifted it and felt the veil. Still damp.

Irena opened her bedroom door. "Excuse you, I need some help in herre."

Lacey and Lydia hid their smiles and went as beckoned. Irena stood in her panties and strapless bra, her white nylons stretched precariously over her abdomen. The triplets were making their presence known. "I can't get in dis drress," she said crossly.

Lydia walked over and lifted the wedding dress off the bed. Made of white satin, the dress was sleeveless, but fitted, with a delicate train at the bottom.

"When is the last time you tried this on?" Lydia asked.

"Dis week. Dun't you worry. De seamstress mek de alterations. It fits."

Lydia knelt down so Irena could step into the dress. Irena pulled it over her bump and halfway over her breasts.

"I can't get it any morre up." She harrumphed.

Lacey took the top of the dress and pulled. It covered Irena's breasts, but just barely. There was not much left to the imagination. Lacey began fastening the satin buttons up the back. Irena was right, the dress fit.

Lydia looked at the little bride. The dress showed off Irena's body beautifully. Her slender arms, full breasts, her slim back, and her perfectly round rear end. She looked like an exquisite mini-mermaid.

"Irena, it's beautiful," Lydia said. "You're beautiful. The satin makes your skin glow, and I like it so much better than if you wore a tent to cover your bump."

"Ov courrse. No tent. My Captain Crrunch luvs my body. Dis is his firrst wedding prresent . . . Just to look et me." She smiled knowingly.

Neither Lacey nor Lydia wanted to hear about anymore "wedding presents."

"Let's do your makeup," Lydia said quickly.

Irena waddled into the kitchen and made an unfortunate discovery. "I can't sit down!" She tried again but failed. "Vat vill I do? I hev to sit for my dinner."

"Let me try something," Lacey said. She unbuttoned the lowest buttons of the dress. "Does that help at all?"

Irena tried to sit again. She bent slightly at her waist and knees and plunked down on the chair.

"It vorks! But vat do I do if I must get up again?"

"We'll be right there," Lacey said. "We'll unbutton when you need to sit, and button you back up when you need to stand. We'll be discreet."

Irena clapped her little hands together with glee. "Now, de face. I hev makeup in dere," she pointed to the bathroom."

"Nope. Not a chance. Not today." Lacey shook her head.

"Vat?"

"You are going to look elegant, my friend. No offense . . . but you will for sure be offended . . . Irena, I don't think you understand the meaning of makeup. I've been wanting to tell you this for quite a while, but you wear makeup like you're a kindergarten art project. No more glitter. No more crazy colors. No more. Just wait and see the miracle I perform."

Irena tried to muster some outrage but couldn't quite do it. She was too curious about how beautiful Lacey could make her.

"Here we go." Lacey opened her makeup case. "I kind of feel like Mary Poppins with her magic satchel."

She laid a towel across Irena's chest to protect the dress and got to work. Lydia picked up the veil and carefully waved it back and forth to get air circulating through.

Thirty luxurious minutes later, Lacey lifted a mirror to Irena's massaged and made-up face. Irena stared at herself, then her whole face crumpled.

"No, no, no!" Lacey said in panic. "Don't cry, Irena. You'll ruin everything. Do you hate it?"

Irena shook her head. She took a deep breath and tried not to cry, but she was overwhelmed. Lacey dabbed a tissue under Irena's eyes and nose until she got a grip.

"I em . . ." *Sniff.* "So verry . . ." *Snort.* "Be-yoo-tee-full! I hev no idea so gorrgeous I em. Ohhhh."

Lacey and Lydia both smiled.

"Yes, you are gorgeous, Irena," Lacey said. "Now, let me repair the tear damage, and we'll put on your veil. I mean, your mother's veil."

Irena almost lost it again, but she bit her lip and held it together. Lacey made her finishing touches, and Lydia brought over the slightly damp veil.

"Now, where is your tiara?" Lydia asked.

Irena contemplated. "I dun't tink de tiarra. I tink just de pearls frum Pastorr Maggie to hold de veil."

Once the veil was in place and Irena was standing and buttoned up once again, Lacey gave her one more blast of hairspray as the doorbell rang. Irena's escort had arrived.

Lydia opened the door for Jack, who was dressed in a sleek black suit, crisp white shirt, and pale-blue tie.

"Hello, Lydia. I believe I have a bride to escort to church."

"Hi, Jack. Yes you do. Irena, are you ready?"

"Wait," Lacey said. "Where are you shoes, Irena? We have to put the leu inside one of them."

"In de box on my drresser. Get it."

"Come on in, Jack." Lydia opened the door wider. "It might be a second."

Finally, Irena was ready with her leu in her shoe and everything else in place. Lacey handed her the bouquet from Sky. Then the bride walked toward Jack.

"Irena, you look stunning." Jack meant it. He had no idea how pretty she was underneath her crazy makeup and kitchen-sink hair disasters. "Keith is a fortunate man."

The four walked to Jack's Jeep, which was decorated with white ribbons draped around the windows and strings of bells hanging from each door handle. Before Irena could get in, Lacey unbuttoned the lower buttons of the dress. It worked.

The drive took less than three minutes, but Irena enjoyed every second. She waved to people on the street like she was the queen of the universe. Jack pulled up to the front of the church, and Lacey and Lydia helped Irena out of the car, buttoned the buttons, and straightened her dress and veil. Jack came around to the other side, and Irena's small hand gripped his bent arm.

"Are you ready for your last walk as a single woman?" He smiled.

"Yes. Ov courrse. Take me to my Captain Crrunch!"

Maggie had been at church for over an hour. Keith arrived at her office door dressed in a black tuxedo with a white French-cuff shirt, black cummerbund, black pearl buttons, and platinum cufflinks with KI (for Keith and Irena) imprinted on each. His thick, silver hair was perfectly coiffed. His nails were impeccably manicured. His vivid blue eyes shone, along with his straight white teeth. Maggie laughed.

"Keith, you look perfectly handsome. You should be a model. You and Irena are quite the couple."

"Thank you, Maggie. I can't wait to see her walk down the aisle today."

"First, I need to ask you a few questions."

She pulled out a blue index card. She'd learned to use traditional colors for this part of the service. Irena's answers were on a pink index card. After she wrote down Keith's answers and slipped the index card into the pocket of her wedding notebook, Maggie's phone buzzed with a text from Jack.

I have the bride and her personal attendants.
We'll see you at the altar! Love you.

22

"Okay, Keith, it's time for us to go. Your bride is on her way," Maggie said with excitement.

They walked to the secret door and heard the organ. At first, Maggie forgot it was a recording of Irena playing.

"It sounds like she's out there right now, perched on the organ bench," she whispered.

"She wasn't going to let anyone else attempt the music. There would have been blood if that happened." He grinned.

Maggie opened the secret door just a crack and peeked out. Once again, the church was packed. She heard noises and saw the guests look toward the gathering area. The music changed. An unfamiliar lilting tune came through the sound system.

"What is this piece?" she asked Keith.

"It's a Romanian wedding song."

"It's beautiful."

Jack and Irena were in the gathering area, with Lacey and Lydia doing their last-minute checks of Irena.

Irena yelped.

"What's the matter?" Jack whispered, hoping his whisper would help her lower her own voice.

"My foot!" Her voice was not lowered.

"Can I help?" Jack had no idea what to do.

"I hev a leu in my shoe. It is hurrting me."

Jack laughed to himself and thought of a Dr. Seuss wedding rhyme:

I have a leu in my shoe.
My fingers are blue.
I'll walk down the aisle,
And then I'll kiss you!

"What shall we do?" Lydia asked.

"Ohhh, nuting. My museek! I must valk now."

Irena gripped Jack's arm and began walking toward the aisle. Then she saw her Captain Crunch waiting. She wanted to run to him, but her belly, dress, and shoe prevented such a flight. Instead, she moved between a waddle and a limp, clinging to Jack's arm.

Maggie looked sideways at Keith. She wondered what he was thinking as Irena made her lurching walk toward him. She looked like a drunken forest fairy as she passed each lighted apple tree. Keith was smiling from ear to ear.

When Jack and Irena finally arrived at the altar, Jack gave Irena a hug, shook Keith's hand, then took Irena's hand and placed it in Keith's. He sat down in the front pew just as Lacey and Lydia slid in from the side aisle. They represented her family in the front row.

"You look amazing," Keith whispered to Irena as Maggie began the service.

"I hev a leu in my shoe," she scream-whispered back. "It hurts!"

Maggie prayed.

"Do you like my hairr?"

"I do. And your makeup and your dress. You are the prettiest bride there has ever been."

Maggie read Scripture.

"I didn't know what dis tuxedo would look like. You arre so handsome, my Captain Crrunch." She wriggled closer to him.

Maggie began her wedding homily.

"Did you have a good morning with Lacey and Lydia?"

206

"Yes. Dey help me with blue tings, new tings, old tings, and, hey, look at de clips in my hair. Dey arre from Pastorr Maggie, yes. She wore dem in herr wedding. She is letting me borrow dem. I put de leu in my shoe, but it is nut working. It must come out beforre dinnerr."

"We'll take care of it. My bride cannot be in pain on her wedding day." He put his arms around her and kissed her.

"Wait! No! No! We cannot kiss yet! We arre nut married!"

This outburst stopped Maggie in midsentence. She was trying to make it to the vows while Keith and Irena enjoyed their happy little chat about the morning, but now Irena was screaming. Of course, Irena screaming about the timing of their nuptial kiss was incredibly humorous as the evidence of previous kisses and other activities were on full display in the midsection of her wedding dress.

Maggie cut her homily short and prayed while Irena pulled herself together.

"Before you say your vows," Maggie said, "I would like to share some special words you told me about one another."

Irena was suddenly quiet and all ears.

"Irena, earlier today I asked you why you were marrying Keith. I asked you what you love about him. Keith, here is what Irena said."

She pulled out the pink index card and read:

"I love my Captain Crunch because he is kind. He must catch the villains, but he is not a mean man. He is a good man. I will marry him today so we can be a family. Our little chicks will know how much they are loved by their daddy. I love that he is clever. I love that he doesn't get angry. I love that his eyes only look at me. I love that he makes me laugh all the time. I love many things I cannot tell you in church. I love that he thinks I'm a great organist, because I am. But there is one thing I love about him that is above the rest. He found my mother for me. He found her and brought me to her, and now I know where she is sleeping forever. She is no longer lost because he found her and gave her back to me."

Maggie looked at Keith. He was clearly moved by her last statement. He took Irena in his arms and held her close. He kissed her again, and she let him. Lacey saw the veil begin to slip out of the clasps and desperately wanted to jump up and fix it but remained seated.

"Now, Irena. Keith said some things he loves about you too."

She pulled out the blue index card:

"I love Irena because she is the most authentic woman I have ever known. She doesn't play games. She is completely honest and genuine. I love her intensity. I never wonder how she is feeling. I love her passion in so many ways. She makes me laugh. I love the mother she already is and will be with our children. I love her commitment to this church. I love how I feel when I'm around her. I am safe, and I am home. I can't wait for all the years we will be able to love each other and raise our family. I love how she sings her Romanian lullaby when she doesn't know I'm listening. I will love and adore her forever."

Irena was beaming. "Yes, I love you. You say beautiful words about me, verry nice words." She looked at Maggie. "What's next?"

Maggie was taken aback. Not only had she spent several hours wordsmithing a beautiful and personal homily for Irena, which Irena and Keith had ignored and merrily chatted all the way through, but she'd written the prayers specifically for her crazy little colleague.

Irena reached out and slapped Maggie's hand. "What's next?"

Maggie's notebook fell out of her hand to the floor. She stooped clumsily down, picked it up, stood back up, and opened the notebook to the vows.

"Please share your vows with one another. You first, Irena," she said flatly.

After the vows—which no one could hear because Irena and Keith practically whispered them to one another—Maggie asked what symbols of love they had brought to the ceremony.

"Rrrings!" Irena shouted while Keith spoke the word like a normal person.

They exchanged rings.

Maggie pronounced them married.

Keith and Irena enjoyed a long, passionate kiss.

Maggie said with as much enthusiasm as she could muster, "Ladies and gentlemen, it is my honor to introduce to you Mr. and Mrs. Keith Crunch and Irena Dalca."

The prerecorded recessional blared through the sound system as the congregation erupted in applause and a few racy whistles. Irena clung to Keith as she limped back down the aisle. Lacey and Lydia were waiting for her.

"Git dis shoe frum my foot!"

Lacey pulled off the shoe and removed the offending leu.

"Hey! Vat is dat?" Irena said, reaching for the shoe. She looked at the bottom and saw written in blue marker and surrounded by a heart:

ID + KC
True Love Forever
8-12-17

"Who wrrote dis?"

"I did," Lacey said. "I just wanted to make sure you were covered for the something blue, in case fingernails didn't count."

Irena grabbed Lacey around the neck and hugged her. "You tink ov all tings to mek de poem come trrue for me. Tank you!"

"You're welcome. Now, let's get your shoe back on and get some pictures taken."

Lacey put the shoe back on and gave Keith the leu. "You keep it for the rest of your wedding day. You might as well take part in the poem too."

Pictures commenced, with Irena shouting out orders and ignoring the photographer completely. Maggie and Jack watched from the back of the church at the crazy chaos Irena rained down.

"How do you feel about the ceremony?" Jack asked.

"I don't know. Did anyone hear anything I said?"

"Yes. You were wearing the microphone, so we all heard you. It's too bad Irena and Keith missed out on their ceremony. Irena was true to form today."

"And the truth is, they are married. Praise be to God for that."

"PASTORR MAGGIE! YOU COME HERRE NOW!"

"Off you go, Pastor Maggie." Jack laughed as Maggie walked down the aisle.

"Now, I vant a picture vit my pastorr. She ees my best frriend een dis vorrld." Maggie could hear Irena's excitement as her accent became more extreme.

Maggie in her white robe and Irena in her white dress stood side by side on the altar. The photographer snapped several shots, but Maggie's favorites were the ones when she and Irena looked at each other and Irena said, "I'm sorry you drropped yourr notebook. You arre clumsy." They both laughed as the camera clicked away.

The caravan of guests drove to the Gandy Dancer in Ann Arbor for the reception. Keith had made the decision for the location and refused to cut corners. He was marrying the love of his life, and their guests would be treated to the best. When he'd made the reservation months in advance, the manager wanted an exact number.

Keith had responded, "Be prepared to serve one hundred fifty people. If there are leftover dinners, I want them taken to the Purple House Homeless Shelter that evening for the residents."

Keith had watched during the past year as Darcy Keller and Maggie worked to bring the Nasab family to Cherish from Syria. He was an astute man. It became clear to him there was more he could do to make the world a more equitable place. He and Irena were already plotting on what to do in Cherish and beyond to create a safer and kinder world.

The Gandy Dancer was set up for one hundred twenty, with extra tables ready to be added as needed. As it turned out, one hundred eighteen people showed up.

"This might be the fanciest reception we ever go to," Maggie said to Jack. "It's beautiful."

"Remember, Darcy and Jennifer are still planning their wedding. We may all fly to Hawaii or Switzerland or someplace."

"Good point."

After the guests were seated, the DJ introduced the newlyweds. They walked into more cheers and applause. Lacey and Lydia were waiting discreetly behind some planters near Keith and Irena's small private table. When Keith and Irena came near, the two women stepped forward. Lydia pretended to fix Irena's veil, while Lacey quickly unfastened the lowest buttons on Irena's dress. Irena sat. Lacey and Lydia faded away to a nearby table.

The cake-cutting ceremony followed the gourmet meal. Lacey and Lydia magically appeared to button up Irena so she could walk to her cake. Then they helped her sit to eat it. They were there when it was time for the first dance.

Maggie waited for the dance to finish before she approached Keith and Irena.

"We need to sign the marriage license. Your photographer is waiting by that tall table."

They walked over to where Maggie had laid out the three copies of the license and three pens.

"Now, who are your witnesses?" Maggie asked.

Irena and Keith looked at each other. They hadn't had anyone stand up with them in the ceremony.

"How about you and Jack?" Keith suggested.

"I will sign it as the officiant," Maggie said. "How about a family member, Keith?"

Keith looked around the room. "I think not." He looked at Irena. "There are two people here who have been involved in this day as much as we have."

"Lydia! Lacey! Come here and sign dis license ov my marriage to my Captain Crunch!" Irena screeched as she searched the room.

Since Lydia and Lacey were only three feet behind the screaming Romanian bride, they moved in quickly.

"Great," Maggie said. "If Keith and Irena could sign all three copies first, then L and L, and I will sign last."

Once it was official, Jack took his wife to the dance floor for one slow dance to "Songbird" by Eva Cassidy. As the music finished, he whispered in her ear, "And I love you, I love you, I love you, like never before." He kissed her on top of her head. "I think it's time for you and baby Elliot to get some sleep."

They were just about to leave when Keith stood up, tapping a glass of champagne with his butter knife.

"Excuse me! May I have a word?" The chatter and laughter settled down. "I would like to thank you all for being part of this incredible day. It means a lot to both of us."

Irena vigorously nodded her head.

"I have one more surprise I'd like to share with you. I have been informed by someone in the know that my lovely bride has never been on a vacation. Not once in her entire life. So, let it be known, tomorrow Irena and I are driving to New York City. We are going on vacation."

Irena's eyes grew round. Many audible gasps could be heard around the room, but none louder than Irena's. The applause began almost immediately. Irena clasped her hands over her heart. And then . . . Irena wept. She'd been able to stifle most of her tears throughout the loving care given her by Sky. She'd remained nearly tearless during the kindnesses Lacey, Lydia, Jack, and Maggie bestowed upon her. Perhaps she didn't want to think of her mother on this day because of the sharp pain of her absence. Perhaps the elegant reception, delicious meal, and delighted faces of her church family allowed her to hold her emotions in check. But now . . . Now every single tear she'd held back during the day rushed to her eyes. They slid down her delicate cheeks. They dripped off her chin. She was going on vacation. Not a honeymoon, a vacation!

Jack and Maggie looked at each other and grinned. Keith had spoken to them weeks earlier.

"I need your input," he'd said as he sat in their farm kitchen sipping an off-duty beer. "Now that I know she's never experienced a vacation, I want to take her somewhere special after we're married, like Europe. But I'm guessing with triplets on board, that's a big no."

"Yes," said Jack. "That's a no."

"So, I think I will take her someplace where we can drive. Like New York City."

Maggie clapped her hands. "Yes! Yes! Yes!"

Keith had been pleased with Maggie's enthusiastic response. "I'll order theater tickets and symphony tickets. We'll tour the city and enjoy the excitement of the Big Apple."

Maggie had never seen so much animation on Keith's face.

"How long will you be away?" she asked.

"Two weeks, including the drive to and from. How does that impact the church?"

"I will speak with Marla. She doesn't play the organ, but she is a good pianist. Don't worry, we'll take care of the music. Just make your wonderful plans."

The secret was shared with Marla, who began to practice familiar hymns on the piano in her living room, not wanting to give anything away by practicing at church when Irena might be lurking.

Now the cat was out of the bag, and Keith tenderly held his crying bride. At the same time, he relished the sure and certain knowledge of being the most creative and thoughtful man in the universe.

23

It was eight a.m. when Maggie pulled into the driveway of Mark and Ann Carlson's home. She heaved out of the car, grabbing a plate of soft gingersnaps she had baked the day before. The Carlson's were early risers, which worked well for Maggie. They had much to celebrate. Bryan and Cate would be home in less than two weeks. Ann opened the front door as Maggie walked up the sidewalk.

"Pastor Maggie, come in. We've been waiting for you. The tea is ready."

Maggie walked into the air-conditioned living room and took a deep breath. She was always hot these August days.

"Hi, you two. How are you feeling about the latest news?"

"Have a seat," Mark said. "We're cautiously optimistic."

"Maggie, you look miserable," Ann said with a sympathetic pat on Maggie's arm.

"I am miserable. And I still have five weeks of miserableness to live through. It's a good thing my brother and your daughter are coming home to take my mind off my misery." She chuckled.

"I can hardly believe they'll be home a week from Friday. I can't wait." Ann's voice longed for her daughter. "I need to see her with my own eyes and hug her with my own arms."

"I thought the email was hopeful," Maggie said as Ann served her a cup of tea.

"We appreciated Bryan's email," Mark said, "with the medical update and the news of what they've done to prepare United Hearts to function on its own. They've worked themselves out of their jobs, just as they intended to from the beginning."

"Jack is pleased with the medical news. Cate will need to continue gaining strength, but no permanent damage, thank goodness. Have you had a chance to talk with her recently?" Maggie asked as she took a sip of her tea.

"Yes," Ann said with a light heart. "They called two nights ago. She's definitely weaker. Her voice gave her away. It was soft and breathy, not our rambunctious girl." Cate would recover completely, and Ann would oversee every second of the healing process as soon as she had her daughter home again. "It's obvious Bryan has done most of the work to pass the torch to Pastor Elisha and Nana, but Cate did help with the nonprofit status application. They are quite a duo."

"Is Cate still planning to go back to school in January? That was the last we heard from Bryan. She's too ambitious to just sit around thinking about being Bryan's wife, once she's feeling back to normal." Maggie laughed.

"Yes," Mark said, "she will finish her Public Health degree at the U second semester. She's going to take the first semester off. She'd like to study for a nursing degree as well. She began college with both degrees in mind. She'll make it happen." Mark's face showed the pride he felt for his youngest daughter.

"I wonder if she'd like to work in the free clinic to get a feel for her new professions," Maggie said, more to herself than to Mark and Ann.

"You may be jumping the gun," Ann said protectively.

"Of course. We need to have them both home and rested." But Maggie planned to call Jack the minute she got to her office and ask him about the possibility of Cate and the clinic. "Bryan will begin volunteer work at the Ann Arbor Refugee Support Services in September, and I'm sure you've heard he has a position there beginning in October. I don't know exactly what he'll be doing, but he's excited. They'll both do good things. That's just who they are."

"Your mom and dad must be just as excited as we are." Ann changed the subject slightly.

"Yes, indeed. They are driving over early on Friday so we can all go to the airport. My mom isn't one to show great heaps of emotion, but I can tell she is on the verge of an emotional outburst whenever she talks about Bryan and Cate. She and my dad have been worried about Cate since her malaria diagnosis. They are also thrilled about the engagement. You can't push that much emotion aside for too long. I, myself, am never short on emotion."

Tea and light conversation continued. Bryan and Cate's homecoming was imminent, and their families could hardly wait.

After her visit with the Carlsons, Maggie drove to church. It was strangely quiet without Irena perched on her organ bench playing something too loudly. Marla had done a very satisfactory job on the piano in church the previous day. Now there was silence. Maggie went to the offices and found Ednah typing at Hank's desk.

"Good morning, Ednah. It was so nice to see you in church yesterday." Maggie had been surprised when she saw Ednah walk into the sanctuary a few minutes before the service began. "Did you get a chance to talk with folks at coffee time?"

Ednah lifted red-rimmed eyes to Maggie. "Yes, I visited with several people. I met the Gutierrez family. Their little boy, Marcos, is so precocious. He's a bright one. He serenaded me with the ABCs and gave me a picture he colored in Sunday school. It's on my refrigerator."

Maggie wondered if Ednah had sought out Juan, Maria, Marcos, and Gabby, or if they initiated the conversation. Did she know Martha had been their landlord and treated them so cruelly?

"They are a wonderful family," Maggie said, "and we're lucky to have them in Cherish and here at Loving the Lord. Maria is a natural teacher and has made significant educational contributions to the childcare center. I love to watch her with her kids too."

"There are nice people here," Ednah said quickly.

"Ednah, are you okay?" From the look of her eyes, something was clearly not quite right.

"I'm fine. Before I forget, Sylvia Baxter was in with her little girl. They left you something in your office."

The door opened, and Doris bustled in with her rolling trash can.

"Good morning, ladies," she said as she emptied Ednah's trash. "It's another gorgeous summer day in Cherish, Michigan."

Maggie wanted to query Ednah some more, but not with Doris around.

"It's a *hot* summer day in Cherish, Michigan," Maggie said, fanning her face with one of yesterday's bulletins.

"Yes, you're pregnant. You really should have planned better, Pastor Maggie. Always plan the third trimester to be in the winter. You can walk around without a coat in a blizzard and feel hunky dory."

"I'll have to remember that. But for now, I'm a ball of sweat."

Ednah laughed. It was natural and somewhat pleasant.

"Only for another month or so, during the absolutely hottest part of the year." Doris winked at Maggie.

"Doris, I banish thee to the basement."

"Okay, okay, let me empty your trash first. I am going to clean out the kitchen cupboards this morning. I think we should begin the fall by returning all the lost pans and utensils left down there after potlucks and Lenten breakfasts."

Ednah's eyebrows raised, but she remained silent. Doris looked right at her.

"Yes, Ednah, you have inspired me in this endeavor. I didn't appreciate your negative comments when you first got here, but I realized you were right about our kitchen. It's a mess. So, I'm somewhat shocked to say, thank you for your observation. The kitchen shall be overhauled and cleaned within an inch of its life." Doris retrieved Maggie's trash can and emptied it into her larger one. "Ta-ta, ladies. Onwards and forwards!"

"What in the world has gotten into her?" Maggie accidentally said out loud.

"She's funny," Ednah said quietly.

The phone rang. "Good morning, Loving the Lord Community Church. May I help you?"

Maggie walked into her office and laughed when she saw a bag of vegetables on her worktable. Sylvia Baxter ran The Garden Shop and made the rounds to her friends with fresh vegetables throughout the summer and fall. She and her husband Bill were the parents of Katharine Marie. There was a note on the bag.

Dear Baby Elliot,
These veggies will make you
healthy and strong.
I can't wait to meet you!
Love,
Katharine

Maggie looked through the bag and knew what she would make for dinner that night. Salad and spaghetti squash with fresh tomatoes, onions, zucchini, and mozzarella. She would pick up a loaf of Mrs. Popkin's Italian bread and call it good. One less thing to worry about. She popped her head out of her office door.

"Ednah, I'm expecting a clergy friend in about an hour. Her name is Pastor Nora Wellman. Just send her in, please." Maggie looked again at Ednah's eyes. "Ednah, are you really okay?"

"I'm just a little tired today. Thanks for asking. I'll send Pastor Nora in as soon as she gets here."

Ednah went back to her typing. She could never tell Pastor Maggie about the phone calls and cruel notes she was getting every day. Martha Babcock left notes on her car, in her mailbox, even under her apartment door. The only place Ednah felt safe was at church. Martha would never set foot in Loving the Lord during work hours or on Sundays. Now Ednah looked forward to being at church and away from the harassment.

An hour later, Nora walked into the office. She was about a foot taller than Maggie and had glossy brown hair, which was bound in a long, curly ponytail. Her bright hazel eyes held a whisper of mischief. Whereas Maggie loved the creativity of drama and the theater, Nora loved the competition of basketball and soccer. Seminary had leveled the playing field. The many -ologies and -isms, along with Greek and Hebrew, had kept both their noses in stacks of books.

"You must be Pastor Nora," Ednah said.

"Yes, and you're Ednah. It's nice to meet you."

Ednah smiled. "Thank you. Pastor Maggie is waiting for you in her office."

Maggie met Nora at the door, and Nora hugged her short, round friend. "It's so good to see you. You are incredibly pregnant."

"It will be easier for you when you have a baby. You're so tall, your baby will just stretch out and no one will know you're pregnant. You'll just show up with a baby one day."

"Hah! Another perk of being a woman of the Amazon. How do you feel?"

"I could whine about the heat, my bladder, my aching lower back, not enough sleep, swollen feet, and being unable to focus on anything for longer than two seconds, but I won't."

"Thank you. It sounds miserable. Will this be your last baby, then?" Nora smiled.

"I'm pretty sure it is. Jack says there is something like amnesia after a baby is born, and I will forget this agony. I won't forget. Now, tell me how things are in Lansing. I'm so excited to hear everything."

"It's incredible. The people of Glory to God Church are a lot like the people here at Loving the Lord, except we have many more of them. They don't wait around for someone else to do the work, they just get the job done with no fuss, no drama. There is a food pantry right inside the church. They get food shipments from the larger food bank in Lansing every other week and serve clients Monday through Thursday each week. I can hardly drag myself out of there. It is an amazing ministry."

Maggie felt . . . What was it? Inspiration, tinged with envy.

"I can't imagine," she said wistfully. "Someday, when you finally have a baby, may I come up and work in your food pantry while you're on maternity leave?"

"You'd have to preach and do pastoral care too." Nora grinned.

"Nope. I'd just live in the food pantry for six weeks or so and feed hungry people and get to know the neighborhood."

"Okay. Sometimes I feel that way too. Besides the work of the pantry, the people are intelligent, curious, faithful, practical, and loving. Dan and I can't believe God plunked us down in such a wonderful church. If you can find the time to drive up before the baby comes, I'd love to show you around. And it's right near the capitol building. We can stroll down there too." Nora beamed. "But let's talk about Loving the Lord. How I can I get myself ready to be of assistance?" She nodded her brown, ponytailed head toward Maggie in obeisance.

"I should probably take you to The Sugarplum first. You will eat many a lunch there. My treat. Are you hungry?"

"Always. Sounds good."

"We'll be back in a bit," Maggie said to Ednah as she and Nora left. "I have my cell phone if you need anything."

"Have fun," Ednah said. *What's it like to have a friend to laugh with and have lunch with and just be yourself with?*

Maggie and Nora crossed the street, involved in conversation and unaware of the car parked in front of the parsonage. The fairy bells of The Sugarplum rang merrily as they entered.

"Mrs. Popkin, this is my dear friend Reverend Nora Wellman, or Pastor Nora."

"Well, hokey tooters! It's a pleasure to meet you, Pastor Nora. I've actually heard about you in a sermon or two."

Nora looked at Maggie, eyebrows raised.

"I talk about my friends in sermons sometimes. Get over it," Maggie quipped.

"What can I get you ladies?" Mrs. Popkin asked.

"I'll have your cherry walnut salad and some water, please," Maggie said.

"I'll have one of those cinnamon buns and a peach yogurt," Nora said.

"I like her," Mrs. Popkin said, pointing at Nora.

Once they had their food, they found a table and talked sermons, pastoral care needs, and how much time Nora would spend at Loving the Lord.

"Half days on Tuesdays, Thursdays, and Sundays will work for me," Nora said, taking a bite of yogurt.

"I didn't realize how much I needed to have this conversation," Maggie said. "I think it's one of the last things on my to-do list before this baby shows up. We'll get Bryan and Cate home and settled, then Hank and Pamela. After they are on the correct time zone, I should be ready to hold this baby in my arms instead of in here." She patted her bump.

"Good. I can let my church folks know how we've set the schedule."

As they walked back across the street, Maggie noticed the car in front of the parsonage.

"Oh, good grief. Hurry, Nora."

They walked quickly across the street, and when they got to the oak doors, Maggie put a finger to her mouth. She opened the door as quietly as she could, and they both heard raised voices. Maggie rushed toward the office much faster than Nora imagined possible.

"You get out of this office and out of this church," Doris roared. "I heard every word you said, and we have no use for that kind of language around here!"

"Shut up, Doris. Go clean something, since that's all you know how to do."

Maggie pushed open the door. Doris stood in the middle of the office, her apron bulging with cleaning supplies. Ednah sat at her desk, head in hands. Martha Babcock stood over Ednah and glared at Doris.

"What's going on here?" Maggie asked. She pulled out her cell phone and hit speed dial. "Hi, Charlotte, could you come to the church, please? I think we have an issue for you to deal with . . . Martha is here, and she's causing some trouble . . . Great. Thank you."

Martha rushed to the door. Nora, who didn't know exactly what was going on, stood in the doorway so Martha couldn't get through. Martha tried to push Nora out of the way, but Nora grabbed her arms and forced them down hard.

"Ow! Get out of my way!" Martha barked.

"I don't think so." Nora quickly grabbed the doorknob and closed the office door. She towered over Martha. "Sit down, Martha."

Martha looked around the office, searching for a way out. She surveyed the four women around her, then resigned herself to taking a chair. They all waited in silence. Maggie wondered what Martha could have been saying to upset both Doris and Ednah so much.

They heard Charlotte before they saw her—the squeak of her leather belt and holster and her heavy boots as she trod across the gathering area. Nora stepped aside as Charlotte reached the office door.

"What's going on here?" Charlotte looked from one face to another. "Martha?"

"What?" Martha stood.

"I don't have time for this. What are you doing here?" Charlotte sounded like a scary mom.

"I just came by to talk to Ednah. We're friends."

Charlotte looked quizzical. "You are?"

"No. We're not," Ednah said quietly.

Martha turned and glared at the red-faced Ednah, but Ednah drew strength from Maggie, Doris, and Nora.

"Martha and I are not friends. I thought we were, but she asked me to do things to disrupt life here at church. I did those things, and I'm sorry. Since I told her I would not continue, she has called me at all hours of the night and day with threats. She came here today to threaten me more." She stared at Charlotte. "I can tell you everything, Officer Tuggle, but what's going to stop her from calling me at midnight tonight?"

"Martha, is this true?" Charlotte asked.

"I think Ednah has mistaken my—"

"Have you been calling and threatening her in the middle of the night, Martha? Yes or no?" Charlotte crossed her arms and stared.

Martha was thinking fast and coming up with nothing. Her plan to claim friendship with Ednah had already collapsed.

"Here's what's going to happen," Charlotte said. "Martha, meet me at the police station now. You and I will have a talk about this issue. You will not call Ednah anymore." She looked around the room. "Ednah, I would like to know if you get any more harassing phone calls or other interactions. Now, let's all get on with our day, shall we?" She turned, then waited for Martha to leave first.

Once Charlotte and Martha were through the large oak doors of the sanctuary, Ednah let out a sigh.

"Are you okay, Ednah?" Maggie asked.

"I think so. I didn't expect anything like that to happen. Officer Tuggle seems to mean business."

"She's a no-nonsense kind of gal," Doris piped up.

"Ednah," Maggie said, "I'm sorry about the phone calls and other abuse you have put up with. Martha obviously has some problems. If she bothers you again, tell us right away. You aren't alone. You've got friends."

"Thank you," Ednah squeaked out, afraid she would burst into tears on the spot.

"It's after noon. Do want to go home?" Maggie asked.

"Would you mind if I stayed for a while longer?"

"Of course not. Stay as long as you like. Nora and I will be in my office if you need anything."

"Thank you. I will," Ednah said. She looked at Nora. "And thank you, Pastor Nora, for standing in Martha's way when she tried to leave."

"My pleasure. We all need a blocker now and then. I'm glad I could be yours today." Nora smiled.

Once the two pastors were in Maggie's office, Doris looked at Ednah and said, "I want to apologize for every mean action, word, and thought I had against you. I didn't understand."

"Thank you, Doris, but I'm sure I was miserable to be around. I'm sorry for being rude and for thinking I knew more than anyone else about how to run this office."

"Let's get coffee or lunch sometime this week," Doris said.

"I'd like that."

∽

Charlotte walked with Martha into the police station, and the chief of police pointed to a chair, where Martha quickly sat down.

"Let's make this simple. We need someone trustworthy to work the police radio. Your conduct with Ednah to damage the church and then to badger her when she refused to help you is unacceptable."

"I can work the radio. No problem there." Martha was surprised her job was in jeopardy.

"I don't think you can. Every private detail that comes through the radio must be handled with the strictest confidence, but you have shown that using private information to harm others is not beneath you. I suspect you were the big brains behind the false email under Pastor Maggie's name sent from church. Unacceptable."

"I'd like another chance."

"It's too risky. We have overlooked your questionable actions in the past, but this is too much. You can pick up your last paycheck on Friday, but you don't need to come in for work anymore."

Martha left the police station seething and drove to her lonely apartment. Her cat, G. Gordon Liddy Kitty, had lived all nine of his lives on the receiving end of his mistress's daily complaints, but he was well-fed and always had a soft cushion on which to lay his small head. One night he'd peacefully made his journey out and beyond to the eternal place of cats—be they wild or tame, large or small, striped, spotted, or solid, house, or feral.

Martha sat alone in her small living room and considered her options. She didn't have much to consider. So she settled into the long afternoon and did what came naturally. She painstakingly gnawed on a list of grievances with the world. It was a bitter meal.

24

"They're coming home today! They're coming home today!" Maggie tried to bounce, but her body would have none of it. She was a month from her due date. Her parents, Dirk and Mimi Elzinga, would be in Cherish any minute. They, Jack, Maggie, and Mark and Ann Carlson would travel to the Detroit Airport to collect Bryan and Cate. *Finally*!

"Are you excited about something?" Jack teased.

"Yes, yes, yes! I can't wait to get my eyeballs on them and my arms around them."

There was a knock on the kitchen door.

"Hi, Mom and Dad! Come in." Maggie hugged and kissed her parents.

Mimi stepped in carrying a large Longaberger basket covered with a white cotton tea towel. As always, she was perfectly dressed for a warm August day in light gray cotton pants and a cap-sleeved white blouse. Her hair was impeccably coiffed, her brown eyes shining.

"What's in there?" Maggie asked, staring at the basket.

"Just a few things to add to your dinner tonight."

Mimi was not a cook or a baker, but she was an excellent purchaser of classic Dutch foods. Maggie peeked under the towel.

"Mmm! You've been to DeBoer's Bakkerij." She rooted around. "Oliebollen, Dutch letters, speculaas, and a Dutch apple pie. Is this all?"

"I know. Stingy." Dirk winked. His gray temples paired well with his blue eyes. He looked at Maggie's roundness. "How are you going to last

225

another month? It doesn't look like you can go another day without popping."

"Yes, I'm very aware. I feel like a pressure cooker."

The front doorbell rang. Jack ushered in Mark and Ann.

"The parents of the bride," he said grandly.

The four parents chatted together as Maggie stole a Dutch letter out of Mimi's basket.

"What have you heard from Cate?" Mimi asked Ann.

"She says she's feeling stronger," Ann said, "but I'll feel better when I can see for myself."

"I'll feel better when *Jack* sees her," Mark piped in. "Once you give her the all clear, we'll all breathe easier."

"It will be good to have them both home. I hope they stay a while," Ann said wistfully. "We raised our girls to be independent. Then they all grew up, went into the world, and never looked back. I guess we did what we intended to do. How stupid!" She laughed.

Soon, two cars drove east to the McNamara Terminal of the Detroit Airport. When they arrived at the cell phone lot, it didn't take long for Maggie's phone to ding.

Sister Margaret, we have arrived. We went through
customs in Atlanta. We'll get our luggage and meet
you at door 3.

Mark followed Jack's car to the terminal. They waited, willing door three to open and dispense Bryan and Cate. A police car with flashing lights came up behind them, and an officer got out.

"You've got to move along. No parking."

Reluctantly, Jack and Mark drove away from door three and made the loop around the airport one more time. Maggie's phone dinged.

Have you gone home without us?
We're at door 3.

Maggie answered,

We know you're at door 3!
We were chased away by an
overzealous police officer. On
our way back to you and your
fiancée.

Do you have any food?

Mom brought a basket of
everything you ate as a Dutch
child. You should probably
pace yourself.

Hey! I see you!

The cars glided to a stop and the passengers emptied out on the sidewalk in front of door three, where two young people eagerly awaited. Maggie held back in utter agony and let her mother and father hug Bryan first, while Cate was embraced by her own parents.

"Excuse me, pregnant lady coming through. Out of the way, folks." She looked into Bryan's eyes, so identical to her own. "Bry!"

Bryan put his arms around his sister as much as he could reach and held on. "Gosh, I've missed you."

"I've missed you too. How are you, and how is Cate? The truth, please."

"We're exhausted," he said, pulling back to face her, "but some of that is from traveling all night. She is a little stronger, but it's been slow. We need to sleep and eat and sleep." He smiled. "And how is my niece or nephew? Are you having twins? One of each? You're huge."

"Thanks. I'm not huge, I'm short. Your niece or nephew is kicking my bladder right now. Such a brat."

Maggie looked over at Cate and was shocked by how thin she was. Her face was tanned by the sun, but there were dark rings around her hollow eyes. Maggie snuck over while Mark and Ann gathered luggage.

"Cate, I'm so glad you're home. We've been waiting to see you with our very own eyes for weeks. How are you feeling?" She hugged Cate and could feel her spinal cord and ribs through her colorful Ghanaian dress.

"Maggie, I am so glad to see you. Look at your baby." Cate gave a wan smile. "Are you so excited?"

Cate hadn't answered Maggie's question, which was answer enough.

"I am excited, I'm glad you will be here, I'm very glad our baby will be calling you 'Aunt Cate,' and I think we need to get you home and fed and then to bed. Here, you get into your parents' car. Bryan will ride with you."

The ride back to Cherish was subdued in the Elliot car.

"I just want to soak them both in," Maggie said, sounding the tiniest bit petulant.

"They need to rest and recover from everything they've been through, but maybe we'll get to visit with Bryan for a little while before he crashes," Mimi said.

"Why are you always so practical?" Maggie asked.

"I'm good at it. It's one of my gifts," her mother said with a self-approving smile. "Plus, you will have all the time you want with Bryan. He'll be living under your roof for who knows how long." Now Mimi sounded the teeny, tiniest bit petulant.

"You two will just have to move to Cherish," Maggie said. "With Bryan's new job in Ann Arbor and Cate finishing school, they'll be here for a while."

"We probably need a new car," Dirk said. "I suspect we'll be driving over here on autopilot."

Once they were back in Cherish, the afternoon slipped away. Cate went to Jack's office for a preliminary checkup and some lab work, then home to her old bedroom and her parents' hovering care. Bryan grabbed a quick snack and was deposited in one of the guestrooms at

Jack and Maggie's. He took a long, relaxing shower and went straight to bed.

Jack, Maggie, Dirk, and Mimi ate a quiet supper.

"I hope he sleeps well," Mimi said. "Traveling is one thing, but worrying about Cate must have taken more of a toll than even he realizes. What can we do to help the two of you? You'll take care of Bryan for now, but the baby will be here soon. It's going to be very busy in this house. Have you done more with the nursery?"

"Yes," Maggie said. "Do you want to see?"

They went upstairs to the small room next to Jack and Maggie's.

"We bought a changing table to match the crib, and we have a sliding rocker coming next week. We're keeping it simple." Maggie looked around at the pastel yellow walls. "Arly Spink painted the Noah's Ark mural all by hand. I love it."

They all gazed at the wall-sized ark and the animals walking off and onto green, lush land after their long journey. Two by two, they looked as if they would march right into the nursery itself. A large rainbow was painted over the ark as a sign of God's promise to creation. Mimi peeked into the closet and saw disposable diapers, onesies, and baby blankets stacked neatly on the shelves. A teddy bear bath towel hung on a hook.

"It's all so cozy," Mimi said. "Won't it be fun next month to have a little someone in here?"

"Yes," Maggie said. "I'm very ready, and I feel like the church is well taken care of because Nora will be there. Jack and I can take care of the baby, and Bryan will have to take care of himself. He's got almost a month to get his nights and days straight and sort out his new job. But until . . ." Maggie almost slipped and said the baby's name. "Uh . . . the baby arrives, I will feed Bry and do his laundry. After the baby, he's on his own." She laughed, knowing she would do anything for him, baby or no baby.

"We have much to be thankful for," Dirk said. "Bryan and Cate are safely home. It sounds like Cate will recover from her malaria, and they both can move forward with their plans for education and work and a wedding. Your mother and I have a grandchild on the way. In fact, we will hold that child in the next month. God is good. So let's not borrow trouble. The interest is too high. The four, I mean five of you are in God's good hands."

"Amen," Mimi said. "But I think I will arrange to have your groceries delivered via Instacart for the next few months."

"I'm glad you're spending the night," Maggie said. "You'll get to have a little more conversation with Bryan, and Jack will make his world-famous omelets for breakfast. I'm going to put together some overnight sticky buns and go to bed."

They all headed back to the kitchen. Her parents and Jack munched on Dutch goodies from the basket while she dumped frozen bread rolls, brown sugar, walnuts, dry butterscotch pudding mix, cinnamon, and melted butter in a Bundt cake pan, covered it with a tea towel, and set it in the oven to rise overnight.

"Done and dusted," she said, washing her hands. "Good night. The baby and I are in need of rest." She kissed all three of them. "Mom, Dad, your room is ready. There are towels on your bed. Sleep well."

"I'll be up in a minute," Jack said.

After Maggie was upstairs, Mimi asked Jack, "Does she have any idea?"

"Not a clue," Jack said with a wink.

He got up and gave the cats their treats. Then he remembered Smudge. Maggie had forgotten all about her furry rescue project. He quickly put some food and water in bowls and walked out to the barn. When he opened the door, there was a rustling noise.

"Hey, Smudge. Here's your dinner." He set down the bowls and picked up the empty ones from breakfast. "Have a nice night."

From the darkness he heard a soft "Meow."

Verna smoothed Pond's Cold Cream on her face as she took stock of her balding head. She knew this was going to happen. She'd had her fourth chemotherapy infusion that morning, and her hair was coming out in clumps. Her heavy bun was no more. Although she had the promise of its regrowth, it was a little frightening to watch long locks wash down the shower drain. Her other side effects were flu-like symptoms that came exactly twenty-four hours after the treatments. She had missed the past three Sundays at church, and that was more painful than anything. She looked over at her nightstand and saw the fourth rose. Last week, she was given the gift of the word "Peace." Today, she'd opened the small white envelope and read "Strength." She needed all she could muster.

"What are you thinking, my love?" Howard came into the bathroom.

"I think those roses mean more to me than I expected. I need to see them on Fridays. I need a word to take with me into the next week. Four down, four more to go. I also think I need some scarves. Not a wig. A wig would be too hot."

He kissed her shoulder. "Scarves it is. We'll find the prettiest and most colorful scarves in all the land." He was getting better at hiding his pain so they could both focus on hers. "I think fuchsia and magenta to begin with."

The next morning was Saturday and felt like Christmas. Although Bryan had been awake since three a.m., he was energetic and ready for sticky buns when Maggie turned the oven on at seven thirty.

"Did you have some bedfellows last night?" Maggie asked as she opened cans of cat food to the demanding meows erupting at her feet.

"Yes, all three beasts made themselves comfortable on my bed, so I was unable to move."

"They wanted you to feel safe and secure. What good kitties," she said in her Snow White voice.

Mimi and Dirk came downstairs—showered, dressed, and ready for the day.

"It smells good in here," Dirk said. "Where are the omelets?"

"Coming right up," Jack said, entering the kitchen. He opened the refrigerator and took out the various ingredients to make personalized omelets, including containers with pre-chopped vegetables and meats, along with cheeses. "I'll begin taking orders. The matriarch of the family first."

"I don't like the word matriarch," Mimi said. "It makes me sound old, which I am not. I would like white cheddar cheese, red bell pepper, and mushrooms, please."

The egg cracking commenced.

Once omelets and sticky buns were consumed, Maggie took Bryan to the barn with bowls of cat food and water.

"You might be able to see him this morning. He's getting a little friendlier, or a little less scared."

Bryan slowly opened the door, and Maggie stepped through.

"Smudge? Are you in here?"

They heard the rustle of hay. From behind a bale, two black ears appeared. Then bright-green eyes. Then long black whiskers. Smudge yawned, then stared.

"Hi, Smudge. Here's your breakfast." Maggie set the two bowls down and backed toward the door where Bryan was still standing.

Smudge waited to see if they would leave him in peace, but it seemed they were not going anywhere. He yawned one more time, then stalked his long, lean frame to the food. He sat back on his haunches and looked up at Maggie. "Meow." Then he slow-blinked at her.

"Did you see that, Bry? He gave me a kitty kiss. When cats blink both eyes at the same time, it's a sign of affection."

"He's in love with you. Congratulations."

Smudge began to eat without haste.

"I love you too, Smudgie," Maggie said quietly as they walked out of the barn with Smudge's empty dishes from the previous night.

"He's a beauty, Megs. That's for sure."

"He's calmed down since we first noticed him. I want to take him to Doctor Drake for a thorough check-up as soon as he's tame enough."

Maggie's phone rang. "Hello, this is Pastor Maggie."

"Pastor Maggie, this is Doris. I'm so sorry to bother you, but we have a problem here at church. I just came in to get things ready for tomorrow, but it looks like the bulletins are missing, and I don't know what to do."

Maggie couldn't help it. All she could think of was Ednah and Martha. One or both had done something with the bulletins.

"I'll be right there, Doris."

Maggie and Bryan went into the house, and Maggie shared the news.

"I'm going to go over to church and see if I can pull up the bulletin on Hank's computer. I'm sorry."

Maggie was tired, frustrated, and sick of wondering when Ednah and Martha were going to strike again. She'd thought it was all handled. She got into her car and drove down the long driveway a little too fast.

Jack, Bryan, Dirk, and Mimi waited till they saw Maggie pull onto Dexter-Cherish Road. Then they quickly got into Jack's Jeep.

When Maggie got to church, she saw the large oak doors open. *Doris must be airing out the sanctuary.* With no air conditioning, the sanctuary was stuffy during these hot summer days. Maggie parked and hurried up the walk. She wanted to get back home to her family.

When she stepped into the sanctuary, she saw Irena standing by the organ, wearing leopard-print maternity leggings topped with a bright-orange maternity blouse. The blouse had puffed sleeves and was low cut so Irena could show off her blossoming bosoms in a hot-pink bra. The only thing Irena had toned down was her hair and makeup. Lydia and Lacey had made more of an impact than they imagined. Irena decided to have her hair done regularly at the We Work Miracles Salon, and she even purchased makeup to replicate her wedding day look.

"Irena, what are you doing here?"

"Yes! Dat's exactly rright! I get de call from Dorris. 'Come to churrch. Your museek is off de organ.' We only got back from ourr vacation last night. I want to sleep, but Dorris wake me up with dis bad news."

Maggie followed Irena's stare. Her music was stacked neatly, where it always was. It didn't look like anything was missing. Maggie looked at the table near the back pew. The bulletins were there, just as they had been when Maggie left church on Thursday.

"I'm glad to see you, Irena, and I want to hear all about your honey . . . um . . . vacation, but what's going on here?" Maggie was totally confused.

Doris walked into the sanctuary. She was not dressed in her cleaning attire. She had on a Sunday dress. "Hello, ladies!"

"Doris, why are you? . . . What's happening? . . . Why did you call us?" Maggie tried to keep her temper.

Irena's eyes narrowed. "Vy you call us down to churrch? I vas coming later to prractice. Nut now." Maggie could hear Irena's accent accelerate.

"Surprise!" Jack, Bryan, Dirk, Mimi, and Keith Crunch came through the oak doors.

Maggie and Irena stared. Nothing made sense.

"Welcome to your baby showers!" Doris exclaimed, ready to burst.

"Baby showers?" Maggie asked, looking at Jack.

"Yes," Doris jumped in. "We have been planning this for weeks. At first, it was just for Pastor Maggie, but then, when we found out about Irena's batch of babies, we decided to have a 'Loving the Lord Staff Baby Shower.' Even though I'm on staff, I'm not having a baby," she concluded. "Let's go downstairs, shall we?"

Maggie and Irena went downstairs and found the members of Loving the Lord sitting at round tables decorated with pale pinks, blues, yellows, and greens. The tables were laden with Mrs. Popkin's baked delicacies and pots of church coffee and tea. Cheers erupted as the two mothers-to-be walked into the celebration. Maggie and Irena were led to what looked like the head table at a wedding. They were seated with Maggie's family and Keith. Jack's family was at one of the round tables, and Maggie beamed at them.

"How long have you known about this?" she whispered to Jack.

"Hank sent the invitations before he and Pamela left for Australia.

Fortunately, Irena's pregnancy was made public so we could double up. Or, I guess, *quadruple* up."

"Sneaky. I'm glad she can feel so much love. She has a lot of happiness owed to her by life."

Doris quieted everyone. She was obviously the mistress of ceremonies and took complete control of the festivities.

"Now, we have gathered here to celebrate the baby boom sitting before us," Doris proclaimed.

More applause and cheers. Irena stood up and waved to everyone.

"Pastor Maggie and Irena, we would like to shower you with good wishes and things to help you with your new additions. Children, will you come in now?"

The children of the church came in carrying two large baskets of cards, wrapped gifts, and a rolling white board. Ryleigh and Zoey carried one of the baskets to Maggie.

"These are cards for you and Doctor Jack," Ryleigh said.

"It's because you are having a baby and people are happy," Zoey chimed in.

"When your baby gets here, are you going to baptism it?" Ryleigh asked, thinking of her own recent baptism.

"Well, yes. I will."

"And will you baptism Irena's babies? She's having a lot of babies. That's what Mommy said." Zoey looked over at Kali and waved.

"Of course, if that's what Irena wants."

Irena was accepting her own basket of cards from Carrie and Carl.

"Tank you, tank you, leetle chicks. Yes, I love de carrds. Also, I love de prresents."

The Nasab children, the M children, the Porter children, Marcos and Gabby Gutierrez, Kay and Shawn Kessler, Hannah Benson, and Jack and Maggie's niece and nephew, Gretchen and Garrett, brought in the gifts as solemnly as the wise men at the birth of Christ. They laid the presents on the table and the floor around Maggie and Irena.

Irena clasped her small hands together and chuckled. "Ve open de presents now?"

"I just want to say," Doris stopped Irena from ripping the paper off the first gift, "we know Pastor Maggie and Doctor Jack have been preparing this summer for their baby. Irena, you and Detective Crunch haven't done much. So, we had to come up with something creative. We'll get to it in a bit. You may open your gifts now, Irena."

Irena tore the paper from a package and marveled at the all-in-one car seat, stroller, and baby carrier.

"Dis is what we need to take de babies to and fro. But we need two-morre.We are heving de triplets."

"Yes, there are two more packages just like the one you have there," Doris said patiently.

Irena spied the other baby carriers and pulled them next to her chair. "Mine."

Maggie and Jack enjoyed opening their gifts, mainly clothing and small baby paraphernalia. It was more fun to watch Irena open her pile. Keith was clearly only an observer. Irena was in baby shower heaven.

By the end of it all, besides the transforming baby carriers, Irena and Keith also had three cribs—not in the room, but promised on a card. The cribs would be delivered to their home. There were three highchairs, three Pack 'n Plays, three Diaper Genies, a baby camera and intercom system for the nursery, boxes of diapers, stacks of onesies, toys, and blankets. Irena was beside herself with glee.

"Ourr babies arre rrich!"

Maggie tearfully surveyed the room. The generosity of her congregation overwhelmed her. She saw Marvin Green sitting in his wheelchair at Howard and Verna's table. They must have picked him up from Friendly Elder Care for the party. Marvin was one of the most generous men she knew. He turned and caught her gaze. "Little one," he mouthed. It was his favorite nickname for her. She blew him a kiss.

"Now, we have one more thing to give you," Doris said, almost giddy. "Carrie and Hannah?"

Carrie and Hannah pushed the rolling white board in front of the head table. It was blank. Then they turned it around. It read:

Meals: We, the congregation of Loving the Lord Church, commit to bringing meals, snacks, and other treats to your houses for as long as you need and want them.

Babysitting: We, the congregation of Loving the Lord Church, commit to helping you with childcare when you need to work or just for a break or a date night.

Cleaning: We, the congregation of Loving the Lord Church, commit to assisting you with housecleaning, yard work, snow removal, car washes, or any other task to ease your life at this very exciting time.

Love: We, the congregation of Loving the Lord Church, commit to loving you and your children as they grow in the grace of God. We will watch them in the nursery, play with them on the lawn after church, teach them in Sunday school, and encourage them in their faith. We want them to always feel surrounded by a caring church family.

Maggie sighed and took Jack's hand. Her church never ceased to surprise her with their kindness and other-focused actions. She was about to speak when Irena stood and lifted her small arms in the air.

"Tank you, you people of de churrch. I hev many storries to tell you of my vacation. De theaterr, de jazz museek, de museums, de dinnerrs in fancy places. I tell you dis another time. For now, you hev alvays been kind to me, yourr organist. Sometimes you annoy me when you talk durring my preludes, but all is forrgiven. No prroblems." Her bottom lip began to wobble.

Keith smiled and looked around the room. "Irena is right. You are kind, and you are thoughtful. I never knew a church could be such a happy place. Irena and I thank you for caring for our family."

Applause erupted, and Maggie thought he looked close to tears. Then she and Jack stood together.

"It looks like next month we will actually be holding our baby in our arms," Maggie said. "We will also hold him or her in the gifts you have given us today. Thank you for being a congregation who constantly surprises us with your expert care and abiding love."

"And thank you for the all the date-night babysitting." Jack smiled playfully. "We will take full advantage of your offer."

Jack's comment brought levity to the room. The party wrapped up, gifts were loaded into cars, and Bryan was brought to his bed for a long nap.

"I'm really getting excited now," Maggie said after her parents left and she and Jack were alone on the deck, piles of gifts waiting to be dealt with later. "In a month, we'll have our baby right here with us. I can hardly believe it."

"Your weekly appointments with Charlene begin next week. I must admit, it's different to be on this side of things. I haven't understood the hopes and fears of parents-to-be before. But now I'm one of them. It's time for you to slow down. What do you think?"

"Yes, I've been texting with Nora. She's ready to preach beginning two weeks before my due date. I can sit in the pew with you. Her Tuesday and Thursday half-days will be full as she does all the shut-in and elder care visitation. She'll also teach adult Sunday school and be available to the congregation for other concerns. I will focus on one more sermon after tomorrow's and that's about it. Except for Hank and Pamela's homecoming on September eighteenth. I will put the finishing touches on their celebration. Then, baby!"

"Sounds good. Shall we take Smudge his dinner?"

Maggie was up quickly for being so round. "Yes."

She opened a can of food and filled the water dish, then she and Jack went to the barn and looked into the darkness until their eyes adjusted. Smudge was sitting on his favorite hay bale. Maggie set down the food and water bowls, walked slowly over, and sat on another bale. She waited. Smudge sniffed the air, then took a step and hesitated. He took another step, and another. He carefully made his way to Maggie. She held out her hand so he could sniff it. He took another step closer and condescended to a soft pat on the head. Maggie kept petting him until she heard what she longed for.

Smudge began to purr.

25

Nora drove back and forth from Lansing beginning September fifth. She and Maggie made visits to those in the Friendly Elder Care Center and those at home who were either ill or needed a little extra care.

The day they first pulled into Howard and Verna Baker's driveway, Maggie said, "Verna has three more chemotherapy treatments. They are every Friday. She hasn't been in church for weeks because she feels ill and doesn't want to expose herself to any cold germs or infection."

"I remember how she treated you when you first got here," Nora said. "It's amazing how life, patience, and care can change things. She's one of your biggest fans now."

They went to the front door, and Maggie rang the bell. Howard opened the door.

"We've been waiting for you." His smile was dimmer than usual. He ushered Maggie and Nora into the living room, where Caroline the cat was curled up on one of the chairs. "Please don't sit on the cat. She always has first choice on where she will reside in any room."

They laughed. Verna came in carrying a tea tray. She wore a bright-blue-and-green scarf on her head. Her eyes had dark circles beneath them, but she smiled at the young women as she set down the tray.

"I'm glad you're here."

Maggie noticed a single white rose on the tea tray. The card with the fifth word was still hanging from the vase: "Assurance." Tea, cookies, and conversation filled the next hour and a half.

"Nora, we look forward to more visits with you while Maggie's on maternity leave," Verna said.

"You can tell us secrets about her from seminary. We want all the dirt," Howard said with a wink.

"Oh, there are so many. I don't know where I'd begin." Nora smiled. "There was that time when she climbed onto the chapel roof and, oh yes, when she broke into one of our professor's office and stole a Hebrew exam. And . . ."

Maggie rolled her eyes. "I'm sure you will have many things to talk about while I'm home. Don't get too carried away, Nora."

"On a serious note," Verna said, "we wish you all the best, Maggie, as you prepare to become a mother. What a joyful time. We will be eager to meet your little one and hope your birthing experience is easier than most." Verna smiled at her pastor.

"Thank you, Verna. Two and a half weeks to go. It seems like a year."

A week and a half later, on September fourteenth, Maggie felt a small twinge just before getting into bed. She went into the bathroom, then called for Jack. When he didn't come, she called again, louder. Finally, she heard his footsteps.

He opened the door and stared.

Maggie stood up from the toilet and grabbed the countertop. Blood seeped down the inside of her thighs and trickled onto the floor.

"Is this normal?" Maggie asked. Her eyes couldn't see clearly. She clutched the countertop with both hands to keep her balance. She struggled, then focused on Jack's face.

The blood drained from his face as quickly as it was draining from her body.

"No," she whispered, looking down. "I didn't think so." Maggie fell back hard on the toilet.

Jack moved quickly, leaned down, and put his index finger on her wrist to get her pulse. He carefully picked her up and carried her to their room, laid her on the bed, and pulled out his cell phone. Charlene answered immediately.

"Hello, Jack. What's up?"

"Maggie's bleeding. Her pulse is . . . I'll bring her to emergency and meet you there."

"I'm on my way, and I'll call ahead. I'll call Alan. He's in surgery. I'll also call Doctor Siegers."

Charlene was moving fast. Jack could hear drawers opening and closing. She clicked off. He stuck his phone in his pocket, then pulled Maggie's nightgown down around her. He quickly changed from his pajamas into jeans and a sweatshirt.

"What are you doing?" Maggie mumbled.

"We're going to the hospital. I'm going to carry you to the car. Are you feeling any pain?"

"Maybe a contraction. I don't know what it's supposed to feel like. But here comes another one."

Jack watched as her teeth clenched and her eyebrows drew together. She groaned with pain. He gently picked her up and carefully maneuvered down the stairs, through the kitchen, and out to his jeep.

"I'm going to put you in the car now," he said softly in her ear.

She groaned again as he slid her awkwardly onto the front seat and strapped her seat belt. He looked at the arm of his sweatshirt and saw her blood. He got in and started the engine. They were at the hospital within minutes, faster than if he'd called an ambulance. Jack had run through every stop sign and red light. He pulled up to the emergency room door and sighed in relief as two nurses with a gurney came rushing out to meet them. Jack released Maggie's seat belt as one of the nurses opened her door. Together, they lifted her onto the gurney as Maggie cried out in pain.

Then she was quiet.

Maggie dreamed she was in her office, getting ready for Pentecost. She put on her white robe and red stole. As she made her way through

Hank's office to the secret door, she heard Irena playing Brahms's "Lullaby." Maggie smiled and put her hand on her baby bump.

Irena's playing for my baby. What a nice thing to do on Pentecost.

Maggie opened the secret door and saw the red streamers. She tried to part them to walk through, but they wouldn't budge. She tried again, but couldn't grip them. They were sticky and warm. She tried again to push them aside, but they stuck to her hands. Then she felt them on her face and reached up to push them away. They were in her mouth. She tasted the streamers. Her mouth was full of blood. She looked down at her beautiful white robe and saw the huge blood stains.

Why can't I get through? I must get to the pulpit and begin the service. But my robe is ruined!

She tried to call for help, but she couldn't catch her breath. She looked through the bloody streamers, searching for Jack. Jack would fix this. He knew all about blood because he was a doctor, she was certain of this.

Wait, is he a doctor? What does Jack do? Maybe he is a baker. He bakes donuts for coffee time.

She tried calling for him, but the blood choked her throat. Then she heard Irena change from the gentle lullaby. No longer was she playing Brahms's "Lullaby," but rather, his *Requiem*.

Blessed are the dead which die in the Lord . . .

Jack quickly parked his car, then ran into the emergency department. He ran through the waiting area and past the front desk. He ran so fast he didn't slow as he turned down the hallway to the surgery rooms and literally slammed into Alan Cocanour, sending the younger doctor across the hall.

"Jack!" Alan's glasses were askew.

"Sorry, Alan. Where's Maggie? Where's Charlene? Are you assisting?"

Alan fixed his glasses as he took Jack's elbow. "Jack, what's going on? Is Maggie in labor?"

"Charlene said she would call you."

"I just finished emergency surgery." He pulled out his phone and saw the missed message. "Is Maggie in labor?" he asked again.

Jack's eyes welled up as he looked at Alan. "I think it's more serious than that. She's, uh, she's bleeding. A lot of blood." Jack put his hands over his face and sobbed. He looked back at Alan. "Where are they?"

Charlene had scrubbed in and was ready to enter the operating room when Alan arrived.

"Good. You're here. We'll need you to be ready to take the baby. Maggie's losing a lot of blood. Hurry. Doctor Siegers is ready to do an emergency section."

Alan scrubbed in as Charlene rushed into the operating room. He looked up as Jack came through the door.

"Jack, what're you doing?"

"I want to be in there with her. Let me scrub in. She can't be in there by herself."

"Jack, you can't come in. You *know* you can't. Let us take care of Maggie and the baby. I swear, I'll find you. Someone will find you immediately. I've got to get in there. Doctor Siegers is waiting for me."

Alan pushed the operating room door open with his shoulder. Jack heard Dr. Siegers' voice: "Hurry! We're losing her!"

Jack slid slowly down the wall of the scrub room and rested his head on his knees. The tears came quickly, and he could barely breathe through his sobs. Maggie was dying. He knew exactly what was happening in the room on the other side of the door. He knew how quickly a hemorrhage could drain the life out of a body. He knew because he had stood over patients in the operating room when bleeding could not be stopped. In just moments, hope was gone, and so was life. Jack knew what was happening and could do nothing to save the life of his wife.

Dr. Siegers shouted more orders, and Jack heard the movements

243

and verbal responses of those on the surgical team. They were fighting for life, but death had a foothold. The gravest battle had commenced.

Jack shook his head, wiped the back of his hand across his eyes, and let out a primal sound of ultimate despair that could be heard down the hallway. He felt arms wrap around him. He looked up. It was Ellen. He hugged her to him, trying to squeeze away the pain he was drowning in.

"Jack, Jack, ouch!"

Jack loosened his grip and looked desperately into his cousin's eyes. "She's dying."

"Doctor Siegers, Charlene, and Alan are doing everything they can."

"I knew when I saw the blood. It's bad. It's so bad."

"Do you think you should call your parents and Maggie's? Where's Bryan?"

Jack stared at the ceiling. "He's with Cate. I don't think I can call anyone right now."

"Would you like me to call them?" Ellen asked quietly as she handed Jack some tissues from her pocket.

Jack wiped his eyes and his nose and took a deep breath. "Just give me a second."

Ellen did.

Jack pulled out his phone. Ellen put her hand on his shoulder as he hit speed dial for Dirk and Mimi.

"Hello, Jack," Mimi said with a smile in her voice.

Silence.

"Jack?"

"Yes, hi, Mimi." His voice broke.

"Jack, what's wrong?"

"We're at the hospital," he heard himself say.

"Jack, is Maggie okay? Is it the baby?" Dirk came quickly to the phone.

Jack squeezed his eyes shut and gritted his teeth to keep from breaking down.

"Jack!"

"Maggie is in emergency surgery. She's bleeding badly. I wish I knew more, but I don't. You and Dirk should come."

"Jack, we're on our way right now. Is anyone with you?"

"Ellen," he whispered. He handed Ellen the phone and laid his head back down on his bent knees.

"Hello, Mimi. It's Ellen. I'll be here with Jack. I don't have any other information. We are waiting to hear. We'll call you when we know something. Are you driving over now?"

"Yes," Mimi said as Dirk grabbed their coats. "Please let us know anything you find out as soon as you know."

"We will. Drive safely."

The phone call ended.

"Would you like me to call your mom and dad?" Ellen asked.

Jack nodded.

Ellen made the call and talked to Bonnie. Jack winced hearing Ellen give the quick summary of no real news, and no real hope either.

"They are on their way, Jack," Ellen said after the call. "What about Bryan, Anne, Leigh and Nathan?"

Jack shook his head. "Let's wait. We can't tell them anything. If Mimi and Mom choose to call them, that's fine. Or once we know something."

They sat together on the floor of the scrub room. The harsh light, sterile metal sinks, and cold floor enhanced their misery. The noises on the other side of the door became more muffled. Machines were beeping and being moved across the floor. They could hear Charlene's voice, but couldn't make out her words. Alan's lower voice answered Charlene's. Jack also heard the surgeon, Dr. Siegers, giving orders of some kind.

Jack clenched his fists and let out a sigh, ending in a desperate sob.

Dirk and Mimi drove silently east. They would have two and a half hours in the car. Mimi held her phone in her hand and looked at it every few seconds, willing it to ring and give her good news about her daughter and grandchild, but it lay mute. She looked at her husband and saw his tightened jaw, and his taut hands gripping the steering wheel. This would be the longest trip of their lives.

Ken and Bonnie, with Jack's younger sister, Leigh, drove north from Blissfield. Bonnie called her other children as they drove—Anne, the oldest, and Nathan, the youngest. With no real information to share, she asked them all to pray for Maggie and the baby. Leigh sat in the backseat of the car and could only think they had entered another nightmare of pain and loss she was sure her family could not bear.

Jack and Ellen remained on the floor in the scrub room. Listening, but not knowing what was happening, tortured them both. Jack tried to get up, but Ellen held him down.

"Jack, you can't go in there. You have to wait."

"What if she dies and I never have the chance to say goodbye?" He sobbed, his worst fear now hanging in the room.

Their heads flew back as they heard Alan shout.

"No!" Jack yelled.

Ellen held his hand as they heard another outburst, but it was not the sound of despair. It was a shout of triumph. Life had won the battle against death's stronghold in the emergency room.

Ever so faintly, Jack and Ellen heard the loveliest sound of all: a newborn baby's cry.

26

Mimi thought she would go mad if her phone didn't ring. So, it did. "Hello," she said tersely.

"Mimi, it's Jack."

"Yes, Jack. What's happening?"

"The baby is here. She's healthy and beautiful." His voice rasped.

"And Maggie?"

"She's in recovery. I'm just about to go in and see her. They are monitoring her carefully. She lost a quart of blood."

He heard Mimi's intake of breath.

"My God," Mimi said weakly. "What's the baby's name? I'd like to pray for her by name."

"Abigail Brynn."

"Abigail Brynn. Beautiful. We'll be there soon." Mimi needed to hang up before she fell apart. She looked at Dirk. "We have a granddaughter."

At the hospital, Ken, Bonnie, and Leigh were in the waiting room. Ellen came out and hugged her aunt, uncle, and cousin. "The baby is healthy. She's beautiful."

"She?" Bonnie began to cry. "We have another granddaughter?"

"Yes, Abigail Brynn."

"Brynn," Leigh whispered. "How thoughtful."

Hearing the name of the daughter-in-law they would never have brought every emotion to the forefront in Ken and Bonnie. Ellen held their hands through the tears.

"Where's Jack?" Ken asked, wiping his eyes.

"He's in with Maggie."

In another part of the hospital, Jack walked into Maggie's recovery room and took his wife's hand. She was still asleep. Her eyelashes looked dark on her white face. He checked her oxygen level and watched the heart monitor making its patterned, jagged line across the screen.

The nurse came in. "Hello, Doctor Elliot. She seems to be holding her own." The nurse checked Maggie's vital signs and typed notes into the computer. "Can I get you anything?"

"No, thank you. I'm fine."

The nurse left and closed the curtain behind her. Jack leaned over and put his cheek against Maggie's. He knew his parents were in the waiting room, and Dirk and Mimi would be there soon. He knew his daughter was in the nursery being cared for by good nurses. But he had agonizingly waited to see Maggie's face. He wasn't going to leave until she knew he was there.

"Maggie," he whispered. "Abby is here. Our little Abby Brynn." He paused. "I saw her, and she's the most beautiful, perfect baby in the world. That's because you're her mother."

He heard a gurney passing on the other side of the curtain. Another patient beginning recovery. He squeezed Maggie's hand.

"I can't wait until you wake up and we can hold her together."

In the waiting room, Dirk and Mimi found Jack's family, along with Bryan and Cate.

"Any more news?" Dirk asked.

"No," Ellen said. "Jack's still in with Maggie. But if you would like, I can take you to your granddaughter."

"Yes, we would like to see her," Mimi said with a tired sigh.

An hour later, Jack found them in the waiting room.

"She's going in and out of sleep, but I told her about Abigail Brynn, and she understood, at least for the moment. They will watch her closely all night. Do you want to just go to our house and rest?"

"We can drive back down to Blissfield," Ken said, knowing there wouldn't be enough room for everyone at Jack and Maggie's. "We'll drive back up tomorrow or the next day, when you think Maggie's strong enough to have visitors."

"We don't need to overwhelm her," Bonnie said, although she felt like grandmas should be the first to see the mother, father, and child together.

"Her recovery is the most important thing," Jack said. "We can celebrate once she's strong enough." Jack hoped his message got across.

"We'll call in the morning and get an update," Ken said. "Got your message loud and clear, Dad."

"Thanks. I'm going back to her. You will have to fend for yourselves." Jack strode off.

The families got into their cars, and the Elliots drove south, while the Elzingas drove to the farm.

The next morning, Jack woke to a dull ache in his neck. He had slept in the chair by Maggie's bed, quite uncomfortably. He wanted to brush his teeth. When he sat up, he saw Maggie's eyes flutter.

"Are you awake?" he asked.

Her eyes fluttered some more, then opened. Her lips were dry. "Water?"

He held the plastic cup of water and put the straw in her mouth. She drank.

"Where is Abby?" she whispered.

"She's in the nursery. I'll ask them to bring her to us."

Within ten minutes, Abigail Brynn Elliot arrived in her mother's room. Jack picked up his daughter and placed her in her mother's arms. Maggie stared into her daughter's face—the delicate eyebrows, long eyelashes, tiny nose, and little rosebud mouth.

"Hello, Abigail Brynn. Welcome to the world." Maggie's exhaustion briefly abated.

The new parents sat with their sleeping daughter and marveled at her existence.

"I never imagined it would feel this way," Jack said. "I've only watched other parents hold their babies like this and cry and laugh. It's always nice to watch, but it's unbelievable to experience."

"She's completely her own little self. Full of promise and potential." Maggie kissed Abby's nose, then laid her head back on the pillow. "I'm so tired."

"I'll take her. You just rest." Jack took the baby and sat back down.

Maggie drifted off to sleep again. She awakened when Dr. Siegers entered the room.

"How is the new family doing?"

"I think we're all pretty tired," Jack said.

"I can't help you or the baby, but I can help the mother. Maggie, your hemoglobin is seven. You lost a lot of blood. To get the number up, we need to start a blood transfusion this morning."

Maggie looked at Jack. He nodded.

"You'll feel better very soon," Dr. Siegers said. "We're going to keep you and Abigail for three or four days. You gave us quite a challenge last night. It's good to have you both here, safe and sound."

"Thank you, Doctor Siegers, for everything."

"You're very welcome, Maggie." He looked like he wanted to say something else, but he only smiled and left the room.

"Do I have to have a blood transfusion?" Maggie asked Jack.

"Yes, you absolutely do. You will feel so much better, I promise."

It wasn't long before someone else's blood was flowing into Maggie's arm. When the transfusion was complete, Maggie fell into a deep sleep.

She dreamed she walked into the sanctuary but had to pass through the red Pentecost streamers. The bloody streamers stained her robe, her face, her hair. She was determined to get to her altar chair behind the pulpit. Baby Abigail was wrapped in a white blanket, lying on the chair. Maggie had to get to her. She fought the heavy streamers and finally reached up and pulled them from the door frame. She kept pulling until the streamers were in a heap on the floor. The mountain of streamers was as tall as she was. She jumped over the bloody mess and ran to the chair. Abby was gone. Maggie had taken too long to fight. Then she heard a cry. She looked at the front pew. Jack was holding the baby.

"Jack, why are you here?"

"You were busy fighting the streamers. I came to take care of Abby. We knew you would win. We just decided to wait here. Let's go home now."

Someone was shaking her shoulder. Maggie opened her eyes.

"Maggie, wake up. You're okay," Mimi said.

"Mom?"

"Yes. Dad and I are here. You seemed quite distressed. Were you having a nightmare?"

"Yes, I think so. I keep dreaming about Pentecost. Not Pentecost, just the streamers." She sighed. "I don't know."

"It's all going to be okay," Dirk said and kissed Maggie's forehead. "You've been through a lot."

"Where's Jack? Where's Abby?"

"Abby is in the nursery. Jack is home taking a shower and getting something to eat. We forced him out of the room." Mimi smiled.

There was a knock in the door, and Ken and Bonnie walked in with Leigh and Nathan.

"Hello, Mama," Leigh said in her normal voice, but it hurt Maggie's ears.

She closed her eyes. *Why are they all here? Too much noise. Too many.* She took a deep breath. *I must be nice. I must be happy.* She opened her eyes and smiled wanly.

Mimi looked at her daughter, then turned to the others. "Hello, Ken, Bonnie, Leigh, and Nathan. I think she's a little tired right now. Jack is home for a bit. Shall we go to the nursery and see Abigail Brynn?" She leaned down and whispered to Maggie, "Get some rest. You will feel better soon."

Although Mimi was the smallest person in the room by far, she marshaled the others into the hallway and closed Maggie's door. She led them down to the nursery like a tiny but mighty general.

Mimi was right. By the next morning, Maggie felt like a different person. Ellen, who was on duty, came to Maggie's room to help her take her first post-birth shower. Moving carefully not to pull bandages or stitches, Maggie gloried in the warm water and soap. Ellen helped her wash her hair, carefully dried her off, and tucked her into a clean nightie. The shower, and all the new blood pumping through her body, made Maggie feel more like herself. Ellen helped her nurse Abby. Both women cooed over the miracle of Abigail Brynn.

"She really is the most beautiful baby, isn't she?" Maggie asked seriously.

"She is. I've never seen a baby as beautiful. And she oozes intelligence."

"I think that's just something in her diaper."

"I'm so happy for you, Maggie."

"I didn't think it would be like this. You know, I had an idea of how birth was going to be, and it was nothing like what we've just been through."

Ellen sat back and listened.

"I feel like I missed everything," Maggie said. "I can never tell her how wonderful it was to hold her the moment she was born. Jack and I didn't kiss and ooh and ahh together in the delivery room. I didn't get to feed her right away. I must rely on other people's first impressions. Mine came after everyone else's."

"But they're yours," Ellen said.

"I wanted to be part of bringing her into the world. I was just the receptacle for someone else to open and remove my baby."

Ellen wanted to disagree but wisely held her tongue. Maggie needed to grieve for the lost dream of childbirth.

"Anyway, I get to hold her in my arms now. I'm thankful." Maggie stared into Abby's face. "We have memories to make now."

One of the most vivid memories occurred three days later. Hank and Pamela landed in Detroit after their three-month trip Down Under. Doris and Chester collected them at the baggage claim door while a contingent from Loving the Lord waited in the cell phone lot.

"Welcome home, Hank and Pamela," Doris said in the car. "It's mighty good to see your tanned faces. Yes, it is."

"Doris, I'm so happy to see you," Hank said. "Tell us everything. How are things at church? Is Ednah still around? How's Pastor Maggie? She must be ready to get to the hospital and have that baby. Yesiree-bob!"

"Well now, Hank, slow yourself down. We certainly have a lot of news for you and Pamela, and we want to hear about your trip too. As far as Pastor Maggie, you won't be seeing her today. She had her little baby girl last week."

Hank looked at Doris's somber face. "She did? Well, this is a little early, isn't it?"

"How are they?" Pamela asked quickly.

"They are both going to be okay," Doris said, "but we had a scare. Pastor Maggie had an emergency C-section and lost a lot of blood. She had a transfusion, and she and the baby are coming home today."

Hank and Pamela took in this information.

"Listen," Doris said, "you both must be so tired and upside down on your time zones. Pastor Maggie and Abigail Brynn, that's the new baby, will be ready to see you in a few days, I'm sure. But for now, you must put up with the rest of us. We sure are glad you're home."

They drove to the cell phone lot. Hank and Pamela rolled down their windows to cheers, applause, and balloon bouquets. The caravan of cars made their way back to Loving the Lord.

"By golly, I've missed this place," Hank said. "It's good to be home."

They got out of the car and walked through the large oak doors into the sanctuary. Both Hank and Pamela breathed in the smells of their church—the musty aroma of age, the faint hint of burned candles, and Murphy's Oil Soap gleaming on the pews.

"Hunk! Hunk! You come herre to me!" Irena yelled from the organ bench.

"Irena, well, my goodness. It is good to see you, yesireebob, it sure is." He strode over to her and got the full view of her new girth. "Irena, when are your babies due? Tomorrow?"

"Dun't be silly. I hev two months to go. Hunk, dun't go away no more. Hello, Pamela. No more trips for you. We just all stay right here where we belong." She rolled off the organ bench. "Now, it's time to eat de food. Hev you hearrd about Pastorr Maggie? Bad times.We worried much for her. But all is well now."

"Yes, Doris told us. Have you seen her?"

"No. Nobody sees her. She got new blood. It's good. We let her get strong now."

"It will be good to all be back together. I've missed you, Irena."

"Ov courrse."

Before going down to the basement for a good old-fashioned church potluck, Hank walked into his office. He was surprised to see everything exactly as he'd left it. His blue tarpaulin was folded neatly on the floor next to his desk. His computer and other items were right where they belonged. Ednah came in through the secret door, leftover bulletins from Sunday in her hands.

"Ednah?" He looked surprised and a little annoyed.

"Welcome home, Hank. It's nice to see you." Ednah reached out her hand to shake his. Hank hesitantly took her hand. "I think things are in good order here. If it's okay, I'll finish out this week for you. Then I'll transition to the clinic opening. But whatever you want to do is fine with me."

Hank stared. Ednah looked almost embarrassed.

Hank smiled kindly. "Well now, Ednah, that sounds just about right. I think I'll need some time to figure out what time it is, yesireebob. If you really don't mind, I'd like to take the week at home to right myself."

"Shall we go down to your welcome home celebration?" Ednah beamed.

The next few days slipped by. Maggie gained her strength back quickly, thanks to the transfusion, and poured all her energy into Abby.

"I'm sorry we missed Hank and Pamela's homecoming party," Maggie said, "but to be honest, I feel relieved not to have to see the congregation quite yet."

"I agree," Jack said. "You've been through a lot."

"*We've* been through a lot."

Maggie had noticed a tenseness in Jack that hadn't been there before. He loved holding and caring for Abby, but sometimes when she looked at him, he was lost in some disturbing thought.

"Jack, are you okay?"

Jack smiled, but before he could answer, Mimi walked in. Dirk and Mimi were staying for a few days to help Maggie rest and to hold their granddaughter as much as possible.

"I thought I'd start dinner," Mimi said. "Will you be hungry in about an hour?"

"Sounds great," Jack said. "Do you need any help?"

"Sure. How are you at chopping vegetables?"

"I chop so well, you'd think I was a doctor."

Jack kissed Maggie on top of her head before he followed Mimi to the kitchen.

Maggie looked at Abby and whispered, "Your daddy had a bad scare, I think. You and I slept through it all. I wonder what we can do to help him?"

The days and weeks after Abby's birth were filled with kind notes, small gifts, and, of course, food. The congregation of Loving the Lord kept their promises to help the new family. The lawn was miraculously mowed while Jack was at the office. Friends called and asked Maggie if they could come and clean the farmhouse.

"We'd love to see you and Abby, but we don't want to intrude," Sylvia said over the phone.

"Thank you, Sylvia. If we're awake, I'll bring her downstairs. Right now, I'm on her schedule."

"I get it. If we don't hear either of you, we'll clean but not vacuum. How does that sound?"

"Perfect."

Maggie wasn't trying to hide Abby from anyone, but she had no intention of parading her baby around because of other people's expectations. Those private days were gently savored by both Jack and Maggie. Their families had received a similar message. They could call ahead of time and drive over for a visit with their new niece and granddaughter, but if they arrived and Abby and Maggie were asleep, they would have to wait until naptime was over.

Bryan was still ensconced at the farmhouse, but work at the Refugee Support Services took him away during the days. Most evenings were spent at the Carlson's home. When he was at the farmhouse, he enjoyed the moments he could hold his niece, was shocked by her smallness, and was glad he didn't have one of these tiny, crying things of his own. There was plenty of time for that later.

One night, Jack heard Maggie and Abby in the nursery. They'd put a small daybed in Abby's room so Maggie could sleep there when Jack went back to work. Jack got up and found Maggie and Abby rocking together. Abby was fussing and squirming.

"She's a little night owl," Jack said.

"Yes. I think she and I will sleep well tomorrow while you're at the office."

"Can I get you anything?"

"Oh, yes. I'd love a bowl of oatmeal and sliced banana."

"I'll bring it right up."

"Hey, Jack, do you think I'll ever want to go back to church and work again?"

"I don't know. Do *you* think you'll ever want to go back to church and work again?"

"Not tonight, I don't. I think I could stay like this for a very long time."

27

Sylvester and Skylar's wedding was exactly one month after Abby's birth.

"Why did I think I could do this?" Maggie asked Jack. "If Abby had been born on her due date, it would have only been three weeks until this wedding. What was I thinking when I said yes?"

"You couldn't have known how it was going to go or how you would feel."

"I'm not ready to show Abby to the world yet."

"Everyone understands."

But Maggie didn't believe this. She was a mess of mixed emotions. She'd agreed months before to officiate Sly and Sky's wedding on October fourteenth and Lacey and Lydia's on November fourth. She loved both couples and wanted to help make their days special. But being away from Abby, even if it was just going into her home office to look over the ceremonies, was too much.

"I only want time with Abby and you. I don't want to spend time on these weddings."

"Let's take them one at a time. I'll have Abby with me while you officiate Sly and Sky's. We'll see how you feel after the wedding is done."

Sly and Sky planned and executed the classiest wedding Cherish had ever seen. The church was packed. Even the gathering area was overflowing due to the connections in town, and beyond, of both bride and the groom. Sylvester's family flew in from Nigeria. They dressed in traditional Nigerian wedding clothing that made everyone else look a little dull. Skylar's wedding dress seemed to be handcrafted by fairies or angels or a collaboration of both. It flowed in waves of the softest creamy lace over her long, lean body. Lacey had worked a miracle with her curling iron, creating an exquisite waterfall of blonde curls down Sky's back. In her long fingers, Sky held a bouquet of her own making—a glorious display of peony, gardenia, peach roses, tulips, baby's breath, and cascading eucalyptus. She was the most breathtaking bride Maggie had ever seen. For the reception, Sky changed into a lovely Nigerian bridal dress gifted to her by Sly's mother. Nigerian music played during dinner and for dancing afterward.

The guests, particularly the members of Loving the Lord, gave Jack and Maggie their space. As much as they wanted to coo over Abby, they chose to guard their pastor and, instead, focus on the bride and groom.

"I'm glad we came," Maggie whispered to Jack. She was holding Abby, who blissfully slept through toasts, family speeches, and the bridal couple's first dance. "It really is impossible to take your eyes off them, isn't it? They're too gorgeous."

Maggie herself was feeling soft and round and short. She tried to walk Abby in a running stroller most days but hadn't been allowed to run yet. Dr. Siegers would have to give her the all clear at her six-week checkup.

"We knew Sly would settle for nothing less than perfection," Jack said. "We should consider ourselves lucky he didn't choose some tropical island for their wedding. We wouldn't have made it there. By the way, you're beautiful. I know the thoughts in your head, and I'm going to continue to chase them away."

"Blah, blah, blah." She kissed him. "Thank you."

Jack, Maggie, and Abby Brynn drove to Dr. Siegers's office for Maggie's six-week checkup. Dr. Siegers was in Cherish one day a week to see his few patients there. Most of his work was done in Ann Arbor. After her exam, he talked with both Maggie and Jack.

"You are healing well, and your blood work came back exactly where it needs to be." He paused. "It was a scary day when Abigail was born."

Maggie could feel Jack's arm tense.

"The week before Abby was born," Dr. Siegers continued, "I encountered the same situation with another young mother. The placenta detached. She lost a lot of blood. Too much blood. We lost her. I sent the baby home with a bereft father."

Jack inhaled raggedly.

Dr. Siegers smiled at him, understanding the stress that night had put him through. "I was afraid we were going to lose you too, Maggie. I thank God we were able to save you."

Abby cooed in Maggie's arms and blew little bubbles with her rosebud mouth.

"I can't stop thinking about how close she came to dying," Jack burst out.

Maggie jumped slightly, and Abigail's eyes widened at the sudden movement.

"I heard you say it in the OR," Jack said. "I heard you say you were losing her. Last year, I lost my brother and his fiancée in a car accident. I didn't think there could be anything worse. It never occurred to me that I could lose my wife."

"Jack," Dr. Siegers said, "I'm telling you this to hopefully give you comfort. Maggie is fine and will be fine. Her body is healing just as it should. There was nothing either of you did to cause the issue with the placenta. There was nothing you could have done to stop the bleeding. I want you to realize your story has a good ending."

"Thank you for everything you did for me and for Abby," Maggie said. "Jack and I both understand the gravity of what happened that night." Then she looked at Jack and said, "It was only the cow."

Jack remembered Betsy's story. *It was only the cow. Yes, it was a horrible night, I thought I'd lost you. But it wasn't the worst night—you and Abby are alive.*

Maggie looked at him and squeezed his hand. He came back from his thoughts and tried to focus. He felt overwhelmed.

Dr. Siegers looked a little confused but carried on. "You can do the things you feel comfortable doing now, Maggie. If you feel too tired or a little bit of pain, stop. Your body will let you know. It's good to see all three of you." He stood.

"Thanks for everything, Cal," Jack said, standing up to leave. "I'm glad I have the opportunity to work with you. And thank you for saving my wife."

As they drove home, Maggie reached for Jack's hand. "Are you okay?"

"I'm better now. Maybe I just needed to hear Cal's words, hear that you're okay. I sometimes dream about that night in the hospital."

"I hope those dreams stop. We have a lot to be thankful for."

After dinner that night, Maggie held Abby, who smiled at her mother. Maggie knew it was a real smile and not just a gas pain.

"What's my little girlie doing?" she cooed. "Who has the prettiest smile? Abby Brynn does, that's who."

Marmalade, Cheerio, and Fruit Loop came into the nursery when they heard Maggie's voice tone but noticed she seemed to be talking to the new kitten again.

"Hello, babies. Have you been neglected lately? I will get you some treats." She handed Abby to Jack. "Come on kitties, downstairs."

Treats were dispensed to the indoor cats. Maggie spooned a can of cat food into a bowl and sprinkled some treats on top. She filled another bowl with water. When she opened the barn door, Smudge was sitting smartly on his bale.

"Hello, sir. Are you ready for something to eat?"

Smudge jumped down and walked with purpose to the food bowl. As he ate, Maggie was able to pet him gently. He didn't flinch.

"I think we're getting close to your checkup with Doctor Drake, mister. Keep trusting me, please."

The walk-through of the Community Matters Free Clinic was held one afternoon in late October.

"Are you excited?" Maggie asked Jack.

"Yes. We've worked hard on this project. Despite Fitch Dervish and the ridiculously late delivery of flooring, we're going to open on November first, as planned."

The ribbon-cutting ceremony and walk-through was more exciting than Maggie had imagined. Sylvester planned the grand opening with the same class and eye for detail he'd used for his wedding. Maggie and Abby, who was snuggled into a baby wrap on Maggie's chest, accompanied Jack up the sidewalk to the front of the clinic. Two small red maple trees flanked the large glass sliding doors. Floor-to-ceiling windows went along the entire front of the building. Sly had hung a large red ribbon, each end tied to one of the maple trees. A string quartet played classical music as guests gathered outside. The sun shone, a gentle breeze blew, and the temperature was delightfully warm.

"How did Sly arrange the perfect weather for today?" Maggie whispered to Jack.

"He's Sly. All the gods seem to smile down on him."

Sly gave Jack a wave.

"I'll be back. Enjoy the ceremony," Jack said to Maggie. Then he walked around one of the maples, along with Charlene, Alan, Aimee, the dental hygienist Sofia, Betsy, Cate, and Ednah. They stood along the ribbon, and Sly handed them each a red-handled pair of scissors.

"Welcome to the Community Matters Free Clinic," Sly said, looking around at the large crowd. He spied his new wife and gave her a wink. "I'd like to introduce you to our staff. Our physicians are Doctor Jack Elliot, Doctor Charlene Kessler, and Doctor Alan Cocanour. These physicians are donating their time to care for people in need of medical care, with or without health insurance. Let's give them a round of applause."

Applause erupted.

"Because we believe in caring for the whole person, we are grateful to have Doctor Betsy Sneller, Psychologist. She is also donating her hours to the clinic to help with mental and emotional issues our patents may struggle with. Thank you, Betsy,"

More applause.

"Doctor Aimee Van Dyke is a local dentist in Manchester and will open another office in Cherish. She will donate time to the dental wing of our clinic. Dental health is something we often overlook, but Aimee is going to make sure we pay attention to our mouths."

Aimee gave two thumbs-up and was applauded. The pink wisps of her hair blew gaily in the wind.

"We do have three paid part-time staff, and we couldn't do our work without them. Sofia Rodriguez is our dental hygienist. She will assist Aimee in all three offices."

Sofia waived at the applause from the guests. She gave a nod to Aimee, who waved her arm like a game show host revealing the prize behind door number one. Both women began to laugh.

They make me want to get my teeth cleaned, Maggie thought. *They must have the happiest dentist's office in the history of the world.*

Sylvester continued, "Cate Carlson will help direct patients and receive training for her nursing degree. Cate is newly back from Ghana."

There was applause and some loud whistles from Bryan as Cate waved from behind the ribbon.

Sly finished his introductions. "Ednah Lemmen will be our office manager and work the front desk. We are grateful for her organizational skills and previous work experience in medical offices."

More applause. They each took their scissors, and Sly signaled the dramatic ribbon cutting. With a series of snips, it was complete.

"Welcome to the Community Matters Free Clinic!" Sly announced. "Please join us inside for a look around and some refreshments."

The members of the string quartet moved into the waiting area of the clinic, opened their music, and began to play. The classical music was a tasteful addition to the opening, along with the heavy hors d'oeuvres and glasses of sparkling champagne. Maggie helped herself to a smoked salmon puff and a crab cake.

"Want a private tour?" Jack asked.

"Yes, lead on." She grabbed a strawberry tart and followed her husband to the right of the waiting room, down a hallway.

"This is the behavioral health wing. We have two offices here, even though Betsy is the only person working in mental health for now."

He led Maggie and Abby into Betsy's spacious office. She had a desk and a little sitting area underneath high, uncovered windows that let in lots of daylight. A thick cream-colored carpet made the room homey, while the light-blue walls and darker-blue trim were soothing.

"It's calming to walk in here," Maggie said. "The blue walls are perfect."

On the other side of the large office was a smaller sitting area. There was a chair an adult could use, but also smaller chairs, a little table, and bins of toys and art supplies.

"This is where Betsy will work with children who are experiencing stress or trauma," Jack said.

Maggie looked at the small furniture and pondered what it must be like to be so small and already have experienced the worst life has to offer.

"I'm thankful for Betsy," she whispered, "but I wish she didn't need this part of her office. Who could willfully hurt a child? It's unthinkable." Maggie kissed Abby's downy head, then said a silent prayer for those who would enter this room in the future. "Betsy will hopefully heal little minds and souls in this safe space."

The second office was being used as a storage room for the time being.

"We'll see how everything goes," Jack said, "but we plan to have another therapist join us here."

They walked down the hallway and through the waiting room full of patrons talking and eating while the string quartet played Handel's *Water Music* in the background. There was a door behind Ednah's new desk, which led into another hallway.

"This is the medical wing. We have three exam rooms and a procedure room, an X-ray room, and a laboratory. We have the capacity for two more exam rooms."

"Won't it be fun to see the additions you'll make a year from now? How smart to build enough space to expand."

"We received an 'anonymous' gift from Darcy Keller. He basically said, 'Plan for the future, it's paid for.'"

"Darcy has done so much for Cherish since he came home. What do you think makes some people generous and others so miserly? It doesn't matter how rich or poor a person is, some people are just better at giving."

"I don't know all the possible reasons, but I think one important reason is empathy. People who can put themselves in another person's situation, feeling the stress or pain or fear, usually want to help. Darcy has shown himself to be an incredibly empathetic man. He also has more money than God."

Maggie laughed. "I'm glad Darcy is in the world, especially our little part of it."

"Yes, this clinic would have happened, but not as easily without Darcy's latest contribution."

They walked down the medical wing hallway and passed others who were touring the facility. There were many oohs and ahhs as people saw Abby sleeping comfortably, snuggled next to her mother. Jack, Maggie, and Abby went to the dental wing and found Aimee. She was showing off her domain with flair.

"We have two exam rooms where my hygienist, Sofia, will do cleanings. We also have a procedure room for me to do my mouth carvings." She winked and laughed maniacally.

"I like Aimee," Maggie said to Jack. "She's going to be a lot of fun to work with. She's one of those people who decides to have a great day every day."

"She's smart, and hilarious. And you're right, she doesn't let anything get her down. If she hits a roadblock, she finds a way around it. When we first planned the office spaces, before Darcy's contribution, we didn't think we could have more than five exam rooms total. Aimee was the one who said it wasn't going to be enough for the clientele we'll serve. She looked at Sly and said, 'Who has the money around here, besides the hospital board?' I told her about Darcy but warned her he had already done several philanthropic projects in Cherish. She made an appointment with him, told him what we needed, and he made his offer to Sly."

"I want to get to know her," Maggie said. "I want to figure out how she stays so positive and creative."

"She'd love to meet you."

Maggie walked up to Aimee and put out her hand. "Hi, Doctor Van Dyke. I'm Maggie Elliot."

Aimee smiled and shook Maggie's hand. "And this must be little Abby. She's precious. It's nice to meet you. Your husband talks about you all the time."

"Don't believe a word he says." Maggie smiled. "I want to invite you to visit our church."

"I know you're the pastor."

"Yes, but I'm still on maternity leave. You would love my friend Nora. She's helping me out for a couple more weeks."

"I'm sure I would, but I'm not really a churchy kind of gal. No offense, but church folks seem hypocritical to me. I don't need it. Too negative."

"I'm sure you don't. But Aimee, I think we need you."

28

Nora had stopped by to see Maggie at least twice a week to share all the updates about life at Loving the Lord. She did the exact same thing every time she walked into the farmhouse. She found Abby, who was usually in her mother's arms, took the baby, and sat down to tell Maggie all the news.

"Hank is a hoot. Don't you just love working with him? He is so happy to be back. It sounds like he and Pamela are planning an evening to share stories and videos of their trip Down Under. I'm going to bring Dan whenever they choose a date. I saw Verna and Howard today. She is getting stronger since her chemotherapy ended. Her hair is growing back too."

Verna's last chemotherapy treatment was completed in September, and all eight cards attached to the white roses were framed together in a collage. It hung in the living room for everyone to see, especially Verna. *Hope. Perseverance. Peace. Strength. Courage. Assurance. Anticipation. Hallelujah—the final rose.*

Sunday services were going well. "People seem to like my sermons okay, but I know they are missing yours. They will love having this little one in the sanctuary on Sundays. They miss you all."

"I have to say, I finally feel a little excited to get back to work. I miss them too."

"I made the rounds today to all the shut-ins. Again, they are very kind to me but always ask when you'll be back. You have great job security. I told Marvin Green you would bring Abby in for a visit, and I thought he was going to cry. He can't wait to meet this little one." She kissed Abby's fingers and got a smile and a gurgle for her troubles.

"I can't thank you enough for all your help. I have felt so comfortable being home with Abby and not worried about one single thing at church."

"How are the plans for Lacey and Lydia's wedding?"

"Funny you should ask. I was just peeking at my notes yesterday. I'm glad I wrote most of their service before Abby entered the world. I know Lydia wanted Lacey's parents and sister to come to the wedding, but I don't think much progress has been made. They have cut Lacey out of their lives, which I can't imagine." Maggie looked at Abby, and her heart grew three sizes. "I'll never understand parents turning on a child."

"It's rough. Especially when it's an LGBTQI issue. We're all born how we're born."

"Lacey's family still thinks it's a choice, as if she could just choose to be heterosexual. It's an attitude of fear. Wouldn't the world be a nicer place if we could be more accepting of others and less judgmental?"

"It would be a much better place. It's the kind of world all our children should grow up in." Nora looked down at Abby. "I think I want one of these."

"Good. Abby needs a clergy friend. Get to work. And when you have your baby, Abby and I will drive up to Lansing and preach for you and work in your food pantry."

"It's a deal. Hey, tomorrow the free clinic opens for real, right?"

"Yes. Jack's there now with the rest of the staff. They are doing all the last-minute things. I wonder how many patients they will see at first."

"The word will spread like crazy. It's a wonderful gift to the surrounding community. It seems like things around here are very different than when you first showed up."

"They are. I think we learned a lot from our trip to Ghana. Then the horrible fallout from the presidential election really showed everyone's true colors. Welcoming the Nasab family was an education. Now they are just part of us and we're part of them. The free childcare center is growing, and parents aren't so stressed. To be honest, Jesus would love to hang out around here, I'm sure of it." Maggie laughed. "It's so much better than being a place where he would just pass through."

"We really get to do great work, don't we?" Nora said.

"Yes. There's nothing like the holy chaos of being in the church, and the hope we share with those who have no use for the church or for us. I envy you and Dan. In Lansing, you have a rich diversity of people. That's what I want for Abby. Too much whiteness isn't good for anyone."

"I agree. I want our children to go to schools that represent, and look like, the world, rather than an episode of *The Brady Bunch*. I don't like what's happening to our country right now. Travel bans and anti-refugee rhetoric help grow the cancer of bigotry."

"The president is exactly who he told us he was. No surprises." Maggie shook political thoughts out of her head. They kept her up at night.

They heard the back door open, and Bryan walked in. "Hey, how's it going?"

"Good. Are you home because your fiancée is at the clinic with my husband?"

"Yep. I came straight home from work. How's my niece?"

"Perfect," Nora said. "Absolutely perfect. How is it going for you, living with her and her parents?"

"It's working great for me. I hope it's working okay for them." He looked at Maggie and winked.

"It works because you are always at the Carlson's house. We never have to see you."

"Well, I hate to break your heart, but I've been looking at apartments online. I think it would probably be a good idea to live in Ann Arbor. I'd be closer to work, and Cate and I can have some time away from so many family members."

Maggie laughed. "Just marry her already."

"Don't worry, I plan to."

"How's she feeling, Bry?" Nora asked.

Abby started to fuss a little, so she was placed back in her mother's arms.

"She's still regaining her strength," Bryan said. "She gets tired easily, but she's so much better than when we got home. The few hours she'll work at the clinic will be enough for now. In January, she'll be back at the U, and soon, she'll be a nurse."

"She looks a lot better," Maggie chimed in. "She had such dark circles under her eyes and was so thin. Now she looks more like herself. I'm excited because she and Addie are going to sing for Christmas Eve."

"You already have Christmas Eve planned?" Nora asked.

"I got a jump on a lot of things before this little one showed up. I'm glad I did. Tomorrow is November. That means we can say next month is Christmas. This will be the first year Irena doesn't do one of her big concerts for the holiday. *She'll* be on maternity leave."

"What else are you going to do for the service?" Nora was looking for ideas.

"I'm actually finishing a little story I began this summer. I hope it works."

She had started to tell Nora and Bryan her idea when the back door opened again and Jack walked in with Cate.

"Hi, all," Jack said with a grin.

Maggie could feel his excitement. "Things must have gone well at the clinic."

Jack looked at Cate. "Yes. We are all ready for tomorrow, whatever tomorrow may bring."

"Every little detail is covered," Cate interjected. "Ednah was in the last few evenings and labeled cupboards and drawers, prepared files for the patients who have already called for appointments, and even brought in fresh flowers for the waiting area. She loves the clinic." It was obvious Cate also loved the clinic.

Maggie pondered the news for a moment. *Ednah has found her place. Amen to that!*

29

Lacey and Lydia's wedding plans had come together only because Maggie had said, "I need to prepare your ceremony before I hatch this baby. You two must settle on a few things."

"We've decided to be married in the church," Lacey had said, "mainly because we want Irena to play the organ. We love that crazy lady."

"We will call Sky this week and get flower suggestions," Lydia said dutifully.

"We'll walk down the aisle together," Lacey said, "you do the ceremony part, and we'll head off to the Cherish Café, which fortunately, we have already booked. We still have to pick out the menu."

"Do you want to write your own vows or go traditional?" Maggie had her pen poised.

"Traditional," they both said.

"Will you have attendants?"

"No. Just us," Lydia said quickly.

Lacey looked down.

"Are you okay, Lacey?" Maggie asked.

"I feel bad because Lydia has a cousin who would be perfect for her to have as a maid of honor. My sister won't be here, but it doesn't mean Lydia's cousin can't participate."

It was obvious they had already discussed this issue.

"Is there someone else you would like as a maid of honor, besides your sister, Lacey?" Maggie asked gently.

"I don't think so."

Maggie jotted a few more notes to herself in the notebook. "Okay, this is enough for me to work with. Thanks, you two. I think your wedding will be beautiful, and I'm so glad you are getting married in the church."

Later that afternoon, just as Maggie had been packing up to go home, Lydia called.

"I was wondering if you could help me," Lydia said. Then she laid out her plan.

"I'll help any way I can," Maggie said.

November fourth arrived. The night before, there had been a twenty-minute rehearsal of the ceremony. With no attendants, it went quickly, except for Irena's demand to play three pieces of music on the organ all the way through.

"You know you won't be doing this tomorrow, right?" Lacey said to the exceedingly round organist.

"I know! Dat's vy I do eet now," Irena barked.

Lydia's family was present at the rehearsal, while Lacey's was conspicuously absent. Following the rehearsal, the small group walked to O'Leary's Pub and enjoyed an evening of bar food and conversation. Maggie connected with Lydia's parents, Dave and Jackie, her brothers, Beau and Travis, and her cousin Elizabeth. She was immediately drawn to them and wished they lived closer to Cherish.

"How long have you lived in Lansing?" Maggie asked Jackie.

"We moved here from Illinois three years ago. I am the chief nursing officer at Sparrow Hospital. We moved so I could take the position. Lydia was heartbroken when we sold her childhood home in Elgin, but she decided having us less than an hour away was an okay compromise."

"What does Dave do?" Maggie asked.

"He's retired, but he keeps himself busy around town. Both of our sons are studying at Michigan State. The move has been good for us all."

"And Elizabeth lives in Lansing too?" Maggie asked.

"My sister, Elizabeth's mother, lives in Okemos. I have to admit, moving to Lansing had more allure than just the work at Sparrow Hospital. You'll meet more of our family tomorrow. Lydia and Elizabeth are like sisters. They were born one day apart and have always been close, even across the miles."

Maggie observed how Lydia's family enveloped Lacey into every conversation and peppered her with questions that demonstrated their interest in her.

At nine o'clock, Maggie took her leave. Jack had been home with Abby all evening.

"Are you ready for tomorrow?" he asked as Maggie cuddled a sleeping Abby.

"I'm ready. I hope it will be a meaningful day for the two brides, especially Lacey."

"What's Lydia's family like?"

"Amazing. They are open and loving and accepting. Lydia has no doubt she is loved, and neither does Lacey. She was treated like a long-lost daughter."

"She deserves that kind of love. It would be nice if her own family was as accepting."

"Yes," Maggie said absently. "I'm going to put Abby down and visit with Smudge. Did you feed him his dinner?"

"Of course. He even let me pet him on the top of his head."

"Lucky you!"

The next afternoon, Maggie arrived at church while Lacey and Lydia were in separate rooms getting dressed. The photographer took photos of each as they put on their makeup and did their hair. Lydia's cousin Elizabeth fussed over and teased her.

"It's too bad the only person who could really do your hair right is the person you're marrying, and you can't see her for another hour."

"I'll have to try to do my hair myself. Woe is me." Lydia laughed. "I'm so glad you're here."

"I am too," Elizabeth said as she placed a wreath of roses around Lydia's head. Her long hair fell in ringlets down her back. The rose wreath made her look like an upscale hippy.

There was a knock on the door. Elizabeth cracked it open. "Hello?"

"Hi," a woman said. "I think I'm lost. Is Lacey there?"

Elizabeth opened the door. "Are you . . . ?"

"Ruth. Campbell."

The young woman looked so much like her sister, Lydia could only stare in disbelief.

"Ruth! I'm so glad to meet you," Lydia said delightedly. "I'm Lydia, and this is my cousin Elizabeth."

"Hello." Ruth took in Lydia's satin wedding dress and the roses in her hair.

"I'm so glad you came," Lydia said. "This will mean everything to Lacey. I have heard so much about you."

Ruth's face warmed slightly.

"Would you like to see Lacey?" Lydia said. "Elizabeth can take you to her."

"Yes. I would like to see her. Does she know I'm coming today?"

Lydia didn't miss a beat. "No. We thought surprising her might be the best wedding gift."

Ruth looked uncomfortable. Lydia was not going to say it would have been too much of a heartbreak if Lacey thought Ruth was coming and then she never showed. Dave and Jackie came into the dressing room with the photographer.

"Hello!" Jackie was bubbling with excitement.

"Ruth, this is my mother, Jackie, and my father, Dave. Mom, Dad, this is Ruth Campbell, Lacey's sister."

No one would have guessed how much Jackie and Dave had worried about whether Ruth would attend the wedding. Jackie opened her arms and flung them around a startled Ruth.

"Ruth, we are thrilled to meet you. Your sister is remarkable, and we consider both of you part of our family."

Dave held out his hand, and Ruth shook it. "It's a pleasure to meet you, Ruth."

His smile was so warm, Ruth couldn't help but smile back. "Thank you."

"Would you like to see your sister?" Elizabeth asked.

"Yes. If she doesn't know I'm here, I don't want to scare her or anything."

"She'll be thrilled," Lydia said with certainty.

In the other dressing room, Lacey put the pearl-encrusted hair clips on each side of her head. Pastor Maggie had given them to her after the rehearsal the night before.

"This is your something borrowed," Maggie had said. "They worked for me, they worked for Irena, and they will work for you."

Irena waddled through the door. "Vat you doing?" She looked at the hair clasps. "Ahh . . . de hairr clasps. Yes, dey arre good luck. De borrowed ting."

Irena had designated herself to be Lacey's "person" for the pre-wedding preparations. Unfortunately, her pregnancy discomfort kept her from being more than an irritant.

"My feet hurt me so much. I must sit. Oh no! I hev to pee again."

Lacey had quietly done her hair, applied her makeup, and was ready to put on her wedding dress when Maggie checked in on her.

"Would you like to help me with my dress, PM?" Lacey asked.

Maggie looked out the door. She'd hoped someone else would be there to help.

"I em herre to help!" Irena screeched, then took a deep breath. "Oh, forget it. I'm too tired."

Maggie looked again out the door and saw Elizabeth with a young woman who looked a lot like Lacey.

"I think there's someone else who could do a better job than either Irena or I."

She stepped aside, and Ruth walked through the door. Lacey gasped. Maggie grabbed Irena's arm and dragged her out of the room.

"Vait!! I vant to see dis. Lacey's gong to crry."

She tried to go back into the room, but Maggie yanked Irena away and pushed the door closed behind them.

"Give them some privacy, for heaven's sake, Irena."

"You came," Lacey whispered.

"I'm so sorry, Hannah, I mean, Lacey. I'm so very sorry."

"Let's not do this, Ruth. You don't need to apologize. I want this day to be the best day, for both of us. You're here, and I am so happy. Can we just pick up where we left off?"

"How can you be so forgiving?"

"Our relationship isn't just the past few years when we've been separated. We're sisters. We've known each other forever. I can't remember a time when you weren't in my life. I'm sorry Mom and Dad made you choose. It must have been hard."

"I hate the fact that I fell for it. I'm mad at myself for believing them instead of listening to you. I can't believe I almost missed your wedding. If Lydia and Pastor Maggie hadn't called me, I never would have known."

"They called you?" Lacey felt her nose sting.

"Yes. They called and gently invited me to be part of the most joyful day of your life. I told them I'd think about it, but I didn't have to. Something just clicked. Mom and Dad's judgmental attitude toward you was one I couldn't go along with anymore. It's a sickness. They are so busy deciding who is 'in' and who is 'out,' as if they have the power to do so. I don't want to be that kind of Christian anymore."

"Do they know you're here?" Lacey asked.

"Yes. I told them last night. I stopped by after work, sat them down, and told them exactly what I thought. Even if they chose to miss their eldest daughter's wedding, I would be with you. Then I went back to my apartment and packed. Do you like my new dress?"

"I love it." Lacey laughed as Ruth spun around. "Thank you, Ruth. Now I have one more thing to ask of you."

∞

Maggie went to the secret door and peeked out into the sanctuary. Full. Of course. I love our church. Lacey and Lydia are so loved by these good people.

Maggie went out to the altar as Irena came to the end of her prelude. She was just switching her music when Maggie saw Elizabeth and Ruth standing together at the back of the sanctuary. When Irena began to play, both young women walked down the aisle together. Then each took their place on either side of Maggie. Irena changed keys in the music, and Jackie stood up to signal the congregation to stand.

"Here they come," Elizabeth whispered to Maggie and Ruth.

Lacey and Lydia walked arm in arm down the sanctuary aisle. The photographer's camera clicked as they smiled at their guests. As they reached Maggie, the music ended.

"Lacey and Lydia, welcome to your wedding day," Maggie said. She was startled when she heard someone clapping their hands. It was Irena from the organ bench. The rest of the congregation joined in until everyone was applauding. Lacey and Lydia turned around and drank in the excitement of their church family. When it finally died down, Maggie continued.

"There isn't usually applause until the end of the ceremony, but what a great way to begin. We have gathered here today to join these two women in marriage. Lacey Campbell and Lydia Marsh have thought-fully and prayerfully decided to be married. Marriage is a holy estate and not to be entered into lightly. I can attest these two women are prepared for the commitment they will make on this day."

The ceremony continued with Scripture readings, Maggie's words of affirmation, and two pink cards with Lacey and Lydia's own loving and hopeful words to one another. Irena played while Maggie read the words of a handfasting ceremony. The handfasting ended with the re-peating of their vows. Lacey and Lydia's hands were wrapped together as each in turn repeated after Maggie.

"I take you, Lacey/Lydia, to be my wife.

To have and to hold.
For better, for worse.
For richer, for poorer.
In sickness and in health.
To love and to cherish.
As long as we both may live.
This I pledge truly, with all my heart."

And then came the final prayer.

"Let us pray for the happy future of these two kind and generous women."

Maggie put down her notebook on the altar table behind her and placed one hand on the shoulder of each woman. She was ready to begin the prayer when she saw Ruth step next to Lacey and put her hand on Lacey's other shoulder. Elizabeth did the same with Lydia. Maggie watched as Dave and Jackie, followed by Beau and Travis, left their front pew and stretched their arms around the four women. It was a protective shield of love for a new family. Maggie swallowed hard and began her prayer.

"Holy God, you have created all of us in your image. Therefore, we have been created to love one another. Thank you for this sanctuary filled with love as we witness this new family being formed by your grace. We pray for Lacey and Lydia and commend their marriage to you as you guide them through the years ahead. Bless them with laughter and joy in their life together. Give them strength for their work. Fill them with understanding and forgiveness on the days when there is misunderstanding. May they find delight in one another. If they choose to be mothers, bless them with children to love and nurture. Thank you for their family members here today, and for their love and support. We thank you for Dave, Jackie, Elizabeth, Ruth, Beau, and Travis. In the years to come, may Lacey and Lydia's good days be many and days of sorrow be few. Guide them in creative ways to share your love in the world around them. We ask in the name of Jesus Christ, the one who taught us all how to love unconditionally. Amen."

Maggie watched as the families moved into a group hug. A tear slid down Lacey's face. Ruth gently wiped it away with her handkerchief.

The applause during the recessional nearly drowned out the organ. But for once, Irena didn't mind.

It wasn't until after the pictures were taken and everyone had made their way to the Cherish Café that Maggie heard a noisy commotion. She and Jack, who was holding Abby, both looked across the restaurant at the disruption. Irena was clinging to Keith and howling.

"Owww! Dis dun't feel good!" She grabbed her midsection.

Jack leapt up, handed the sleeping Abby to Maggie, and ran across the room. "What's happening, Irena?"

"I dun't know. It hurrts! Yourr de doctorr. You tell me!"

Jack looked at Keith. "I'll call Doctor Siegers. Get her to the hospital. I'll follow."

It quickly became clear to all the guests, as well as the two brides, that Irena was going to have her babies earlier than expected.

Lacey looked at Lydia. "What do you think?"

Lydia looked around the room at her family and all the guests. "We're her people. We've got to go."

Lacey clinked a knife against her champagne glass. "Quiet, quiet please! We would like to thank everyone for joining us today. Lydia and I are both overwhelmed by your love, but we're going to disappear for a while. This little lady," she pointed to Irena, who was leaning on Keith as they walked toward the door, "is about to become a mother. She is family to us, and we are going to go to the hospital with her. Enjoy your dinners. Save us some cake, and if you're still here when we get back, we'll all enjoy some dancing."

Another eruption of applause filled the room.

Lacey hugged Ruth. "I'll be back. Please don't go anywhere. We aren't going on a honeymoon until next year sometime. Can you stay with us for a while?"

"Yes! Thank you. I'll be here when you get back. Go take care of Irena."

Maggie grabbed Jack's arm. "I want to go too. Irena is one of my best friends."

"Okay, come on. We've got to hurry."

As they left, Maggie heard Dave's voice through the microphone. She turned and saw both Dave and Jackie in front of the guests.

"Well, folks, even though we have apparently lost both brides, we're going to have a reception in their absence. I'd like to make a toast."

Maggie heard the laughter from the crowd. Dave and Jackie Marsh would celebrate their daughter's wedding, no matter what.

The operating room was filled with Irena's shrieking voice as she described every pain she felt every single second. "It is hurrting me! My back! Oww!"

Dr. Siegers and Jack were scrubbing in and could hear Irena's screeches.

"She needs to be sedated," Dr. Siegers said.

Jack laughed as a nurse helped him with his gloves. "I'm sure it's happening now."

"Neonatal is ready, doctor," another nurse announced.

"Let's go," Dr. Siegers said as they entered the chaotic room.

Keith was masked, gowned, and holding Irena's hand. She had indeed received sedation and was fighting the effects, but finally she lost the battle and drifted off to sleep.

An hour and a half later, Jack went out to the waiting room to find Maggie and Abby sitting with Lacey and Lydia, still beautifully dressed in their wedding gowns.

"They're all here. The surgery went well, and everyone is fine. Irena is in recovery."

"What did she have?" Maggie, Lacey, and Lydia asked in surround sound.

"Keith and Irena have three daughters," Jack said, grinning. "Three little Irenas. Would you like to see them? They're in the NICU."

Jack led them to the nursery. He went in and spoke to one of the nurses, and soon three little incubators were wheeled over to the window for Maggie, Lydia, and Lacey to see. There were handwritten cards on the sides of the incubators: "Baby Girl Crunch 1" followed by 2 and 3. Maggie looked at how much each baby weighed. Four pounds five ounces. Four pounds seven ounces. Five pounds.

"How long will they to stay in the hospital?" Maggie asked Jack.

"My guess is four to five days. They are all doing well and can breathe on their own. They'll need to be monitored, but I think Keith and Irena will have a full house in less than a week."

It was over another hour before they were able to go back and visit Irena in her room. She was still a little groggy but smiled happily when she saw her friends.

"I hev tree babies. Tree leetle girrl chicks."

"Congratulations, Irena!" Gentle hugs and kisses followed.

"Congratulations to you too, Keith. How are you feeling?" Maggie asked.

"Like the luckiest man alive. I have three daughters and the most beautiful wife. Life is incredible."

"My Captain Crrunch is good to me," Irena said, yawning.

"We're so happy for you both," Lydia said.

"Irena, they are certainly small," Maggie marveled, "but still, that's a lot of baby you were carrying around. No wonder you were in such pain at the reception."

"No, I was feeling bits ov pain since dis morning, but I nut miss de wedding ov my frriends. No. I play for today."

Lacey and Lydia both hugged Irena again, and baby girls 1, 2, and 3, were exclaimed over.

"Irena, they are beautiful. They have so much dark hair for babies," Lydia said.

"They are so tiny. Wait until you see their little fingers," Maggie chimed in.

"You know," Lacey said, looking at Keith and Irena, "you two are outnumbered right from the get-go. Those three miniature humans are going to give you a run for your money."

"I vant to see dem!" Irena yelped, then she yawned again.

"You'll see them soon," Jack said. "You might want to rest while you can."

Maggie filled the small room with a prayer of thanksgiving, then she looked at Irena, Lacey, and Lydia.

"Today is one that binds the three of you together. A wedding and three babies. Someone should write a book about it."

"Do you have any names picked out?" Jack asked.

"We do," said Keith. "Do you want to tell them, Irena?"

"Yes. I want to tell. First, de leetlest chick, her name is Catrina Maria."

"Oh, for your mother," Maggie said quietly. "How beautiful."

Irena nodded. "Den de next one is Alina Lydia."

Lydia's mouth opened in surprise. "Really?"

Irena nodded again. "And den, what is de last baby? Daria Lacey."

"No. Really?" Lacey began to tear up.

"Yes. Leetle Alina Lydia and Leetle Daria Lacey. You arre my peoples. Tank you for missing yourr reception to be with me."

"This was so much better than a reception," Lacey said, brushing a stray tear from her cheek.

There were hugs and kisses, goodbyes were said, and Keith and Irena were left alone, waiting for their new "leetle chicks" to be wheeled into the room.

The others all went back to the wedding reception. Jack, Maggie, and Abby stayed long enough to eat some wedding cake and dance one slow dance—Abby happily sandwiched between her parents as they swayed back and forth. Lacey and Lydia would dance with their heartier guests until four a.m.

When Jack and Maggie finally got home, they put Abby down, fed Smudge in the barn, and shared treats with the indoor kitties after many obnoxious demands.

Jack put his arms around Maggie. "I love you."

"I love you too."

"I'm glad we only have one baby."

"Amen."

∽

On Monday morning, Maggie finally lured Smudge into a large cat carrier with a delectable piece of liver. He wasn't thrilled about being locked in the cage, and less thrilled by his visit to Dr. Dana Drake. Many embarrassments were endured by the proud tomcat.

"He's been dewormed, had his shots, I cleaned his teeth, and I removed other bits of his anatomy so he won't be making any kittens. He's in fine shape, Maggie. I think it was the good food you gave him over the last few months. You'll have to see how he likes being inside. He may just be your neutered barn cat." Dana gave Smudge a loving scratch behind the ears. "He's a beauty, that's for sure."

"I love this cat so much," Maggie said. "There's something about watching a scared, wild animal figure out he doesn't have to be scared or quite so wild. He's changed so much from when I first met him."

Despite Dana's concerns, Smudge had no problem becoming an indoor cat. Of course, there were a few hissing matches when he first encountered the other felines. It took a while for him to accept that Marmalade was the alpha kitty, even though Smudge was the larger of the two. After a few weeks—in the evenings, when Jack lit the fire—the four beasts would meander over and flop down in front of the dancing flames.

Smudge always had the warmest spot.

30

Christmas Eve seemed to sneak up on Maggie. The service was in four hours, and she felt scattered and unfocused.

"What are you thinking?" Jack asked. He watched his wife as she fed their daughter.

"I'm not fully in church mode yet. I can go for hours and not think about anything that has to do with the church. It feels more like a chore than a calling. Nora was so kind to preach longer than expected, but even the last four weeks have been a struggle for me. I just want to be with Abby." Maggie took a moment to enjoy feeling sorry for herself.

Jack decided not to indulge Maggie's self-pity. "Well, no one would know it from your sermons. You have brought us through Advent beautifully. I thought you were ready for Christmas Eve."

"I am. I'm glad I prepared before Abby was born. I just don't have any enthusiasm."

"You have four hours to change your attitude."

"Harrumph!" Maggie tried to look irritated but ended up laughing instead.

"I'm glad you love being a mother. I'm glad you love being a wife. You are an excellent pastor, and you still have the capacity to be a fantastic daughter, sister, friend, et cetera."

Maggie kissed Abby's soft head. "Did you ever imagine what it would feel like to be a parent? I knew it must be wonderful or people would have stopped having children a long time ago, but I never imagined this kind of love. I would do anything to protect this baby girl. I don't want to miss a single second with her."

Jack understood exactly what Maggie was talking about. "I would do anything for her and for you too. It's surprising how much life has changed since Abby came along."

"I'm thankful for the way the church has given me so much latitude to care for Abby and for them. I know not every mom can have a crib in her office and take her baby to visit shut-ins. I'll get it together and change my attitude."

In a couple of hours, Maggie's attitude changed completely. Despite being on maternity leave for three more weeks, Irena was perched on the organ bench when Maggie walked through the large oak sanctuary doors. Irena played and sang:

Infant holy, infant lowly, for his bed a cattle stall;
oxen lowing, little knowing Christ the babe is Lord of all.
Swift are winging angels singing, nowells ringing, tidings bringing;
Christ the babe is Lord of all; Christ the babe is Lord of all!

Flocks were sleeping, shepherds keeping vigil till the morning new;
saw the glory, heard the story—tidings of a gospel true.
Thus rejoicing, free from sorrow, praises voicing, greet the morrow;
Christ the babe was born for you; Christ the babe was born for you!

Maggie had not heard Irena sing before. Her voice was high and sweet. Maggie walked to the organ and wrapped her arms around Irena, who immediately stopped playing.

"Irena, you sing so beautifully, and that's one of my favorite Christmas carols. You gave me chills."

"I em a good singer. I sing to my leetle chicks all de days."

Irena's hair was still a lovely auburn. *She must have had Lacey color it again.* She had some sparkles on her eyelids, but for the most part she looked like a normal human.

"You look beautiful. How are you feeling?"

"I em good. I feel healed in my tum, no more pain. My boobs arre too big and always full of milk. I'm a cow mama. But it's okay."

Maggie laughed. "It's amazing how you hear a baby cry, any baby, and your milk comes rushing in. I only hear one baby, but you hear three."

"Yes. Leetle chicks. My Captain Crrunch has dem in de nursery. We'll see if dey come out for church or stay in dere."

"I'll tell Jack. Maybe he and Abby would like to join Keith and your litter."

Maggie walked to her office and sat with her Christmas Eve service. She heard Irena play through the carols for the evening, then she heard voices as the ushers arrived to make sure the bulletins and individual candles were in order. There was a knock on her door.

"Come in."

Jack and Abby Brynn came in, followed by Dirk, Mimi, Bryan, and Cate.

"Hello, family!" Maggie got up and hugged everyone. "What a fun Christmas."

"We just wanted to say hello," Mimi said. "We know you're busy, so we'll leave you alone. See you afterward."

Mimi led the others out of Maggie's office but not before Jack gave his wife a kiss and whispered, "It's going to be a beautiful service. Aren't you glad Irena's here?"

"I am. I've missed her since she's been on maternity leave."

"Well, break a leg."

"That's for thespians, not pastors. Do you really want me to break my leg?"

Jack answered with a kiss on the top of her head.

Finally, it was time to put on her robe, white stole, and gold cross. She walked to the secret door, said a prayer, and entered into a full sanctuary.

Cate and Addie had spent time during their break from school practicing a duet of "Away in a Manger." The service began with their clear soprano voices filling the sanctuary. Carols were sung, lessons were read, and the miracle of Christmas was revealed. Finally, Maggie invited the children to come and sit with her on the altar steps. She opened her notebook and read aloud.

LILLY

A long time ago, before there was Christmas, there was a little lamb named Lilly. Lilly and her mother and sister lived in a stall. Other sheep and lambs had stalls too. There were cows, donkeys, and goats in stalls near Lilly's. And there were chickens, who just got to run around anywhere they pleased. In the daytime, the cows went out to a field and the donkeys went to work in the city of Bethlehem, but the sheep and the goats spent the days in a very large pen. The chickens were there too.

Lilly was a happy lamb who loved to be helpful. In the mornings, she would race to the very large pen where the other lambs and baby goats played. The baby goats were called kids. Lilly would play for a while, then she would look for something helpful to do. She would follow the kids and watch them as they ran and jumped. They were good at jumping. She would say to them, "Be careful, kids. Don't jump too high or too far!"

Everything Lilly saw and heard in the pen made her want to help others. She would organize games for the other lambs to keep them from getting bored. She would push straw with her nose and her front hooves to make a bed for one of the old grandma goats. She never went first to the water trough, but she always let the oldest sheep and goats have their morning drink first.

Her best friend was Gertie the Goat. Gertie was the best jumper of all the kids. Gertie liked to run and jump. Lilly and Gertie found each other every morning and played together with the other lambs and kids. Then Lilly would say, "Let's see if we can help the mama sheep and goats." Gertie sometimes liked to help, but she usually just wanted to play. She would say, "Lilly, why do you always want to help? It's more fun to run and jump and play."

One time, Lilly's helpfulness got her into some trouble. She was trying to help Ethel, the oldest grandma goat in the pen. Ethel couldn't bend her crackly old knees to lie down in the sunshine. Lilly thought she could help Ethel, but she ended up pushing the old goat over on her head.

"Quit trying to help! You just pushed me over on my head," Ethel said sternly. "I know you want to be helpful, Lilly, but you're not big enough. You're just a little lamb. Wait until you get older, then maybe you can be helpful."

Lilly felt bad. The only thing she ever wanted to do was be helpful. Then she saw Gertie and the lambs and the kids, and she followed them, telling them to be careful as they jumped on top of every small shed in the pen. The other animals sat under the small sheds to get out of the sun if they felt hot. Trip, trap, trip, trap went the lambs' and the kids' hooves. Trip, trap, trip, trap went Lilly's little lamb hooves. Up and down, up and down went the kids and the lambs and Gertie and Lilly.

"Stop!" some of the mother sheep bleated. "You're too noisy."

"Don't!" the mother goats complained. "We're trying to take a rest."

Lilly said, "Gertie, you and the other kids must stop." But they only stopped for a minute before their hooves went trip, trap, trip, trap again. Lilly said to herself, "I wonder how I can help the lambs and kids do something less noisy?" She decided she would keep the lambs and kids quiet all day tomorrow.

That night, Lilly, her mother, and her sister walked into their stall, ate some hay out of a manger, and snuggled down in the nice clean straw to sleep. But when Lilly was asleep, she dreamed of the lambs and kids. Her hooves moved and kicked as she dreamt about them going trip, trap, trip, trap on the sheds in the pen. She accidentally kicked her mother and her sister.

"Ouch!" they cried. "Lilly, stop kicking. Just sleep."

The next day, Lilly tried to be helpful and made all the lambs and kids sit down and be quiet, but Gertie and the rest of the kids ran away and jumped on all the sheds.

Lilly was perturbed. "Come back, kids! Come back, Gertie!" But the kids decided to play leapfrog. They all lined up, and one would jump over all the others. They took turns jumping over each other until Lilly tried to stop them by standing in front of the leapfrog line. Oops! Gertie jumped and landed hard on top of her very best friend.

Lilly fell and felt her back leg bend awkwardly. "Owwww!!" Lilly cried. "My leg! I can't stand up, and it hurts so!" Lilly began to cry.

Her mother came over and looked at Lilly's leg. "This isn't good, Lilly. You need to come to our stall and rest your leg." Her mother and her sister helped her limp to the stall. Lilly cried the whole way. "I just wanted to help all the mamas and grandmas by keeping the lambs and kids quiet."

For days and days Lilly couldn't go out and help. She had to stay in the stall and rest her leg. When she tried to stand up, she fell right back down. Gertie came over every morning and asked, "Can you come out today, Lilly?"

But Lilly could only say, "Not yet, Gertie."

Then Gertie would go and play with the lambs and kids.

One night, Lilly was asleep under the straw (her mother covered her up because the nights were getting cold), but Lilly was startled awake when she heard voices she didn't recognize.

"Come this way, please. This is the stall closest to the inn. I'll move the sheep."

Lilly stayed under the straw while her mother and sister were led out of their stall. They had to sleep with another mama sheep and her babies.

Lilly peeked slyly from under the straw. She saw two humans. They had a donkey, who stayed close to them. Lilly watched as the man helped the woman lie down in the straw. She was lying very close to Lilly. She sounded like she didn't feel well.

"I wonder if she hurt her leg, like me?" Lilly said to herself.

The cow in the next stall saw Lilly's white ears and said, "Lilly, what are you doing in your stall? The humans need it."

"I can't walk yet," Lilly bleated.

The man and the woman looked down at the bleating straw.

"It's a lamb," the woman said. "Leave it be."

The man let Lilly stay.

The donkey who came with the humans said to the cow and to Lilly, "She's going to have a baby. We've come a long way, but when we got here, there was no place for them in the inn. That's why they're out here."

Lilly felt bad for the woman. She probably needed a better place to have a baby. But then Lilly said, "I was born here in this stall. All the kids and the calves and the baby donkeys were born in stalls. We were all born here. Maybe I can help while this new baby is born."

As the night went on, Lilly saw a beautiful star slowly rise in the sky. It was the brightest star she had ever seen. It bathed the stall in a beautiful light. The woman didn't feel very well at all. She cried out sometimes.

"I wish I could help," Lilly said to herself as she yawned. "I will sit closer to her and be her friend. Maybe that will help." Lilly pulled herself up and dragged her bad leg as she moved closer to the woman. She let the woman pet her soft white wool. In the starlight, she could see the woman smile.

"Thank you, little lamb. You are so soft, and you give me comfort," the woman whispered.

The man asked, "Mary, what can I bring you?"

"Water, please, Joseph."

He brought her water.

When the woman seemed to be in more pain, Lilly moved closer to her. Lilly dragged herself to the woman and let the woman rest her head on the soft wool of her tummy.

Finally, after a long time, the woman stopped crying. There was a different cry. It was a baby cry. The cry was very soft.

"Mary, it's baby Jesus," Joseph said. He wrapped the baby in cloths and handed him to Mary. She used more water from a bucket Joseph brought to wash the baby and re-wrapped him in the cloths. Then Lilly watched as she laid the baby right in the manger where Lilly and her mother and her sister ate. The baby made little snorting sounds.

Lilly looked at Mary's face. She looked happy and tired. Mary kept staring at the baby. Then she looked at Lilly.

"Thank you, little stable lamb. You let me rest my head on your soft wool, and it comforted me. You are a very helpful lamb."

Lilly was so happy inside. She couldn't wait to see her mother and her sister and tell them about her night in the stall. She couldn't wait to tell Gertie and even old grumpy grandma Ethel.

She had helped Mary.

The next morning was so busy. Lilly watched as many shepherds came from the hillsides to the stable. They stood by the stalls of all the animals, and they brought their own sheep and lambs to see the baby.

"We heard a special baby was here," one shepherd said. "An angel told us all about him while we watched our flocks last night. The angel told us to go to Bethlehem and find the babe lying in a manger. And here he is!"

Then the shepherds knelt and bowed their heads. One of them cried with happiness. They stayed for a while and talked with Mary and Joseph and the innkeeper. Lilly stayed very close to Mary and the baby. Mary said, "Don't disturb this little lamb. She has an injured leg. She can stay right here. She helped me all through the night."

Finally, all the shepherds left to go back to the hillsides. They took their sheep and lambs with them, but they walked with cheer. They walked with joy in their steps because they had met the baby who changed the world.

The innkeeper said Mary and Joseph could come inside. Apparently, there was room in the inn after all. Before they went in, Joseph took one of the cloths wrapped around the baby and wrapped it around Lilly's leg. "There you go, little one. Thank you for helping Mary through the night."

Lilly's mother and sister were brought back to their stall.

"What happened?" her mother asked, looking at Lilly's bandaged leg.

"Why did all the shepherds and sheep come to visit from the hillsides?" her sister wondered.

Lilly thought for a moment of all the things she had seen and heard throughout the night and morning. "After the humans rested in our stall, there was the brightest star I have ever seen. This morning, shepherds came from the hillside to see something amazing. Something they have waited for."

"What?" her mother and sister asked together.

Lilly remembered the baby's cry. "A baby human. An angel said to the shepherds on the hillside, 'Do not be afraid; for see, I am bringing you good news of great joy for all the people. To you is born this day in the city of David a Savior, who is Christ the Lord.' So, you see, Mary had a little lamb right here in our stall. And she wrapped him in cloths, and he slept in our manger. And I helped. I really helped."

Lilly's leg healed completely. She was able to play with Gertie again. She kept being helpful. She grew into a beautiful sheep and had little lambs of her own.

But Lilly never forgot the night in the manger when she met Mary, Joseph, and baby Jesus. She never forgot how she let Mary lie on her soft, white tummy. She never forgot all the shepherds and their flocks. She never forgot the brightest star she had ever seen. She never forgot how Joseph wrapped her painful leg with one of the baby's cloths. And she never forgot what the angel said about Christ the Lord. Jesus, the little lamb born in a stall and lying in the manger.

The Savior of the world.

Maggie looked at the children's faces.

"I liked that story," Zoey said. "Can you tell us another one?"

"Maybe sometime. But this is our story for Christmas tonight. I'd like you to stay up here with me while we sing our last carol, 'Silent Night, Holy Night.'"

"We know that one," Carrie said.

"I'd like you to see what I get to see every year."

The children stood around Maggie as the lights in the sanctuary were dimmed. Slowly, the candles were lit, one by one, by all the people in the pews. The children's eyes widened when they saw all the candles alight. Everyone sang the verses with reverence. Then Irena stopped playing the organ, and they sang the last verse a cappella. Slowly, the candles were raised toward heaven.

Silent night, holy night!
Wondrous star, lend thy light;
With the angels let us sing,
Alleluia to our King;
Christ the Savior is born,
Christ the Savior is born.

There was only beautiful silence as the candles shone out in the darkness of the sanctuary. Until Zoey said, "And Lilly was there!"

Abigail Brynn slept through her first Christmas Eve. The farmhouse was filled with all her relatives, and she blissfully knew nothing of the celebration. Although wide awake during the church service, once Maggie fed her up in the cozy farmhouse nursery, little Abby went down for the night.

Mimi helped Maggie set out platters of pigs in a blanket and sticky buns. Large bowls of fruit salad sprinkled with bright-red pomegranate seeds were at each end of the kitchen island.

"It was a beautiful service tonight," Mimi said. "When did you write the Lilly story?"

"Before Abby was born. I worked on the service early, suspecting I wouldn't want to after the baby. I knew we were having a girl, so I started thinking about who was at the manger and decided it would be a little lamb name Lilly."

"Have you ever thought of publishing some of your children's stories? You have written quite a few now. Maybe you could compile them into a book," Mimi said as she stirred the spiced apple cider.

"I wouldn't know where to begin. Besides, I don't have time."

"Maybe someday." Mimi decided to do a little private investigation herself.

After their Christmas supper, small gifts were exchanged. Jack and Maggie had decided this year they would just celebrate Abby as their gift.

Jack's family bundled up for the drives back down to Blissfield and Adrian. Dirk and Mimi would spend the night at the farmhouse.

"Merry Christmas," Jack said the next morning as he hugged his sleeping wife.

"Mmm? Oh, Merry Christmas. I love you, Jack." She yawned.

"I love you the most."

31

Maggie found the weeks after Christmas filling up with visits to shut-ins, sermon study and preparation, and Abby. When she could, she brought Abby with her on her visits. Conversations revolved around every little thing Abby did. She brought smiles to the faces of those parishioners who were having a rough day.

When Maggie needed time to study and write, she had Cate, Marla, and Sylvia to help with babysitting. Sylvia's little one, Katharine, was toddling around, and Abby was learning to crawl. They were obsessed with each other. Katharine shared toys and would bring Abby her blanket if she cried.

At the farmhouse, a crawling Abby meant unwelcomed surprises for the cats, who were her favorite targets.

"How did she get so big?" Maggie asked one snowy evening after settling Abby to sleep in her crib. Jack and Maggie sat by a crackling fire while snow fell outside.

"You fed her, and she grew," Jack said practically.

"When she was first born, it seemed like time stood still. It was such a sleepy, dreamy time. I never wanted it to end. Then she smiled for the first time. She startled herself when she made a shouting sound, then kept shouting and laughing. She found her toes. She rolled over! That was a big day. Now she's scooting herself around and putting cat toys in her mouth."

Jack made a face. "I think the cat toys need to disappear."

"I already hid them in the basement. Anyway, Christmas came and went, and now we're halfway through Lent. I didn't think I'd be happy going back to work, but I'm thankful to be able to spend so much time with her while I work."

"I think it's good for her too. She's not afraid of people. Growing up in the church means she has a very large extended family. What could be better?" Jack gave his wife a hug. "These are good days, Maggie. I think we have a lot of good days ahead of us. Now, are you going to be traumatized when she takes her first step?"

"Oh! Don't even say it." She kissed him and snuggled into his arms. "She is the cutest baby of all the babies, isn't she?"

"Oh, yes. She's the most adorable baby in the history of the world. She's got your blue eyes and my dark hair. It's too bad she'll never be allowed to date."

"No. No dating. She'll just live with us forever, right?"

Jack laughed. "It's a good thing no one can hear us."

One evening, Jack and Maggie were enjoying bowls of turkey-pota-to-corn chowder and slices of cinnamon bread while Abby was in her highchair eating bites of avocado and banana.

"How was your day?" Maggie asked.

"Interesting. We received the patient numbers for the past four months at the clinic. We are now averaging ten patients per day. And that's with our part-time hours. We are obviously meeting a need that has gone unmet in our rural areas. People need medical care."

"Are they mainly medical patients? How are Aimee and Betsy doing?"

Maggie watched as Abby dropped a piece of banana on the floor and giggled.

"They both have full hours as well. Betsy sees many of her Cherish clients at the clinic because the drive is shorter. It's working out well. Aimee is busy too. It took a little longer for people to catch on that there is dental care at the clinic, but she and Sofia are taking care of a lot of mouths."

He took a big bite of chowder. Abby put some avocado in her mouth, then spit it out and smashed it on the highchair tray.

"It's your dream come true," Maggie said. "You're doing the work you really love to do for those who need it so desperately."

"To be honest, I wish I could work at the clinic full-time."

"Maybe Sylvester can spin some magic one more time. He seems to be able to pull money and dreams right out of thin air." Maggie laughed. "But you can't forget the people who live here in Cherish who love you and need you. It's a good thing you, Charlene, and Alan are all taking hours at the clinic. We don't want to lose any of you."

Abby banged her little fists on the tray and shouted. When her mother smiled at her, she banged louder and laughed.

"Abby Brynn! Who's a little monkey?" Jack got up and grabbed some baby wipes. He cleaned Abby's face and hands, removed her bib, and put her down on the floor so she could hunt for cats.

He turned back to Maggie. "Everything at the clinic is good work. It's such good work." Jack's energy was contagious. "Cate and Ednah are both assets to the team. I can't imagine not having either one of them there. They are excellent with the patients, and Ednah runs the office so efficiently, we never have to worry about supplies, scheduling, or anything else. She's nice to work with, and she makes our jobs much easier."

"Ednah is living her best life," Maggie said. "I'm happy for her and for you."

"Okay, tell me, how was your day, wife?"

"I worked on the Easter service for next month. I wrote another story."

"May I read it?" Jack asked.

"I think I'll make you wait. I hope we all have a special Easter. But I will need you to help me at the beginning of the service, as usual. I also asked Addie and Cate to sing again. They were so beautiful on Christmas Eve."

"It will be a beautiful day. What are we doing for Easter dinner with the family?"

"I'll work on that tomorrow. But the most important question is, shall we do an Easter egg hunt for our little peanut?"

They heard a cat screech.

"I think our little peanut just pulled somebody's tail."

32

Cecelia pulled into the parking lot of the free clinic for her appointment with Dr. Sneller. The sun was setting, and Cecelia was thankful for Betsy's evening hours. Between studying for her degree in architecture and caring for Naomi and Bobby, her days felt over-filled. She gripped the steering wheel before getting out of her car. Jim had been released from prison the previous week. The whole family knew there was a restraining order, but Cecelia knew Jim didn't bother himself with laws or orders. She got out of her car and walked into the clinic. Ednah greeted her at the front desk.

"Good evening."

"Good evening, Ednah. I'm here for Doctor Sneller."

"She'll be right with you. Won't you have a seat?"

"Thank you." Cecelia took a seat in the waiting room, where four other people waited for different services.

Ednah pressed a button on her phone and said quietly, "Doctor Sneller, your next client is here."

A few minutes later, Betsy came to the waiting room. "Come on back."

Cecelia followed Betsy into her office, and Betsy closed the door. They walked over to the small sitting area and each took one of the comfortable chairs. Betsy had her pad and pen sitting on the arm of her chair.

"How are you doing since Jim's release?"

Cecelia always appreciated how Betsy didn't waste time with chatter. She got right down to business.

"It's messing with my head. It hasn't even been a year since he was arrested. I feel like all the progress I've made with you has drained away. It feels like he's watching us, but I have no proof, of course."

"How are the kids doing?"

"They're anxious too. He's done a number on all three of us. They are at Marla's this evening. I don't leave them alone at the house now that he's free. I'm scared."

"The restraining order is in place."

"Yes, but there is nothing to keep him from coming after us anyway. I can't call the police until he violates the order. He's a ticking time bomb. I don't understand why this is so backward. He broke his daughter's arm. He abused me for years. Now he's as free as a bird. It doesn't make sense."

"If he tries to harm any of you, he will be immediately arrested and put back in prison."

"What if he actually harms us before the police find him?"

Cate stepped into the waiting room. She smiled at a young mother and her five-year-old son. "Doctor Van Dyke will see you now. Follow me." The mother and son followed Cate to the dental office where Aimee practiced. Sofia, the dental hygienist, then took them to an exam room.

Cate went back out to the lobby and called the next patient's name. She led an elderly man to the medical wing of the building, where Dr. Jack was seeing patients that evening. Cate enjoyed working with the medical patients. She studied diligently in the nursing program at the U, and Jack had made it clear she would be offered a job in the medical wing of the clinic once she graduated. Cate was thrilled to be helping in the clinic but looked forward to helping as an RN.

She returned to the lobby and brought the last patient back to the medical wing.

Cate was in the lobby to check the rest of the night's schedule with Ednah when they both saw a car pull into the parking lot.

"Do we have another appointment scheduled for tonight?" Cate asked.

"No, it must be a walk-in."

"I'm going to grab a granola bar," Cate said. "I'll be right back. Doctor Aimee won't be done for another half hour at least, and neither will Doctor Jack."

"No problem. I'll get this person registered and tell them the wait time."

Cate went to the staff room to get her snack. Ednah watched the man get out of his car, make his way into the clinic, and then to the front desk.

"May I help you?"

"What is your action plan?" Betsy asked.

"Right now, I'm doing the practical things. All the doors and windows are locked. Thank goodness it's March—too cold for open windows. I make sure the kids are never home alone. But I don't want to scare them either. I'm trying to be, I don't know, normal."

"It's good if they are aware. He may surprise them at school. Or somewhere else."

"I have informed the school and my neighbors. Of course, Marla and Pastor Maggie are involved. Naomi loves to go to Pastor Maggie's after school to play with Abby. Bobby is doing some fence painting for Doctor Jack. Marla has them over often. Did I tell you about the roses?"

"No. What roses?"

"It took me a while to figure it out, but Pastor Maggie has sent me a white rose every month since Jim was arrested. With each rose she attached a word of encouragement. I have nine encouraging words on my refrigerator. It's been such a quiet, thoughtful, hopeful gift every month. I told her she doesn't need to send one anymore, but it is so comforting to open the door and see a white rose."

Betsy wrote this down on her pad. *What a great idea. I'm going to remember this.*

"Days are okay, even good. It's just at night that I get jumpy." Cecelia protectively wrapped her arms around herself.

"Do you have outdoor lights to illumine the exterior of your house?" Betsy asked.

"Yes. The neighbors do also. Of course, I changed all the locks after he was arrested. Once I graduate from school and find a job, I want to move into town. I don't think we will ever get rid of the ghost of Jim and the nightmares he caused in our home."

"That's a good idea. A fresh start." Betsy jotted more notes.

"I wish we could have moved last year when he was arrested, but there was no way."

"The police are aware of the situation. Chief Tuggle and Officer Bumble are your allies. They will receive every update regarding Jim, and they are able to surveil your home."

"It still seems backward. Why does he get to make a contact, or an attack, before we are protected? I can't get my head around it." Cecelia could feel a weariness descending. She often felt this way in the evening. Her days were full, and her emotional labor output was becoming too much.

"I wish there was a way to promise you safety. If Jim is foolish enough—"

"He is. And he's not just foolish, he's vengeful. There will have to be a payback. It's just a matter of where and when."

"I'm here for my wife." His voice was hoarse.

"And your name?"

"Jim Chance."

Ednah felt a chill rush down her spine. *Jim Chance. Oh my God. He's here for Cecelia.*

"Please have a seat," she said, trying to sound calm. "I'll see if your wife is here."

"She's here. Her car is right there." He pointed to the parking lot. "I'll wait right here, and I'd like you to wait right where you are."

Jim reached in the back of his jeans and produced the handgun that had been missing from his gun safe. He let Ednah get a good, long look.

"Sir, guns are not allowed in this building." Ednah tried her best to use her know-it-all voice, but she couldn't quite pull it off.

"Well, what are you going to do about it?"

"I'll have to call the police. Please leave now." Ednah reached for the phone.

"I wouldn't do that if I were you." Jim was quickly next to the desk. He grabbed Ednah's hand and bent it backward until she yelped. "Quiet!"

"Let go of me!" Ednah yelled as loudly as she could.

"Dumb bitch. Shut up!" he growled.

Cate entered the waiting room. "Ednah, do you need—"

"Sit down right there." Jim used his gun to point Cate to a chair.

She sat and looked at Ednah, whose face was red and blotchy, her eyes wet with fear.

"I'm sorry, Cate," she whispered.

"Shut up! No more out of you!" He pushed the nozzle of the gun into Ednah's cheek.

Ednah jumped and pulled her head away, but Jim grabbed her hair and slammed her face down on the desk.

Cate screamed.

The scream traveled through the hallways of the clinic.

Betsy jumped up. "Stay here, Cecelia. Don't come out of my office."

Betsy raced into the hallway. When she entered the waiting room, she spotted Jack running in from the medical wing and Aimee from the dental wing. They all saw Jim Chance holding Ednah by her hair, her face bloodied.

"Stay where you are!" Jim yelled.

Jack, Betsy, and Aimee froze. Jack looked over at Cate, who was white as a ghost.

Jack took a step forward. "Jim, don't do this. You don't want to hurt anyone now that you're out of prison. You can move on with your life."

"I'm going to move on. Just as soon as I find my wife. I have a few things to say. Stop walking, doctor." He spat out the last word.

"You'll be sent back to prison, Jim," Betsy said. "You'll be there for the rest of your life. You don't want that." Betsy spoke clearly, without emotion.

"No, I won't go back. Where's my wife?"

Silence.

"I SAID, WHERE'S MY WIFE?!"

Still in Betsy's office, Cecelia's blood ran cold. "Jim," she whispered as she closed her eyes. She sat frozen for a moment, then looked around the room, becoming more frantic by the second. *I've got to get out of here. I've got to get the kids.* Maybe if she stood on a chair, she could climb out the window and get to her car before Jim found her. There was no other way out except through the waiting room.

"CECELIA!"

She jumped. His voice sounded close.

"Cecelia, I've got the doctors all lined up! I'll give you one minute to get out here before I shoot!"

Cecelia didn't know what to do. She needed to protect her kids. She needed to protect herself. *But what about everyone else here?* She knew he would shoot them all without batting an eye.

Jim raised his gun to the ceiling. He cocked it, his finger on the trigger, ready to fire his warning shot.

"I'm not shitting around. Betsy will be the first to go!" He lowered the gun and pointed it at Betsy's head. "This is fun." He grunted. "You're the one who's been telling her how to get rid of me. Now I can get rid of you. Forever."

Betsy didn't move. Her heart was racing, but she kept her face calm and stared Jim straight in the eyes.

"You wanna have a stare down?" Jim asked. He stepped forward and put his gun to the side of her head.

"Stop." Cecelia walked down the hall to the waiting room. "I'm right here."

Jim turned. "Well, well, well. You thought you could hide from me? I've been following you for days. I've even been in the house when you were gone. I noticed you keep the kids somewhere else. Bitch! I thought they might like to come with me for a while. Once you're gone, they'll be with me forever."

"No, they won't. You scare them, and they've worked hard to understand and believe they are not to blame for your cruelty." Her voice was steady, but her shaking hands gave her away.

"I hate you." He seethed. "Do you know what you've done? You ruined my life. You turned my kids against me. Do you know what prison is like? I wish I could send *you* there. But I think I'll send you to that god you follow. Are you ready?"

"No, I'm not. Put the gun down. You will never get away with this. You have already done enough damage to us."

"Shut your mouth. Nothing's going to stop me from making sure you go straight into the ground. I've been waiting for this moment. I've dreamed about putting a bullet right into your ugly face."

"Where did you hide the guns?" Cecelia needed to keep him talking, needed more time.

"Oh, so you noticed they were gone? Where did I hide them? I hid them in the box springs of Bobby's bed. They were under him when he slept, night after night. The guns were tucked right in his bed." He let out a snort, then laughed.

Cecelia tried to keep a straight face, but the thought of the weapons being hidden under her sleeping son made her nauseous. She saw movement. Jack was slowly shifting from his chair to get behind Jim. Jim followed Cecelia's eyes and turned quickly.

"You want to die too? I'd love to make that stupid pastor a widow."

Jack sat back down.

"Jim." Betsy took over the questioning to buy more time. "How can we work this out so that you get what you want and deserve without violence?"

"I came for Cecelia. You all helped sabotage my life, but I came for her."

I came for the wife, Betsy thought. Yes, he had come for the wife. And he was going to kill her.

Cecelia had been straining her ears since entering the waiting room, but now she heard it more clearly. Sirens.

Jim heard the sirens too and became enraged. His face flushed red, and he stepped closer, spit in Cecelia's face, then raised the gun to her head.

The Manchester police arrived, followed by Charlotte, Bernie, and Detective Keith Crunch with his team. Charlotte had preemptively called for an ambulance, praying one wouldn't be needed. She had also called Keith.

Cars, lights, and sirens pulled up to the front doors. The officers got out of their cars and took stock of the situation. Keith peered through the floor-to-ceiling windows and watched in horror.

Jim pulled the trigger of the gun just as Jack tackled him from behind. Jim writhed and twisted over on his back. He aimed the gun and fired again. There was a scream, and everyone fell to the ground and tried to hide or crawl out of the waiting room. He aimed at Betsy and fired. He aimed at Cate and was ready to fire when Ednah ran forward and kicked him the ribs. The gun fired one more time. Ednah fell. Then, there was one last shot.

As soon as Keith had seen Jack make his move toward Jim, he'd given the signal for the team to enter the clinic. Keith raced to subdue Jim. The ambulance pulled into the parking lot, and Charlotte grabbed her phone to call for more ambulances. She looked at the beautiful clinic and only saw carnage.

33

Maggie put Abby in her crib with a full tummy and smelling like baby bubble bath. She watched her daughter's eyes grow heavy, and finally, with her thumb in her mouth, Abby fell into a blissful sleep. Maggie smiled and sighed, completely satisfied with life.

"I love you, Abby Brynn," she whispered.

She heard her phone ring in the kitchen, took one more look at her baby girl, and went to answer the call.

"Hello, this is Pastor Maggie."

"Maggie, it's Keith."

His voice sounded odd.

"Keith, what's the matter?"

"There's been a shooting at the clinic."

"At the clinic?" Maggie asked.

"Yes. Jim Chance came in looking for Cecelia. He had a gun. The doctors and staff were in the waiting room. He began shooting." Keith failed at the attempt to keep emotion out of his voice.

"Oh God. Where's Jack?" Maggie felt herself go cold.

"Jack is in an ambulance, Maggie. He's on his way to the hospital, as are Cecelia and Ednah."

Maggie clutched the kitchen counter. *Cecelia and Ednah too?*

Bryan, who had stopped by after work to wait for Cate to get home, watched Maggie's face, trying to put together what had happened.

"Which hospital, Keith?"

"They're taking him to St. Joe's."

"Keith, is Jack . . . is Jack badly injured?" Maggie didn't hold back her tears.

"All three were shot," Keith answered. "Jack was the only one conscious at the scene. I don't know more than that. Maggie, who can take you to the hospital?"

"Uh . . . Bryan is here now."

"Have him drive you. I'll call you if I know more."

As Keith hung up, Bryan's cell phone rang. "Cate! Cate, are you okay? What's going on?"

"I'm not hurt." Cate's voice broke. "It's horrible. You can't believe what happened here in our beautiful clinic. My parents are driving down here to get me. We'll drive back up to Cherish with my car."

Bryan was torn. He wanted to go to Cate and bring her home, but he couldn't leave Maggie alone. "I want to see you, Cate. I need to see you."

"Stay with Maggie. I think you may need to drive her to Ypsilanti. Jack was . . ." Cate took a deep breath. "Call Ellen and see if she can watch Abby. You've got to take care of Maggie now. I love you."

"I love you too. I'll call you when we get to the hospital. Bye."

He turned to Maggie. "Let's call Ellen. Then I'll drive you down to Jack."

"Okay."

Maggie was in shock. The beautiful clinic. A place meant to bring healing and wholeness to mind, body, and soul. Poor Cecelia. She was healing from years of pain and moving forward with her life. Poor Ednah, who finally knew her worth and felt the love of human kindness. And Jack . . . her Jack. Her darling husband and Abby's father.

Bryan searched through Maggie's phone contacts for Ellen's number and tapped it.

"Hello?"

"Ellen? This is Bryan. I have some rough news. There's been a shooting at the free clinic. Three people are on their way to St. Joe's. Jack is one of them. We don't know anything else yet. Can you come over and watch Abby so I can take Maggie to Jack?"

"I'll be right there." Ellen hung up.

"Maggie, Ellen's on her way. Let's get ready to go."

Maggie stood up. "Okay. I'll write down a few things for Ellen. Bryan, how long will we be there?" Her brain was moving in slow motion.

"I don't know. We'll find out when we get there. Are you okay?"

Maggie didn't answer. She made a list of Abby information for Ellen, who arrived with Harold five minutes later.

"Have you heard any updates?" Ellen asked.

"We don't know anything more," Bryan said, "but we'll call you from the hospital when we do. Maggie wrote a list for you." He handed the list to Ellen, then looked at Maggie. "Shall we go?"

Harold and Ellen hugged them both as they left. Bryan drove out of the farmhouse driveway next to a silent Maggie.

Ellen looked over the list of instructions and saw the last word on the bottom of the page: PRAY.

Ellen prayed for her cousin. Then she and Harold peeked in at Abby, who was fast asleep. Ellen knew the only thing they could do was wait, which was the hardest thing of all.

Betsy Sneller sat in her office at the clinic. She stared at her desk where Cecelia's cell phone lay. It was the last thing Cecelia did before she walked into the waiting area. She had dialed 911. The reality of what had just happened swirled around her, and she felt lightheaded. *I've got to call Marla. Get a grip, Betsy!* She touched Marla's number on her phone and listened as it rang once, twice, three times . . .

"Hello, Betsy. How are you?"

"Marla, I've got some serious news. Naomi and Bobby are still with you, correct?"

"Yes. What's wrong?"

"There has been a shooting at the clinic." She heard Marla's intake of breath. "Jim came in with a gun and—"

"Who did he shoot?" Marla's voice rose. "Cecelia? He shot Cecelia?"

"Yes, and Ednah, and Doctor Jack. They are all on their way to the hospital."

"Oh my God. Are they alive?" Marla grabbed the back of a chair to steady herself.

"There was only one fatality. Jim turned the gun on himself after he shot the others." Saying it out loud for the first time gave Betsy strength. "Cecelia told me the kids were with you tonight. They may need you for a while. I'm going to the hospital to find out what I can. I'll call as soon as I know anything."

"But what am I supposed to tell Naomi and Bobby?" How could she possibly tell them their mother had been shot and their father was dead?

"Tell them there was a shooting at the clinic. Answer their questions honestly. There's no way to know how they will respond, just be there for them. I'll meet with them as soon as I can."

"I can't do this."

"You can."

"They were talking tonight about how they were afraid their dad would just show up now that he was out of prison. We came up with some strategies for how to cope. But this news is horrific. Is Cecelia going to be okay?"

"I have no idea. As I said, she was unconscious when they put her in the ambulance. I promise I will let you know the minute I find out anything."

"Okay. I'll tell them. We'll wait to hear from you. God bless you, Betsy."

"Thank you."

Cate saw her parents drive into the clinic parking lot. They were stopped by the Manchester Police, then let through to park near Cate's car. Cate stepped out into the cold spring air. Seeing her parents allowed her tears to flow freely. She ran to their open arms and poured out the horror story of what she'd witnessed. Every detail of Jim's threats, the gun, the shots, bodies falling, blood splattered on the walls and floor. The final shot. Mark and Ann both held it together, even as they were repulsed by every detail their daughter shared—saddened and infuriated that their child had to witness such trauma. Once again, they couldn't protect her from the shocks and griefs life delivered.

"Let's get you home," Mark said. "I'll drive your car, and you ride with Mom."

Cate got into the car with Ann. Then she felt her mother's hand wrap around hers. Cate looked up and said, "Something in my spirit is sick."

Bryan and Maggie pulled into the emergency entrance parking lot. They hadn't spoken a word during the entire twenty-eight minute drive. They got out of the car and quickly walked in tandem to the entrance.

"We're here because of an accident," Maggie said at the admittance desk. "My husband is . . . here. He's been shot." She felt a wave of nausea.

"What's his name, please?" the receptionist asked.

"Doctor Jack Elliot."

The receptionist typed in the name. "He's in surgery. I will make the OR team aware you're here. Please have a seat."

Bryan led Maggie to a quiet corner of the waiting room.

"What do you think?" Bryan asked. "Should we call Mom and Dad, or Jack's parents?"

Maggie sighed. "I think we should wait. We have nothing to tell them, and Ken and Bonnie don't need a call like this with no answers. They will be terrified."

The emergency room entrance door opened, and Betsy walked in. She went straight to the reception desk. Once she received a similar message to Maggie's, she turned to the waiting room.

"Betsy," Maggie said with a half-hearted wave.

Betsy walked over and sat with Bryan and Maggie. "How are you?" she asked.

"Shocked and afraid," Maggie said starkly.

"No word about Jack?"

"He's in surgery. We don't know anything. Are you okay, Betsy? What are you doing here?" Maggie asked.

"I'm here for Cecelia."

"What happened in the clinic?" Maggie needed more answers.

"Jim Chance came for Cecelia. He kept the staff in the waiting room. We had patients in the dental office, and Jack was seeing a patient in the medical office, but they were not hurt. They were kept in their exam rooms. Jim was agitated, of course, and when he heard the sirens, he began shooting. He shot Cecelia, Jack, Ednah, and then himself. He's dead."

Maggie gasped.

"Yes, it was terrifying. Detective Crunch and the police were there, ambulances arrived, Aimee, Cate, and I answered as many questions as we could. Then we waited. They finally allowed the patients to go home. They left through the staff entrance at the back and did not have to come through the waiting room. Then we made phone calls. Keith called you. Cate called her parents and Bryan. I called Marla. Aimee was still there when I left to come here."

"This is something you read about happening in another town. Not here," Maggie whispered.

A doctor came into the waiting room. "Is the family here for Cecelia Chance?" she asked, looking around.

Betsy raised her hand and stood up. The doctor walked over. "Hi, I'm Doctor Marna Wilson."

"I'm Doctor Betsy Sneller. I'm Cecelia Chance's therapist. I was with her at the shooting. She has two minor children and no other family nearby." She gestured to Maggie. "This is Reverend Maggie Elliot. She is Cecelia's pastor. And this is Bryan Elzinga, Maggie's brother."

"So none of you are relatives?"

"No."

"Is there a guardian for the underage children?"

"Yes."

Maggie looked at Betsy, surprised. "There is?"

"Yes. Cecelia was worried something might happen when Jim got out of prison. She and Tom and Marla agreed that if something happened to Cecelia, Tom and Marla would be the guardians of Naomi and Bobby. They are having papers drawn up with their lawyer."

"And where are Tom and Marla?" Dr. Wilson asked.

"In Cherish. The children are with them right now. Would you like to call them?"

"Yes. I would also like to speak to you, Reverend."

Maggie followed Dr. Wilson to a small private waiting room. Then she gave the doctor Marla's phone number. Dr. Wilson put the phone on speaker.

"Hello?"

"Hello, is this Marla Wiggins?"

"Yes, it is."

"This is Doctor Marna Wilson at St. Joseph Hospital. I'm with your pastor."

"Hi, Marla," Maggie said.

"Maggie!" Marla sounded terrified.

"I'd like to talk to you about Cecelia Chance," Dr. Wilson said.

"How is she?"

"She's been critically wounded. From the X-ray, we determined the bullet hit her clavicle and ricocheted to her lung, which then collapsed. We inserted a chest tube. She will be taken back to surgery shortly to retrieve the bullet and check for other internal injuries."

Silence.

"I wish I could tell you more, but we need to get inside before we know the whole scope of her injuries."

"Thank you, doctor. I'll let the children know what's going on. Should I bring them to the hospital?"

"The surgery will last around two and a half hours. I can call you when it's over, if you like. It might be easier than waiting here."

"I'll be here," Maggie said to Marla.

"How's Jack?" Marla asked.

"I . . . uh . . . I don't know. He's in surgery. I haven't heard from a doctor yet."

Dr. Wilson looked confused.

"I'll call you when I know anything about either one of them," Maggie said.

"Good. We're praying for all of you, Maggie."

"I know. Thank you."

The call ended. Dr. Wilson looked at Maggie. "Do you have a loved one here? Was he one of the multiple gunshot victims?"

"Yes. My husband, Doctor Jack Elliot."

"I'll go back right now and find out what's going on. I'm sorry I didn't know about this. So you aren't here as a pastor. You're here as a wife."

"Both. I also know the other woman who was shot, Ednah Lemmen. She worked at the church and attends services. I don't think she has any family. I'd appreciate any word on her condition."

"I'll be back." Dr. Wilson stepped out of the room.

Maggie sat for a moment and said a prayer for Jack, Cecelia, Ednah, the doctors and nurses, and the congregation of Loving the Lord. This was going to be rough on the whole community. She thought of Jack's face and the kiss he gave her on the top of her head before he left for the clinic that afternoon. She pictured him holding Abby last night and how Abby's tiny hand was wrapped around his thumb. She closed her eyes. She couldn't tell if time stood still or was on fast forward. She had no idea how much time had passed when Dr. Wilson entered the private waiting room again and sat down.

"Pastor Elliot, Jack is in surgery still. The bullet went into his abdomen. The surgeons are performing exploratory surgery and searching for internal damage. As of now, they found minor damage to a small portion of Jack's bowel. They have resected the damaged area. The good news, and there is good news, is that the wound is through and through. The bullet exited Jack's back."

Maggie was reeling. The words sickened her. *Exploratory surgery to search for internal damage. Through and through. Something about his bowel.* These were words from a television crime drama. People in Cherish didn't experience these things. Her husband was a doctor, not a gunshot victim.

"Are you okay? Do you need some water?"

"We have a baby," Maggie said, her hands shaking. "She's six months old. She needs her father. Do you understand?" Her eyes pleaded with Dr. Wilson.

"Yes. I do." Dr. Wilson took Maggie's hands to steady them. "It sounds trite to say the surgeons are doing everything they can, but they are. He is getting the best care by experts."

"But is he going to live or die? Even the best doctors lose patients. You can't fix everything."

"No. We can't. I will check on Jack again. As for Cecelia, we're taking her to surgery now. We will put a plate on her shattered clavicle and repair her lung."

Maggie was able to focus better when they weren't talking about Jack. "What about Ednah?"

"Ednah is more complicated. She has lost a great deal of blood and does have significant internal injuries. Her surgery will take quite a bit longer. I'm here through the night. I'll be out with more news as soon as I have something to tell you. May I ask you something?"

"Yes."

"I'm a praying woman, and I'd like to pray with you. May I?"

"Yes. Thank you, Doctor Wilson."

"Please, call me Marna."

Marna prayed. Maggie wept.

After Marna said "Amen," she walked quickly from the room. Then Maggie went back to Betsy and Bryan and told them the updates. They settled in for the long wait.

∞

Dr. Aimee Van Dyke was still at the clinic. It was midnight. Keith Crunch's team, assisted by the Manchester and Cherish Police, had retrieved the evidence they needed and no longer declared the clinic a crime scene. There was no mystery. The witnesses saw and heard everything regarding the murder/suicide. The police themselves had seen it all unfold through the windows. The bloodstained walls told the worst of the story.

"May I stay here for a while?" Aimee asked Keith as he prepared to leave. "I'd like to put a few things back in order."

"You may stay, but aren't you tired?"

"I'm very awake. Adrenaline, I guess. There's nothing to be afraid of. The bad guy is dead. Thank God."

Keith was surprised by Aimee's candor. "Yes, you may stay, but get some rest tonight. The shock of the shootings will show up in interesting and unsuspecting ways." He left and Aimee locked the doors behind him.

Then Aimee went to the cleaning closet in the medical wing and pulled out a bucket and bottles of cleansers. She filled the bucket with hot water and bleach. She carried a scrub brush and some rubber gloves to the waiting room. Pulling on the rubber gloves, she swished the brush in the bucket and began to scrub the wall where the worst bloodstains were splattered. The wall ran pink as she scrubbed and rinsed the blood away. Aimee methodically went from bloodstain to bloodstain, dipped her brush, and scrubbed. When the water got too red, she poured it down the utility sink and refilled it again. She washed the walls. Then she moved on to Ednah's desk, chairs in the waiting area, and finally she took a mop and cleaned the dirty, bloody floor. It took five moppings to remove the stains.

She walked around the waiting room and surveyed her work. There were only a few places where paint would be needed to cover the stubborn stains. And the bullet holes. They would have to be dealt with later.

Then Aimee sat in one of the visitor chairs, put her head in her hands, and wept. At four a.m., after putting the cleaning supplies away and straightening every room, she turned off the lights, locked the doors of the clinic, and drove home.

It was three hours before Dr. Wilson reappeared with Jack's surgeon. Maggie, Bryan, and Betsy all sat up, shaking off their exhaustion.

"Doctor Sneller, Bryan Elzinga, and Reverend Elliot, this is Doctor Grant. She performed Jack's surgery."

"Hello, Reverend Elliot." Dr. Grant, who was still in her scrubs, looked kindly at Maggie. "I have good news. Jack should recover without major repercussions. There were no other internal injuries besides the bowel. I expect him to be in the hospital for the next ten days. He will need to be on IV antibiotics during that time. He'll have to take it easy for a while, maybe two to three weeks, but he'll be able to hold your daughter with no problem." It was clear Dr. Grant had received the details of her patient and his family from Marna.

The relief was immense. Maggie had gone to the dark places in her mind, thinking of the worst outcomes. She'd made mental plans for different scenarios in order to cope. *Jack will recover without major repercussions. Jack will live. Jack will hold Abby. Jack will hold me.*

Marna continued. "Cecelia will have a longer recovery. We repaired her lung and her clavicle and removed the bullet. She'll also be in for at least ten days on antibiotics, but as of now, I expect a slow but full recovery."

"Will you call Marla so she can tell the children?" Betsy asked Dr. Wilson.

"Of course."

Marna and Maggie went back to the private waiting room and gave Marla the updated news in a brief call. Marla could now tell Naomi and Bobby their mother would recover.

"As for Ednah Lemmen," Marna said. "I can't give you good news. She's out of surgery and in the ICU, but she's unable to breathe on her own and is on a ventilator. Her blood loss was extreme, along with the internal damage she sustained. We will watch her closely, but it doesn't look good. We'll know more in the next forty-eight hours."

"Is there a possibility she'll still survive?" Maggie asked.

"A possibility."

Maggie sat with the thought of Ednah's injuries and unknown outcome.

"Would you like to go back and see Jack?" Marna asked. "He's in recovery."

Maggie nodded and followed Marna through the hospital.

Jack's eyes were closed as machines beeped and hissed around him. Maggie took his hand and stared into his pale face.

"Jack, I'm here." She struggled to keep her voice steady. "You are going to be okay. Abby and I love you so much." She leaned over and kissed his mouth. "You are going to be okay. I hope you can hear me." She sat with him until the nurse suggested she take a break and come back once Jack was awake.

It was six a.m. by the time Bryan and Maggie got back to the farmhouse. Maggie let Ellen and Harold sleep but snuck in and got Abby out of her crib. Abby clutched Maggie's hair and let Maggie kiss her several times. She carried Abby down to the kitchen, got her into her highchair, and gave her some Cheerios.

"I made you a cup of tea," Bryan said. "When are you going to call the families?"

"I thought I'd wait a couple of hours. They might as well sleep. I know they will all be shocked, but at least I can begin by saying Jack is going to be fine." She felt her eyes sting.

Abby was eating her Cheerios and drinking apple juice from a sippy cup. "Dah! Bah!" She looked at Maggie for a positive response.

"Oh! Dah! Bah!" Maggie said.

Abby giggled and pushed another Cheerio into her mouth.

"Dah! Bah!" Ellen said as she walked into the kitchen and put her arms around Maggie. "Tell me everything. Is Jack going to be okay?"

34

Jack came home ten days later. His biggest challenge before being released was a properly functioning GI tract. His biggest challenge once he was home was intense fatigue.

He'd had many visits from his family while in the hospital. Maggie was there with Abby each day. Ken, Bonnie, Leigh, and Nathan came in the evenings so Maggie could rest and take care of Abby. Dirk and Mimi came to help at the farmhouse and made their visits to the hospital.

Cecelia went home three days after Jack. Marla, Naomi, and Bobby had visited each day she was in the hospital, then cleaned the house for her return—making sure the other guns were removed. A home health nurse was hired to help Cecelia recover.

Jack and Cecelia both made good progress. After two weeks at home, Jack was able to go to his office for a few hours each morning. Cecelia was catching up with her studies online.

Ednah was a different story. Ednah was still hospitalized.

The morning of Good Friday, Maggie went into Ednah's room. A "No Visitors" sign hung on the door, but Ednah had finally communicated through a whisper. Dr. Wilson heard her say "Pastor Maggie." So Maggie had been summoned.

Going back to the hospital after Jack's return home was difficult and seeing Ednah tethered to so many machines made Maggie feel sick.

The only good thing was Ednah had finally begun to breathe on her own, and the ventilator had been removed. She was wearing an oxygen mask.

"Ednah, it's Pastor Maggie here. Can you hear me?"

Ednah's eyes opened. She looked into Maggie's face, then two large tears slid down her cheeks. She gave a small nod.

"Oh, Ednah. I'm so sorry for all that happened to you. Everyone at Loving the Lord is praying for you and waiting for your return."

Ednah shook her head slowly.

Maggie rubbed Ednah's arm. "Yes," she said quietly. "We are all praying for you. We miss you. I miss you."

Ednah closed her eyes.

"Would you like to know what I pray for?" Maggie was determined to give Ednah some modicum of hope. "I pray you will be able to walk into church one Sunday morning and feel the hugs from a congregation of people who love you. I pray you will be able to breathe without the help of an oxygen mask. My prayer for your ventilator to be removed has already happened. I pray you will be able to taste your favorite foods again. I pray we will be able to walk to The Sugarplum and have lunch together. I pray you will run the clinic again, if that's the work you still want to do. I pray to God that I will hear you laugh again."

Ednah opened her eyes. Then she mouthed the words "Thank you."

Maggie walked through the secret door and smiled. Chairs filled the center aisle and were along the back and sides of the sanctuary. The pews were packed, every extra chair filled. More people were seated in the gathering area, but she couldn't see how far back the chairs went. *This must break every fire code.* She was thrilled to see that Betsy, Cecelia, Naomi, and Bobby were sitting with Marla and her family. Abby, Catrina, Daria, and Alina were in the nursery under the watchful eye of Doris.

Maggie smiled and set her sermon on her chair behind the pulpit. She stood on the top altar step and watched Jack carefully rise from the front pew and walk toward her. The pulpit, baptismal font, communion table, and lectern were covered in black cloths from the Good Friday evening service. Maggie looked at Irena as soon as Jack was in place. Irena began to play "Were You There?" slowly as Addie and Cate sang the lamenting words together from the back of the sanctuary.

Were you there when they crucified my Lord?
Were you there when they crucified my Lord?
Oh! Sometimes it causes me to tremble, tremble, tremble.
Were you there when they crucified my Lord?

As they sang, Jack and Maggie removed the black cloths to reveal bright, white paraments. Harold and Ellen came forward to light the altar candles and the Christ candle while the black cloths were folded and set behind the secret door. Then Maggie invited everyone to stand as Irena changed keys and opened all the stops on the organ. Addie and Cate sang in harmony:

Were you there when he rose up from the grave?
Were you there when he rose up from the grave?
Oh! Sometimes it causes me to tremble, tremble, tremble.
Were you there when he rose up from the grave?

When the music ended, Maggie spoke. "This is the day the Lord has made. Let us rejoice and be glad in it. We can be glad because our help is in the name of the Lord, who made heaven and earth."

"Amen!" A voice came from the gathering area.

Maggie smiled. "Jesus Christ is risen!"

The congregation responded, "He is risen indeed!"

Jack sat back down in the front pew, surrounded by family.

"Please join together as we sing our opening hymn, 'Christ the Lord is Risen Today.'"

Irena went wild. Her fingers danced on the organ keys, and her feet glided easily over the pedals. The sound of the organ and the many voices lifted together on this happy Easter morn gave Maggie chills.

The joyful service continued until it was time for the sermon. Maggie sat on the top step of the altar and said, "I would like to invite all the children and youth to come up front. I realize we have many people here today, but please let the children come up here and join me on the altar."

After some squeezing and even a couple of boys crawling under the pews, the children of Loving the Lord gathered around their pastor.

"I've written a story for you this Easter," Maggie said. "I hope this tale about Humphrey the Donkey makes today special for you." She took out her sermon.

HUMPHREY

Many years ago, under a blue sky and a golden sun, a tiny gray donkey opened his eyes for the first time. At first things were a little fuzzy, but then he saw the most beautiful brown eyes looking back at him. It was his mother. She leaned forward and snuzzled him with her soft gray nose and said, "Hello, little one. I'm so glad you're here."

The tiny gray donkey felt warm inside. His mother helped him stand up on his wobbly legs, and he began to toddle around. She looked at him and licked his nose. "I'm going to call you Humphrey."

Humphrey loved being with his mother, and as his legs got stronger, he learned how to run and kick and play. His mother would smile, as only a donkey can, and say, "Humphrey, you are getting so big and strong. Someday you will be able to work for our master."

Then she would look from her big brown eyes into

his and snuzzle his little gray nose with her big one, because that's how donkeys kiss.

"Mother," Humphrey said, "I have a funny feeling in my tummy."

She kissed him again and said, "That's called 'happy.'"

Humphrey fell asleep smiling. "Happy," he said.

In the mornings, their master would come and take Humphrey's mother to the bazaar in Jerusalem to fetch grain and other necessities. Sometimes he would strap large loads on her back, and she would carry them down the crowded streets.

Humphrey always followed behind, running and jumping and kicking. "When I get bigger, I will be able to work for the master too, just like mother."

After long days in the bazaar, the master would finally put Humphrey and his mother in their pen with a bucket of grain for their supper. Humphrey was tired from his day of running and playing. He ate his supper and then lay down by his mother.

"Mother, I know what 'happy' is, but being with you right now feels different. My tummy is full, and I'm so sleepy." (He said this while he yawned.)

His mother looked into his big brown eyes and snuzzled him with her soft gray nose and said, "That's called 'contentment.'"

"Contentment," he said. Humphrey fell asleep smiling.

One day, the master came to the pen and put baskets on Humphrey's mother, as usual, but then . . . he put two small baskets on Humphrey's back too! Humphrey could hardly believe it. His big brown eyes opened wide. He was going to finally work like the other donkeys! He said, "Mother, I know what 'happy' is, and I know what 'contentment' is, but my tummy feels so different today. What is it?"

His mother gave him a quick snuzzle and said, "That's 'excitement.' Today is your first day to work for the master, and you are excited."

Humphrey smiled, as only donkeys can. He also jumped up and down a little bit. "Excitement!"

Humphrey worked hard with his mother each day. Sometimes he would carry the baskets full of things from the bazaar in Jerusalem, and the master would ride on his mother's back. But he never rode on Humphrey's back. Humphrey carried many important things for the master's house. Humphrey carried many important things his master sold in the bazaar.

At night, when Humphrey and his mother went back into their pen, he would eat his supper and then lie down, barely able to keep his big brown eyes open.

"You are 'tired' my little donkey," said his mother as she snuzzled him.

"Tired," Humphrey whispered as he drifted off to sleep.

One day, Humphrey and his mother were in their pen. This was a day when there was no work to do. Everyone had a day to rest, even the animals. Surprisingly, two men came up to the pen.

"It must be the smaller one," one of the men said.

"Yes, he must be the one," said the other man. They opened the pen and began to lead Humphrey out.

The master came out to the pen and asked, "Why are you taking my donkey?"

The first man said, "The Lord needs him."

The master seemed to understand and let the two men take Humphrey away. Humphrey looked at his mother and said, "Mother, my tummy feels funny, but not good. I don't want to leave."

His mother said, "Humphrey, you feel 'scared,' but you will be fine. These are good men, or the master wouldn't let them take you. Be brave, my little donkey." She looked into his big brown eyes and then snuzzled him as he left the pen.

"Scared," Humphrey thought.

The two men led Humphrey through the quiet town and up a hill. Humphrey had never been here before. His hooves went click-clack on the rocks as they climbed. When they reached the top of the hill, there were other men gathered. They were speaking quietly together. They turned when they saw Humphrey and the two men.

Now Humphrey was really scared, but one of the men came closer. The man walked slowly, and when he got to Humphrey, he knelt down and looked into Humphrey's big brown eyes.

"Hi, little fellow," the man said, and then he began to scratch behind Humphrey's long gray ears (because that is where all donkeys like to be scratched). It felt so good to have his ears scratched that Humphrey wasn't scared anymore. He felt happy. This was a Good Man.

The Good Man talked softly to Humphrey. He patted Humphrey's soft gray nose and then he said, "Will you take me for a ride, little fellow?"

A ride? Oh, Humphrey felt excited! No one had ever ridden on his back before. He felt the other men put soft cloaks on his back, and he stood as straight and strong as he could.

Finally, the Good Man gave Humphrey a pat and climbed on his back. Humphrey could hardly wait to tell his mother about the Good Man. Humphrey felt content and happy and excited!

They began to walk down the hill and back into town. But the town wasn't quiet anymore. Humphrey was surprised to see many people in the streets. They shouted and cheered, and they waved branches from the trees. They cheered for the Good Man.

"Hosanna!" they cried.

"Save us!" they shouted.

"Blessed is he who comes in the name of the Lord!"

The people threw their soft cloaks on the ground. Humphrey walked on the cloaks with the Good Man on his back.

When they walked through Jerusalem, the people followed and danced and shouted. The Good Man finally stopped Humphrey and climbed off his back. The Good Man knelt down again and looked Humphrey in the eyes.

Through all the noise and excitement, Humphrey heard the Good Man say, "Thank you, little fellow, for bringing me to Jerusalem. You are strong and brave. You did a very important thing for me today." Then he scratched Humphrey behind the ears one more time.

The Good Man was gone in the crowd.

One of the men who'd fetched Humphrey from his pen now led him back to his master's house. He opened the pen, and Humphrey was with his mother. Oh! He had so much to tell her! He felt happy and content and excited and tired all at the same time. His mother listened to Humphrey's story. She snuzzled his nose with her nose. She was so happy to have her little one home and to hear of the Good Man who was so kind to him.

"And mother, he rode on my back. MY back," Humphrey said. "I carried him down the hill and through the town. He said I was strong and brave."

"And so you are, my Humphrey. You are strong and brave, and you are good."

His mother gave him one more snuzzle with her soft gray nose, and then Humphrey was asleep.

It was a few days later when Humphrey and his mother went with their master. Humphrey and his mother carried baskets on their backs while the master led them into town.

The town was more crowded than usual. It reminded Humphrey of when the Good Man was on his back and all the people were shouting and happy in the streets. But people didn't seem to be happy today. The master was asking some of the people why it was so crowded and why people looked so angry.

The master kept walking. He led his two donkeys to the edge of town, the place Humphrey had walked with the Good Man. There was a crowd of people standing. Some were shouting. Some were sitting on the ground. Then Humphrey looked up. He was so surprised.

Humphrey saw the Good Man. But the Good Man was hurt. Some people were shouting mean things at him, and some people were trying to reach him and touch him because the Good Man was not on the ground walking around. The Good Man was on a cross.

Humphrey felt something he had never felt before. He felt it in his tummy, it wasn't good. But he felt it somewhere else too, in his eyes. Humphrey couldn't see because his big brown eyes were filled with tears. The tears rolled from his eyes down his soft gray nose and fell onto the dusty road.

"Mother," he said, "that is the Good Man."

His mother looked up and saw the man who had been so kind to her little donkey. Her eyes filled with tears too. Just then, the Good Man looked down. He

327

looked right at Humphrey! Then the Good Man's eyes closed and didn't open again.

"Mother, I don't feel good. I have never felt like this before. What is it?"

His mother looked at him and said, "Humphrey, you feel 'sad.' You feel very, very sad." Then his mother gently snuzzled him.

The master walked them back to their pen. Humphrey didn't eat his grain that night. He lay down next to his mother and thought about the Good Man until he fell asleep.

"I'm very, very sad," Humphrey whispered.

But this isn't the end of the story about Humphrey or the Good Man. No, it's not!

On the third day, under a blue sky and a golden sun, a little gray donkey opened his brown eyes. It took Humphrey a moment to wake up, and then he remembered what had happened three days ago. He remembered being sad. He got up and walked over to his mother, who looked into his brown eyes and snuzzled his little gray nose with her bigger one. Her brown eyes looked sad too.

Today was the day when there was no work. Everyone rested, even the animals. It would be a long day.

Humphrey walked around his pen and then lay down again. At least the sun was shining, and the sky was blue. It was better than the dark skies and the rain of yesterday. Humphrey and his mother had worked hard with their master in the rain. They'd carried heavy loads and slipped in the puddles. They were glad to be in their pen last night.

Humphrey was dozing in the sunshine when he thought he heard footsteps. Maybe it was the master walking outside in the morning sun. Humphrey opened his eyes to see.

It wasn't the master. Do you know who it was?

It was the Good Man. Yes, it really was. He walked toward Humphrey's pen, and he wasn't hurt anymore. He smiled. He smiled at Humphrey.

Humphrey jumped up and ran to the edge of the pen where the Good Man stood. His mother came over too. She couldn't believe what she saw.

The Good Man walked inside the pen and knelt down in front of Humphrey. He reached up and scratched Humphrey behind his ears, where donkeys love to be scratched. He said softly, "Hey, little fellow, I was looking for you. I saw you three days ago. That was a sad day. I wanted you to know I am alive. The sad day is over. I have done my work, and you helped me by letting me ride on your strong back into the city. You are a good donkey." Then he tickled Humphrey's nose. The Good Man reached up and scratched behind Humphrey's mother's ears and tickled her nose too. He said, "You have a brave little donkey."

And then he did something amazing. He touched Humphrey's back from his neck to his tail and then from one shoulder to the other. After the Good Man touched him, Humphrey had a dark-gray cross on his soft gray back!

"This is to remember the important journey you made with me on your back."

And that is why donkeys have a cross on their back to this very day.

The Good Man stood up and scratched Humphrey one more time. "Thank you, Humphrey." And then he left the pen and went on his way.

"Mother!" Humphrey exclaimed. "He knew my name! How did he know my name? And mother, look at the cross on my back! Oh Mother, how did he do that?"

Humphrey was feeling something new. It was a funny feeling in his tummy, but different from all the other feelings he had before.

"Mother, I feel something in my tummy. It is not bad. But it's new."

"Humphrey," his mother said, "what you are feeling is 'joy.' It is better than any other feeling because it means everything is okay, even on bad days or scary days or sad days. Joy reminds you there will always be good days to come. The Good Man has made it so." Then she looked into his big brown eyes with hers and snuzzled his little gray nose. "Humphrey, I am so proud of you. You are a good little donkey."

Humphrey lived many years and worked hard for his master. He had days that were happy, content, exciting, tiring, scary, and even sad. But no matter what the day was like, Humphrey always had joy because he never forgot the most special day of all.

The day he walked into Jerusalem with the Good Man on his back.

Just as happened on Christmas Eve, there had not been one interruption during the story. Maggie looked at Naomi and Bobby. Naomi held Ryleigh in her lap, and Bobby held Zoey. She surveyed the rest of her smallest congregants and said, "I hope you can always live with joy, even on the bad days and the sad days. Everyone in this place loves you very much. God loves you very much because you are worth loving."

The children remained where they were as the congregation sang the next Easter hymn. Maggie watched as Jack, with Mimi holding Abigail Brynn, walked down the aisle. Behind them were Keith, holding Catrina, Lydia, holding her namesake, and Lacey, holding hers. They all walked to the altar and the baptismal font. When the hymn was done, Irena hopped off the organ bench and flew down the aisle to her family. Lydia and Lacey handed over their two charges to Irena.Maggie poured warm water into the font and began the baptismal liturgy. When she got to the part of the actual baptism, she took Abby from Mimi. Maggie dipped her fingers in the warm water.

"Abigail Brynn Elliot, I baptize you in the name of the Father, and of the Son, and of the Holy Spirit."

Abby gazed up at her mother, then grabbed Maggie's hair and pulled. Maggie kissed her baby, then gave Abby back to Mimi. Jack, who was still healing, watched the baptism, then also kissed his daughter in Mimi's arms.

Maggie then took Catrina from Keith. As she made the three tiny crosses on Catrina's forehead, the baby began to cry. Her two sisters took her cue and began to wail in Irena's arms. Abby, not to be left out, looked at Mimi and also raised her small voice in protest. Maggie soldiered on. As the babies howled, she baptized each one. She wanted to walk them up and down the aisles, but the abundance of parishioners and distraught babies kept her where she was. Finally, Keith and Mimi brought the babies back to the nursery.

After church, when they were all settled in the farmhouse, both families had a good laugh at the unorthodox baptism of Abigail Brynn and her three little cohorts.

The week after Easter, Maggie took a day off. She packed Abby into the car and drove up to Lansing. She pulled into the parking lot of the Glory to God Church, excited to be finally visit the food pantry and meet some of Nora and Dan's parishioners. She took Abby out of her car seat and walked to the side door. Nora was waiting for her.

"Maggie, you're here! Hi, Abby." She kissed Abby on the head. "I'm so glad you made it. I'd like to introduce you to some of the great workers here at the food pantry."

Maggie looked around at the people in the large welcome area. Everyone was smiling and obviously had heard about Maggie from Nora.

"This is the Wednesday crowd. We have many volunteers, so you'll have to come back to meet them all. These two are Jerry and Linda."

Maggie smiled. "Hi, Jerry and Linda."

"Your baby is just adorable," Linda said. "She has your eyes."

"Thank you. I hope she looks a little bit like me. She's got her father's darker hair."

"This is Pastor Maggie, of course," Nora said. "That's Sharon at the desk. She answers the phone and helps keep the books on Wednesdays." Sharon was actually taking a call but waved at Maggie.

"This one is Brian. He sings a lot while we're working. Fortunately, he's got a great voice. And this is Katie. She's an animal nut, like you, Maggie. How many pets do you have, Katie?"

"Three dogs and four cats," Katie said, grinning.

"Hello, Brian and Katie," Maggie said. "And Katie, all I need is three dogs and I'll match you."

Nora continued, "This is Ron. He runs the whole show around here. He tries to sound rough and tough, but he's a big teddy bear. Aren't you, Ron?"

Ron just laughed. "I get the job done."

"You'll have to come on other days of the week. We have many more volunteers," Nora said.

"I look forward to meeting all of them," Maggie said.

Doors to an elevator opened, and a man walked off pushing a grocery cart full of frozen meat. Maggie recognized him, but the context was all wrong. "Dave?"

"Why, Pastor Maggie, what are you doing here?"

Lydia's father walked over and gave Maggie a hug.

"What are *you* doing here?" she asked.

"I volunteer here. It's the best work under the sun."

Nora stared from Dave to Maggie. "How do you two know each other?"

"Dave is Lydia's dad. I met him and Jackie at Lacey and Lydia's wedding. Remember when I told you we all ditched the reception to wait for Irena to have her babies? Dave and Jackie became master and mistress of ceremonies, even without the bridal couple."

Dave laughed boisterously. "The most fun I've had in a long, long time."

Maggie's afternoon at the food pantry was a delightful respite from the work in Cherish. Nora and Dan gave her a tour of the large church building, and before she left, Nora walked with her to the Michigan State Capitol just a couple of blocks away.

"Thank you, Nora, for a soul-healing afternoon. I'd like to sneak back up here again and meet the other workers. I can't wait to tell Lydia I saw her dad. It's a small world."

"Please come back again. And don't forget to bring this little one." Nora held Abby and gave her a kiss, then her voice became conspiratorial. "I have something to tell you."

Maggie carried Nora and Dan's happy secret home to Jack. "Abby is going to have a little clergy baby friend!"

Epilogue

Healing occurred in Cherish and at Loving the Lord. The free clinic reopened and continued meeting the needs of the surrounding community. Patients often asked about the shooting, wanting to know the gory details, as some humans are wont to do. The staff said little about it. They all had their own visible and invisible wounds from that deadly night. A strong bond had grown between them through what they had endured, but caring for others helped their personal healing begin.

Betsy Sneller kept up her work at the clinic and in Manchester. She also joined in with political campaigns of candidates who wanted to protect the rights of all people, end hatred and bigotry, and welcome refugees into the country and the community. News of immigrant babies being locked in cages horrified all decent people. For Betsy, the way to move forward was through politics. She fought hard for justice and mercy.

Cecelia sold her house. She could only think of it as a house of horrors. After accepting the offer of a job in a small architectural firm while she finished her degree, she began doing the work she had dreamed of for years. She, Naomi, and Bobby moved into a pretty little home on Middle Street, just three doors down from church.

One afternoon, Marla brought a large, beautifully wrapped box to Cecelia's new house. She was surprised and pleased to see Julia Benson sitting in Cecelia's living room.

"I was hoping you two would find each other," Marla said.

"We have a few things in common." Julia smiled. "We both know how to knit, for one thing."

Marla laughed. "The test of a true friendship, indeed. Cecelia, I bought this for you. It's a housewarming gift." She set the box down on the coffee table.

Cecelia unwrapped the lovely pink paper and looked at the gift. Her hand immediately went to her throat. "The china. My china."

"I hope it's close to your grandmother's pattern."

Cecelia removed a delicate coffee cup and saucer. The snowy white china was covered in purple pansies and yellow roses.

"It's beautiful. It's perfect." Cecelia sighed. "Thank you."

On the third Sunday of May 2018, Pentecost Sunday, Jack and Maggie arrived at church early in the morning. Eight-month-old Abby Brynn watched from her Pack 'n Play as her mommy and daddy hung red streamers from the doorways. She watched as red candles were placed around the sanctuary, along with fans with red ribbons.

Maggie set the readings on the altar for the children to read in different languages. The sanctuary was ready.

"Can you believe it's been a year since we did this?" she asked Jack.

"I can't believe all the year held for us since then. I'll take a little less excitement this year, please."

He was feeling almost completely normal now. Maggie was the one who still shuddered when she saw his scars. One on his abdomen, and the other on his back. Through and through.

"We each thought we would lose the other," Maggie said. "We each took our own trips to hell and back. I don't ever want to do that again."

"No. Never." Jack hugged his wife.

"It was only the cow," Maggie said.

The large oak doors opened, and Irena walked in, carrying a stack of music. She wore tight red leather pants and a low-cut red blouse accompanied by a red lace push-up bra. Her breasts really didn't need the extra help. On her right shoulder was a splotch of baby throw up.

"I'm herre! Ready for de Pentecost!" Her stilettos carried her to the organ bench. "I'm ready to play de Holy Spirrit songs."

As the congregation arrived, Maggie noticed a bit of a commotion near the oak doors. She walked over and saw Ednah Lemmen, dressed in red for the day. Ednah was leaning on a walker, but her face was glowing. She accepted the hugs and well-wishes of her church family. Finally, everyone came back to the sanctuary, and Maggie helped Ednah to the front pew.

Ednah turned to the congregation. She saw a sea of red and smiled at the beauty of it.

"Thank you," she said. Her voice was soft, and she struggled to catch her breath. "Pastor Maggie visited me in the hospital every day. And when I moved to the rehabilitation center, she visited me there. She told me during every visit that you were all praying for me." Ednah paused, filled with emotion. Maggie put an arm around her. "I believe your prayers are what healed me. I believed you were thinking about me and asking God to heal all my wounds. I believe God did just that. I have been dreaming of this day. The day I could come here and say thank you. You kept me from giving up."

Maggie watched as the members of Loving the Lord Community Church rose to their feet. With shining eyes, the congregation applauded Ednah's words, her healing, and God's grace. Maggie helped Ednah sit down in the front pew.

Maggie looked out and saw Aimee Van Dyke in church for the very first time. Aimee and Sofia were sitting with Betsy. Lacey and Lydia were sitting with Keith and the triplets. Cecelia and Marla's families were intermingled together with Julia and Hannah Benson. Bryan and Cate sat with Mark and Ann. Irena climbed back onto her bench and began playing "On Pentecost They Gathered."

On Pentecost they gathered
Quite early in the day,

A band of Christ's disciples,
To worship, sing, and pray.
A mighty wind came blowing,
Filled all the swirling air,
And tongues of fire a-glowing
Inspired each person there.

Maggie felt the rustling of a breeze. The red streamers fluttered in the doorways.

The Holy Spirit was there—the sustainer, the healer, and the giver of life.

God whispered a message of peace, love, and new beginnings, and Maggie heard it.

For Maggie, the way to move forward after all of life's traumas was to remind herself and her parishioners of Jesus' commands to love one another. Maggie's mission for herself and her church was emboldened. She had printed his words and hung them in the farmhouse kitchen and in the church sanctuary:

For when I was hungry you gave me food,
I was thirsty and you gave me something to drink,
I was a stranger and you welcomed me,
I was naked and you gave me clothing,
I was sick and you took care of me,
I was in prison and you visited me.
Truly I tell you,
just as you did it to one of the least of these,
you did it to me.

May it be so.

-The End-

TO LOVE AND TO CHERISH
BOOK ONE

What's a young, idealistic, novice pastor got to learn from the congregation at Loving the Lord Community Church? A lot!

Twenty-six and single, Maggie Elzinga has just graduated from seminary and received a call to pastor a church in the town of Cherish, Michigan. Idealistic, impetuous, enthusiastic, and short on life experience, Maggie jumps in with both feet.

With her on the journey are a cast of colorful characters who support, amuse, and challenge her daily.

For Maggie it's a year of firsts: first funeral, first baptism, and the hope of a first wedding. But much more awaits her at Loving the Lord Community Church and in the little town of Cherish. Parking tickets, abandoned cats, and little white lies pop up to make her question what she believes is right and good, and a sprinkling of romance provides a happy distraction.

Maggie faces her happiest moments and her deepest sorrow while serving the good people of her little church. She learns that being part of a community can be simultaneously suffocating and life-giving. Her bright attitude and hopefulness carry her through the difficult times, as she becomes a full-fledged pastor.

To Have and To Hold
Book Two

Welcome back, Pastor Maggie!

Pastor Maggie of Loving the Lord Community Church has settled into her new position and finally gained the trust and respect of her congregation, but they will all be tested when the church comes under attack through a series of malicious break-ins and vandalism. Maggie tries to hold everyone together and determine if the threat is from an outsider or someone actually sitting in the pews of her church each Sunday. Can she keep her beautiful church safe? Will she still be able to accomplish the planned mission trip to Ghana if the money from a fundraiser is stolen?

While Maggie desperately waits for a whisper from God, she also fears that a major event will be ruined by the well-meaning, very loving members of the church. How will she maintain her own blossoming romance with tall, dark, and scrumptious Dr. Jack Elliot and support the daily needs of her congregation through life-and-death matters when it all feels one step away from collapsing?

Will they catch the villain before he ruins everything?

Get your ebook or print copy today at
www.Pen-L.com/ToHaveAndToHold.html

FOR RICHER, FOR POORER
BOOK THREE

What's Pastor Maggie up to now?

Life at Loving the Lord Community Church in Cherish, Michigan, isn't always easy. Learning how to adjust to a new marriage while caring for her many parishioners keeps Pastor Maggie on her toes. And things get more complicated as she prepares a group of church folks for the coming holidays—AND a two-week mission trip to Ghana, Africa.

While in Ghana, the expectations of good-hearted people clash with the real needs of the villagers. Maggie's frustration boils over and her plans begin to crumble. All her beliefs about rich and poor, success and failure, poverty and wealth, opened hearts and closed minds get turned upside down. The lessons learned in Bawjiase are life changing for all.

As her spiritual beliefs are threatened, Maggie knows her ministry will be transformed once she returns from her time in Ghana. But will she be the richer or the poorer for it?

GET YOUR EBOOK OR PRINT COPY TODAY AT
WWW.PEN-L.COM/FORRICHERFORPOORER.HTML

FOR BETTER, FOR WORSE
BOOK FOUR

Is America at war?

It is the summer of 2016 and Pastor Maggie finds herself challenged in unimaginable ways. A national election is dividing the country, the city of Cherish, and Loving the Lord Community Church into splintered factions. To complicate matters, she is working with a local business owner to resettle a refugee family from Syria, but not everyone is happy to see the new arrivals. Maggie tries to guide her discordant flock but careens from one crisis to another. She knows that much good happens in a community where love and kindness reign, but how can she possibly overcome the judgment, divisiveness, and hate that permeates her parishioners and the nation? Can she hold her flock together through the storm?

In this fourth book of the series, the determined young pastor must marshal all the patience and fortitude she can to hold the vision of a harmonious and loving society.

GET YOUR EBOOK OR PRINT COPY TODAY AT
WWW.PEN-L.COM/FORBETTERFORWORSE.PHP

Recipes

Maggie's Cinnamon Roll Bread Pudding

6 baked cinnamon rolls, unfrosted (use your favorite recipe or something like Pillsbury cinnamon rolls)

Preheat oven to 300*

Tear the prebaked rolls into bite-sized pieces and spread in a single layer on a cookie sheet.

Bake for 10 minutes until golden brown. Stir once during baking. Remove from oven and set aside.

Adjust oven to 350*

In a medium bowl, mix together:
    2 beaten eggs
    1 ½ cups whole milk
    ¼ cup whipping cream
    ½ cup brown sugar
    ¼ cup melted butter
    1 tsp. cinnamon
    1 tsp. vanilla

Place the cinnamon rolls in a buttered 2-quart baking dish and pour the custard over the rolls. Push the rolls down with a spoon until they have absorbed the custard. Sprinkle with a dusting of cinnamon.

Bake for 45-50 minutes until puffy and golden.

If desired, top with blobs of cream cheese frosting, vanilla ice cream, or fresh whipped cream.

Yum!

Maggie's Pie Plate Cheese Cake

Preheat oven to 350*

> 1 ½ cups graham cracker crumbs
> 2 Tbs. sugar
> 3 Tbs. melted butter

Place first three ingredients in a 9-inch pie plate, mix with a fork, and press around bottom and sides. Bake for 10 minutes.

Adjust oven to 300*

In medium bowl, mix at medium speed:
> 24 oz. of softened cream cheese
> 1 cup sugar
> 1 ½ tsp. vanilla

Add 3 room-temperature extra-large eggs, one at a time, and beat well after each addition.

Pour into prepared crust and bake for one hour.

Let cool, then refrigerate.

Top with anything you love: hot fudge, berry compote, salted caramel sauce.

Maggie's Turkey-Potato-Corn Chowder

Heat two teaspoons olive oil in a large Dutch oven, then add:

> 1 medium white or yellow onion, diced
> 2 stalks celery, diced
> 1 garlic clove, diced
> 1 orange bell pepper, diced
> 4 medium potatoes, unpeeled and diced

Cook, stirring occasionally for five minutes.

Add:

>½ cup canned diced mild green chilies (4 oz.)
>3 1/2 cups turkey or chicken broth
>Simmer for 10 minutes.

Add:

>1 to 1 ½ cups of frozen corn kernels, depending how much corn you like

Simmer for four minutes.

Put ¼ cup flour in medium-size bowl and add:

>½ tsp. salt
>¼ tsp. ground pepper
>Whisk in:
>2 cups milk

Whisk until smooth, then whisk into chowder and continue to cook until thickened, whisking frequently, about 15 minutes.

Add:

>2 ½ cups shredded or diced cooked turkey
>1 cup shredded cheddar cheese
>¼ tsp. cayenne pepper

Cook and stir until cheese is melted.

Serve with some of Mrs. Popkin's ginger scones (recipe found in *To Have and To Hold*) or crusty bread.

Delish!

Cinnamon Butterscotch Ring

30 oz. frozen bread rolls, such as Rhodes
1 (3 oz.) box of cook & serve butterscotch pudding (not instant)
1 stick butter melted and mixed with ½ cup brown sugar
1 cup walnuts or pecans, chopped
Cinnamon

Before Bed:
Place frozen rolls in a greased Bundt pan.
Sprinkle with dry pudding mix and generously with cinnamon.
Pour the melted butter and brown sugar over the top.
Sprinkle with nuts.

Cover with a tea towel and let sit overnight. In the morning, bake at 350 for 35-40 minutes.

Let stand for 5 minutes, then turn out on a platter.

Discussion Questions

1. When you hear or read the word "sickness," what comes to mind? What did you find in the layers of sickness Maggie encountered in her congregation and her family?

2. Which characters evoked your empathy? Which characters surprised you?

3. How has illness, yours or a loved one's, impacted your life? What changes did you have to make?

4. Where do mental, emotional, and spiritual health or illness find recognition in our society?

5. What are creative and helpful ways to care for a family going through a crisis? What have you done or experienced?

6. Lacey and Lydia's wedding was a true celebration for the congregation of Loving the Lord. How did their wedding affect you?

7. What parts of the book brought you joy? What was frustrating in the story?

8. Will you share a personal story of illness, healing, and redemption in your own life?

Acknowledgments

I am thankful for God's continual presence and encouraging whispers.

To everyone at Pen-L Publishing. Duke, Kimberly, Meg, and Kelsey, you take pages of my words and make beautiful books! Kimberly, thank you for your friendship.

Dr. Judith Balswick, Susan Matheson, Ethan Ellenberg, and G.M. Malliet.

I'm a strong believer in surrounding myself with people more knowledgeable than I. My first readers are some of the most intelligent, thoughtful, honest people I know. My mother, Dr. Mimi Elzinga Keller; Lori Nelson Spielman, *New York Times* best-selling author of *The Life List*; the Reverend Dr. Annemarie Kidder; the Reverend Dr. Jeffrey O'Neill; Dr. Charlene Kushler; and Dr. Doug Edema.

I used names of friends and family as characters in this novel. Thank you, Dr. Betsy Sneller; son-in-law Alan Cocanour; son-in-law Sylvester Fejokwu; my cousin, Aimee Van Dyke; Charlie, Kali, Ryleigh, and Zoey Teater; and Mark and Ann Sneller.

To my dear friends at the food pantry of the First Presbyterian Church of Lansing, Michigan. Working with you throughout the pandemic has been a daily inspiration. Feeding hungry families during these difficult times has been my greatest ministry experience. I'll see you all in the next book.

Doug, I love you. Thank you for your brilliant editing, medical knowledge, patience, and for talking to the cats when you don't think I can hear you.

About the Author

The Reverend Dr. Barbara Edema has been a pastor for over twenty seven years. Barb is the pastor of The First Congregational Church of Chelsea, Michigan. The Pastor Maggie Series is inspired by this beautiful church and loving congregation. Being a pastor has inspired Barb to write about the joy, sadness, craziness, and hilarity of life in a church family. Barb lives in DeWitt, Michigan with her husband, Doug, and their four rescue cats.

VISIT BARB AT:
www.Barbara-Edema.com
Blog: www.BarbaraEdema.blogspot.com
Facebook: The Pastor Maggie Series
Twitter: @BarbaraEdema1

Find more great reads at
Pen-L.com